# THE
# LENTIL TREE

*By Gordon G. Kinghorn*

# THE
# LENTIL TREE

*By Gordon G. Kinghorn*

Heiliger Boden Publishing

Dedicated to the one who meant most. Only death brings release from the emptiness of a loveless, barren existence; the longer I yearn for the lost glory of yesterday, the more I crave the serenity of eternal peace.

*I leave you my portrait so that you will have my presence all the days and nights that I am away from you - Frida Kahlo*

# CONTENTS

# CHAPTER 1:
## British Airways Flight 0147, 2016

Angela Mortimer drummed her long, slender fingers on the lid of the antiquated biscuit tin resting on her lap. For all she knew, she may have been doing so for a considerable period of time. Since they'd reached cruising altitude, maybe, or perhaps just prior to take-off, as her aircraft had sat temporarily inactive on the Heathrow tarmac, positioned under dismal grey skies and buffeted by sheets of sweeping Middlesex rain. It was only a few moments ago that she had become conscious as to what her moistened hands had been unconsciously doing.

The simple, steady, reliable rattle of her willowy extremities against the metal container's lid, plus the satisfying click that punctuated the beat whenever her wedding ring made contact with the delicate layer of tinplate, afforded little more than minimal relief, her continual tapping inadequately masking the symptoms of anxiety swirling inside her mind as if a sullied or tarnished rope were being thrown to a doomed, drowning swimmer.

Linking into the sound, Angela strove desperately to loiter with the distraction of its reverberation, thus enabling its unchanging regularity to wrench her free from the inundation of fear that was currently and mercilessly seething throughout her troubled cranium. She closed her eyes so tightly that tiny coloured blurs swam across the inside of her eyelids, then she leant her head against the body of the plane, granting its gentle vibration to soothingly massage her forehead for a moment before reopening her eyes and gazing wearily out of the aircraft's window once more.

Thousands of feet below, what she considered to be the south-eastern edge of Western Europe sped by, the lush, verdant green giving way to the increasing runniness of brown, tan, and dun textured topographical features.

*Desert colours*, she silently contemplated, *already? We must have at least two more hours to go, surely?* And then, another thought: that for countless hours—days, even—the recurrent nagging doubts lodged in her psyche had sat as if a lurid, intermittently flickering neon sign, now superimposing itself over the peaceable rap of her matrimonial gold band as it hit the hollow but evocative casket, so immense and blinding and loud that it frightened her inner thoughts. She ceased drumming her fingers entirely. *What the hell am I doing?*

To imply this was the most appalling excursion of Angela's life would not have been entirely accurate. Reuters, after all, had placed her aboard multitudinous aeronautical transportations over the extensive duration of her journalistic past. Come the period she had steadfastly opted to pursue her career in a freelance capacity, she had unashamedly developed a genus of Pavlovian response, one that surfaced each and every instance she heeded to a voice that uttered the words, "Now Boarding," perplexingly transmitted over a muffled, near-incoherent tannoy system.

Angela Mortimer harboured no irrational fear of flying; it was simply her abhorrence of being forlornly ensnared at 35,000 feet that drove her to the point of despair. Not to mention being wedged in an undersized and inadequate seating arrangement, ultimately kissing goodbye to the liberty of individual mobility, other than the odd visitation to the coffin-like WC. To Angela, air travel ironically represented a piqued, motionless, needs-must occurrence, as if she were having to serve an intolerable stretch of aeronautical penal servitude, miserably incarcerated some five miles above Mother Earth.

Dolefully, she reflected on those earlier voyages.

Each had been ghastly undertakings, notwithstanding the despairing occasion when she'd logged over twenty-eight hours of journeying to cover a 'scoop' about a VIP British hiker who had inexplicably disappeared somewhere in the rugged, mountainous terrain of New Zealand's North Island. After that, Angela swore— wherever and whenever possible—to never repeat the damning, tiring inconvenience of long-haul flights, and had subsequently elected to stop over in Thailand from Auckland following her fruitless, investigative travail in the land of the kiwi. There she pleasurably engaged in a week of devouring delicate and succulent

Asian cuisine, imbibing on imported French wine, and sharing catch-up gossip with Geoff, a rendezvous that provided a soulful combination of laughter and tears, unashamedly portraying a special bond of togetherness, a spiritual union laced in unpretentious love and life-long devotion for one another.

British Airways Flight 0147 from Heathrow to Amman's Queen Alia International Airport was over five hours in duration and non-stop. It should have been an uncomplicated means of transportation for Angela, but with each passing minute her flying flirtation with the BA carrier ascended higher on Angela's hit-list of Worst Flights Ever. The disagreeable category of awfulness that soaked her fitful, internal framework was now immovably rooted, unpleasantly distinct, and curiously odd.

In a feeble attempt to quell the devouring effects of self-persecution, she toyed with the idea of flicking through the paper sheets of her complimentary copy of *The Daily Telegraph*, although this notion was hastily jettisoned from her anguished cerebrum when a brief glance at the front page headline ruthlessly generated a further flutter of interior disquiet and laxative-like nervousness to rise inside her: '*Assad Scents Victory in Aleppo amid Shattered Souls*'.

She freed the broadsheet newspaper from her clasp, letting it fall rather unceremoniously from her trembling hands.

For a moment she pondered examining the inventory of the on-demand entertainment, scanning the in-flight movies available, or possibly engaging in polite chatter with a fellow passenger—anything at all to initiate more psychological space between the present moment and whatever awaited her on Arabic soil in the coming hours.

"Madam? Can I offer you something to drink? Excuse me, madam?"

For a second Angela was oblivious to the presence of the trolley-pushing female member of the cabin crew, who was now standing over her. Then she temporarily extinguished the trouble lights that had flickered and jiggled within her conscious and contemplated requesting a glass of wine, or possibly something stronger. "Just some water, thank you," she said, timidly.

The stewardess displayed a warm smile of acknowledgement on receiving Angela's request, and rapidly placed a brimming plastic cup into her quivering hand. The flight attendant then repeated the same question to Angela's fellow passengers, this time in Arabic.

*Splendid. I already stand out as the foreigner*, Angela thought.

She stood for a moment and scanned the aircraft, instantaneously shrinking back into her seat, embarrassed by her uncovered head. Looking around, there were more *abayas* and *burkas* than hair. Lots of full black beards. Not to mention numerous sweeping sheets of fabric in blacks, whites, and dizzying patterns. It was as if she'd already passed under and through the portcullis of a whole new world, one in which she had no standing or identity of her own.

She wasn't prepared for any of this, and in that moment she craved the unlikely possibility that the scheduled arrival time would be delayed by yet another few hours, delaying her inevitable confrontation with the quivering suspicion that she'd be significantly out of place in a land she knew nothing about.

Her imminent and pressing need to erase the frightening notion of non-acceptance or intolerance of her presence on the Arabian Peninsula instinctively saw her hand extend to the touch screen and begin flipping through the visual smorgasbord of televised distraction. As she scrolled, images of couples locked in passionate embraces gave way to assault rifles bristling on miniature movie posters, decorated in blood red and flame orange. On these thumbnails muscled men stood in gallant formations, their mouths wide open in silent battle cries.

As Angela browsed, stress-related bile rose up in her parched mouth, and she glanced at the seatbelt sign to see that, mercifully, it was turned off. She simply couldn't bear the situation any longer. She raised herself, then scaled over the young woman and small boy with whom she shared the row and, astutely making sure not to step on the woman's black *abaya*, hurriedly made her way along the aisle and into the first available toilet cubicle.

She locked the door and assessed her reflection in the mirror, forcing a puny smile on her face and sighing in a manner more associated with unconditional surrender. Her teeth had been as white as the stewardess', once upon a time. Her face, too, had been un-roughened and devoid of skin creases, once upon a time. Her blonde hair (now flecked with silvery strands), which rested just above her neckline, used to tumble down in a lustrous cascade of gold, once upon a time.

Despite this cold appraisal of herself, Angela took solace from a scrutinising deliberation and investigative analysis of her optical components. At least they, thank God, continued to retain an iridescent, innate rich sparkle and permanent dynamism. The shallow lines that were faintly etched around them were obvious, though scarcely detectable from a distance.

*I may not be that old,* she sensitively surmised, *but I'm far too old to be doing something like this. Too bloody old to be going on adventures. Too bloody old to be going to war!*

"Oh God," she whimpered aloud, stooping over the small sink and tightly gripping its rounded rim for support. "Why? Why am I doing this? Why am I here?"

As she fastened her eyes into voluntary stricture, the potpourri of luxuriant colours from earlier was not in evidence. In their place, a picture of Miles came into focus, the image growing sharper and clearer the longer she held it in her mind's eye. His strong jaw. His salt and pepper stubble. His beautiful chin. His full lips. His jade-green eyes, those ever-smiling eyes. All these human characteristics combined to emit a breathtaking, intoxicating representation of unique physical harmony, the most stunning synchronisation of mature manhood that had ever come to rest upon her eyes.

Elevating her hands from the porcelain basin, Angela gently bit down on her bottom lip before lifting her head and opening her eyelids. Some inner 'oomph' was reversing the deformity of her uncharacteristic stooped stance; she straightened herself, standing upright as if a soldier on a military parade. It was the physical manifestation of the confidence and self-worth she'd experienced during each occasion when Miles had, with orgiastic gratification, placed his arms around her thirsting body, thus registering an unmistakable sureness that no matter what happened, something in her life was unequivocally strong and pure and right: solely, their indissoluble and interminable love for one another.

As she clinched the treasured memories and removed the looming clot of dread that was forming inside her, a voice echoed in her mind with such clarity that she almost jumped, wrongfully believing that someone had entered the tiny latrine to unwelcomingly accompany her.

It wasn't Miles' tones she was hearing, but an invigorating oration that was defiantly drenched in unabashed boldness, an unfaltering force of will and flawless potency.

*Geh nach Aleppo und bring ihn nach hause!* The words of her *Oma* steadied her hands of their involuntary shaking. *Geh nach Aleppo und bring ihn nach hause!*

The dulcet-yet-commanding voice in which the German phrase reached her had been her guiding polestar ever since birth. Angela accepted that the language (and all it forcefully announced) was all she required to get through the upcoming ordeal. No—not just to get through it. To face it head on, and to bring Miles home.

"I am a member of the Schaeffer dynasty," Angela patriotically declared to herself as she stared at her reflection. "My Germanic roots are my strength, the strength of my *Oma.*" She sprinkled water on her face and dried off with a paper towel before glancing at her reflection again, the glint in her eyes now burning brighter than ever. Leaning close to the mirror, she repeated her *Oma*'s message in her own words. "Go to Aleppo and bring him home," she said to her reflection. "Go to Aleppo and bring him home! That's just what you're going to do, Angela."

Walking back down the aisle and sinking into her window

seat, she finally submitted to the intrinsic weariness that engulfed her exhausted carcass, willing Morpheus to dreamily transport her into the stalwart clutches of Miles—a fleeting aspiration that instilled a refreshing sense of tranquillity across her anatomy, inviting the reality of meaningful and sensuous slumber to settle gently down upon her.

This, however, proved to be an impossible venture. The young boy sitting next to her had grown restless, and whatever he was doing to amuse himself, it involved spreading his small legs wide and kicking Angela repeatedly in the process. She was forced to frequently shift her position in an ineffective attempt to make herself as small a target as possible.

"I'm so sorry," remarked a throaty female voice.

Angela gazed over at the young lady sitting in the aisle seat. She'd been so wracked by her level of fretfulness that she hadn't paid the woman any attention since take-off. But now she saw her, remarkably beautiful with an appealing ovoid face, her body shrouded in the *abaya's* black fabric, her compassionate brown eyes set cavernously into her flawless copper crown. All of her features untied, radiating a womanly camaraderie as she smiled apologetically at Angela.

"Oh, it's quite alright," Angela replied. "I get the same way occasionally on lengthy flights."

The woman's smile widened. "I'm Aairah. What's your name?"

"Angela." She unravelled herself from her sleeping stance and extended her arm past the boy to shake hands. "Angela Mortimer. I'm pleased to meet you."

"A pleasure," said Aairah, taking Angela's hand in her own. A slight accent clung to her speech; it made her voice sound richer, as if it had been dipped in honey. "What brings you to Jordan, Mrs. Mortimer?"

Angela dallied for a moment, caught off guard by the reference to "Mrs.", and then a brief flurry of recollections were conjured up in her mind, recollections that she didn't have the energy to even think about, let alone talk about. What could she tell this woman? The truth? *She'll think I'm insane*, figured Angela, *but maybe I am. I mean, I'm here, aren't I? Then, after a pause: What have I got to lose?*

"Well," she began with noticeable trepidation, "Amman is not quite my final destination. I'm meeting someone there who will ferry me across the border. To Syria. To Aleppo."

Aairah's eyebrows rose towards the ebony textile material that shrouded her head. "To Aleppo? Oh my goodness. You must be a journalist. It's terrible what's been going on there. Few things in this world are uglier than a civil war."

"I agree. It's horrifying, and, if this had been a few years ago, you would have been correct in your assumption about me. I *was* a journalist, although I seldom reported from an active war zone. I'm retired now."

Aairah regarded her for a moment with expectant optimism, and when Angela offered nothing more, she said, "Well then, if you don't mind me asking, why are you going into a battle arena now? An active war zone, I mean. Because I trust you know that Aleppo is very, very dangerous. There was just a story in the paper about more than fifty people being killed by—"

Angela raised her arm to interrupt. "Yes, I read it. I know

15

how precarious it is." She heaved a loud sigh, fully conscious of how absurd her story was, particularly coming from a woman in her late fifties, and one with an old, dented biscuit tin resting on her lap at that. "I'm going there to locate someone. Someone I… someone I care about." Even as the indolent explanation tripped from her mouth, the guarded utterance resounded as if it were an imaginary falsehood. Yet something about this young woman made her want to tell the truth. So, Angela quietly exhaled and added further, "Someone I love."

Again, Aairah waited for Angela to continue.

"He actually is a war journalist, and quite a celebrated reporter in his prime. Miles Dunbar. Maybe you've heard of him? Before he took a job in Aleppo, he was officially retired."

"Is that him?" asked Aairah, pointing at the small diamond on Angela's ring finger.

Angela had only ever confided in two people about this particular subject—Geoff and her *Oma*—but as fears about what this young Islamic mother may surmise began to swirl around inside her head, Angela noticed how small and insignificant they seemed when compared to the fears she'd just vanquished in the WC with the help of her *Oma*'s words. What did it matter if she openly spoke with this woman? *I could be dead within the week*, she thought. *I don't wish to spend my final friendly conversation lying.*

"No," said Angela, "it's not. We were having—well, there's no other way to say it, is there? We were in a relationship."

The brown eyes looked at her inquisitively.

Angela went on. "God, I hate the word 'affair'. It sounds so… empty, doesn't it? Like something you do in the shadows for a while until you get bored of it and then move on to the next one. It wasn't like that. My husband and I shared a good and lengthy association. I'd thought I was in love with him when we married, and in a manner of speaking, I suppose I was. I never stopped loving him in my kind of way, but my way was in an oblique style that some may find confusing and shallow. But I was never introduced to what dynamic, true love could be until I met Miles. When I did, I realised I'd never felt so… so…"

"Alive?" Aairah was smiling at her with a poignant beam of entrenched accepting.

"Yes! Exactly. It was like I was seeing colour for the very first time. Or as if an optician had just handed me a pair of spectacles, following a lifetime of blurred dim-sightedness. I knew that everything I'd done previously had been worth it because it had brought me to him. Do you understand?"

Aairah blinked a few times and tilted her head back, dabbing at her eyes with the knuckle of her index finger. "I do. Completely," she supportively responded. She stared piercingly at Angela. "And your husband? Did he ever discover or learn about your relationship with Miles?"

Angela hesitated slightly before answering. "Not exactly, but I'm sure he knew. He had cancer. I felt so guilty, for drifting off course, but more so for not being there for him when he needed me the most. Miles is my love, but William was my partner in life. We had children together, after all. I was so morbidly decomposed about what I was doing that when William's condition mortally worsened, I heartbreakingly walked away from Miles. I just *had* to nurse William." She looked away from Aairah, staring through the glassed porthole at the endless carpet of clouds below. "Miles didn't take it well. In truth, I suffered too, more than I could ever have conceived possible, and I believe that he accepted the job—one last job, he said—to try and rid his mind of the shattering consequences of our split, and to keep him busy elsewhere. But then, he just... disappeared. Vanished. No one's heard from him since."

"And now you're going to find him?"

Angela nodded, still gazing out the window.

"When you were talking about your husband, you said he *was* your partner. Is he...?"

"Yes, he passed. He has passed away."

It was so extraordinary. Angela had been sure that telling her tale—that setting it free from the subjective world of her mind into reality—would make her appear a ridiculous and fantasy-driven lady. But now, by finally distributing the emotional complexity of her existence, her path felt solid, real, and inevitable. She simply had to do what she was doing.

As she reflected on the events that had led her this far, stringently examining the endless adoration she held for Miles and he for her, that horrible, blaring question, *'What the hell am I doing?'* evolved into a past problem, more unreal than anything she'd just shared with Aairah. She knew what she was doing. She knew what she had to do for the man she'd come to love, as she'd loved no other man before him. There was nothing else for it.

She twisted back in the direction of Aairah, ready to continue, but then stopped, startled by the tears flowing down the young woman's face.

"I'm sorry," Aairah said, "it's just, you're so brave. And I—"

She cast a furtive peek at her son, now peacefully asleep in the seats between them. "And I am not. I'm returning to Jordan, to my elderly husband. He is twenty-nine years older than me. *My* love, my Miles, resides in Birmingham." She unapologetically informed Angela about the Pakistani engineering student who'd regularly visited the family restaurant where she worked in the Midlands. Their first secret outing. Their first kiss in a car park. The maudlin reaction on his face when she'd bid him adieu, only yesterday.

"I'm going the wrong way, don't you see?" she asked Angela. "My husband is similar to yours. He too is ill and I need to go back to him. To be a good wife. But I wish I could be as brave as you. To put true love above everything else."

Reaching out, Angela placed the palm of her hand on the side of the woman's face. "Aairah. If I hadn't taken care of William in his last days I would never have forgiven myself. You're doing what you have to do." She took a deep breath and exhaled slowly. "And I'm not as brave as I may sound. I'm terrified. I'm barely holding myself together right now. I would never, ever have boarded this aircraft and addressed what my heart beckoned me to do if it hadn't been for my *Oma*." She smiled. "She's the primary source of my supposed bravery."

"*Oma*? What does it mean?"

"Oh, sorry dear. It's 'grandmother' in German. She grew up there and that's what everyone calls her. My kids address her in this way too. I haven't heard anyone call her by her Christian name since I was a small child. Nina… it doesn't sound right to me, not like *Oma* does. She's the strongest woman I know. The strongest one can possibly imagine. The horrors she witnessed and survived

19

when so young…"

"Did she survive the war unscathed? World War Two?"

"Yes. She survived it. And she survived so much more too, over the years that followed."

The seatbelt light illuminated and a stoutly robust voice announced to the cabin crew that the pilot was preparing for their final descent. The information was then repeated in Arabic.

The hopeless unfamiliarity of the language set Angela's hands shaking again. All the defiant purpose and self-assurance that had been growing within her as she relayed her tale of love and longing was suddenly and rapidly pulled out from under her feet.

As the aircraft descended towards the desert floor, Angela found herself returning to an anguished sphere of uncertainty. She gripped the biscuit tin until her knuckles turned white; the palms of her hands grated against its metallic surface, her stiff fingers implanting fresh indentations next to the existing depressions indelibly embedded there by previous custodians of the tin from years gone by.

Sensing Angela's unease, Aairah placed a hand on her arm. "Hey, it's OK." Her gaze moved downwards, to Angela's lap. "What do you have in the tin?"

Angela glanced down at the aged rectangular box, running her hand over its familiar, dark red borders and the faded image of a long-forgotten German mill in its centre. As she looked at it, an expression of serene satisfaction appeared on her face. "Nothing but lunch, just lunch," she said and flimsily laughed. "I had to bring it with me. This biscuit tin has been in my family for generations. It belonged to my *Oma*. It saw her through a war; a good luck charm of sorts. I don't know." She smiled as she thought of her *Oma* again, sighing slightly. "Maybe it will do the same for me as it did for her."

# CHAPTER 2:
## GERMANY, 1938

The fiery intensity contained within the ironclad, wood-fired oven extended a temperate discharge throughout the entire Schaeffer habitat, providing a snug, swathing blanket of measured conviviality and cheer. It fanned the effects of its interior hotness across the entire kitchen, enveloping each square centimetre of the modest 18th century apartment in a clement and approving embrace. The antiquated cookery area within the home was redolent of lavender and heated brown sugar, its small-paned windows fogged over with heavy condensation.

Erna Schaeffer removed the last baking tray from the stove and, after placing it on a corrugated stand, she dusted the small crescent moons of sweet dough with a generous quantity of sugary crystalline grains. Once the cookies were cool and covered with a snow-white layer of caster sugar, she began transferring the newly produced confections into a shiny red biscuit tin that stood on the wooden preparation area, careful not to snap or break any of the delicate treats as she went.

Nina sat cross-legged on the kitchen floor, a few footsteps distant from her mother's ankles, papers and pencils splayed out in front of her. The small girl hummed to herself as she sketched with one hand, absentmindedly stroking her cat, Minka, with the other. She peeked up at her mother and giggled softly, noticing that not only did Erna have white smudges all over her pleated blue dress, but that sugary fingerprints also peppered the typically immaculate brown curls that adorned her head.

The otherwise peaceful atmosphere within the cooking chamber was soon compromised by hurried, thumping footfalls vigorously descending the staircase, delivering a disagreeable din that was all too common in this little house.

Nina felt a hand settle on top of her head as her elder brother Werner playfully ran his fingers through her dishevelled blonde hair. "Thanks a lot, *bruder*!" she said, giggling even harder.

Her brother didn't respond. The smell of baking had avariciously drawn him into the scent-laden *spülküche* and he had only one thing on his mind. With his football tucked under his arm, he paced speedily up to the culinary worktop and reached for one of the cookies that had yet to be safely deposited into the biscuit tin.

"Not yet, Werner!" Erna said, gently slapping her son's determined hand away and stopping him from clutching a sample of the abundant booty of newly created delicacies. She glanced at him quizzically and shook her head. "How can you be hungry already? You've only just eaten lunch. They'll be better once they've had a chance to harden a little, anyway."

"But Mama, I like *vanillekipferl* better when they're soft. Please?"

Erna peered into her son's bright blue eyes, identical replicas of her own deep aquamarine irises, and swallowing the emotions rising in her throat she said, "Alright, alright. Take one, *mein kind*. Then go out and play with your football and leave the *keks* to rest."

Werner grinned at his mother. He popped one of the *vanillekipferl* into his mouth and then, with the ball still clasped under his arm, he sprinted out the door. "Bye, Nina!" he called over his shoulder, unintentionally slamming the door behind him.

Nina chuckled and returned to her drawing. There was no one else in the whole wide world she loved more than her brother. The five years that separated them in age weren't a barrier for their friendship at all. In fact, they served to make her admire and worship him even more. Everything he did appeared as the actions of a hero, and when he asked her to read to him, or make tea for him, or play, she felt a level of pride that was higher than the loftiest peak in the nearby Harz Mountain Range.

"He is always hungry, your brother, always! He's like a train engine that never stops and constantly needs refuelling." Erna closed the biscuit tin with a little pop, blowing some errant sugar off the bright image of a water-powered mill that was etched on its lid.

"Mama, why are you making *vanillekipferl* when it's not even Christmas?" Nina questioned.

Erna paused for a moment. The luminosity of the day had begun to transform into the orange-gold textures of late afternoon, and it wouldn't be too long before Johannes arrived home. Then, they would relay the truth to Nina together, as husband and wife, as mother and father. It was an undertaking she certainly did not relish, and one she couldn't possibly handle alone. The news would unquestionably break Nina's heart just as much as it was breaking her own—and that of her spouse. "*Vanillekipferl* are delicious no matter when you make them," she replied. "Tell me, Nina. What is it you're most excited about for Christmas this year?"

Nina snorted. What a silly question! Her mother surely knew what she adored most about the holiday season. "The Christmas market, of course!" In uttering the passionate response to her mother, Nina instantaneously created a picture in her mind's eye, lucidly imagining the annual Yuletide transformation of the vibrant municipality of Braunschweig, and the vast swathes of people from the surrounding farmland who would converge on the town square. She envisaged the enchanting sight of horse-drawn carts with their large wooden wheels clicking over cobbled stones, laden down with sweets and toys and an entire universe of colourful, sparkling things. It was as if, for those few days each December, the whole world—with its full spectrum of exotic mystery—was transported into the centre of the historic settlement, spreading itself out specifically for the delight of Nina's senses.

"Ah, yes. The market is special, isn't it? But Nina, you should be excited for something else this year."

"I should?"

"Of course! By the time it's Christmas you will have turned ten years old. That means that when you write your letter to *Cristkindl*, you should ask for a very special present." Erna saw the excitement shining in her daughter's eyes and smiled. The least she could do was to make her girl as happy as possible, prior to ripping her world apart. "Oh, yes," continued Erna. "Your father was just saying the other day that he's sure you'll be given something extra special on your tenth birthday."

At the mention of Johannes, the glow in Nina's face clouded over. Suddenly, she looked far too serious than any little girl had the right to look.

Erna knew that look. It was a look that inevitably preceded a difficult question.

"Mama?"

"Yes, child?"

"Why does Papa hate the Führer so much?"

Erna leaned back against the kitchen counter and glanced out the window, examining the colour of the light again and wishing that Johannes were there to assist with delivering an explanation. Even during the best of times, discussing politics with her nine-year-old daughter wouldn't be Erna's idea of fun. But these days, as evil appeared to be rotting her country from the inside out, and as inconceivable event after improbable horror came to pass, she hardly knew where to start.

*Ever since that awful man came along, things have become worse*, Erna inwardly mused, *and now he's driving us into the unthinkable. The country won't survive it a second time.*

But these thoughts were sequestered within her mind. She

could not disclose such overwhelming fears to her daughter, not when her mission in life was to protect her children from the sordid, adult darkness that was cloaking the German nation completely.

"Well, darling, Herr Hitler has done some bad things," she said eventually.

"Like what?"

It seemed Erna wasn't going to get away that easily. She sighed in despair, wishing Johannes and his father wouldn't become so animated whenever they discussed politics within the household. She recognised that the current political climate unsettled the children, and that difficult questions from them would ultimately have to be responded to coherently, but what could she comprehensively divulge to a nine-year-old child about the movement of troops to the Rhineland? To Austria? To the Sudetenland? How could she clarify it in a way where she didn't have to use that dreaded, horrifying word: War?

"Is it because Papa thinks the Führer is going to start a new war?" Nina asked, her voice uncharacteristically faint as she spoke the very word Erna had been dreading. "And will lots of people die, like in the last one? And will Papa have to go away?" She doodled listlessly as she spoke; not meeting her mother's now distressed gaze.

Erna shuddered. Hearing her daughter's deepest fears being spoken aloud—and from her own mouth, no less—frightened Erna more than she had previously anticipated. *I can't protect her from it*, she thought, *I just can't.*

"Look, *mein kind*," she said, "there's no need to worry about any of that. Don't be concerned about your papa. He's a very, very strong man. Have I ever told you the story of our wedding day?"

Nina nodded silently.

"Well," Erna continued, dredging up some reluctant cheerfulness from some subterranean reserve inside of her and willing it into her power of speech, "it was a glorious spring day. Your grandfather played the organ at the church and all of us wept with happiness. After we were married and the rice was thrown over us, we strolled into a sunny, lush green clearing for the *Baumstamm sägen* ceremony. Do you remember what that is?"

"It's when you cut a tree in half."

"That's right, darling! A log is placed on a sawhorse and husband and wife work together to saw through the log. Each of us held one side of the sharp cutting tool with one hand, and we worked together to demonstrate our unified strength and ability to work through future challenges."

She paused for an instant, lost in the memory of a simpler time. Then, recalling why she was telling the story, she continued with her recollections.

"Your papa was so strong he cut into the log as easily as he shears his customers' hair. My weakened arm was just flying back and forth while he hacked away all by himself. You don't need to worry about him. No matter what happens, he'll take care of himself."

Nina's face lit up and she stifled a laugh. She was imagining her father cutting a log in half, not with a saw but with a pair of scissors, just like the ones he used in his barbershop—only these were giant clippers, large enough to split a tree in two.

Seeing the attitudinal change in her daughter, Erna exhaled deeply and returned to her tasks in the kitchen. While Nina sketched, Erna asked her questions about what she was learning in school, if her teacher Frau Möller had recovered from a brief bout of the flu, and other such quotidian inquires—simple things to try and reinforce a sense of normalcy in her daughter's life.

For a while, it felt as if she was succeeding.

"Mama?"

"Yes, dear?"

"Where did Sami Cohen go?"

"What?"

"Werner's best friend. Sami. Sami Cohen. He and his whole family are gone."

"That's strange," said Erna, frowning. "I had no idea. How do you know this, Nina?"

"Sami hasn't been at school for days. Last night, Werner was crying in his bed because he went to Sami's house and the whole family was gone. There was no one there," Nina explained.

An uncomfortable chill coursed through Erna's body. She'd heard rumours, of course, but hadn't been able to believe they were true. *Could it be?* After all, so many horrible things that had previously seemed impossible had already happened. *Could it really be?*

"Did they leave because they know there'll be a war, Mama? Is that why Sami's gone?"

Erna closed her eyes and took a deep breath, trying to restore her voice and heart rate back to normal before answering her daughter. "I don't know, dear… maybe they went to visit some of their family in Wolfsburg?"

"But then why didn't Sami tell Werner?" Nina pressed.

"I don't know."

"And why were most of their things not in their house when Werner went to check on them?"

Erna turned away from her daughter and looked out the window again. The condensation had now cleared, and the sky was burning a deep, dark crimson as the sun set. "I don't know, *mein kind.*"

"And why were things missing from Mr. Cohen's shop when Werner checked there? And why were there mean things written on the windows?"

"I don't know! I don't know!" Erna brought her hand down hard on the counter, causing a small puff of powdered sugar to fly into the air. "You'll just—you'll have to ask your father!"

"Ask me what?"

Johannes' tall, slender torso was peeking halfway through the entrance to the kitchen, a troubled look playing over his face. He closed the door behind him and ran his fingers through his yellow blond hair. He usually kept it neat and smartly parted to the side, but at that moment it was almost as messy as Nina's. He scanned his distraught wife's appearance, caught sight of his daughter's trembling lip, and cocked his head to one side in confusion, like a dog that doesn't understand why it's being punished.

"I thought we were going to tell her together, Erna," he said.

It was Erna's turn to look confused. "Tell her what?"

Johannes looked at her in shock. As he began to answer he witnessed Erna's facial features crumple under the weight of the realisation; her hand flew to her mouth, embarrassed and stunned that she'd forgotten even for a moment why she'd been baking *vanillekipferl* in the first place. It was because they were Werner's favourite. It was the only thing she could do, the only thing she had any control over. Her best attempt at providing a farewell gift—a final, lavender-seasoned taste of home.

"I'm sorry," Erna said to her husband. "Nina began asking questions about politics and… and war, and…"

Johannes hung his head. "It's quite alright." He turned towards his daughter. "But since you've already touched on the subject, I guess we might as well get this over with."

"What? What is it, Papa?" Nina looked from her father to her mother, searching their faces for some kind of indication as to what was troubling her forlorn parents.

Johannes perched on the wooden floor next to his daughter, picking up Nina's cat with one hand and depositing the small animal into Nina's lap.

Hugging Minka to her chest, Nina looked up at Johannes expectantly but anxiously.

"Nina," Johannes sighed. "Nina, you know that our country is going through a… a difficult time at the moment."

"Mama said that the Führer did some bad things, but she wouldn't say what they were."

Johannes peered at his wife, who shrugged at him helplessly, and he allowed his eyes to survey the room. He'd dwelt in this house his entire life; it had belonged to his parents until they'd bestowed it to him and Erna as a wedding present and moved to a smaller apartment nearby. The aged furniture that had accumulated over the years gave him a sense of comfort, of rightness. The row of porcelain vases that had sat atop a shelf against the far wall for as long as he could recollect appeared exactly as they had when he'd been Nina's age. And then there was the huge Bechstein Art Nouveau grand piano—the family's most valuable possession, which had been handed down through generations and had dominated the lounge area ever since he'd been a boy—which provided unquantifiable cheer and happiness to himself and his family whenever he stroked one of the thirty-two Beethoven sonatas he knew by heart (or the works of Chopin, Mozart, or Rachmaninoff) from its ivory keys.

But so much had altered since those bygone days, not least the Great War—or the Great Disgrace, as his father liked to call it—followed by years filled with mourning. Then there was a time of madding uncertainty laced with faint hope. And now, the possibility of a new war, a new disgrace.

He turned his attention back to Nina. "Your mother is correct. Herr Hitler has done some very bad things. And I need to tell you about one of them right now. Do you know what the *Hitlerjugend* is?"

"A boy at school told me it's like an army for children. He said he couldn't wait to join."

"It is something of that sort, I suppose." He looked to Erna to see if she could facilitate any assistance, but she just stared back at him, still biting her lower lip, as tears welled in her eyes. "Nina," he continued. "Herr Hitler has made a law that all boys of a certain age must join the *Hitlerjugend*. That age is fourteen. Do you remember how at your brother's birthday last week he seemed upset? Well—"

"No," Nina said, suddenly understanding where the conversation was leading. "No, you can't! *He* can't. He didn't even tell me!" Nina clutched Minka tighter to her chest and shook her head in disbelief.

Johannes reached out to calm his daughter but she vigorously pulled away. "We made him promise not to say anything, Nina. This is terribly hard for all of us. For Werner, most of all. But we knew this would be especially hard for you and thought it best to talk it through like adults. So, please, darling. Please just—Nina!"

But she was already running to her bedroom, preceded up the stairs by her loud, heaving sobs.

Johannes bowed his head and gasped. Then, glancing downwards, he noticed his daughter's drawing on the floor in front of him.

It depicted a small girl. A slightly larger boy was standing next to her, kicking a football. The paper was dotted with little wet circles where Nina's tears had fallen.

The following evening, when Nina sauntered past the bathroom on her way to bed, she noticed that the door was ajar. She opened it quietly and found Werner inside, regarding himself in the mirror. He was dressed in a crisp new uniform: a khaki brown shirt with black tie, knee-length socks, and thick shorts.

Nina thought it made him look strange—so much older than he had been just that morning—but he didn't quite look like a soldier… just a boy, pretending to be one.

In spite of the terrible mix of emotions the sight stirred inside her, Nina almost giggled at the strange figure her brother cut whilst standing there in uniform, oblivious to her presence. But her girlish mirth died the instant she saw the dark look on his face. He appeared unnaturally sombre as he rigidly raised his right arm arrow straight, pointing his fingers towards the ceiling.

"*Heil Hitler!*" he barked in a voice that was not his own.

His arm remained erect for several seconds, reflecting a chilling grimace that Nina never would have believed could ever grace the features of her older brother. The fingers of his hand curled into a fist and he punched the bathroom wall with all his strength.

The abrupt flash of violence, and the crash of its reverberation, made Nina squeal.

Werner whipped around and immediately embraced his troubled sister, allowing his own teardrops to fall freely from his crimson cheeks. "Oh, Nina. I'm sorry I frightened you," he mumbled into her shoulder. "I'm frightened too. I don't want to go."

Nina pulled back, unable to speak, and reached into a pocket of her dress to pull out a new drawing. It illustrated the Schaeffer family standing together, each member smiling brightly.

Werner hugged her again and led her into their bedroom, their arms still wound tightly around each other. They climbed into their respective beds and, as was their nightly tradition, Nina pulled out her favourite book, *Die Biene Maja*.

She began to read, and she continued reading until the first light of dawn started to reflect on her brother's frowning, sleeping face. Then she closed the book and lapsed into a restless and troubled sleep of her own.

By the time she awoke, her brother was gone. She would never lay eyes on him again.

# Chapter 3:
## Jordan, 2016

T he oppressive heat immediately engulfed Angela's body as she stepped off the bus, utterly exhausted.

Without the luxury of air conditioning, the brief excursion from the airport to the city centre had been stuffy and stale. Yet it bore little comparison to the abrupt shock of being immersed in a boiling cauldron of Middle Eastern conflagration; the afternoon desert sun made an intense impact on Angela's pastel, English-marble skin.

Angela's eyes strained under the powder-blue skies and squint-inducing sunshine, struggling to identify the precise location of the ticket office as she peered over and through the swaying shoulders of disembarking passengers. She eventually unearthed the relevant building as she wearily trundled across the vast parking lot, and upon finally sighting it, she increased her jaded pedestrian pace and hastily strode towards the booth with accelerated strides.

All around her churned the chaos of contemporary international travel. Hordes of people—alone, grouped in families, or with friends—all on the move. They dragged rolling luggage or carried black briefcases and bulky vinyl bags as they made their way to or from the rows of buses that filed along the superheated concrete pavement. The persistent cries and wails of infant children sliced through the babble of numerous alien languages. Teenage boys barked the prices and brand names of various snacks and trinkets whilst waving their wares over their heads and optimistically wading through a tide of potential customers. Men shouldered past one another, some in light, short-sleeved button-downs, some resplendently adorned in shimmering white *thawb* robes, others dressed in faded t-shirts, which unabashedly bore the logos of American sportswear organisations. Some women were dressed in skimpy vests and denim leggings—similar to Angela's choice of attire—but the majority of them moved through the crowd as elegant, mysterious shadows in their black, full-length *abayas*.

Protection from the searing high temperatures was soon afforded to Angela courtesy of the merciful shade of the ticket office's awning. Drenched in bodily dampness and slightly panting, Angela was thankful she hadn't brought much baggage: just a backpack with a change of clothing and underwear, various toiletries and a towel, together with the biscuit tin that bumped and knocked around awkwardly within the far reaches of her

Scandinavian Bergen. The rucksack alone, however, was enough to make her suffer as if she were an over-encumbered camel traversing an interminable desert landscape. Using the back of her hand, she swabbed another deposit of sweat from her heavily perspiring brow.

Fortunately, the file of soon-to-be bus passengers impatiently loitering ahead of her was not particularly lengthy, but unfortunately, it wasn't moving very fast. As she stood dejectedly motionless behind them and anxiously shifted her body weight back and forth in her Nike training shoes, she imbibed the very last liquid remnants from her tepid water bottle. Slowly, she raised her eyes to the unforgiving sky and pleaded for divine intervention to ensure the queue would start shuffling along with immediate effect.

In the meantime, Angela reaffirmed the hour on her phone and thumbed to her Notes app to confirm the scheduled time of the bus' departure. She was fragmenting her agenda into desperately fine margins.

Attempting to distract herself from the unpleasant feeling of running late, she spied a family standing adjacent to one of the long-wheeled coaches, impeding a line of passengers who were attempting to board the mechanised craft.

A young boy stood next to the open bus door, weeping. He clung to his smaller sister while the mother and father gently tried to separate them and usher the boy onto the coach. Ultimately, they were successful. The boy then appeared at the window directly above them, pressing both his hands against the glass while the remaining passengers filed on. The three family members held each other tightly. The bus then moved away, generating a large cloud of dust, while the little girl wiped at her tears with the hem of her mother's robe.

As Angela arrived at the window of the ticket office she tried to shake off the emotions of the incident.

The jowly face of the attendant fixed her with a bored, bureaucratic gaze. A few strands of his thin hair were being blown straight up off his scalp by the small fan next to him.

"English?" asked Angela.

He shook his head. This time, she didn't reach for the Arabic phrasebook she'd purchased at Heathrow; after withdrawing a small amount of local currency and navigating her way through Amman's surprisingly sleek airport, playing linguistic games with her Arabic lexicon had made her miss the first transport from the airport to the city coach terminal, pre-empting a long, tense, but mercifully air-conditioned wait for the next coach into town. The woman who'd sold her the ticket had been valiantly patient with Angela's semantic bumbling, smiling at her encouragingly as she thumbed through the challenging pages of her translation tome, but her aim to be understood had proved to be far more trouble than it was worth. If Angela was going to have any hope of meeting the man she'd hired to ferry her over the Syrian border and into Aleppo, she couldn't pass up any more buses. "Irbid, please," she uttered with firm and determined confidence. The attendant raised his eyebrows and shrugged. "Irbid," she repeated louder, trying to enunciate each letter. "The next bus to *Irbid*."

Comprehension dawned on the man's face and he repeated the name of the small northern city back to her as a question. She nodded, and he began to type on his computer keyboard, moving the mouse around slowly as he squinted at the screen. Some moments later, his eyes widened and engaged with Angela's.

"Irbid?" he said again, replete with a draconian tone that made Angela's heart pound.

"Yes. Please."

He responded rather agitatedly by speaking rapidly to her in Arabic and gesticulating wildly as he did so.

Angela sighed, failing to decipher a solitary word he uttered, yet it was obvious to those waiting in line behind her what he was striving to relay. He jabbed his watch and then pointed to a bus positioned at the far end of the parking lot. Angela looked over and saw that the procession of passengers in the process of boarding it was becoming smaller by the second.

Anxiously, she passed several colourful banknotes through the narrow slit in the window and quickly snatched the slip of paper that appeared in return. "Thank you!" she called over her shoulder as she ran back into the sun's fury and towards the public means of transportation. The man at the ticket office was still shouting at her—she had fled without collecting her change. Angela ignored him, and she still had some ground to cover when she heard the hiss of release from the bus' breaking system.

"Wait!" she yelled, feeling ridiculous to be calling out desperately in a language the bus driver probably wouldn't understand, even if he did hear her. She slammed into the door of the craft just as it was nudging forward, and through the doors the driver gave her an affronted look. She waved her ticket, pressing it up against the glass pane. In response, the disgruntled operator rolled his eyes and, after a moment, the door swung open. She exhaled noisily with relief and stepped aboard.

Her new chauffeur then barked something rashly as she handed over her ticket, a derogatory comment that she assumed was less than flattering, but she didn't care. She'd made it.

Finding an empty seat, she gratefully collapsed onto its lumpy surface, breathing heavily and waiting for her pulse rate to restore itself to normality.

By the time the last of Amman's rectangular, beige apartment buildings had given way to open desert, Angela was reunited with her old self once more. And not just her current self—the suburban mother of two who resided in a comfortable domicile in Wimbledon—but her younger self, a person she'd almost forgotten had existed: the sharp-witted correspondent who'd asked the tough questions, who'd travelled the world chasing stories, interviews, and truth, who'd gritted her teeth in the face of difficult assignments and who'd excelled in her professional life. On this occasion, she grappled with the fact that she still had a long way to go if her mission to find Miles was to be successful, but having negotiated the first hurdle in connecting with her dilapidated carrier to Irbid, she felt accomplished, energised, and extraordinarily exhilarated.

In reality, this was not a promising journalistic assignment. This was not a job her editor would commend her for doing well. This was a life or death rescue mission into the unknown. The very existence of the man she loved hung in the balance. All she had achieved thus far was boarding a bus in a foreign land, and she had nearly failed to execute that otherwise routine task.

Now, what lay ahead of her—and the possible consequences of her Herculean quest—came to occupy her mind once more. For the first time since closing the front door to her home in South West London, she mournfully pondered what and whom she had left behind in England.

Again, she felt blameworthy. What would her children think if they knew what she was undertaking and how utterly unprepared she was to even think of attempting such madness? They had no knowledge of her current whereabouts, as she had deliberately not confided in them before her departure. If they knew… if they only knew…

John, her youngest child, would probably consider this outlandish action to be typical of his nomadic matriarch, dashing off far from home once more. As a boy, he had frequently become maudlin and mawkish, weeping pitifully and confusedly at the merest suggestion that she would soon abandon him for another overseas journalistic assignment, and he'd also sulk for a day or so when she returned to the home front.

When she finally decided to retire from her career their relationship had improved considerably, and over time, Angela had come face-to-face with the emotional costs of her international media career. She had been conspicuously absent at too many of John's football games, had consistently failed to attend Parent & Teacher meetings during the school term, and seldom was present to encourage him at the annual school sports day. For the majority of John's young life, it was *Oma* who had tucked him into bed for an incalculable number of lonely nights over many, many years, while Angela was off chasing her next assignment.

Christina probably wouldn't approve either. She was dedicated, responsible, and practical in a way that made Angela incredibly proud. From a very young age, Christina proved to be a loving and conscientious daughter and a source of great comfort for her parents, earning top marks in school and spending an equal proportion of time with her friends and family as she grew older. There were boyfriends, of course, but no admiring *beau* had managed to stir the heart of her daughter—the man to ultimately do so was yet to be revealed to her. Christina had never known true love. Therefore, how could she possibly understand what Angela was embarking on? How could she even start to comprehend why her mother had inexplicably chosen to head for one of the world's most dangerous cities to reach, quite possibly, an already dead lover?

All Angela could hope for was that somehow, some day, she'd be able to make them understand.

Her thoughts then transferred to her late husband, William. While their relationship had never quite had the explosive, magnetic appeal that her connection with Miles so effortlessly exhibited, she and William had nurtured a bottomless understanding and genuine appreciation for one another, a profound friendship forged by a respectful, even-keeled love. William had identified early on in their relationship that he loved Angela for what was at the core of her being. He accepted her tenacious and adventurous spirit and had continually remained a vital source of encouragement as she prepared to travel abroad to cover various stories. There existed within Angela an inherent hunger to live life and to narrate the horrors of life—it undeniably filled her.

William had been a fine man, a loving and supportive human being, one to whom she had remained devoutly loyal and faithful since their very first date, many decades previously—that was, until she met Miles. The marital situation was a workable means of survival, and a worthwhile expediency in pursuit of domestic harmony and the successful upbringing of their children.

William also determined that he would struggle to keep pace with Angela. Especially as the years rolled by, his personal tastes in excitement leaned more towards watching a football match on TV, participating in a game of golf, or pottering in the garden. Only during the children's pre-school years did William push her harder to adopt the role of a stay-at-home mother. He respected her dedication to her demanding profession, but would often plead with her—or, eventually, argue with her—about placing the family first, strenuously advising that it was time to enter into a life of domestic routine and motherly commitment. It was just natural, a task for a mother and not that of an aging *Oma*.

As the children began to develop and grow, William's attitude tempered and he bestowed on Angela his blessing to advance further in the news reporting industry. *He was a better, more understanding man than I ever gave him credit for*, she poignantly reflected, sighing slightly.

Peering through the dust-encrusted window, her attention was caught by the pinks and purples of dusk, which were starting to propagate across the sky. She smiled briefly at yet another recollection of her late spouse; William adored the multi-coloured radiance that exuded from a late evening summer sky. As she took in the colours, the encumbrance of guilt—which had weighed on her mind since her departure from London—slowly began to ebb.

*What good will I do here if I keep dwelling in the past?* she thought to herself. *I'm going to do this. No, I am doing this. And I'm going to do it well. It doesn't matter if people think I'm right or wrong. That's the nature of confidence, which I'll need in order to get through this and to find Miles. I'm going to bloody well use every ounce of strength I have to reach the man I love.*

When Angela adjusted her posture on the badly upholstered seat, she spotted a few male passengers staring at her. Her blonde hair and deep blue eyes had made her the human focal point on board, to say nothing of her sartorial choices. *Let them stare*, she thought. It didn't matter. She was on her way. She was moving forward. Maybe, just maybe, she was capable enough to find Miles.

If she could disregard for just a moment the horrible circumstances that had resulted in her being transported through the Jordanian desert, if she was able to just barely overlook the grave danger or life-threatening duress that Miles may be enduring, if she could prompt the lightness and freedom of adventure to course through her veins and then hold it close to her bosom, she would be successful.

The bus slowly manoeuvred into the Irbid coach terminal just as the first stars came into view, brightly spread across the vast cobalt sky.

Angela retrieved her bag and as she alighted from her second form of wheeled transportation of the day, she craved that her next step would be just as straightforward, as she'd been informed it would be several weeks earlier. When Angela had been endlessly transmitting flurries of emails to a plethora of journalists she was once acquainted with—particularly those that had worked in the Middle East—several of her past colleagues cautiously informed Angela that, while it wouldn't be easy to reach Aleppo, it was certainly possible. Some people even made a prosperous living by transporting journalists into hard-to-reach, war-ravaged destinations, and fortunately for Angela, a friend of a friend who'd recently returned from Aleppo had hesitantly agreed to arrange the services of one such transporter for her.

Following the journalist's instructions, Angela had converted a considerable sum of money into digital currency and had then forwarded it to an address consisting of a long string of letters and numbers, which she'd been guaranteed was the transporter's account. Once the funds had gone through, the journalist had informed her that her 'ride' would be waiting at Irbid, but there was no more information than that.

Irbid's bus station was less significant than the terminal at Amman, but somehow more chaotic; it was as if all the intensity of Amman's central terminal had been condensed and, thereby, intensified. She manoeuvred around the crush of bodies (most of them emitting disagreeable odours and chattering incessantly in their native tongues), and after fighting her way to the periphery of the crowded assembly, she abruptly stopped.

What was she supposed to do? Go to the front of the bus station? Wait here? She gazed over at the small kiosks packed tightly together around the station (and at the shadowy thoroughfares leading away from them), and then cast her eyes back to the congested terminal. The idea of drifting around the city alone at night in search of someone she'd never met before had no appeal whatsoever.

"Boo!" said a voice behind her.

She whipped around and found herself examining a tall, lanky, yet muscular man. He wore an orange baseball cap and had, perched on his snub-nose, a pair of aviator sunglasses, even though it was now, most definitively, night-time. Below his darkened lenses he sported a scraggly beard and a huge, mischievous grin. In his hand, he held a rectangle of white cardboard upon which the words 'ANGELA MORTIMER' had been etched in thick black felt-tip pen.

"Boy, oh boy, you sure looked lost there for a moment—or three." He spoke with a southern American accent.

*Texas, probably*, she confidently ascertained.

"You're the man? The transporter?"

"*The Transporter*'s an action flick that I dare say I'm a fan of. But the dude in the movie gets shot at a hell of a lot more than I do. Plus, he's bald. So no, I'm not 'the transporter'. I'm Tommy."

"Hello, Tommy. I'm—"

He waved his sign at her. "Angela Mortimer, I'd guess. Not many other folks around here who fit the description. Caucasian woman, fifties, blonde hair, blue eyes... see anybody else like that 'round here?" He winked at her. "Shall we?"

He led her out of and away from the terminal, traversing a busy avenue lit by buzzing fluorescent streetlamps before turning a corner and coming to a halt in front of a dusty silver Toyota

Hilux pickup truck.

"This is us," he ardently announced.

Angela tugged at the locked door of the vehicle, getting frustrated when she realised it was locked.

"Hold your horses, now," he said. "We must get a few things straight first."

"Alright," she said, letting go of the handle. "You're to drive me to Aleppo. Let's start there."

"Yes, ma'am, and it's none of my business why a nice lady like you wishes to go to that godforsaken place. I don't get paid to ask questions. Or at least I'm not getting paid for that today." He chuckled to himself.

"What exactly is it that you do?" she asked.

"Well, that's what we're about to straighten out, right here right now. I don't have anything as official as a job description. No business card. I'm just Tommy and I do lots of things for people that need them done." He leaned forward against the bed of the truck with his upper body, emphasising his sentences by patting the side of the vehicle with the flat of his hand. "Sometimes I'm a fixer. Sometimes I'm a translator. Sometimes I just sit and watch things happen and remember them real carefully. But today, I'm none of those things. Today, I'm a driver. A ferryman. Understood?"

He waited for Angela to nod and then continued, "First I'm going to drive you approximately twenty minutes north to the border. When we get there, I intend to ferry us across an imaginary river of political bullshit, into Syria—"

"And how exactly will you do that?" Angela interjected.

He gave her a blank stare and said dryly, "I know people.

Those people know other people whose salaries are not what they could be. Now, where was I? Right. Once we're in Syria, I'm going to drive us through a whole lot of nothing for, oh, about seven hours or so, until we reach Aleppo. On arrival, I'm taking you to a Red Cross outpost in the centre of town. Those fifteen minutes of the trip are the expensive part," he smiled at her. "This here taxi's got variable rates. Anyway, we get to the Red Cross. We shake hands. You get out. I turn around and leave. Are we clear?"

"Yes. Very clear," Angela replied, a little taken aback. "I mean, I thought that was the deal in the first place."

Tommy unlocked the truck and pulled his door open. "Well, be that as it may, I always want to make sure my customers know exactly what they've signed up for before we start. Especially when they don't look like they've got what you'd call... 'operational experience'. No offence. Go on, get in."

Angela did so, shutting the door carefully behind her once she was in. The car smelled of a fragrant combination of pine air freshener and strong French cigarettes. *Gauloises, more than likely*, she thought to herself.

Tommy perched himself on the driver's seat and closed the door. "You see, where you're going, it's... well... dangerous, OK? And I don't mean dangerous like walking around in a bad neighbourhood after darkness descends, or riding your motorcycle without a helmet—not that kind of dangerous." He removed his sunglasses and revealed his sharp hazel eyes, which he fixed directly on hers. "I mean seriously *dangerous*. I'm not trying to scare you, but you've booked a trip to a location where probably, right now—right this very second—some poor bastard just got

49

his head blown clean off. Boom! Tick-tock. Boom! Another second, another dead guy. Another dead *kid*, understood? Right now. Right this very minute. Limbs lost. Orphans in the making. Mortars, shrapnel, grenades. Day or night. It's not a city anymore. It's a 24/7 battleground."

Angela held his gaze and nodded weakly. She swallowed. "I know."

"You keep telling yourself that, but I'd be willing to bet my mama's pet Chihuahua that you don't. Not yet, anyway. And my mama loves that damn dog."

Angela nodded once more.

"But you *will* know," said Tommy. "I'm going to get you there and then you're going to learn real quick what Aleppo is really all about. And, if you happen to learn that unpleasant lesson while we're still rolling together, you have to know in advance that the answer is no. No, I will not translate for you. No, I will not take you anywhere else besides that Red Cross Office. No, I will not be picking you up in a few days, running errands, laying down covering fire, gathering intelligence, or executing any covert missions on your behalf for any amount of money or teary-eyed begging. *Comprende*, woman? I'm your driver. Nothing more. Alright?"

"Yes," Angela replied, "you've made yourself quite clear, Tommy. Thank you for your forthrightness."

He grinned at her and winked. "I like to think of it as part of my job, Angie. Can I call you Angie? Anyway, great," he said, starting the truck, which came to life with a thrust of considerable power. "Now we've got that out of the way, the only thing left to discuss is the money. You brought it in cash, right?"

So far, Angela had been doing everything she could to keep from visibly shaking following Tommy's graphic speech regarding dismembered children and hostile ammunition inflicting such misery on its victims, but this question tipped her right over the edge.

Tommy caught the look on her face, lifted his eyebrows, and cut the engine. He stared at her in silence.

"What?!" she shouted at him. "What do you mean, the money? I didn't bring you any cash! I thought I already paid! On the internet!"

"Is that right?" he said pensively, his eyes boring into hers. Then, after a very long moment, his face split into a grin and his hysterical laughter filled the cabin. "Ha!" he barked, struggling to catch his breath around the spasms of hilarity, shaking his scarecrow frame and starting the vehicle a second time. "Boy, you should see your face, Angie! Don't worry, don't worry. I got the money. I got it. It was a joke, alright? I was just trying to lift the mood a little. You just relax now—and buckle your darned seatbelt."

Angela just sat there, shaking, both angry and relieved at the same time.

Tommy pulled away from the curb and didn't stop laughing until they'd turned onto the highway.

Hours passed, and miles of depressing nothingness passed

with them. Outside the Hilux was just pure, deep ebony blackness. Only the headlights and the illuminated few metres of road ahead could be seen.

It had taken Angela a while to calm herself after Tommy's practical joke, but once that initial spike of fear and anger had subsided, she realised—with an element of surprise—that she had developed a fondness for her unusual driver. Somehow, for some reason, she trusted him. Not only did it take a certain level of bravery to maintain a sense of humour in the world in which Tommy thrived, thought Angela, but he probably used it as a survival mechanism, as a way to not let his humanity be crushed by the terrible things he must have seen and experienced.

"Tommy," she said after a while, "I take it you came here with the military, correct?"

"Yes, ma'am. I finished my tour with the Marines and had no real wish to go home. Never had any real skills for civilian life. But out here I get by OK."

"And do you do most of your work in Aleppo?"

"No, ma'am. I try and go there as rarely as I possibly can, to tell the truth. I had enough close calls when I was on active duty in Iraq and Afghanistan; I try to keep them to a minimum these days."

"If you've been there recently," she said, delicately, "you wouldn't happen to have crossed paths with a correspondent named Miles Dunbar, would you?"

"Miles," he said thoughtfully. "Miles, Miles, Miles." Each time Tommy said the name, Angela's heart beat faster. "I knew a Miles in Aleppo."

"You do? Or you did?" Hope, fear, pain, and desperation all ganged up on Angela, twisting her voice into a drawl she hardly acknowledged as her own.

"Did. He got hit."

Angela's stomach lurched.

"Good old boy down from just outside of Memphis," Tommy continued. "Not in the same division as me, but a Marine. Real good at poker, Miles was."

Angela bit her lip and exhaled out of her nose in frustration. It seemed as if every conversation she had with this man turned into an emotional rollercoaster. "I said a *correspondent* named Miles. Miles Dunbar. He's Scottish."

"Oh, that's right. You did, didn't you? No, I can't say I know him. Don't think I ever crossed paths with a Scotsman in Aleppo."

They drove in silence for a few more minutes, then Tommy said, "Listen, Angie. I know I said I don't get paid to ask questions, so feel free to blow this one off, but is that what you're doing down here? A woman your age—begging your pardon, but it *is* outside the norm—heading straight for a warzone, alone. I couldn't help but ask myself, why? You out here looking for this Miles?"

"Yes."

Tommy glanced at her wedding ring. "Is he your husband?"

"No. He isn't."

"But you love him, don't you?"

Angela closed her eyes. To simply say 'yes' hardly seemed sufficient. Her feelings for Miles couldn't fit inside a four-letter word like 'love', let alone be confirmed with a simple three-letter affirmation. Just a single glance into Miles' eyes was worth an entire library of words. But right now, with him gone, words were all she had.

"Yes. Yes, I do," she said.

Tommy let out a long, low whistle. "Angie, you're wilder than you look. And I mean that as a compliment." He winked at her again.

"Do you… do you think there's a chance? Of finding him, I mean?"

"Well, I'll be straight with you, Angie," Tommy said. "The odds are stacked against you. They say war is hell—and believe me, it is—but even more than that, it's chaos. And getting anything done in that level of chaos is a tough ask."

Sighing, she sank back into her seat and stared at the emptiness flying by outside.

"But I'll also say this," Tommy went on, glancing at her, "I told you I do lots of different jobs out here. Some of those jobs are what you might call intelligence-gathering operations, and I'm damn good at those kinds of tasks, if I do say so myself. And the reason why I'm so good at them is because I can read people like proverbial open books. Understood?"

She looked at him concurringly.

"I don't know if you'll find your Miles or not, I can't say. Too many variables. But I do know that from the second I saw you, I could tell that you have it in you to do whatever it was you came here to do. You've got the fire. Some people got it, some people don't. I look at you and I feel I can say—pretty damn confidently— that you got it."

Angela smiled shyly at him. "Thanks, Tommy."

"Don't mention it. But be careful. Don't go running head first into gunfire because you think I said you're Superwoman. Right now, my advice to you would be to try and get some rest." He patted the armrest of the truck. "This here mechanised puppy is armoured and 100% bulletproof. I doubt you'll be able to say the same about any of the sleeping arrangements you're going to find yourself with once you get to where you're going. Best take advantage while you can."

The instant he referred to sleep, Angela accepted that she was exhausted. A plane, two buses, and now this long ride through the desert—several days' worth of travel had all been crammed into a single, incredibly long twenty-four hours. She leaned back into her seat and attempted to relax.

Sleep did not, however, come immediately to Angela, and her mind inevitably started to wander. Maybe it was Tommy's mischievous hazel eyes or maybe it was his effortless and playful confidence, but something about him reminded her of Geoff. This was decidedly not her best friend's kind of environment, but she desperately wished he was here with her, making her laugh even in her worst moments, just as he'd done since they were small children growing up in Geoff's family estate on the fringes of London, so many decades previously.

Suddenly missing her life-long companion very much, Angela addressed the urge to communicate with him. She pulled out her phone and tapped the text conversation labelled 'Bug'—a pet name for Geoff that had endured since distant childhood. To her, he'd always be 'Bug' and to him, she'd always be 'Mouse'. She began to key out a message informing him that she'd arrived in

Jordan, but quickly discovered that there was no service where they were, which was the middle of nowhere.

To secure the semblance of comfort that his words perpetually brought to her, she began to scroll up and read a number of their old 'Signal' conversations, and soon she was silently laughing to herself at his past replies, almost able to hear his voice echoing in her head.

Eventually she came to a message that was many months old, written a lifetime ago, from the night she'd met Miles, mere hours before she'd laid eyes on him for the very first time.

Angela shook her head, unable to believe the words she had written, complaining to Geoff of how bored she had become with her retiree, suburban lifestyle, and informing him of her longing to sample the excitement, the adventure, and the exotic travel schedules that shaped his existence.

*Oh, Bug,* she thought, *it looks as if your grouchy, petulant mouse finally got her wish, and then some. This is much more excitement than I ever envisaged for myself – and more than I'm capable of handling, I think.*

With that scrutinising thought cradled in her head, she drifted into a shallow and restless slumber as the vehicle continued its journey towards a violent netherworld of terrifying uncertainty.

# CHAPTER 4:
## ENGLAND, 2015

Angela's thoughts drifted towards the special evening that lay ahead. With the restaurant having been booked weeks ago, the guest list already confirmed, and the taxi expected to arrive shortly before seven, she could now focus on her wardrobe selection—a problematic uncertainty that would focus solely on just two pieces of clothing.

She juggled between the all-black apparel with a silver neckline, and the perky floral yellow dress without sleeves. The same predictable poser seldom made her concluding verdict any simpler these days. The ebony evening gown held special appeal, extolling Angela's luscious, light-haired, Germanic feminine appearance and sublimely highlighting a bounty of shimmering blonde hair, especially when tastefully accompanied with a pair of black diamond-shaped earrings, which emitted a quartz-like sparkle that few in her company ever failed to notice. But the yellow dress would no doubt be cooler, she determined, and the evening ahead was intended to be a colourful, enchanting experience.

"No place for black, therefore," she quietly muttered to herself. "Yellow it is."

Her major concern lay with the exposed arms of the floral costume. Angela's overall appearance seemed wan to her these days, replete with minor facial skin blemishes that had recently broken out due to Angela's anxiety of her demanding actuality. But these were no more concerning than the paleness of her upper limbs, which the yellow dress would expose. Still, she elected for the brighter option as being more suitable.

As she perched on the edge of the bed, pondering the conscious exposure of her milky skin, her thoughts drifted to her need to expose herself emotionally to anyone capable of listening to her ever-increasing woes. She knew that she could reveal her pure, irrational, raw feelings to Geoff without incurring unwanted wrath or condescending judgment, but tonight was not the night for that. He had just touched down in London—now finally back in England following a lengthy absence—and it would be wrong to do so before a party, on a night that must exclusively belong to her *Oma*. Angela had to withhold that nagging deduction that she'd steered her own life into a corner of plainness, a disinfected nook of nothingness, a suffocating corner of leafy suburbia located on the apex of a hilly thoroughfare in the city. And yet she had. And now she was simply too old and too tired to escape from it all.

Angela remained seated on the edge of the duvet-clad divan, clutching her phone in one hand and fondling an earring with the other. There had been specific, poignant occasions in the past where it had been appropriate to confidently relay her doubts and apprehensions to Geoff—to cry, to curse, to open her soul and permit him to absorb the weakest, most childish, most fearful components of her internal framework. Nothing she could do or say would ever affect him. After all, he had witnessed an abundance of her childish choler throughout the years of their adolescence. They'd grown up together under the same roof, and in all those years no tantrum or demonstrative mood had seen him back away or reverse hurriedly from her. They'd shared the fullest, happiest moments of their respective lives as members of an extended family, and had innocently borne and endured some of their darkest interludes as one. Geoff was her rock, her confidant, her anchor. Her saviour.

She ultimately decided that she would confide in him, stating the truth behind her deep-seated disquiet, but that she'd temper the difficulties it generated inside her. Geoff would surely soon pry and question her relentlessly, eventually reaching the source of the problem and astonishingly getting to the root of establishing a solution. He always had, after all, and Angela knew he always would.

She tapped his number into her phone, and he answered on the first ring. "Welcome back you nomadic, lovable mystery of a man!" cried Angela. "I've missed you so terribly!"

"Greetings, Mouse, how the hell are you?" Geoff's croaky voice responded, indisputable evidence of fatigue saturating his reply. "My plane landed an hour ago. I'm now sitting in a cab making my way to you. I just can't begin to tell you how I'm so looking forward to this evening." Geoff paused in his exuberant conversational exchange with Angela, sensing that something was amiss in the tone of her greeting. "Okay, Mouse. Weary I may be, yet I can still detect when my favourite lady is not at one with the world. What's up, girl?"

"Oh, Bug," she sighed, "I just feel so stuck, confined, marooned… you know? Each day is the same as the one before, and as the one to follow tomorrow. It's as if I'm in a *Groundhog Day* loop. It's all so predictable. No surprises, no excitement, no nothing."

"Oh, don't be such a drama queen, Mouse!" yelled Geoff, before continuing firmly, "You have a satisfying life. You have William, you've got the kids—and your book club!"

The book club! Was this well-meaning, throwaway comment intended to invigorate or re-direct her in a sympathetic kind of way? No! Geoff knew Angela all too well to simply believe that he would, or possibly could, raise her from the mire of inner discontent that horrendously languished in the pit of her stomach simply by mentioning her book club. He had, in recent times, frequently dwelt on Angela's current continuation in Wimbledon. Time was passing her by and her moment to reflect and take stock of her anticipated future survival had duly arrived. She was asking questions of herself, with no meaningful answers forthcoming.

"*A menopausal flirtation with one's mortality,*" Geoff often mused.

"Well, sure. It could be worse," Angela said. "I'll give you that.

But the kids are away, and… poor William. It destroys me to see him so pathetically weak."

"How is he? The poor dear."

Since the cancerous diagnosis had been confirmed, and with William's lungs in a state of advanced, poisonous deterioration, he had elected not to undergo needless treatment that would no doubt fail to provide any likelihood of achieving extended longevity.

His physical decline had initially been a moderately slow journey, but then it had picked up pace with alarming impetus. His ceaseless weight loss through lack of appetite was leading to the inexorable erasure of the energetic and good-looking man whom Angela had wed so many years before. She'd watched as his flesh had embarked on a ruthless exodus from his skeletal structure and as his tolerance for sustenance had waned even further, as had his vigour. Angela couldn't even begin to imagine how much thinner and exhausted he'd become before death would mercilessly claim what was left of his once robust and healthy body, and nor did she want to.

To Angela, the most heartbreaking aspect of her husband's illness was that upon being confronted with the unassailable prospect of his premature termination, William had developed a strange lust for life, much greater than ever before. Initially, he desperately yearned to embark on all he'd never achieved throughout his actuality, before his time ultimately eroded. Yet, as the weeks and months wore on and his condition decidedly exacerbated, he transformed into an enfeebled carcass, one incapable of taking care of even his most basic of needs.

Only days earlier, while Angela had spied him impotently

attempting some basic gardening chores through the kitchen window, William had collapsed in a gasping, wheezing heap right next to the compost bin at the foot of his beloved square yardage of escapism. Angela fled to his aid and assisted him to the top of the stairs, struggling to ease him into bed.

The thought of losing the steady presence of her husband made Angela's vision of a sterile future of household chores, general maintenance, reading, and little else, feel all the more oppressive.

"He's stable, but he's involved in a battle he can't possibly win," she murmured into the phone.

"He hasn't changed his mind about the proposed treatment, then?" asked Geoff.

"No. He's too ridiculously obstinate... too stubborn. But at the same time he's too frail to continue much further without the therapy he requires." Angela flitted into the bathroom whilst continuing to chat with Geoff, picking up the second earring from the dark granite counter and threading it through her ear. "Oh, Bug! I just wish my life was more like yours. I'd just, you know, like some detachment from it all, for a while at least. I feel so decrepit at times, and I've become scared that everything—everything good— is now behind me. I'm struggling with the reality that I'm just an old lady with nothing more to look forward to than steering my bloody book club in a more productive direction and caring for a beautiful, infirm man until the grave eventually beckons me too."

After listening to the despondency that filtered through each of Angela's beseeching words, Geoff promptly attempted to lighten the mood. "Well, look here, Mouse," he said, "you *do* have something to look forward to – right at this very moment, in fact. A party! A grand party to honour *Oma*! Eighty-five years young, our grand lady, and still as much of an angel as ever, I'll bet. Doesn't that rekindle at least a smidgeon of youth's sparkle within you?"

Angela giggled at Geoff's lifelong ability to conveniently sidestep (or change the subject) when circumstances did not productively prevail, and with irritated happiness, she retorted to his comment, "That reminds me: I haven't seriously tried to apply make-up in far too long. Just get here and make me laugh again. See you soon! The back door is open, come straight in!"

With their conversation concluded, she glanced at herself in the mirror and sighed. The earrings had been a gift from Geoff's mother, Lady Dorothy Ashley-Cooper, for Angela's sixteenth birthday. Although Nina's salary had been ample for a governess, Nina could never have afforded such a lavish gift, but the Ashley-Coopers were generous and grateful employers. Lady Dorothy had spent many years defiantly striving to bridge the social divide between her privileged family and that of their loyal governess, one Nina Schaeffer.

Hitherto, Angela hadn't been thinking of Lady Dorothy as she peered at the earrings. Instead, she'd recalled wearing them to one of the rare social dances she'd reluctantly attended while studying journalism at Cambridge. She couldn't quite recall, however, the precise occasion or why she'd chosen to dress for it so spectacularly. Possibly, she'd done so out of curiosity.

In her youth, Angela had accepted that she was attractive, but she had been entirely unprepared for the jaw-dropping reaction she received as she crossed the threshold of the ballroom, the manner in which the boys stuttered when requesting to dance with her later in the evening, or the looks on the faces of the girls who enviously whispered amongst themselves as she graciously strode by. It had all injected into her a heady but not entirely pleasant feeling, especially when she briefly sensed an element of power over those who cast their darting eyes in her direction. It was an ephemeral flirtation with unforeseen power that would last but mere moments, a level of supremacy she'd felt she had not truly earned.

Her *Oma* had once informed Angela never to indulge or share in anything that was not richly deserving of her, and over her entire lifetime, Angela never had. But now, seeing how the earrings dangled from her lobes, book-ending a face that was starting to wrinkle and crease as it treacherously and none-too-spectacularly submitted to the ravages of time, the way they hung limply above a neckline that was intimating imminent sagging—and an upper-chest region that was spottily peppered with the skin signatures of unprotected intervals under a hot sun—she found herself longing to return to that special night.

Just one more opportunity to interrupt a male stranger's inhalation and exhalation capabilities. Just one more night where she could drink from the fountain of youth prior to attending a glistening ball and be locked in the arms of someone incredible, stealthily dancing the night away with an unknown other as they tenderly massaged their bodies to the unhurried musical accompaniment. Just one more time when they ran fingers and hands across the contours of their excited anatomies, developing a carnally ignited entanglement that would transport them both to an out-of-this-world destination, sensually and sexually higher than that of the moon above.

Emerging from her daydreaming, Angela privately scolded herself for entertaining such ludicrous hallucinations, though she failed to quell a mild form of embarrassment rising within her, confirmed by the light crimson flushing of her cheeks she saw in the mirror. The thought struck her as silly and girlish; it was so long ago and it would certainly never happen again.

"Aging is such a horrible burden!" she yelled in frustration at the ceiling. *They tell you it'll happen to you eventually,* she despairingly thought, *yet we never believe it. Not until it's dropped on us.*

Up to a point, she mournfully analysed, both she and William had enjoyed regular physical links and, long after the kids had been born, the sexual element to their marriage occupied a vital niche of bodily fulfilment, something that offered meaning and stimulus to their ongoing togetherness. Eventually, the regularity of intercourse began to wane—ebbing into oblivion, almost—notwithstanding the nocturnal moments following a late night out when William had relentlessly quaffed too much wine at whatever social gathering they'd attended, or after a neighbourly banquet or summer barbecue held within the confines of their home. At these times, her semi-inebriated spouse would attempt to arouse her when they finally reached their bed, but with little effect.

The last time such an undertaking was attempted by William, his briefly erect penis had significantly diminished inside her within seconds. He'd gasped in frustration and then rolled away from Angela, falling asleep immediately. She had silently wept throughout the crass and loveless act, and she'd continued weeping for the remainder of the night. They never made love again; for the previous seven years, their relationship had taken the mutational form of a sibling connection, nothing more.

Her reluctant submission to encroaching antiquity had placed upon Angela the encumbrance of female uselessness. She couldn't recollect when she'd last experienced an urge to covertly masturbate—most certainly, it had been long before both she and William ultimately bid *adieu* to the act of marital copulation. She had obviously dried up, her once-fertile body now a barren land incapable of feeling or delivering love. *Nothing grows on a parched and arid field of dust*, she dejectedly contemplated.

It wasn't sex she craved, though; she missed feeling loved.

Angela glanced at the sundry jars, brushes, and cases that comprised her make-up bag, the vast majority of the cosmetics not having seen daylight for some considerable time. She reached for a pink-coloured, conical container that encased a bold shade of eyeshadow, then she shook her head, reconsidering. *What am I thinking? That's all over, as are the days of my once-ingénue existence*, she inwardly mused.

Instead she applied the eyeliner pencil, lightly brushing with a technique that was subtle but ponderous. On completion of this uncommon cosmetic assignment Angela examined her handiwork with an element of satisfaction, and then, at the behest of an inner—possibly dangerous—impulse, she applied a faint coat of lipstick.

As she pulled the knee-length, floral yellow dress over her shoulders and let it fall into its natural position on her body, she meandered over to the corner of the room and stood upright in front of the tall Cheval mirror, which swung as required on an upright wooden frame. She reminded herself that the long mirror took its name from a French Cheval horse. *A carthorse, in my particular case*, Angela chided herself. Her appearance looked plain and, on second thoughts, the dress was not the style of garment that would catch anyone's attention.

She sighed, reminding herself again that tonight was all about her *Oma,* not about her. No matter how she was feeling about her personal life, her outer shell, or her age, she would don a happy, sincere face for her *Oma.* After all, she'd do anything for her.

She checked the hour on the bedside clock. Not late, but time to get moving; the German restaurant she'd chosen was deep in the city and it would take a considerable while to reach.

As a concluding touch, she removed her wedding ring and slipped on a 22 carat gold band set with a dark green gemstone. It had been yet another bequest from Lady Dorothy, but not one that had been gifted to her directly. It had belonged to her mother, Hjördis; it was special, and thus, it made her feel special too.

"All ready, *mein kind*?"

Her *Oma*'s voice drifted to her through the door, somewhat tremulous as a result of her advanced age, yet still laced with a hint of youthful excitement. Angela smiled; her *Oma* was thrilled by the prospect of the party.

"Yes, *Oma*! Coming!" she called.

As she ran her fingers through her hair and took one last appraising examination of herself, her phone burst into life. It was Geoff.

"Where are you, Bug? You should be here by now," Angela said worriedly.

"I'm sitting in a beautiful garden somewhere in Wimbledon," he replied. "It is a breathtaking sight. I intend to rename this exquisite backyard The Garden of a Thousand Sighs. Here I am, squatting under a blossoming apple tree. Hey, it must be your place as there's a wooden plaque pinned to its trunk proudly displaying the information that this is 'Angela's Garden'. Hey Mouse, you forgot to leave the French Windows open. I'm locked out!"

She immediately fled downstairs, tears of welcoming release filling her eyes.

Nothing mattered now. Geoff was here to make everything so much better.

As the waiters cleared the last of the empty dessert plates, the relative calm that had settled over the long wooden dining table soon gave way to an increasingly boisterous rumble of voices. Mouths that had been filled with beef roulade, sauerbraten, red cabbage, fluffy dumplings and, finally, a large slice of birthday cake, suddenly found themselves free to resume the conversations they'd been exchanging before dinner.

Nina Schaeffer was poised at the head of the table, Christina and John to her left and Angela and William to her right. The aged German lady was glowing with pride. Though her posture was slightly hunched under the weight of her long and demanding life, and though her hair had thinned and greyed, an infectious energy still radiated from her physically diminutive stature. She said little, happy just to quietly survey the scene of contentment in those positioned before her—sated, laughing, drinking, and conversing, gathered within the restaurant's dark-panelled, wooden embrace, all on her account.

Nina thought to herself, *Eine Nacht zum Erinnern*—and a night to remember it certainly was. A night never to be forgotten, in fact. At that thought a graceful beam lit her withering facial features, her grey-blue eyes sparkling under the candlelight. Finally, harmony in life had been secured.

In a contemplative transfer of thought, Nina returned to her home in Braunschweig, so many years before. *Was würden Mama, Papa, und Werner jetzt von mir denken?* she pondered. Even after all these years, the memory of Nina's lost family had never been lost or tarnished to her; they lived within her, never gone, just in another place, waiting to be reunited as an undivided family unit once more.

Angela quaffed a sip of beer from a small, decorative German stein and glanced over at her *Oma*. She strived to emulate her grandmother's beam of acceptance, and while it was harder than it looked, she was coping. Everyone at the table seemed to be engaged in lively chatter—all except Angela.

Trying to remedy this, Angela asked John about his architecture exams. He told her they'd gone well and then, before she could try and learn anything else about his life at university, he turned away from her and began exchanging chit-chat with one of William's partners from the accounting office. Next, she tried Christina. How had things been going with the boy who'd asked her on a date? Angela received a snort for her trouble, Christina replying dismissively that she'd never taken the boy up on his offer and that had been weeks ago.

Leaning in and looking down the length of the table, past the twenty or so guests, Angela caught Geoff's eye. He'd said something that had made the attractive young waiter—with whom he'd been flirting since the appetisers had been served—laugh loudly. Geoff looked at her, winked, and then beckoned her over with his index finger.

"Mouse, darling, we were just talking about you!" he said when she arrived. Geoff took a generous sip of wine and continued, "I was telling—" he squinted at the waiter's name tag, "Barry here about how when we were small, you'd spend hours playing chess with *Oma*—that's the birthday girl over there, by the way," he added for Barry's benefit. "I'd get so jealous for your attention that sometimes I'd nick a knight or a bishop out of the box of pieces and hide it, trying to end your game before it had begun. It never stopped you two, though." He smiled. "You'd just find a stray button or bobby pin and start up a game all the same."

"You always were a scamp," she said, also smiling at the memory.

"Why don't you give us a story from our golden youth, Mouse?" Geoff suggested. "Something fun for my new, dear friend, Barry."

Just then, the high-pitched sound of someone tapping an empty glass with an item of cutlery rang out, causing silence to fall across the table.

Christina arose from her seat, her face slightly flushed, then she raised her beer with one hand and took Nina's hand in her other.

"Welcome everyone," Christina began, "and I hope this is the first of many heartfelt toasts to our guest of honour. Now, I'm not much for public speaking, but I'll give it my best shot." She paused for a moment, looking down at the woman sitting next to her. "All I want to say is that I can't think of a more amazing woman than my *Oma*—or my great-*Oma*, rather, if anyone's keeping score. Nina Schaeffer has taught me the rudiments of life and has endured things most of us shall, thankfully, never have to experience. I'll never be able to thank her enough for being there for me through each and every phase of my life."

Christina paused for a moment to lubricate her dry throat with a small sip of beer. "We love her with all our hearts. To Nina, everyone's *Oma!*"

As a chorus of *'To Nina!'* erupted from around the dining table, Angela wiped her moist eyes. Initially, she'd been moved by her daughter's public display of love for her *Oma*, but hearing her daughter announce that Nina had raised her had hit her with a piercing thud. It hurt, mostly as Angela knew it to be true.

Geoff glanced at her, covertly sharing her distress. "Alright, let's have it, Mouse. Tell us a story from the good old days."

"Another time, Bug," she replied. "I can't think of anything right now and I should go see if William needs anything. Why don't you regale your friend with some tales of your adventures in India or Thailand? I'm going to want to hear it all in excruciating detail later." She squeezed his shoulder. "Nice to meet you, Barry," she added to the waiter.

Arriving back at the head of the table, Angela bent to kiss Nina on the cheek, striving not to make eye contact with Christina lest her tears return. She then gave William a soft squeeze on the shoulder; he looked much paler than he had when they'd arrived.

"You alright, Will?"

"I'm fine, dear, just fine."

It was clear that William was incapable of admitting to the unpleasant rising symptoms within himself. When he didn't feel right, he chose not to make his discomfort or distress known, though his wracked facial features often spoke for themselves.

"Well, I'm headed to the bar for another drink," said Angela. "Can I get you anything?"

"Water, if you're going," he said, "but it's not urgent." He patted her hand weakly and she crossed the restaurant to the bar.

As insipid as her life appeared, this particular pipeline of stimulation was suddenly creating the stifling characteristics of a suffocating enclosure. Angela scanned the chattering guests— colleagues from William's office and their wives, a handful of Christina's friends, and some of her old journalism colleagues. All of them seemed so normal, aptly occupying the various roles that life had applied to them. Angela sighed.

Just then the small, antiquated brass bell above the restaurant's front door tinkled, drawing Angela's attention from the assembled troupe of guests. Thankful for the momentary distraction, she viewed a rather tall, bohemian-looking man, adorned in a brown leather jacket, a blue jumper, and faded black jeans. He strode assertively into the restaurant and responded cheerily to the head waiter's familiar acknowledgement. His grey-flecked hair matched the swarthy five o'clock shadow that prominently shrouded his pronounced cheekbones.

Angela couldn't gauge how old this man was. *Probably fifty-something*, she ascertained as he terminated his conversation with the *Oberkellner* and ambled into the bustling eatery. He did so, however, with the confident, strutting gait of a thirty-year-old, one who'd quite possibly achieved success in each venture he'd undertaken during the course of his mature lifetime.

Angela monitored his short journey across the darkened hardwood floor with interest, even from a distance being drawn into his bright green eyes. He was surely there to meet some younger woman for a date, or to discuss an upcoming art exhibition or similar project with a like-minded associate. Whatever he was there for, he was none of her business. An interesting person, living an interesting life—for all intents and purposes, another species of human being, and certainly not one of her breeding.

*I will turn away and order my beer,* Angela told herself. *I will turn away and…*

But her eyes never left him; they *couldn't* leave him. Her mouth was now slightly open and, with a shudder of self-consciousness, she promptly closed it.

With each step he took, the impossible became more and more likely: he was heading directly for their table, getting closer and closer.

Once it seemed inevitable that Nina's birthday party was indeed his intended destination, Angela's shocked interest turned to overpowering curiosity. Who at the party did she and this mystery man have in common? She had certainly never been introduced to him before. She would have remembered.

His link to the evening's events was explained when he greeted a crowd of her old colleagues, particularly Mary, a younger reporter Angela had known from her time at Reuters.

Mary stood up and threw her arms around him.

*Ah, that explains it*, thought Angela. *Nothing to get excited about. It's just pretty, perky, young Mary's husband.* She let herself watch for a few more moments as various expressions tugged the man's striking features into many different shapes—all of them appealing—when, with a start, Angela accepted that she wasn't just staring at him, but smiling at the man as if she were a love-struck schoolgirl!

Her inherent awkwardness proved enough for her to finally wrest control of her motor functions from whatever strange and inappropriate entity had taken over her body. "A Malbec when you have a moment, please," Angela requested from a member of the bar staff.

"Well, look who's here all by her lonesome!"

Angela jolted as Mary's hand came to rest on the small of her back. "Oh, yes. Hi, Mary. Just after another round," she said, doing everything in her power to keep her gaze fixed on Mary's small, blue eyes so as not to drown once more in the man's large, round pupils, which were currently regarding her from some two feet above Mary's shoulder line.

"You know, I've always been partial to a Malbec," he said. "Wine with a real personality to it."

His vocal tones were a smoky, rich baritone with just a hint of an obscure accent. *Scottish*, she thought. *Possibly Glaswegian.*

His dulcet timbre was made for dry wit and slow-spoken wisdom. It was a voice that would put anyone at ease, emitting vibrations that could convince most people that everything was serene in his capable hands.

She cursed herself for the superficial make-up routine of earlier. Why hadn't she opted for the eyeshadow? A more assertive shade of lipstick, at least? *Oh, that's right,* she reflected. *I felt too old. I feel too old. Too old and too unappealing to merit a full complement of cosmetics.*

"I hope you don't mind that I brought a plus-one."

"Nonsense," said Angela. "I'm sure I mentioned that spouses were invited."

At that, the pair blushed in unison and Mary giggled, "What? Spouse? Angela, you met my husband Tom at the fundraiser a couple of years back. Don't you remember?"

"Oh, goodness! I'm so sorry. How silly of me. That's right. Tom. Your husband."

"Don't worry about it. I'm sure you've had plenty on your mind with the party. If only I could forget my husband so easily myself." Mary giggled again and turned to look up at the man beside her, a half-smile now playing lightly on his lips. "What do you say, Miles? In another time, another life, would we have made a good couple?"

"Well, I dare say we'd—"

Before he could finish, Mary jumped back in. "My word! How rude of me! I still haven't introduced you two. Angela, this is Miles Dunbar—award-winning correspondent, dear friend, and the United Kingdom's most eligible bachelor... over the age of sixty. Miles, this is Angela. We worked together before she retired and buggered off to the suburbs."

*That was the best she could come up with?* Angela thought, inwardly fuming.

Under the weight of the insecurities regarding her appearance, and now Mary's lacklustre introduction, she couldn't help but feel rather small and plain.

"Charmed," Miles said, taking her hand in his.

The second he touched her, Angela felt herself falling into his jade green eyes for the umpteenth time, and as she did, all the smallness and plainness she'd been feeling simply and immediately evaporated. No underwhelming summary of her past could dim this feeling of importance and bubbling possibility she felt coursing through her entire body. She clasped his hand for slightly longer than was customary, then let go.

Had he given her the slightest squeeze as he released his gentle grip?

"What a lovely wedding band," he commented. It was more than just a compliment. It was spoken like a connoisseur appreciating an exquisite item of jewellery.

"Thank you, but this isn't my wedding ring," responded Angela. "It's a family heirloom I choose to wear sometimes. That's all."

"Always the charmer," Mary said, scooting around Angela to collect a tray of mixed drinks from the bartender before turning back towards the table. "Miles, are you coming?" she asked.

"You know," he responded rather hesitantly, "I believe I'd rather have a goblet of wine. A Malbec sounds lovely. You go on. I'll be with you all in a tick."

Before Angela could even begin to question what had just happened, Miles said, "It's from Argentina, you know? Malbec. Have you been?"

"The closest I came was Bolivia. Working on a story about some ancient mines they have down there."

"Ah, yes. Potosí."

"That's right! Not many people have heard about them."

He shrugged. "Someone told me about them when I was down in Buenos Aires. Wonderful city. Vibrant people, just like the *vino* they so expertly produce. It's where I purloined this old jacket." He tugged at the leather collar. "Although, I must say, this beautiful yellow dress of yours is making me feel as if I'm a little underdressed."

"Really?" Angela said, laughing. "I think you're the first person to have ever commented on my sartorial sense of judgment."

"It glows," said Miles enthusiastically.

"Well," she began, mildly blushing, "you look…" She sifted through the pile of flattering descriptors that were currently stacking up in her head, trying to find a suitable word that wasn't inappropriate, and finally settled on, "nice."

"Why thank you," he responded playfully. "That's better than shabby and outmoded. Which is how I feel most of the time, I'm afraid. To be honest, at sixty-two, I've been thinking about retiring to the suburbs myself—for quite some time, in fact. It sounds divine."

Angela chuckled loudly, causing Miles to raise an eyebrow.

"Are my suburban aspirations that humorous? Maybe that'll be my post-retirement hobby. I'll be the sad old comedian doing unsolicited stand-up at the local pub, telling jokes no one wants to hear."

"I'd love to hear them. Are they all knock-knock jokes or are you slightly more sophisticated?"

"Challenge accepted," he said with a grin. "Let me order you another glass of wine and I'll try some of my material on you."

Twenty minutes passed before Angela remembered where she was and why. The entire restaurant and party had melted away, leaving her and Miles floating in their private world of wine and shimmering light, but then reality broke over her body like a cold wave of freezing seawater. Flustered, she made a cursory glance at the table, certain that everyone would be staring at her with disapproving looks fixed on their faces at the negligence of her duties as hostess.

But, no. Everything appeared conventionally normal. *Oma* was speaking slowly to Christina and one of her friends. William was smiling and nodding as one of his fellow accountants spoke to him. Geoff tore himself away from Barry for a moment to send her a wicked grin, a crimson veil of embarrassment quickly swamping her glowing cheeks.

"What?" asked Miles. "Do you find my tales of life a little too mutant for a first conversation?"

Angela placed her hand on his forearm. "Not at all," she said. "Go on, please. I'm listening."

They ended up sitting at the bar for more than an hour, trading stories about their respective pasts, about journalism, about London, about literature and life as a whole. As Angela chatted with Miles, the world around her receded into a realm of secondary importance; they'd slipped its bonds by the simple act of listening to each other. But each time she recalled where she was, who she was, and what she was doing, the opposite occurred: the clock sped up, the precious moments slipping through her fingers faster than the finest grains of sand.

Between them they had drained a bottle of wine, and by now Angela felt comfortingly warm and radiant, as if conditioned and accepting of a change occurring within her, and in her life ahead as well.

"I didn't intend to interrupt this little love affair, but I'm afraid the jetlag has finally claimed me as a casualty."

Angela choked on the last remnants in her wine glass as Geoff's words smothered the blissful haze in her brain. Unable to speak for a moment, she turned and smiled.

"Thank you for a smashing evening, Mouse," he continued. "I'll see you again soon. If not, I'll be sure to give you the details of my travels over Skype." He leaned in for an embrace and whispered in her ear, "And I'll be expecting to hear some details of your own as well."

Following Geoff's departure, Angela and Miles briefly gazed at one another in a humorously guilty fashion—as though they were two children who'd been caught talking in class and chastised by an ever-vigilant pedagogue, both searching for the threads of the conversation they'd previously been engaged in—until Angela felt a tug on her elbow.

"*Mein kind*, it's getting a little late, and after all the excitement, I am quite tired."

Peering past her *Oma*, Angela saw that almost all the

guests had departed the bistro, heading for home. Christina was recovering several gifts that had been bequeathed to Nina, while John stood near the exit with an impatient expression on his face. William remained in his seat at the large dining table, looking decidedly exhausted.

Angela resigned herself to the vexing verity that the party was finally over, and as she did so a hint of sadness leaked into her expression, igniting a level of gloom that was hastened by the stale odour of spent, emotional euphoria.

"Ah, responsibilities," said Miles, rising from his perch, "an essential part of life, but frequently, so irritating."

"Yes, it would seem that duty calls," Angela replied, spying William settling the bill while the remaining guests moved towards the exit.

"Will I see you again?"

She winced, avoiding answering Miles' query while at the same time trying not to search for tones of attraction in his voice.

"Come find me at the nearest pub," he continued. "I'll be the comedian getting booed off stage."

She giggled at the thought of this man getting booed for anything; just the thought of him doing something awkward seemed ridiculous. But she loved that this first little in-joke existed between them, and she'd nurture it no matter how absurd.

"I'll reserve a table right up front," she said.

Just then, William came up behind her and put his hand on her back, asking if she was ready to leave. A hint of weariness laced his voice. He hardly even looked at Miles, clearly oblivious to any subtle undertones in the atmosphere. He always moved through the world inside his own bubble of blissful ignorance to nuance, one of her husband's endearing little quirks.

Angela bid *adieu* to Miles as casually and coolly as possible. Following the effortless intimacy of their conversation, to simply offer Miles a commonplace farewell—as one would a family friend or shopkeeper—struck Angela as being wholly inappropriate and inadequate, but she managed to wrestle control of herself back from the intimacy of the evening.

As William led her away from Miles and toward Nina, who was waiting at the entrance, she struggled not to cast a glance back over her shoulder. Even so, Angela was certain that his eyes were resting forlornly on her retreating figure, watching until she was out the door, the restaurant's aged bell resounding behind her.

Angela climbed out of her car at the parking lot of Maison St. Cassien. Her hands were trembling slightly, though not with the same severity as they had done when she'd covertly met Miles some weeks earlier for the first time following Nina's celebration dinner. Ever since, they had rendezvoused at the out-of-the-way French café each time she could conjure up a passable excuse to leave the house for an hour or two.

During their long and engaging conversations, she had learned more and more about Miles. She'd listened to him as he talked about growing up in Paisley—a bustling Renfrewshire town situated on the periphery of Glasgow—and about the many places he'd travelled in order to cover various military conflicts the world over. She heard him speak about his haberdashery mother and his electrician father—whose wages at the weaving factory were barely sufficient to support and feed his kin during the early years of his Caledonian childhood. In turn, she'd freely confided in Miles about herself, revelling in the way his attentive gaze would unabashedly confirm that her existence was not mundane. Each utterance she voiced seemed to provoke within him a fully charged stimulus and unswerving fascination.

The café was sufficiently distant from her house, an unlikely destination that meant they wouldn't be intercepted by people known to her, or to him. In time, however, the light subterfuge started to feel a little silly. After all, she wasn't doing anything wrong, anything that could be construed as wrongfully extra-marital; they had engaged in nothing other than conversation and a shared platonic kiss on the cheek when saying hello or goodbye to one another.

But, as each departure from Miles became increasingly difficult, Angela failed to shake the feeling that her meetings with him were, indeed, a subtle sort of infidelity. The familiarity between them grew with every meeting, and during the days she didn't see him Angela found herself lost in thoughts about him, longing for the next opportunity when his handsome face would be placed just a few feet away from her own, yearning for that magical sensation of knowing that their ideas, beliefs, and tastes in everything from art, to literature, to music, to life in general, were perfectly in sync. *Well*, she reminded herself as she strolled through the door of the café, *we may just talk, but the last time we met, that kiss had felt different. What* was *that?*

It hadn't been a real kiss. Not really. Just a goodbye peck

on the cheek. It had come shortly after Miles had informed her about the death of his brother in a car accident when Miles was just thirteen years old. She'd seen the emotions stir themselves up in his eyes and had reached out to take his hand across the table, basking in both the electricity this generated within her and the thrill of seeing him so exposed.

Then, his lips had lingered a moment longer than necessary, and unbidden, her fingers had dug into his shoulder.

The phantom shadow of the kiss had lived on her cheek for days, an indelible—if invisible—mark that things were maybe moving towards something more than long chats over espresso in a crowded bistro. Just thinking about it made Angela's heart race.

She'd felt the urge to tell Geoff, embarrassed at reading so deeply into a little peck on the cheek, and when they'd spoken late that night via Skype, he'd poked at her and pried away, and eventually it had come out. She hadn't been able to admit it to herself, but to Geoff, she could admit anything: that this feeling, which was so gigantic and powerful, had been tugging at her with a planetary force of gravity.

"Bug," she'd said in disbelief, "I think I may be falling in love with him."

She sauntered out of the hot July humidity and into the café, and there he was. The same brown leather jacket, the same piercing green eyes, looking up at her with their usual intensity. The skin around his eyes crinkled into a smile that made her catch her breath as he walked to the counter to order them coffee.

"I thought you'd never get here. Go sit down and I'll bring over the drinks," he said to her, grinning.

"What? I'm not late." She laughed.

"Oh, I know. But still, waiting for you is strangely unbearable."

It took an almost Herculean feat of will for Angela not to admit that she felt the same, that almost every hour of every day was a lonely and unbearable pause in her life until she met up with him again.

They sipped their dark, hot beverages and relayed their accounts on the happenings of the past week, their innocent chit-chat consisting of William's continuing struggles with poor health and the astronomical expense of herbal remedies, while Miles confessed to arguments with an editor over the wording of a piece he was expected to produce by the following morning.

Angela's sudden mixed feelings about middle age and all that it entailed had long since evaporated—now, in this very moment, she was a girl once again, in the company of a magnificent boy, both secretly pained for a truthful moment when they may confess that life would or could never be the same again without the presence of the other.

The conversation soon turned to another fierce combat recollection, and that of the hardest job Miles had ever undertaken. As he conveyed his memories to Angela about covering the war in Bosnia and Herzegovina, about witnessing the Markale Massacre erupt on the streets of Sarajevo, grabbing his camera to capture harrowing images that he'd later offer to *National Geographic* at a price, and about the subsequent feeling of survivor guilt and of profiteering from a tragedy that had left him melancholic and questioning his professional scruples for several months afterward, Angela was swept away with admiration for this brave, complex, self-reflective man.

She craved to express her admiration somehow. To grab him, to shake him, to make him understand just how special he was. His intoxicating conversation, and the reaction it created within her, had placed the surprise she'd prepared for Miles in the back of her mind; she'd been thinking about extending an overdue alteration to their conversational, coffee-drinking routine—one that had electrified Angela's senses all morning—and now she accepted that it must come to fruition.

So, Angela made her proposal.

"While I do so love this café," she said casually, "I was thinking that today, since William, *Oma*, and the kids are engaged in their idea of adventurous activity, we too could embark on an adventure of our choosing."

Miles' eyes widened. "An adventure? Outside the sanctuary of our bistro hideaway? How scandalous and bold. I love it."

She laughed. "Not so scandalous. Just a picnic. There's a lovely park near to where I live. I've even made some German treats for lunch."

Miles grinned at her. "You spoil me, and you already know of my weakness for German cuisine." He shook his head in mock disappointment. "How have I left myself so exposed?"

"I like you that way." She pushed her chair back and promptly stood up. "Shall we?"

# CHAPTER 5:
## SYRIA, 2016

Tommy's hand gently stirred Angela's shoulder and, slowly, her sleepy disorientation melted away in the bleak light of dawn.

Squinting out of the grimy cab window, she caught sight of a block of scorched, splintered apartment buildings, crudely congregating under the grey-blue sky. The burnt-out husks of two cars sat in a blackened tangle beneath the buildings, as if disintegrated—mechanised sentinels that appeared as if they'd once stood guard over the devastated architecture. An unnatural silence enveloped the stricken landscape, accompanied by a ghostly, spine-chilling eeriness that registered fear-provoking alarm deep within her.

"Welcome to Aleppo, my Sleeping Beauty," Tommy crooned from the driver's seat.

Angela repositioned herself and promptly sat up, rubbing her encrusted eyes. "We're here? What about the border?"

"You slept through it, Angie, just like a baby. No problems. All silky smooth."

She looked through the windshield, gazing around at all the desolation. Twin, unbroken piles of rubble lined the street as far as the eye could see, swept to either side of the road as if it were household debris brushed into the corners of a neglected dwelling. Large, yawning apertures on the sides of buildings indicated the position where balconies had once existed, at least until the moment they'd suddenly and explosively disintegrated.

"You see that building over there?" Tommy pointed to a small, squat rectangle of shattered cement across the street. "There's your Red Cross Office. And, just like we agreed, I'm afraid this is where I leave you."

The harrowing spectacle of the ravaged outlying district proved sufficient to set Angela's nerves on edge. Now, the prospect of venturing away from the Hilux's armour-plated safety—coupled with the thought that the only person she knew in the entire country was about to depart, leaving her utterly alone in this terrible place—made her mouth as parched as the desert sand.

"Alright," she said, trying to steady herself. "What was it you said we do? Shake hands, I get out of the car, and you drive off into the distance?"

"Beauty of a memory you've got there, Angie." He held out his hand.

"Thank you for everything, Tommy. I appreciate it."

"Don't mention it, sister. I hope you find your Miles."

On releasing their mutual palmed grasp, Angela hesitatingly alighted from the vehicle. Once outside, she stood shivering in the morning chill for a moment, staring at the leaving silver transporter until it was finally out of sight. She then turned in the direction of the mangled Red Cross Office and started walking.

The door was locked and her series of knocks went unanswered. Perhaps she was too early. The sun was in the process of rising, and knowing that its early warmth would soon have an impact on her shivering frame, Angela told herself to remain calm. Looking around, she caught sight of a lone bench at the far end of the fractured edifice, deciding to wait there until the sun—or a person—appeared.

Angela had no idea if the bleak sense of being in a ghost town was due to the early hour, or if this part of the city was just always this deserted. Whatever the reason, from her perch on the bench she felt as if she were the sole survivor of the apocalypse. She was surrounded by substantial evidence of human habitation and yet she was completely alone, as if she'd transcended into a parallel universe, a bizarre version of a sordid underworld in which she was doomed to dwell in solitude, uncertainty and apprehension her only companions.

She began to detect irregular fluctuations filling the auditory void, a combination of nippy airstream whistling its way through the canyon-like streets and the crippled, twisted steel straining under its deformed stress. The mild bellow created a confused but subtle medley of urban tones, peculiarly soothing in an unexpected way. She closed her eyes to the strained accompaniment and drifted into a phase of brief meditation.

A thundering boom in the distance immediately lifted Angela from her drowsy repose.

It was a piercing, ear-splitting commotion that resembled a forceful crash of thunder, and as it pulverised the bleak peacefulness of the deserted locality its echoes resounded across the destroyed, lifeless architecture. Then, another ferocious blast shook the ground beneath her, followed by a trickle of smoke that she could see rising in the distance.

The initial detonation had rendered her rigid and frozen, stuck to the spot in a state of sheer terror. The second powerful blast had the opposite effect; she leaped off the bench and pounded on the door of the Red Cross Office, shouting, "Please! Please! Open the bloody door!"

Then, another explosion with sonic-boom similarity. It was the loudest of them all, and sufficiently close enough to displace each bone and joint within her anatomy.

Angela's throat became raw from yelling, her knuckles bloodied and bruised. After a few more seconds she gave up on the door and sought cover beneath the bench, adopting the posture of a foetus in the womb—with her back curved forward and her limbs folded in front of her body—while the avalanche of smaller tremors transmitted their fearsome pulsation.

The artillery barrage ceased as suddenly as it had commenced.

Several moments passed before Angela acknowledged that the thuds she could now detect were that of her heart—vibrating, racing, and quivering in response to the salvo of indiscriminate bombing. Still, she couldn't move; she attempted to unfold her body from under the bench, but her limbs failed to obey her. They shook as leaves on a tree, involuntary reacting to a placid summer zephyr.

She was uncertain how long she'd been positioned under the bench, ensnared in uncontrollable fear, when the door to the building finally and hesitantly creaked open. At last, the prospect of protective cover freed her body from its terrified pose.

"Oh my God!" said a man's voice from above her as she pulled herself out from under the bench. "What are you doing out here? Are you alright?"

Angela found herself looking at the narrow, tanned face of a young man a few inches shorter than her. He was of slight build, had bright blue eyes and curly blond hair, and he was looking at her with an expression of pure shock.

"Hurry, hurry. Come inside!" He slammed the heavy metal door behind them, locked it, then turned around to face her. "How long were you waiting out there?"

"Oh, I—I'm not sure. Fifteen minutes? Half an hour?"

"I'm so sorry, I had no idea you were outside! We don't get many walk-ins here." He smiled at her. "Would you care for some coffee? A little breakfast?"

Angela had not endured any hunger pangs throughout her recent ordeal, food being low on the list of her survival priorities, but the mere mention of hot sustenance triggered uncharacteristic hypoglycemic symptoms within her exhausted body.

"That would be lovely, thank you," she responded wearily.

"Be back in a minute. Please, sit down. It's not a five-star hotel, but do try to make yourself comfortable." Briskly, he stepped through a door to the rear of the room and disappeared.

Angela scanned the small, dimly lit space.

Pale early morning light seeped through the bars and grates that covered the windows, landing softly on the two rows of metal folding chairs that had been placed on one side of the room to form a waiting area. A wooden bureau was nestled in the corner of the room, covered with official-looking paperwork, plus several archaic black-coloured telephones. At the centre of the desk lay an aged laptop, one from a bygone era, but seemingly still functional. To the other side of the reception area, a burnished and glittering saxophone rested on a metallic easel specifically designed to support the musical instrument when not being played by its owner.

The faint aroma of coffee wafted in through the slightly ajar door, indicating to Angela that the dilapidated pied-à-terre afforded a modest living space, or at least a utilitarian food preparation area.

The man re-entered the room, clutching a Styrofoam cup in one hand and a small plastic container in the other. "Coffee's not great, but it's hot. These kebabs here are better warm, but I figured you'd be hungry and wouldn't want to wait."

"You were correct." Angela bit into the cold seasoned meat and allowed herself to relax a little after quaffing her first sip of the hot, sweet coffee. "Thank you. It's all delicious."

The man smiled. "Glad to hear it. I'm Hans."

"I'm Angela Mortimer. Nice to meet you, Hans. You're German, right? I thought I heard an accent in your voice. That's where my grandmother's from." She smiled at him between generous bites of the kebab. "So… do people actually live in this neighbourhood? I thought it was completely deserted when I arrived."

"Not completely. But there's not much footfall, or traffic, these days. Especially at night, in the evening, and around dawn. Those are statistically the most dangerous times to be a pedestrian around here, as you have recently experienced."

"Good to know. How long have you been down here? And where in Germany are you from?"

"I was born in Remscheid, south side of the Ruhr region, but my family moved around a lot when I was young," he explained. "Leipzig for a while, then Bonn, and finally Dortmund. I studied English Literature for three years at Leeds University in England, then figured I needed to forge a big change in my life. I eventually returned to Remscheid and played a bit of sax here and there, secretly craving the opportunity to perform alongside my hero, Peter Brötzmann. He too was born in the Remscheid area, but I never got the chance."

He shrugged, and Angela smiled at him between sips of her coffee.

"I guess I became bored with myself," he continued. "On a whim, I volunteered for a position with the Red Cross, wanting to do something that would really make a difference in the world. Three years later, here I am." He smiled at her again. His beaming expression was warm and pleasing to the eye, the kind that carries an implicit element of generosity and helpfulness. "Where is your grandmother from, Angela?"

"Braunschweig. She was born there but had to flee during the war."

A sombre look fell on Hans' face. "From the bombing, or…?"

"She was Jewish. Or, well, not exactly. Her grandmother was Jewish, but the whole family didn't know until it was almost too late. Her parents learned of their heritage under the Nazi regime, and within the space of a day or two they plotted the escape of their daughter—my grandmother. She survived, but she never saw her parents again."

"And I take it she escaped successfully?" he asked.

"Oh, yes. She's the strongest woman you can imagine."

"What happened to her parents?"

Angela shook her head. "Gone, like millions of others. All gone!"

Hans nodded slowly. "A dark, dark stain on our history. What a horrible time. What a horrible thing, war. The things I've seen since I've been here… you wouldn't believe half of them if I told you."

They sat in silence while Angela sipped her coffee, and after a few moments, Hans restored himself into the cheerful, friendly individual he'd been before the conversation had turned to war. It was a visible, physical change—he shook his head as if to clear it, shuddered slightly, and then straightened his posture, looking over at her.

*He must need to force himself to stay positive*, Angela mused. *Otherwise, living in a place like this, he'd go mad.*

"Please," he said, his voice mildly pleading, "let us remain seated and you can tell me what I can help you with. I take it you're not here as a tourist."

Angela informed Hans about Miles Dunbar—the correspondent who'd gone missing several weeks ago in Aleppo—and told him that she'd made her way to Syria to take him home.

She then explained how she'd been smuggled across the border the night before and dropped off earlier, having been reliably informed that the Red Cross might be able to assist her.

"He must be pretty important to you to come all this way," Hans commented. "We are asked to look for people pretty often, but I've never met someone brave enough to come and actually do it in person." He learned forward towards her, over the desk. "I can't promise you anything and I don't want to get your hopes up, but you have come to the right place. If there's anything I can do to help you find this Miles Dunbar, I'll do it. But I'm sorry to say that the name doesn't ring a bell. Do you have any photos of him?"

Angela retrieved her phone from the battered Bergen and presented Hans with an image of Miles, a picture she'd copied from the internet. It was a source of vexation for Angela that they'd never once posed for photographs together before his departure to Syria, and not for the first time she dwelt on the vacuous possibility that this single, promotional illustration of Miles was the only visual artefact she possessed of him.

"Hmm. No. I have no recollection of laying eyes on him before," said Hans, "but don't fret," he continued quickly, after glimpsing how Angela's face had developed a crestfallen appearance, "I just work on the administrative side of things. One of our emergency workers or fixers would have a far better chance of knowing who he is. When did you say he went missing again?"

"I don't know exactly," Angela admitted, shaking her head. "Maybe six to seven weeks ago?"

Hans dwelt in silence for a moment. "Five weeks ago there was a lot of action near to the Al-Nuqtah Mosque on Mount

Jawshan. It's a half-hour car journey from here. Any journalist in the area would have been there to cover all the fighting—and the aftermath. I think starting there would be your best bet."

"Alright, thank you. Was it—was it bad? The fighting in that area?"

Hans nodded slowly, a look of uneasiness developing on his bronzed face. Then he shook his head again, pushing the subject away once more. "I wish Idi was here," he announced in despair. "He's a fixer, a translator, and a senior member of the emergency response team. He was also born and raised in this neighbourhood—in fact, you were just eating some of his aunt's cooking. He spends a lot of time with journalists and international TV crews. If anyone at the Red Cross knows where Miles is, I think it would be Idi."

Angela felt a warm glimmer of hope course through her veins. Maybe this wouldn't be so impossible after all. "Where is Idi? When will he be back?"

"Hard to say, really," Hans sighed. "He speaks English impeccably and, because he's so familiar with the territory, he's frequently rotated through the different sectors. At this moment, he's working at an orphanage in the north-east part of town. I doubt he'll be back for a least a few days."

Angela's transitory taste of optimism vanished immediately when taking receipt of the crushing words uttered by Hans. A few days? What would she do for a few days? In this godforsaken place? Over that time frame, anything could happen to Miles, or to herself. She couldn't possibly dally that long. She had to get mobile with undeterred alacrity.

As this notion crossed her mind, the trembling returned with increased momentum. What had she been thinking? She couldn't undertake this trek alone, and now, the only person who could aid her was indisposed. What if Miles had been killed covering the fighting around the mosque? What if he'd been taken prisoner? What if he was just waking up at that very moment, safe in some hospitable host's apartment, sitting down to write up whatever piece he'd been working on this whole time? Would he be thinking of her? Would he have forgiven her? She needed to know and she needed to know *now*. If she didn't find out what had happened to him, she felt as if her entire body would cease functioning. She couldn't wait for Idi. She couldn't wait at all.

"I can't… I can't…" When the sentence had formed in her mind, it had ended in the words *'wait for several days'*, but in the time it took the thought to reach her mouth, the sentence's operative verb had changed. "I can't… I can't breathe. I can't breathe," she gasped.

"Hey! Hey, hey, it's OK. It's OK." Hans jumped up and knelt next to her chair, placing his hand gently on her shoulder. "Deep breaths through your nose and out through your mouth. That's it. Another one. That's it. It's all going to be fine."

She nodded unconvincingly and waited for the blackness at the periphery of her mind (and vision) to vacate. When it had, she said, "Thank you, Hans. I'm alright now. I'm just… I've never done anything like this before. I've never experienced war on this scale. It—it just hit me that I'm in way over my head. I don't know how I'm going to be able to do this without support."

Hans sat across from her and picked up the phone on the desk's receiver. It was connected to the phone's base with a helix cable, something Angela hadn't seen in years. Hans pointed the phone at Angela. "Look at me. You're not alone. First, let me start by giving you some advice. What just happened to you, that panic attack, is totally natural. It happened to me a dozen times when I first got here. Don't feel embarrassed. But it won't help you. Panicking will impair your judgment, will lead you to make rash decisions. It could cost you or someone else their life. When you feel panic taking hold of you, just try to breathe and remind yourself that you're here. You," he jabbed the phone towards her, "are here," he pointed the phone towards the floor, "in this room. In this building. Standing on solid ground. All thoughts about what could happen, what may happen, what might have already happened… those are all out of your hands. Try to remember that you, your brain, and your body are in this physical space and that you can only use them to do so much. Trust me, they'll be of more use to you if you can keep a level head."

Angela took another deep breath and nodded slowly.

"Now," Hans went on, "let's see what we can do about Miles. I don't have any of my regular drivers available, but let me make a few calls. I think we'll be able to get you to Mount Jawshan by this afternoon. How does that sound?"

While Hans made several phone calls and spoke to his various contacts in halting Arabic, Angela connected to the Red Cross' Wi-Fi and sent two text messages. The first one was to Geoff—just a quick assurance that she'd arrived in Syria and that she was with good people who were trying to help her.

Once she'd handled that, she opened her text message conversation with her daughter. She hadn't told Christina that she was even leaving, let alone where to, or why. Thinking for a moment, Angela struggled for a way to explain where she was without scaring or shocking her daughter, but it was hopeless. Finally, she settled for something simple and direct:

> *Hello love. I had to take an emergency trip*
> *to the Middle East. I'm sorry I didn't have time*
> *to tell you before I left and I'm sorry I*
> *can't explain more now. Just know that I'm fine*
> *and that I love you. If you don't hear from me*
> *in the next day or two, it will be due to*
> *connection difficulties, nothing more.*
> *I'll be back soon. Love, Mum. xxx*

She pressed 'Send', saying a little prayer that Christina wouldn't enter a stage of shock and trauma when she read the message.

"Good news," said Hans, holding the phone away from his face and cupping the mouthpiece with his hand, "I've found you a driver. And not just that, but a driver who speaks English! I think."

"Well, I think that's good news then," said Angela, smiling.

"I've never worked with him before, but he was the only English-speaking driver available. So I can't directly vouch for him, but he's supposedly reliable. If that makes you uncomfortable I can keep looking. Or—"

"How long would it take him to get here?"

Hans spoke into the phone. He listened. Then he looked back at Angela. "Ten minutes," he said.

"Let's go with that, then."

Hans uttered a few more words into the phone, then mouthed the words *two-hundred dollars* at her, holding up two fingers.

She nodded, grateful that she'd converted her pounds back at Heathrow.

Hans hung up. "OK. He'll be here in a few minutes."

"Wonderful. I can't thank you enough, Hans."

He shrugged. "I'm happy to help. And I'm not done yet. When he gets here I'll make sure there's no funny business going on as best I can, and I'll ensure everything gets straightened out with the payment too. Some people here are, understandably, quite desperate."

"Thank you. If he can take me where I need to go and translate for me, then I don't care how desperate he is."

Hans gave her a long look and nodded his head slowly. "You're very determined," he said. "Miles is lucky to have a friend like you."

Angela winced. *Maybe he is. Maybe he isn't*, she thought. *After all, I'm part of the reason he ended up here in the first place. I think—I think I might have broken his heart, and mine along with it.* She was too worked up by the prospect of venturing out of the office and into the city, however, to explain all this to Hans.

Before long, they heard tyres crunching over the patina of debris outside.

"That will be him," Hans said. He moved to the door and pulled it open.

In the threshold stood a stocky man, his black beard neatly trimmed and his hair a nest of unruly waves. He was wearing a dirty grey jumper under a faded red vest, blue jeans, and work boots. As Hans ushered him inside and greeted him in Arabic, the man's eyes seemed to dart around the office space, as if he was already searching for an exit route should the building spontaneously collapse.

"Angela, this is Saad. Saad, meet Angela."

"Nice to meet you," said Saad, holding out his hand. His accent was thick and his words didn't quite flow together, but he seemed to speak English well enough.

Angela accepted his hand. "And you as well. Thank you so much for agreeing to drive me."

"And be translator," he said, smiling at her. "I take you to Mount Jawshan. To Al-Nuqtah. I will help ask for you where went who you are looking for."

She smiled back. "That's fantastic, Saad. I deeply appreciate it."

He nodded nervously and then quickly looked away. His presence was almost the complete opposite of Tommy's. In place of carefree confidence, Saad radiated a hyperawareness and intensity that put Angela on edge. But if this was how she was going to get one step closer to Miles, so be it.

Hans and Saad spoke for a while in Arabic and then Hans turned to Angela, beckoning her over and asking her to show Saad the photo of Miles.

Saad frowned as he shook his head, making Angela bite her lip, a little disappointed as she slid the phone back into her pocket. Then Hans and Saad went back to hammering out the details of the arrangement.

After a while they shook hands, and Hans turned to Angela, lowering his voice as he explained, "OK. So pay him one hundred dollars now and then the other hundred once you've asked around at the mosque and know where you're going next. He seems like a good guy. A little jumpy, but who knows what he's been through?"

"Sounds fair to me," she said, rummaging through her backpack for her emergency wad of cash. "Hans, I can't thank you enough."

"Don't mention it," he said patting her on the arm. "Just be careful. I hope you find him. *Viel Glück!*"

"Thank you," she said again. "I'll need all the luck I can get, but I think I've already had plenty of it in meeting you." She picked her backpack up off the floor and slung it over her shoulder.

"We go?" Saad asked.

Angela handed him the money. "Yes. Let's get moving."

"Hold on," said Hans, "just one moment."

He ran into the rear of the building, appearing a few seconds later with a white t-shirt and a dark-coloured shawl. After unfolding the garments he held them out to Angela, showing her the Red Cross insignia emblazoned across each item of clothing.

"Both the regime and the rebels respect Red Cross workers... for the most part," he told her. "Hopefully, seeing the symbol will make them think twice if things should get... unpleasant."

She reached out and grabbed the items of clothing from Hans, slipping the shirt over the one she was already wearing. It was a little too large, making her feel like a child. "I feel safer already," she said.

"These are not body armour," Hans said, shrugging, "but it's the best I can offer."

Saad's red sedan crept down the ruined street. He drove slowly, constantly looking to either side of the road, his head swivelling back and forth as he searched for obstacles, signs of imminent danger, and the odd pedestrian darting into the car's path from behind small mounds of broken concrete and twisted rebar.

The city wasn't deserted after all; as several people moved between various points of cover—completing whatever errands still existed for them amidst the chaos of war—each one Angela laid eyes on had the same pensive look about them that Saad did, the tension in their calculated movements evident in the fear-honed sharpness of their gaze.

They drove past small shops and little kiosks that were actively conducting business; despite the threat of more attacks and aerial bombardment, the selling and purchasing of simple food items to the sparse population of beleaguered city dwellers continued, as it must.

The sight of quotidian commerce taking place between collapsed buildings, and around knots of blackened metal so thoroughly damaged that their previous function was completely unidentifiable, seemed utterly bizarre to Angela. And yet, retail trade thrived between walls riddled with many thousands of bullet holes. It felt incongruous, perverse, and simply wrong to demand of people that their daily lives continue whilst they were surrounded by ineradicable proof that civilian normalcy had been irrevocably and barbarically violated.

But people were carrying on, walking down the street at a brisk pace. Holding little plastic bags and looking over their shoulders. Smoking cigarettes in doorways and casting apprehensive looks over the sky above. A trio of children ambled out of one of the makeshift booths as the car rolled past them. They waved to Saad with one hand, each of them holding a bar of ice cream in the other.

The air in the car was superheated, stiflingly close, and smelling faintly of petroleum, and it wasn't long before Angela's backside became stuck to the vinyl passenger seat. She shifted around uncomfortably, trying to find a position that limited the amount of sunlight hitting her bare forearms.

As she did so, Saad looked over at her, his eyes lingering on her left hand. He hadn't said anything since they'd departed the Red Cross Office, but now he cleared his throat and narrowed his eyes, searching for the right words in English. "This man you are looking for. He is your husband? Your husband gives you a nice ring. Very… pretty."

As Angela fixed her eyes on the wedding ring and the clear, one carat solitaire diamond, she twisted it around with her right hand, an absentminded habit she'd indulged in ever since William had first slid it onto her finger. After having worn it nearly every day for so many years, it had become a ubiquitous addition to her body, as well as—in recent times—her mother's golden band with the green gemstone, which was her most treasured piece of jewellery. But now she tried to see her wedding band through Saad's eyes, the sunlight catching the shimmering diamond and refracting it into a miniature nova of multi-coloured sparkles.

She belatedly responded to Saad's questioning. "Yes, he did, didn't he? It is a pretty ring. But I'm not looking for my husband. I'm looking for someone else. My husband is dead."

Saad's eyes lingered on the diamond for a moment longer and then he bowed his head—*or, at least,* as much as he could while still keeping his eyes on the dusty, pot-holed road.

"I am sorry," he said, after a brief pause. "I have hope that he shall find peace in paradise."

"I appreciate that. Thank you, Saad."

They rounded a corner and a large, white shopping mall came into view. It appeared unscathed and pleasingly intact, and although it was encircled by a vast amount of destruction, the building itself had managed to escape bombardment damage and continued to trade, providing for the great swathes of fast-moving customers.

Saad seemed to relax slightly at the sight of the mall, sinking back into the driver's seat a little and taking one of his hands from the steering wheel. "Over there is Al-Nuqtah," he said, pointing straight ahead. "It has been attacked several times in past years. But, sometimes, the imam still offers prayers from here. We go see if he is now, then we ask him and people inside questions about your man."

Angela nodded, glad to be getting somewhere but anxious about getting out of the car.

They parked and crossed the street to the mosque, which was fronted by an open, rectangular courtyard, sparsely populated with worshippers. The sun beat down on its pale yellow stone blocks. Looking up, Angela saw that an entire corner of the mosque was missing and that the stone around the place it had once stood was scorched. Scaffolding lined one of its walls, and also wound up the full height of the minaret.

Saad pointed upwards to the minaret. "Collapsed from missile two years ago. Early in the war, this mosque attacked a lot. Very dangerous place. Now, it is sort of OK. They have almost finish fixing it."

They approached the arched entrance to the mosque, and when Saad beckoned her to follow him, they veered away from the entryway.

They threaded their way around the courtyard, asking the local people within if they'd seen Miles. Saad repeated the same words in Arabic to each one of them before gesturing for Angela to show them the photo on her phone. Some of the interviewees developed an excited look on their faces, right up until the moment Angela showed them the picture, at which point their smiles fell and they shook their heads, clasping Angela's hands in their own and offering her encouraging words that Saad translated. Others started giving Angela a pitying look from the moment Saad made it obvious what was being asked of them. It was as if they were already shaking their heads before she'd even revealed to them the photograph of Miles.

Once this process had been undertaken, Angela was beginning to lose hope. The words she spoke to Saad for him to translate became more and more desperate, tumbling from her mouth in agonised clumps. After they received what Angela had intuited as a particularly pessimistic response from one of the people— *a response* Saad hadn't even bothered to fully translate for her—she hung her head, exhausted by their lack of success.

Saad noticed her distress. "Not too be worried, Angela. I go inside now and find the imam. Maybe he will know. You wait here."

"Here?" she asked uncertainly.

"You must not come inside," he said, gesturing to her uncovered head. "I am sorry."

Realising that she was the only woman in the courtyard not wearing traditional dress, Angela suddenly became incredibly self-conscious.

As if reading her mind, Saad stopped just before the threshold and turned to face her. "It is OK. Most people around now know why you are here because we talk to them. They understand. They have missing people too. They know what it is to search." He gave her a curt nod. "I come back," he said and then removed his footwear and walked into the mosque.

When he emerged around thirty minutes later, an elderly man with a long white beard, bedecked in a white robe, with rimless spectacles and a black turban atop his head, followed behind him.

Saad introduced the imam to Angela and then Angela to the imam in their respective languages. When the elder, weather-beaten gentleman nodded slightly in her direction she noticed a flash of the kindly intelligence in his eyes that she associated closely with her *Oma*.

"Please," said Saad, "show the photo."

The imam smiled at Angela encouragingly while she wrestled the phone from the pocket of her jeans. As she unlocked it, she finally accepted that she had no plan as to what she would do next if her inquiries around the mosque didn't lead her to Miles. She would have come to a dead end and have no other option but to return to the Red Cross Office, unsuccessful and utterly demoralised. She could not afford to part with much more money for transportation. What if she needed to pay Miles' ransom? What if she needed to pay her own? She took a deep breath, trying to exhale each of these possible catastrophes from her mind, and then handed the imam her phone.

He squinted at the small screen, removed his spectacles, held the phone further away from his face, and squinted again. He regarded the picture for a third time, and then, wordlessly, he returned the device to Angela. The holy man turned to Saad, and in a calm and even tone of voice, spoke to him for several minutes.

Initially, the imam's neutral manner heralded the increased possibility of a negative response. But, with each passing second that he continued to converse with Saad, with every respectful nod her driver offered him in reply, Angela's heart began to swell in excited anticipation.

Finally, the imam's oratory delivery came to an end and, still showing no sign of emotion, he moved his open palm from Saad to Angela.

"He has seen him," Saad said.

"Really?! Oh my God. Oh, thank you! Where? Where was he? Does he know where he is?"

At last, a sign! Her first concrete proof that Miles had been in Aleppo. That he'd been seen here alive. It was as if the weight of all her anxieties and doubts had compressed her mother lode of hopes into spine-tingling relief.

"He was here a little more than a week ago, shortly after a government missile nearly hit the mosque," Saad explained. "The imam saw him interview several people in the neighbourhood. They too had an interview together. He said the man you seek was very respectful, very kind." Angela glowed. It had to be Miles. "Soon after they speak, the media man left this place. He went directly east. Into the worst of fighting. The imam knows not what happened to this man afterward."

Saad registered that the words 'worst of the fighting' had caused Angela's bright, rousing smile to dim considerably, so he added quickly, "But he has information that could be helpful. The translator the man used—his fixer, I think—he is member of the imam's congregation. He knows him well. He says the fixer drives an old big car. SUV. Dark blue Renault. With a big wound in its side. No—not wound. Injury? How you say, car injury?"

"A dent?" Angela offered.

"Dent! Yes, a dent. Big dent filled with red paint from the car that hit it."

"Okay," said Angela. "Okay, that's something. Please thank him for me." She turned to the imam and smiled.

He smiled back at Angela, looking her in the eyes for the first time. He then began to speak directly to her. When he finished, he bowed his head again.

"He says he wishes you the blessing of Allah in your search. But he warns you to be careful. He says there is more than one way to die in war."

With that the imam turned and walked back across the courtyard, disappearing through the threshold of the mosque.

"This is wonderful, Saad. We know where to go now!" Angela exclaimed, feeling a little giddy. "Well, more or less, I suppose. How far east do you think he meant we should go?" She looked over at Saad and was surprised to see none of her triumphant excitement reflected in his face. In fact, the slightest trace of pity peeked through his otherwise impassive expression.

"You do not understand," he said softly.

After a moment, Angela replied, "Alright. Explain it to me then."

"He said Miles moved east of here. Right now, we stand on the edge of rebel territory. The more east we go, the more fighting we see. More danger."

"Yes, that's what he said, and I don't like the sound of it either, but if that's where Miles has gone, that's where I have to go too."

"I say you should not go," Saad said forcefully, exhibiting more firmness than he had all day. "Hire military contractor. Hire fixer or just wait for this man to come back to you on his own. You do not know of it, the danger. You do not know the east. People go there and, *if* they return, they do so in little bits. You are a nice woman. Do not waste yourself." He was almost begging her.

"But I don't have a choice," she whispered, her voice cracking. "I won't go back without him."

"Then it is like you say," sighed Saad. "You do not have a choice. Yet *I* do. I do not go any further east. Not for our price. Rebel territory, more price. I am sorry. But it is very, very dangerous."

Angela exhaled sharply. She should have known it wouldn't be as easy as simply following successive breadcrumbs of information until she found Miles. "I can pay you another two hundred dollars," she said after a moment of mental maths, "but I can't spare any more cash. What if he's been captured and I need to pay his captors to release him?"

Saad shrugged, shaking his head. "Two hundred to go east, I

cannot. Six hundred. Maybe. Once more, I am sorry. But you ask me to maybe sell my life. I have a family. I have a daughter."

Angela bit down again on her bottom lip, her mind racing. Should she try to negotiate with him? See if she could bring the price down and then hope that the rest of her cash would last? Or should she just pay him his asking price and hope for the best?

What if her search saw him killed, leaving his daughter without a father? She wasn't sure she could live with that.

The decision wrapped its dark wings around her mind, squeezing it tighter and tighter until she felt paralysed.

Finally, Saad broke the silence. "Your ring," he said. "Two hundred and your wedding ring. All upfront. For that price, I will take you into the east." He didn't sound the least bit happy about his proposal, but this was all they had left to negotiate a settlement.

Angela looked down at the ring. How many times had she seen it on her finger? How many years had it lived on her hand, representing a bond sworn to last until severed by death?

She twisted the ring with pensive reservation, recalling William's funeral, and then thinking of the sensation of Miles' fingers sliding between hers. How, when holding Miles' hand, the band and stone had felt like it was intruding on their intimacy, impeding the tiniest part of their skin from touching. She heard the answer to the questions echo within her skull, and she knew what she had to do.

*Enough!*

She pulled. The ring slid from her finger without difficulty, and she placed it into Saad's palm.

He looked at it admiringly and sighed, his fingers closing

around the piece of jewellery before depositing it into his shirt's breast pocket and buttoning it tightly.

With this piece of business done, they entered the car once more, and Angela handed Saad the two hundred dollars, plus the extra hundred she owed him from the first journey.

He placed it in the glove compartment and turned the ignition. For several moments he stared through the windshield, bemused and unsure of what they'd agreed upon. His eyes closed and his lips moved soundlessly in prayer. Then, opening his eyes, he twisted his upper body around in the seat and began rummaging around through the car. When he returned he held a glass bottle of dark gold liquid.

He hastily removed the cap and took a long sip from the flagon. Then, with his eyes watering, he passed the bottle to Angela and put the car into first gear. "Drink now please," he croaked. "Now we go east."

She did as he asked, the liquid having an immediate searing effect on her palate, burning her throat as if molten lava.

# CHAPTER 6:
## GERMANY, 1945

Nina leaped out of her chair the instant she heard the baby's first groggy gurgle. She'd only just finished putting the last of the children to sleep for their afternoon nap and if one of them woke and started crying, it would set off a chain reaction of premature wakefulness and subsequent crankiness that would reverberate throughout the makeshift nursery in the Schaeffer living room for hours to come—until the first of the mothers came to collect Nina's infant charges.

The baby was soft and warm in her arms as she held up his head to her lips and whispered a lullaby into his ear, rocking him back and forth in the way she'd learned was most effective at swiftly inducing sleep. It took all of two minutes; the gurgles and inquisitive noises that had issued from the child slowly melted away into blissful dreams. Gently, she set him back down in his cradle and returned to her seat in the old green armchair.

She had become proficient at this, Nina thought happily to herself. It was the first time in her fourteen years that she'd felt she had actually learned a skill, one that she'd been able to watch as it grew from mere competence to a near effortless mastery. She was more than a little proud of how well the children took to her, and of the fact that, even in these unspeakably dark times, she was able to be of some help to both her bomb-ravaged community and her family.

She hadn't always been so productive. In the years since Werner had left home, Nina had been caught in a vicious downward spiral, spurred on by terrible events totally out of her control. She had nearly drowned in a sea of depression as life in the Schaeffer home took a succession of turns from bad, to worse, to nearly apocalyptic. Werner's absence had stolen her childhood innocence, robbing her of her best friend and transforming her from a polite and inquisitive little girl into one quick to anger, with downcast eyes that always seemed to simmer at the world's injustice. But that wasn't the worst thing. Since he'd left, the war had stretched its iron fingers out towards every remaining member of her family, breaking off another piece of her soul with every one it touched.

Her father had been drafted into the army, wrenched from her life for two long years before returning to her as a husk of his former self. Not only had Johannes' mind been devastated by the horrors of war; his body had paid an even higher price. An artillery shell had ripped off his right arm at the shoulder, ending his career as Braunschweig's jolly barber in a hot flash of smoke, blood, and agony. Unable to work, he spent most of his days sunk into the same green armchair in which Nina now sat, his hollow eyes fixed on the living room's opposite wall. He could no longer play the Chopin, Rachmaninoff, or even Beethoven sonatas he'd once loved so dearly on their grand piano, which now sat forlorn and forgotten in a living room it was much too large for. Even Nina, who'd used to love playing duets with Werner, couldn't bring herself to touch the keys.

In order to put food on the table Erna had taken a job as a nurse, meaning she was rarely ever home, her favourite pastimes of baking and embroidery having been replaced by long hours stitching up civilian casualties from the frequent bombing runs that made large chunks of Braunschweig—its population and its architecture—disappear overnight.

One of those terrifying nights, a bomb had landed directly on the apartment in which Johannes' parents lived, obliterating everything and everyone. Days later, Nina had silently laid flowers atop their symbolic graves; nothing substantial had been recovered from the rubble, so there was nothing to bury. Soon after, Erna's parents had simply vanished in the chaos of the war.

All of it had driven Nina farther and farther into her darkening self. She rarely uttered a word to her parents (or anyone) for elongated periods anymore, and she shunned friendships with the young girls her age who remained in the shattered principality. During those long, bleak years she had felt as if the war was slowly grinding her down to nothing, like a rock face being gradually eroded by a torrential waterfall.

How strange, thought Nina as she watched the babies sleep, that it had been the worst news of all that had brought her back to herself, that had given her a second chance at life.

Neither of her parents had been home when the letter arrived, and just looking at the envelope, she knew. Some dormant protective instinct to spare her mother and father the first shock had caused her to tear it open and read it. Her brother's name, the answer to the constant, nagging question of whether or not he was alright, the words 'honour' and 'glory' and 'duty.'

She had spent the next half hour drinking as much of the alcohol in the kitchen cabinet as she could get down between sobs, and had then spent an indeterminate amount of time vomiting it all back up.

When her parents returned and ultimately read the contents of the letter, Nina witnessed the last flicker of hope fade from their eyes, and when she'd heard the unearthly wail rip from the deepest part of her mother and seen her crippled father sink to his knees, everything changed for her. It had happened in an instant.

For years she'd been acting as if she had been a casualty of war, another victim whose identity had been completely and utterly destroyed. In that moment, however, she saw that if she continued to do so, her parents would have effectively lost both of their children to the war—and she refused to be a source of any more of their pain.

And so she changed, forcing herself to be the reason for her parents to continue, and helping them in any way she could. Whilst still in mourning, she cooked and maintained the home. Then she started the nursery to help bring in some extra money, and to inject some much-needed life into the Schaeffer house. And, in the process, she discovered that within her lay the strength to decide whether the person she'd been before things began to fall apart— the person she was growing back into—would survive the war or not. It was a decision she had to force herself to make every day.

Today that decision would be particularly difficult, but her parents would need her to be strong. Hopefully, after they'd held a funeral for Werner (once his body had been returned to them), Erna and Johannes would have some closure.

Nina sat in the chair in the quiet calm of the living room, watching the shadows lengthen and waiting for her father to return from the bomb-damaged *Rathaus*, from his unpleasant errand of submitting the paperwork required to get Werner's remains back to Braunschweig.

Soon after, the front door opened in the halting and jerky fashion that had announced Johannes' return ever since he'd lost his arm. He shoved it inward with his shoulder, a large stack of papers in his remaining hand.

"Hello, Papa! How was it?" Nina said quietly, forcing all the cheerfulness she could muster into her voice without waking the sleeping children. It was important to her that the first thing Johannes saw when he walked into the house was his daughter's smile. "When did they say they would return Werner's… Werner to us?"

Johannes' face was deathly pale—a sheen of sweat shone on his cheeks, beads of it dotting his brow— and for a moment he just stared at Nina, his mouth falling open slowly without a sound. A distressing series of emotions cycled across his features as he looked at her: fear, pain, pity, guilt. Finally, he regained his senses and shrugged his way through the threshold, dropping the papers on the ground so that he could use his remaining hand to slam the door shut. He jumped at the noise he made, casting a furtive look over his shoulder at the row of cribs. As his trembling hand struggled with the lock, he began to speak. But the words came out distractedly, as though his thoughts were far, far away.

"Oh. Yes," he said. "Everything's fine. Everything will be fine, darling. I just—I just have to go. Go and—go and speak with your mother."

Nina spent the next two days completely baffled by her parents' strange behaviour. She had feared that the subject of Werner's body might stir up their feelings of loss, still very much raw for the whole family, but they were acting completely differently than they had in those horrible weeks immediately after they'd learned of their son's death.

Her mother hadn't reported to the hospital for her duties in days, instead staying home with Nina and more or less demanding that they bake biscuits together, and afterward, that Nina join her on the couch, where Erna wrapped her arms tightly around her daughter and stroked her head for nearly an hour. For his part, Johannes had mysteriously disappeared several times (which was strange as he seldom left the house these days), and when Nina asked him where he'd been or questioned her mother as to where he'd gone, they gave her vague and often conflicting answers. When he was home, Nina would catch Johannes staring at her with a look of tragedy etched on his face, making her shudder. Passing her parents' bedroom, she heard raised voices, and faint, stifled weeping whilst they whispered to each other. They stopped talking when they noticed her, immediately striking up conversations about the most trivial things, a desperate, strained tone having taken hold of their voices.

On the third day, Nina woke early and made her way downstairs for breakfast. As she approached the kitchen, she heard more cautious whispering.

"No!" her father was hissing. "No, you don't understand. It could be at any time. They could be coming today for all we know, Erna! We have to do it now."

"But Johannes, how will we tell her? How can—"

One of the floorboards creaked under Nina's foot, and when she stepped into the kitchen she was greeted by her parents' unconvincing, smiling faces, as if a puppeteer was tugging on strings attached to the corners of their mouths. It looked strange and unnatural and deeply, deeply disturbing.

"Would you like some breakfast?" Erna asked, beginning to dart around the kitchen. "I'm running a little behind, but I can have something ready for you in no time. I have some eggs, you like eggs, or maybe some—?"

"What is going on?" For the first time since they'd learned of Werner's death, some of the old anger had returned to Nina's voice. Her tone was filled with fear and disbelief. What could be so much worse than everything they'd already suffered, that her parents felt the need to hide it from her?

Johannes and Erna looked at each other as if they were about to begin arguing. Then, after a tense moment of silence, Johannes opened his mouth to speak.

There was a knock at the door.

Erna and Johannes froze. An ice-cold sensation crept up Nina's spine. All three held their breath. Then came another knock.

"Under the bed!" Johannes hissed, grabbing his wife with his one hand and shoving her at Nina, hard. "Go!"

Erna grabbed her daughter and pushed her up the stairs with a strength Nina had never suspected her mother possessed. She tried to cry out as Erna's fingers dug into her shoulders, but Erna clamped a hand over Nina's mouth to stop her. The bedroom door flew open and mother and daughter tumbled inside, falling into a heap on the ground.

"Get under the bed, Nina! Now!"

Seeing the desperation in her mother's eyes, Nina subserviently complied with her anguished directive.

"The floorboard!" whispered Erna. She motioned for Nina to pry it up, and on doing so, Erna helped squeeze Nina into the filthy, cobweb-lined crawlspace. "Not a sound!" she said, and then put the board back into place, plunging Nina into darkness.

"Herr Schaeffer?" A young man's voice trickled through the bedroom window and into Nina's hiding place. "*Herr und Frau Schaeffer?*" The voice sounded unsure and a little embarrassed. "My name is Dieter! I served with your son!"

Nina heard the creak of the front door opening and then a murmur of voices. Several moments later, her mother's shaking hands lifted the floorboard and caressed Nina's face, wiping at the mixture of dust and tears now caking her cheeks.

"It's alright, *mein kind*, you can come out."

Gently, Erna led her daughter downstairs.

Nina's clothes and hair were covered with grime, but she was still too stricken by the adrenaline coursing through her body to feel embarrassed when the eyes of the young soldier standing awkwardly in the living room widened in shock at her appearance. He couldn't have been more than nineteen years old.

He did not comment on how she looked. Instead, he smiled tentatively and said, "Ah. You must be Nina. Werner never stopped talking about you."

Johannes walked into the living room, a coffee pot trembling in his hand. "S-some coffee? I'm sorry; you said your name was…"

"Dieter," responded the young soldier. "And yes, thank you. I'm sorry if I've interrupted your Sunday morning, Herr Schaeffer."

"Nonsense," said Erna. "Please, sit down." She had regained her composure more rapidly than Johannes or Nina, the instinctual terror that had transformed her mere moments ago giving way to years of conditioning as the gracious hostess. "What brings you here, Dieter?"

"Werner made me promise," said Dieter, his face darkening as a memory invaded his thoughts, "he made me promise to come tell you in person. How he… how he…"

"How he died?" asked Nina, walking across the room and sitting down on the couch close to Dieter, the events of the preceding, frantic minutes momentarily forgotten at the prospect of finally hearing the truth of what happened to her beloved brother. "You were with him?"

Dieter swallowed and nodded. "He was the bravest man I

have ever known. He gave his life for me." With that, Dieter fell silent again, and Nina gently urged him to go on. "We were on the outskirts of Antwerp," he continued. "Our mission was to destroy the enemy forces between ourselves and the city. It was the largest operation I have been involved in. From our position and the numbers of the enemy, we all knew the effort was mostly hopeless. My commander said that the Führer expected us to throw everything we had at the enemy, to fight with dignity for the Fatherland."

"Dignity?!" Johannes turned bright red, as if he were about to explode.

"Johannes, please. Let the boy continue," said Erna.

Dieter resumed his account, speaking with his eyes cast downward, unable to meet the gazes of the family. "Er—yes. Well. Werner and I served in the same unit on the main offensive line. Our tank—he was the gunner and I drove—um, our tank's tracks were destroyed by an American sticky bomb. The tank tipped on its side. We managed to crawl out and rejoin a small group of dispersed soldiers from other units. We were pinned down by a machine gun nest and Werner volunteered to flank it. I went with him. We manoeuvred around the kop they were firing from but we couldn't move from cover. We huddled there for a while as bullets flew over our heads. Werner told me to go. To run. He then broke cover and began firing, and within seconds he was hit, in the leg. Luckily, the rest of our forces were advancing and the enemy was so preoccupied with us two that they were quickly wiped out by our men. I did everything I could for him. But he was losing too much blood. He—he knew. He knew he was not going to live. And he made me swear that I would find you, his family, and inform you of the nature of his death."

For the first time, he looked up from the floor and straight into Nina's eyes.

"With his last words, he said that you should never stop reading *Die Biene Maja* because, in the book's words, you will always find your brother."

Dieter fell silent then, the only sound that remained in the room being the soft weeping of Johannes and Erna. Johannes put his arm around his wife and used his shoulder to clumsily wipe at his face. Nina went to him and wiped away his tears. She then turned to Dieter and took his hand.

"I cannot thank you enough for carrying out my brother's wishes," she said.

"I am so sorry to have brought your family such pain. But it was my duty to him."

"No," said Nina. "We are very grateful. It was more painful not knowing what happened to him."

"Yes," Johannes added. "You have done us a great service in coming. You have our deepest thanks."

When Dieter was framed in the doorway and about to leave, Nina called after him, "We'll be holding a funeral service for Werner sometime soon. You must come! How can we contact you?"

As Dieter wrote down his address and handed it to Johannes, Nina detected that upon hearing mention of Werner's funeral, the normalcy she had slowly seen return to her parents had vanished once again.

When the door shut behind the young soldier, the three surviving Schaeffers stood together in silence. Nina looked down at her dress. It was smudged all over with dirt. She raised her eyes to her father.

"Tell me," she said, "what is it? What's happened? What's going on?"

Johannes and Erna exchanged sad, solemn glances, then Johannes hung his head and positioned his hand over his eyes. He walked back to his armchair and sank into it.

"Please, Erna. I can't," he whispered. "You do it."

Erna turned to Nina and, reaching up, pulled a clump of filth from her daughter's hair. "I don't know how else to say this, my love, but you must leave us. Tomorrow morning. At first light."

"What?" asked Nina. "Why? Where am I to go?"

Erna held up her hand to stop the questions and led Nina to the threadbare couch, where they both sat down. Through the window, the sky was a clear blue, as if nature couldn't fathom the darkness that had invaded the Schaeffer household.

"When your father went to the *Rathaus* to see about Werner, he learned something terrible. Something that puts us all in grave danger. The 'lieutenant' he was speaking to was scanning through family documents and noticed that his grandmother wasn't—she wasn't German."

"What do you mean, she wasn't German? Where was she from?"

"She was Jewish," Johannes said without lifting his hand from his eyes. "She was a wonderful woman. A wonderful grandmother. But her blood—or what that damned Hitler thinks of it anyway—

has written our death warrants, Nina."

"Johannes!" snapped Erna. "Don't scare the poor child any more than she already is!"

"She needs to know the gravity of the situation!" he shot back. Then, finally, he looked up at his daughter. "Nina, you must understand. You are all your mother and I have left. The only thing we want less than to be parted from you, is to lose you completely, do you understand?"

From the moment Nina had heard the word 'Jewish' she'd felt the tremor of death run through her. Now, suddenly, she also felt light-headed, the walls spinning around her clumsily. As the war had drawn on, she'd been able to guess at what had prompted the mysterious disappearance of Werner's friend Sami Cohen and his family. The rumours had made her ill, and she'd prayed that the Cohens had fled, knowing that flight was by far the best outcome for someone of Jewish ancestry in these times.

*Not just for 'someone', she thought now. For us.*

In that moment, the resolute strength she had worked so hard to cultivate collided with the old sense of helpless terror, of anger, of loss. She touched her face and felt tears on her cheeks. She looked around the room. At the porcelain vases, the pieces of furniture—each of which carried its own unique history—the family portraits, the dining table, the huge piano. She'd never once imagined the idea of this not being her home.

"But why must we separate? Where will you two go? I can't leave you behind!" she cried.

"You can and you will," said Johannes firmly. "We were only able to arrange for the escape of one person. There was no other way. A smuggler will take you to Saarbrücken, and from there you will be brought to the Americans. They will take care of you. We will follow as soon as we can." Nina opened her mouth to protest, but he cut her off, saying, "We will find you. I promise, my love. This is the only way."

A deathly stillness fell over the living room, a silence on which pivoted entire lives and futures, a silence like acid, melting away the past clarity of one's identity and leaving someone vague and abstract in its place.

Erna then spoke up softly, "*Wir lieben dich Nina, das ist das beste.*"

A sob caught in Nina's throat and she reached out to grab her mother's hand, squeezing it tightly as though wishing she never had to let it go.

Erna's trembling hands worked their way inside each of Nina's pockets. Into them she secreted a small number of loose pearls, two golden earrings, a gem-studded brooch, plus a number of gold rings and a silver necklace, which Nina had never seen before.

"Where have all these come from?"

"Most of them have been in the family for generations," said Erna breathlessly. "But don't think about that. If your money runs out, you use them to pay for whatever you need."

Nina felt faint. None of them had slept the previous night. They'd huddled together in bed, talking about the past, the future… anything but the present.

A loud knock at the door thudded through the house.

"Come now," said Erna, "it's time."

Descending the stairs, jingling slightly with every step, Nina regarded the man who would take her to safety as Johannes hurriedly ushered him inside and closed the door behind him. He was short and broad-shouldered, his fleshy round head topped with closely cropped brown hair. He looked up at Nina and nodded curtly, then turned his gaze back to Johannes.

"The payment now," he said. "We must leave immediately."

Johannes squeezed past Nina and bounded up the stairs while Erna walked out of the kitchen, the red biscuit tin clutched tightly in her hands. She crossed the room and handed it to Nina. It was heavy.

Nina opened the lid and saw that it was filled with the biscuits they'd baked the previous day, as well as with salami, bread, and cheese. Tucked beneath the food was a layer of banknotes, more than Nina had ever seen in one place in her entire life.

Erna took the lid from her, closed the tin, and then wrapped her daughter in a tight, final embrace.

Johannes ran down the stairs, his hands clutching an even greater quantity of bills than were hidden in the tin, then placed the cash into a briefcase the smuggler had opened on the dining table.

The man closed the case, picked it up, and looked at Nina. "*Alles ist gut,*" he unfeelingly uttered.

Johannes wrapped his arms around both his wife and his daughter. "We'll see each other again before you know it, my love.

This isn't goodbye. We will find you."

Nina struggled to speak through her tears.

Just then, an air raid siren sliced through the delicate morning air, and she and the man left quickly. It was only after she had climbed into the front seat of the black car—when it began to carry her away from everything she'd ever known and everything she'd ever cared for—that she was finally able to shout through the open window and over the siren's wail, "I love you!" to the two shrinking figures standing in the doorway in the half-light of dawn.

The man drove without saying a word, which didn't affect Nina; she was in no mood for conversation anyway. The white-hot pain of leaving had been replaced by first a dull ache in her chest and then, once the outskirts of Braunschweig had given way to countryside, a vision that she would never again see or dwell in the city in which she was raised—nor cast eyes on her mother and father again. There was no blurriness in her mental vision; it was as irrevocably real as it was crystal clear.

After a while, she saw the green pastures and gentle hillsides giving way to concrete buildings. They were entering the edge of a city, and judging by the size of the buildings in the distance, it was a large one.

This was wrong, terribly wrong. Saarbrücken should still be hours away.

In a sudden panic, she looked for the sun and saw it, still approaching its zenith directly ahead. Saarbrücken was to the west, but they were heading due east, towards plumes of smoke and flashes of harsh light, which made it abundantly clear that instead of being driven to safety, she was being taken straight into a battle. The city they were approaching was, could only be, Berlin.

"Excuse me, sir. Sir? Where are we going? Isn't Saarbrücken in the other direction?" Nina's voice was small and saturated in pleading disbelief.

The man said nothing and continued to stare straight ahead, his eyes fixed on the concrete and smokestacks growing larger with each revolution of the car's wheels.

"Sir? Sir! Hello?! Where are you taking me?" she screamed.

This time, the hysterical tone of Nina's words prompted a response; the man calmly reached into his coat and withdrew a pistol. He pointed it at Nina's face and her screams died on her lips. In the span of an instant, her saviour had become her captor.

"No. No, no, no," she whispered, as tears poured hot down her cheeks.

They drove towards the centre of Berlin, the pistol still pointed at Nina and the sounds of war growing ever louder. Artillery fire boomed in the distance, and the closer they got, the more explosions of bombs and mortars could be heard, accompanying the resounding orchestra of death only a kilometre or two ahead.

Without warning, the man pulled the car over on a deserted side street, parking it next to what remained of a warehouse's red brick wall.

"Get out."

The first words the man had said to her since they'd left her home made every hair on Nina's body stand on end. She tried to obey the order but she was paralysed with fear.

"Get out!" he growled again, turning to face her.

"What—what are you going to do with me?"

In response, he cocked the gun and gestured for her to exit the car.

As she opened the door and stepped out into the cold air of the street, the sounds of war were amplified. She heard the distant screams of wounded victims, and the pungent smell of cordite stained the air.

The man got out of the car behind her and, without a word— and keeping the pistol fixed on her the entire time—he walked right up to Nina and dug through her clothes with his free hand. He pulled out the pearls, the gold, and the silver. When his pockets were full, he started throwing the stolen bounty through his car window. Then, dispassionately and casually, he reached into her underwear while she shook and sobbed, withdrawing every last gem and earring. After patting her down a final time, he turned on his heel and started walking back to the car. While he'd been searching her, the gunfire had become more intense.

Nina ran after the man and grabbed his arm with all her strength. "Please! Please, *please* take me with you!" she screamed. Nasal discharge ran into her mouth and throat, slightly slurring her words as she spoke. "You can have everything, just don't leave me here!"

She felt the man's shoulders rise and fall from a single, heavy sigh, then he whipped around speedily and, with clenched fist, rammed a heavy punch onto her trembling jaw.

Flashes of light, similar to those bursting across the city, exploded behind her closed eyelids. She staggered backwards, tasting blood and feeling its sticky wetness pouring from her nose, then she stumbled over a piece of rubble and fell to her knees in the deserted, destroyed street.

After catching her breath she struggled to her feet, choking and sobbing, and through her blurred vision she watched him climb back into the vehicle and examine the contents of the red metal container before driving off.

Seconds later, he placed the vehicle into gear and drove past the bruised and wretched child he had just brutalised, throwing the biscuit tin from his open window in Nina's direction.

It was empty.

# CHAPTER 7:
## SYRIA, 2016

Angela and Miles were strolling arm in arm along the park's tree-lined path, passing through rays of golden light that sliced between the leaves arching elegantly above them. Miles was telling a story about something—a past assignment, maybe— but Angela could not specifically recall the subject matter. As he spoke, gesturing with his free hand and glancing back and forth from Angela to the path ahead, Angela struggled to hear a single word emerging out of his mouth. She repeatedly told him to stop and return to the beginning of what he was attempting to relay to her, yet he seemed oblivious to her cries of frustration.

Miles simply continued to talk and gesture, leading her further down the never-ending pathway.

Forcefully, she tugged on his arm to catch his attention, but his upper limb evaporated in her hands, as if it were made of candy floss. When she glanced down in horror at the disembodied limb, it faded and vanished. Alarmed, she looked back at Miles to see his other arm disappearing too. Then his left foot, then his right, both his legs, his torso—all gone, until he was nothing more than a floating head, speaking unheard words with a casually oblivious look on his face.

Finally, Angela managed to scream.

As the sound came out of her mouth, Miles' head dissolved. He was gone. She was alone in the park, screaming his name over and over for hours or weeks or years.

She awoke on the floor, gasping for breath.

Still in the grip of the dream's terror, her eyes flew around the dimly lit room. She was lying on a pile of thick, dusty carpets, the uppermost of which was a faded burgundy, covered with intricate arabesques and the dampness of her sweat. Next to her head sat a golden oil lamp and an incense burner filled with ashes. Light entered the room through a horizontal slit in the wall no taller than her hand, which served as a window. Above her, a ceiling fan's wooden panels spread themselves in all directions, inert despite the stuffy hot air inside the room. A low bookshelf in one of the corners was stuffed with thick books bound in black leather, squiggly lines of silver running down their spines. Nothing she saw made her feel any less afraid or any less like she was still trapped in some disorienting, inexplicable nightmare. Where was she? How had she arrived here?

It was only when she glimpsed her backpack, tucked away

in a corner, that it all came flooding back. She took a deep breath and exhaled slowly, allowing her head to fall back onto the pillow as her memories of the previous evening dripped their way back into her head.

"Saad?" she called. "Saad?"

No answer. *He must be in the other room*, she thought. *Or maybe he's gone to find breakfast? To begin asking the neighbours if they'd seen Miles or his fixer?*

She sat up and rubbed at her eyes, hoping Saad hadn't gone far.

After they'd left the mosque, Saad had driven Angela deep into the rubble-strewn chaos of east Aleppo. Twice they had pulled over to the side of the road, killed the engine, and ducked down beneath the seats when gunfire had erupted mere blocks away. As the sun had begun to set, Saad told her they couldn't go on, as it would be far too dangerous to be on the streets after nightfall. He'd made a series of turns and had then parked the car, pointing across the street at an apartment, explaining that it belonged to his cousin.

Saad's cousin and his cousin's family had received them warmly, setting two extra places at the dinner table as if surprise visits in wartime were a matter of course.

One of the cousin's two small sons had gaped open-mouthed at Angela's blonde hair all throughout dinner, and she'd bent her head towards him to let him touch it, giggling when the boy squeezed it in his hand. Their hosts spoke no English, and therefore Angela had needed to thank them for the warm meal and their hospitality through Saad. When he wasn't translating, Saad had said little and eaten less. After dinner, he'd indicated the small room in which Angela was to sleep and had then disappeared behind a slit tapestry that hung between two walls, serving as a bedroom door.

Squinting into the room's semi-darkness, Angela rose up from the heap of carpets and walked into the narrow hallway. There, she pulled aside a corner of the tapestry that led to the room Saad had slept in, peeking inside. It was almost identical to hers. And it was empty.

Swallowing her mounting anxiety, Angela cautiously ambled down the hall to the apartment's sole bathroom, taking a moment to relieve herself. When she went to the sink to wash her hands and to scrub some of the desert grime off her face, she noticed for the first time the pale strip of skin on her ring finger—the tan line her wedding band had marked her with after many years of marriage.

She hoped Saad would be back soon, wherever it was he'd gone off to.

As she turned off the water supply, she detected the crackly sound of a television coming from the apartment's main room. Following the sound, she found the entire family that had taken her in, minus Saad, sitting around the kitchen table. The TV was tucked in a corner and neither of the two young boys looked up from the television's grainy images as she entered. In the centre of the far wall was a large window, covered by what looked like a bed sheet. Weak light oozed through it, into the room.

Saad's cousin and his wife both smiled at Angela and nodded good morning. The woman then gestured towards some bread that sat on the table next to a steaming cup of mint tea.

"Thank you so much," Angela said, smiling, ignoring the fact that they wouldn't understand her words. She took a bite of the bread and a sip of the tea.

"Saad?" she asked.

The man held out his palms and shrugged. His wife reached for the teapot and refilled Angela's cup. There was a brief whistling sound and a momentary sucking sensation that lasted for a fraction of a second, and then the cup flew from Angela's hand. It shattered on the floor, which shook and rolled beneath her feet, nearly toppling her over.

The sound of the explosion had erased her hearing.

Through blurred vision and ringing ears, she watched the children dive under the table, followed closely by their parents, who beckoned Angela to take cover under it as well. The five of them stayed like that for a full ten minutes, none of them saying a word. Angela felt the bodies pressed against hers rising and falling with their rapid breathing.

When it seemed clear that no more explosions would follow, the father said something quietly in Arabic and climbed out from under the table. He walked tentatively over to the window and pulled aside the sheet, revealing glass riddled with spidery cracks. He turned and looked at Angela, beckoning her over.

She walked across the room and, following the man's pointing finger with her eyes, saw where the mortar shell had hit. It had taken a huge chunk out of the apartment building directly across the street, ripping out its front wall and revealing the interior of a dust-coated room on the third floor.

Saad's cousin was speaking to her in animated tones, the

language barrier forgotten as he pointed his finger at various parts of the destruction.

However, although the sight of the ruined apartment—so close to the one in which they stood—was both shocking and fearsome, it wasn't what had stolen Angela's breath, and nor was it the object of her gaze. She was staring at a space on ground level, directly below the stricken building. It was the very spot where Saad had parked his car the night before. The car wasn't there.

On the one hand, this was a relief because a giant, jagged hunk of concrete had taken the car's place and surely would have crushed anything that had been there. But on the other...

*Where is he?* Angela thought desperately. *Where has he gone?*

By noon the following day, Angela had run out of excuses for Saad.

She'd spent most of the previous twenty-six hours watching the contorted shadows cast by the cracked window crawl across the living room wall, utterly helpless as her thoughts mimicked their twisted, ill-defined shapes. Each explanation for her guide's disappearance only led to more fear and uncertainty. But, as she sifted through various potential chains of events that may have resulted in Saad strolling through the apartment's front door with an embarrassed or traumatised or apologetic look on his face, she knew that each scenario was growing more outlandish and less likely than the previous one.

Her foot tapped rapidly against the floor as she took another sip of tea. She was running out of time and simply had to face facts. Of all the many, many reasons for Saad's disappearance that she'd come up with the previous day—sitting exactly where she sat now, or tossing and turning on the floor as night had bled into dawn— only two made sense: he was dead, or he had abandoned her.

She had reached this horrifying conclusion enough times by now that rather than causing her mind to go blank with despair, cracks were starting to form in the dead end that this reality had seemed, at first, to present. Lodged in those cracks, Angela was beginning to find a question that would prove productive. Through deep breathing and more sips of tea, she was slowly building up the strength to ask it, and to try to find some workable answers.

She set the teacup down on the lid of the biscuit tin, which she'd tugged out of her backpack and placed on her lap, letting the memories of her *Oma* it generated build up in her until she felt fortified enough to whisper that all-important question aloud. "What now? What now? Think, Angela, think. What do you do now?"

If Saad were with her, they would be walking or driving through the desolate streets, asking passersby if they'd seen Miles or his fixer. Without a translator, however, and as a lone woman in a Muslim country, Angela couldn't do that; she could show his picture all she wanted, but she wouldn't be able to understand any useful information she was provided with. She needed to be with someone who spoke both Arabic and English.

Once again, she ran the events of the past three days over in her mind. She'd made it this far in her search. She'd found some sign of Miles, the tiniest of breadcrumbs leading her east. She had survived until now. She'd made progress. This was merely a setback. All she needed was to forge on, to repeat the small successes she'd managed up until now again and again until they led her to her love.

*But how? How do I get back on track?*

With a trembling hand, she lifted the teacup from the tin and brought the liquid up to her mouth. As she did so, her shaking spilt a little bit of tea onto her shirt. She looked down and her eyes fell on the bright Red Cross logo.

That was it. That was how she'd do it.

Hans had said there were other Red Cross Offices, just like the one in which he worked, spread throughout the war-torn city. Though Saad had left her stranded, either due to greed or fear or some terrible event that Angela couldn't even bring herself to imagine, working with him had at least provided some results. For whatever reason, she had lost her guide and, with him, a considerable amount of her funds. But she wouldn't let money stop her. All she needed to do now was find a new Saad. She'd figure out how to pay him later. If she made her way to the nearest Red Cross Office, if she told them what had happened to her, surely they'd help her contact someone who could help her.

She remembered that she'd even been able to text Geoff and Christina at the last office; if the next place she found also had internet, she might be able to reach out to journalists as she had before leaving England and be put in touch with a real fixer, someone like Tommy. For all she knew, she might connect to the Red Cross Wi-Fi and find an email from Miles waiting for her.

Perhaps his phone had been lost, destroyed, stolen. He'd

forgotten the password to his email. He'd been so consumed with working on a story, human lives hanging in the balance and bombs going off as he furiously typed away, that he hadn't even thought to contact anyone. Oh, how they would hold each other and laugh and laugh in their French café over how a little miscommunication had caused Angela to fly straight into one of the most dangerous places in the world. How sweet it would be to come home and see him waiting for her at the airport, the true understanding of just how uncompromising her love for him was shining in his eyes, the months in which she'd pulled away from him now completely forgotten, all the pain she'd read in his text messages after she'd broken off their relationship burned away by the flames of her brave search for him.

She stood up suddenly, almost knocking the chair over and sending the biscuit tin clattering to the floor.

Four heads whipped away from the TV, turning to her. The mother gasped at the sudden noise.

Angela picked up the biscuit tin and smiled at them bashfully. But even though it was a smile of embarrassment, it was a real smile. As she'd waited anxiously for Saad's return she'd feared she may never smile again. Now she was ready. Now she was armed, once more, with a plan. She'd find him. She'd do what her *Oma* had told her. She'd bring him home.

Moments later she was in the street, tripping her way over the rubble and drawing disconcerting looks from anyone and everyone she passed. Saad's car had provided a modicum of safety and much-needed speed, but those were things she could do without. She was determined to find Miles and was willing to do

139

so at any cost. She would continue on foot.

Through a rudimentary ballet of sign language and gestures at the insignia on her shirt, she'd communicated her desired destination to Saad's cousin. Then, once understanding had dawned on his face, he'd drawn a rough map in the notebook she kept in her backpack. It had indicated that a Red Cross outpost was about twenty blocks away. She'd thanked the family profusely, returned the biscuit tin to her backpack, tucked the notebook under her arm, and had gone on her way.

Not a single car passed Angela as she counted block after block, looking at the map every so often to check her progress. Aleppo was quiet. No gunfire, bombs, or screams shook the hot afternoon air. But still, the signs of war were everywhere she looked. A wall riddled with bullet holes bore a dark, rusty stain, the sight of which made Angela's blood run cold. She thought back to what Hans had told her when he'd given her the Red Cross t-shirt, and she agreed with him; she'd feel much safer if it were bulletproof.

She turned left, then walked three blocks and turned right. Another five blocks and the street ended suddenly in a mountain of pulverised cinderblocks. She checked her map. She was meant to continue straight down this street, but the way forward was completely blocked. She walked off to her left until she found an alley, turning once more toward the direction she was meant to be walking in. After several tense city blocks she came to an open plaza, one that she recognised on the map in her hand. The Red Cross Office was located just on the other side of it.

Angela ventured out into the open space of the plaza, feeling completely exposed. She fought the urge to run across it, settling instead for a brisk walking pace. As she scanned the balconies above her and the streets on the other side of the open square for any signs of danger, however, her eyes fell on something that made her stop in her tracks.

All thoughts of sniper fire disappeared from her mind as she stared quizzically at a car parked to her left, positioned out the front of a shop that appeared as if it had been a functioning restaurant before its glass façade had imploded, covering the tables inside with a layer of greenish-blue shards. The car was an SUV. A Renault. It was dark blue. A vicious dent was grooved in its side, etched with red paint from the car that had caused it. The dent looked exactly like a wound.

*Miles' fixer*, she thought, her heart leaping into her throat. *That's it. It has to be!* She turned to face the vehicle and took a confident stride forward.

As her foot made contact with the pavement, something impossible seemed to happen. It was as if a capricious deity had suddenly tilted the world onto its side.

Angela had just taken a step forward, felt the solid ground under the sole of her shoe, so how could she possibly be lying on her back?

For a moment she felt and heard nothing. The only sense she had was of the thought, *How odd*, squeezing its way through her brain like molasses. Then, as if someone had pressed the fast-forward button on the entire universe, awareness flew back to her too fast for her to grasp the disorienting sensory input she was now being subjected to.

Her ears were screaming, ringing like they never had before in her entire life. When she tried to breathe in she felt as if a huge rock were pressing down on her chest. Terrified, she looked down and saw that there was nothing on top of her besides a thick layer of dust. She gasped for breath, feeling as if every one of her ribs had been badly bruised. Only when the ringing in her ears gave way enough for her to hear the clatter of gunfire did she begin to connect everything she was feeling with what must have just happened.

A bomb. Or a mortar. Or something. It must have gone off just far enough away that she'd escaped any serious injury.

Dazed, she rolled over onto her stomach, desperately trying to figure out which directions the gunshots were coming from so that she could get up and run in the opposite one, but they seemed to be coming from all around her. In front of, behind, to her left and right.

Rising to her hands and knees, she realised she was almost in the exact centre of the plaza and, irrespective of which direction the bullets were coming from, she couldn't possibly find a more dangerous position than she was in now.

*Move. Move. Move! Run!* she screamed inwardly to her legs, which seemed to want to do nothing more than shake so uncontrollably that she worried they wouldn't support her weight. *Go!*

Finally, her lower limbs responded.

She ran. In which direction, she wasn't sure. All she knew was that there was a half-destroyed apartment building directly ahead and that she needed to put its broken slabs of concrete between herself and the bullets whizzing all around her.

Her foot stepped on something that gave unpleasantly under her weight and she fell forward. Picking herself back up, she looked behind her and saw most of a torso, the shirt it had been wearing still smouldering. She ran faster. In the exact moment that she crossed from the hot air of the plaza into the shade of the high rise she'd been running to for cover, an explosion behind her lifted her feet from the ground and sent her flying the rest of the way through the gaping opening in the building's front wall.

Leaping up, she whirled around and looked back the way she'd come. The building directly across the plaza from hers was dotted with little blooms of fire. Gunfire. Pointed in her direction.

She turned and ran deeper into the building, swerving through its collapsed corridors and clambering over bits of drywall, metal, and other assorted building materials. She ran and ran up half a flight of stairs that led to nothing more than scorched handrails and open sky. She backtracked, saw a small hole in the wall to her right, and crawled through it, cutting her hands on little bits of glass as she went. She stood and ran some more. Left, right, straight. It didn't matter. This was her flight instinct kicked into high gear. Everything inside of her was screaming *RUN!* and Angela was listening.

She flew around a corner and stopped, unsuccessfully trying to stifle the gasp of horror that was rising rapidly in her throat.

Three men dressed in grimy t-shirts and jeans—with checked scarves wrapped around the lower halves of their faces—were right there, not ten feet from her. The farthest from where she stood was lying on his stomach and operating a machine gun directed down towards the plaza, looking in the opposite direction from Angela.

The second was squatting down next to the gunner, pointing out targets, his attention similarly directed away from her.

The third man was staring right at her.

She took a step back, her eyes widening in horror. The man's eyes were wide too, but more in shock and disbelief than anything else.

He screamed something in Arabic, loud enough for the other two to hear him over the cacophony, and their heads whipped around, three pairs of eyes boring into Angela with the unparalleled intensity of adrenaline and bloodlust.

The man closest to her yelled again as he drew his pistol, pointing it at Angela's chest.

She held up her hands and took another step back. She shook her head, unable to speak, and backed up further. He bawled at her once more, cocking the pistol. She took another step away, tripping over debris and falling hard on her back.

She looked up into the man's burning eyes, into the black void at the tip of the pistol. There was a faint whistling sound. And then the three men in front of her disappeared.

She blinked several times, tasting blood and looking in disbelief at the space the men had occupied just seconds before. There was nothing there. Not even the machine gun. The air was too thick, too blurry. Coughing, Angela realised that it was filled with dust, pulverised matter from the explosion that had just erupted mere feet in front of her.

She tried to move, but couldn't do more than groan. Her whole body felt as if a prize fighter had punched every square inch of it with all his strength. Except for her left leg. Somehow that felt even worse.

Again, she attempted to stand, or even just to roll over, a scream ripping out of her mouth as a hot knife of pain sliced upwards from her leg to her brain. Suddenly, she realised she didn't want to look down at her body. But she forced herself to.

The left leg of her once light-blue jeans was now darkened with bloodstains, mixing with the layer of dust that covered her entire body. She had felt disoriented before, but the sight of her leg caused the entire world to start spinning.

Angela laid her head back and groaned, and when blackness started to swirl at the edges of her vision, she closed her eyes. She knew she was drifting in and out of consciousness because, every so often, the distant oceanic rumble she was hearing would resolve into loud, terrifying sounds and the blackness before her eyes would flash red and yellow with sudden bursts of impossible pain. Then it would all fade again and she'd float back off to wherever it was she went.

She had no idea how many times this had already happened when one of the eruptions of pain and noise brought with it the sound of hurried footsteps. They were getting louder. She whimpered and tried to wriggle herself away from the approaching steps, but it was hopeless. Even trying to move made her feel like she'd nearly vomit from the pain.

The footsteps stopped when they were right next to her head.

"Hey! Hey!" a voice was saying from the other side of the solar system. "Can you hear me? You're going to be alright. Stay with me now. Stay with me."

A finger pulled back one of her eyelids and then the other. She managed to lift her hands to try and fend off whatever the fingers were doing, but she could barely lift her arms.

As her hands flailed weakly against those touching her face, her eyes fell on that unfamiliar tan line where her wedding ring used to be. Then, sudden pressure on her leg caused a burst of agony so great that darkness swept over her vision, swift and heavy and complete.

# Chapter 8:
## England, 1999

The sound of Angela's wedding ring tapping against the wooden table echoed throughout the kitchen. It was a snug space, tastefully designed with nice large windows that let in ample light.

Her eyes met William's and, at the same time, both of them looked away, searching for the right words to fill the tense silence that hung over them, weighing them down.

"Please stop doing that," William said in a soft voice, nodding towards Angela's drumming fingers, "it makes it ever so difficult to think."

"I'm sorry," said Angela, even more quietly. "I'm sorry we're even having this conversation."

William removed his gardening gloves and placed them in the sink. He then turned away from his wife and leaned on the counter, looking through the window at the fledgling tomato plants he'd just put into the garden. The clear light of late morning struck their green leaves, as well as the freshly turned earth beneath them. He wished everything in life was as simple and straightforward as caring for plants.

He opened his mouth to say as much to his wife, but then thought better of it and sighed instead. He wasn't good at this at all, fighting with her. After all, they'd had so little practice at it until recently. For years their marriage had gone as smoothly as his work in the garden; just as he'd give his plants the water, soil, and nutrients they needed to thrive, he'd always given Angela what she needed—the space, freedom, support, and encouragement necessary for her career to grow as tall and bright as a sunflower. He'd loved watching it grow, and her with it.

But things had become more complicated over the last few years. Christina had started reception, and now that John was gurgling out his first syllables, William thought Angela should turn her attention to her family. She'd had plenty of time to prove herself as a consummate professional, to travel the world, to be an independent woman. But now, William found himself wishing that Angela could act a little more like his mother had. Even though he knew Angela could never be happy as a domesticated housewife, and even though he saw how much joy her career brought her, he found himself wishing—secretly—that she would give it all up. He'd never say as much to her, but he wanted his children to have a mother who wasn't just there some of the time, but all of the time.

Like his had been for him. And so, he'd found himself reluctantly pushing her harder and harder to give up the thing he knew she loved with all her heart.

Finally, at a loss for anything more nuanced to say, he spoke. "I just don't see why you can't take more time off," he said, pleadingly. "You have a child. Two children, now. Don't you think they'd be happier with their mother around?"

"I *am* around," she said. "I've just been around for a whole year of maternity leave! And I'll be around in the future, I promise." She stood up and walked over to him, putting her hand gently on his back. "It's just for a week, Will. They need me out there. And I just took so much time off I have to get back into the swing of things. Otherwise, I'll go crazy. You know I love the children, that I love you, but my work is my life as well. Without it, I'm just not me, you know?"

He looked down at his gloves in the sink, nodding slowly. "I just remembered," he said abruptly, "I forgot to get extra fertiliser from the garden centre." He gave her a light peck on the cheek— without meeting her eyes—and then started towards the door.

"Oh, William," Angela sighed.

"I'll be back inside an hour," he mumbled in response.

She listened to him start the car, heard the crunch of gravel in the driveway, the car accelerating slowly and carefully onto the street. As much as it hurt her to see William upset—and not just upset, but upset by *her* actions—she felt that there was nothing she could do about it. Or, rather, that she was already doing everything in her power to meet him halfway, to be as close a thing to the perfect housewife he'd recently wanted her to be as she could without completely erasing her identity.

She'd taken much more time off after having John than she had after Christina was born. And even back then, when Christina was still learning to walk, hadn't she been there to hold her daughter's hand as she'd taken her first steps? Hadn't she been there for her first words? Hadn't she turned down the kinds of assignments she would have killed for when she was younger, all in exchange for changing nappies and pushing a pram through the park?

It wasn't that she hadn't enjoyed raising Christina, and each time she thought about carrying out those same motherly activities with John she was filled with joy, but she needed balance in her life. She couldn't be one or the other—a mother or a journalist. Both were parts of her identity, in equal measure. Why couldn't William see that?

If in continuing with her work she had been asking him to neglect his job at the accounting firm, if she was forcing him to take care of the children in her place, well, then she would have understood his sudden passive-aggressive tones and the obvious disappointment in his voice whenever she told him she'd gotten a new assignment. But that simply wasn't the case; her *Oma* lived with them and loved nothing more than to care for the children. Since they'd moved out of the main city and into the quaint house in Wimbledon, Nina had occupied the downstairs bedroom next to the nursery, which the aged woman had decorated with charming old-fashioned wallpaper and prints of famous landscapes painted by Bierman and Friedrich.

Nina had seemed to grow ten, fifteen years younger the instant she held Christina in her arms for the first time. She was like a savant with the children, always able to get them to stop crying, always knowing exactly what it was they were asking for, even with their pre-linguistic failings.

On occasion, Angela fretted that her *Oma* was a better mother than she could ever hope to be, but whenever that thought arose in her mind, she reminded herself that Nina had had more practice, having raised two girls and cared for the Ashley-Coopers' children as well. To have someone with such a preternatural talent for childrearing to take care of Christina and John while she was away made Angela feel so much better about her choice to continue working.

*Why doesn't William see it that way?* she thought to herself, walking to the cupboard and pulling down the old biscuit tin, where—when it wasn't filled with baked goods—she liked to keep her tea bags, mainly to have an excuse to see and to touch her *Oma*'s old totem every day. She started the kettle boiling and placed a tea bag into the empty mug. *He's never been like this before. We've always got along so well.*

It was true. Their marriage had always been a stable, reliable series of mutual compromises and kind smiles. Every morning when she saw William, she'd feel a warm wave of loving comfort wash over her. He was a good man. No one could argue with that. A fine man, who'd given her everything she'd ever expected or wanted from a husband.

Since the early days of their relationship, Angela had felt that all the movies about love had been hopelessly wrong. Love didn't make you do crazy things. It didn't turn you into some irrational addict for another person, desperate to do anything for your partner. Her marriage to William had taught her that love was a dependable potpourri of wellbeing from being around another person, a comprehensive understanding and a respectful admiration for who they were at their core. *That* was love. Her love for William had never felt like something that could take over her life, something that would encompass all aspects of who she'd been before she'd met him and make them seem irrelevant; it was simply another part of who she was, rather than how she'd come to define herself as the years had worn on.

William, her work, her *Oma*, and her children were the pillars of her life, without any of which the essence of who Angela Schaeffer was threatened to come crashing down.

*It's a balance. A balance between all of them is what I need*, she thought. *He'll see that eventually. He has to. He's a good man. He's just being stubborn right now.*

Pouring the hot water and giving the tea bag a few frustrated dunks, Angela found herself casting her mind back to her and William's wedding day.

It had been a beautiful ceremony, held out of doors in the gorgeous gardens of Hathaway Hall, where she and Geoff had played as children. Everything about that day had been magical and she'd been extremely happy. But, as she burnt her tongue slightly on the tea, she realised she couldn't say with conviction that it had been the happi*est* day of her life. Wasn't that what people were supposed to say about their wedding day? Or about love, even? That the love of their partner makes them happier than anything else in the whole wide world? Her love for William made her extremely happy, of course it did, but happier than anything else in the world? Of that, she wasn't sure.

She remembered how, throughout all the wedding festivities, the only time she'd ever found herself crying from happiness was when she'd seen William and her *Oma* dancing together. Even then, it was the way William fit so neatly, so politely, so perfectly into the life she already possessed that had filled her with such joy. And it *had* been a joy. Pure joy, watching the pair of them dancing together.

She sighed and removed the tea bag. If there was a type of love that could be the source of such joy all on its own, if it wasn't just an invention of Hollywood, Angela had never known it. Now, at her age, she probably never would.

She wondered what it would feel like for a moment but then shook her head, convincing herself that if she'd missed out on such an obliterating force as that kind of love, it was probably for the best. She had her wonderful husband, the children, her *Oma*, and her work—her pillars. Honestly, she found the thought of a force so powerful it could destabilise the balance of those pillars to be a little scary.

She clicked her tongue and tossed the spent tea bag into the bin. William would come around. He always did. Things would smooth themselves out and she'd fly off to Budapest to cover her new story. *Oma* would watch the children while she was gone, and when she'd return Angela would feel pure elation at seeing their little faces. What more could she want than that?

*My dearest Mouse, I think I've*
*died and gone to bloody heaven!*

*You wouldn't believe this place*

*Where are you now? Still in
Kashmir?*

*Goa! And oh my little mouse it's
better than I ever dreamed*

*The colours! The smells! The food!*

*The beach!!!!!*

Angela set her phone down on the kitchen table and frowned at the screen. She wanted nothing more than to be happy for Geoff, to share in the joy of his professional adventures in the oil industry, but each one of his breathless dispatches from India— or wherever—only added more weight to the faint depression that had been getting heavier and heavier within her with every passing month since she'd retired from journalism.

For the first time in her life, Angela sensed age creeping up on her. Perhaps she'd been too busy with work in the previous years to notice the wrinkles sneaking onto her face. Or maybe just the very act of moving through the world with a purpose, of feeling needed by a cause greater than oneself, had kept the ravages of time at bay. Or perhaps, now that John was taking the bus to primary school all on his own, she'd passed into some new phase of motherhood, a time in her life where nature had deemed it unnecessary for her to feel any sense of verve or vitality. She looked at the backs of her hands, sighing. How long had they been this rough? How long had it been since she'd applied nail polish? Since she'd had anywhere new or exciting to go?

Her phone vibrated on the wooden table.

*I think I have no choice but to
set up shop here for a while. And
you must come and visit me here*

*That's not an invitation. That is
a demand*

*Get thee on a plane little Mouse
and join me in my sunny mimosa
and samosa kingdom! Your Bug
hath thus decreed it and you shall obey!*

*Hahaha*

*If only. I've sworn off all
international adventures. I'm a
full-time housewife now, my
good Lord Bug. Sorry*

*No more excitement for this
entrapped mouse*

*Oh stop it. Retirement can't be
that bad, can it?*

Angela felt tears welling up in her eyes. What was wrong with her? The truth was, yes, it *was* that bad. She'd retired to spend more time with the children, and when she was with them she did feel fulfilled, but the children were so accustomed to having Nina take care of them—and Nina was so accustomed to doing so—that much of the time, Angela felt like an extra presence in the house.

While the children were at school and William was at work, she'd read or play chess with her *Oma*. But each afternoon she found herself anxiously waiting for her husband and the children to come home. Then, when they finally did arrive, she'd pepper them with questions about school and work, and delight in hearing them tell her all about their respective days. And yet, there was always that bitter moment when they'd ask how her day had been.

In years past, she'd always had something interesting to say. She'd been doing so many exciting things—writing articles, interviewing sources, running around the globe chasing leads… new stories and new information had always been flowing into her. But now, what could she possibly say? That she'd dusted the bookshelves, tended the garden, and completed a bit of shopping?

She couldn't help but feel that she'd made a terrible mistake in retiring, one that felt all the more depressing because a part of her had known it was a mistake even as she was making it. But she hadn't been able to stomach the notion that William had been right, that maybe she wasn't being as good a mother as she could have been. And, as her relationship with her husband became more and more strained, and as her guilt over spending time away from home had grown and grown, finally she'd given in and had decided to make a change.

She picked up the phone and started to type a message out to Geoff, saying as much: that she'd made a terrible mistake and didn't know how to undo it; that she knew she'd eventually adjust to this new, drab life but that so far it was terribly hard; that she felt old and tired, and utterly unlike herself.

The shuffling footsteps that could only belong to her *Oma* sounded from the hallway, causing Angela to look up from the screen and into the kind eyes of her grandmother as she entered the kitchen. "Hi, *Oma*. Are they asleep?"

Nina's wrinkled face wrinkled further as it folded itself into a smile. "Oh yes, dear, they are both sleeping like little angels. They fall asleep to those old German fairy tales. Just like you did when you were their age."

"Well, that's good. Would you like me to fix you something to eat?" Angela asked. "There are leftovers I could heat up, or—"

"*Mein kind*," said Nina, her wrinkles rearranging themselves into a look of tender concern that immediately made Angela feel slightly better, "what is troubling you?"

"Nothing, *Oma*. I'm fine."

"Nonsense. I see it in your face. And hear it in your voice. Tell me. Has something happened?"

Angela sighed. There was no point in trying to hide anything from her *Oma*; she knew her too well. So, she took a moment to sit there, trying to compose her thoughts.

"Is it that you miss your job?" Nina asked, sitting down with her granddaughter at the table. "I've noticed you haven't seemed yourself ever since you stopped working."

"Yes," Angela admitted, "I feel lost without anything to do.

But it's not just that. I feel…" Her voice trailed off as she looked away, into the darkness outside. "I feel like I'm not a good mother."

"But Angela, those two things do not add up. Giving up your job was a sacrifice you made to be a better mother, was it not?"

Angela, who could feel the tears starting to flow from her eyes, looked back at her *Oma*. "Yes, but I feel so guilty that I still wish I was working. I wish I was getting on a plane tomorrow, or that I was rushing to hit a deadline right now. I'm not happy like this. And you do a better job with the children than I ever could. I don't think I was cut out to be a mother the way you were."

Nina reached across the table, taking Angela's hands in hers. "I have raised two children all by myself. Your mother, and then you. Taking care of Christina and John has not been the same. You are their mother and you have done a wonderful job with them. You've done all that you can. I know what it is to be a mother and I see that you are succeeding much more than you think."

"But I wasn't around enough when they were small," Angela pointed out, "and now that I'm here, it's like I'm not needed anymore. They have you. I should have been there all the time!"

Nina smiled and said, "If you had, you would have been so unhappy. Is that the way you would have wanted the children to see their mother?"

Angela thought about this for a moment, knowing her *Oma* was right, as usual. She shook her head and wiped at her eyes.

"You know," Nina continued, "I tried to be there for *your* mother constantly. She was the only thing in my world that mattered. I was obsessed with making sure she became the woman I wanted her to. And look what happened to her—I failed as completely as a parent can. There is such a thing as doing too much, child."

Angela stared at Nina in shock. Then, squeezing the old woman's delicate hands, she felt a commanding tone rise in her voice as she said, "*Oma*, you can't blame yourself for what happened to my mother. You just can't."

"Oh, I don't, dear," Nina said, wistfully. "I don't. I did my best. What led to Hjördis' problems was the war; even though it was long over, your mother always felt excluded from English society because she was of German descent. She always felt like she needed to prove that she belonged. I know it wasn't my fault. But still, when a parent loses a child like that, no matter what the reason, they have failed."

Nina lifted a hand to her eyes and dabbed at the tears that had started to form there.

The two Schaeffer women sat at the table in silence for several moments, still holding hands. Thunder rumbled in the distance. The first few inquisitive drops of rain clicked against the roof. Before long, the rain was pelting the house in a full-on downpour. Nina and Angela let the sound fill the space between them, let it wash away some of their sorrows, past and present.

After a while, and looking at her grandmother lovingly, Angela spoke. "I don't know how you turned out the way you did, *Oma*. After all you've been through; after all you've survived, after all that's happened. How are you still so wonderful? I can hardly get through my own life without your help. You've overcome more than I could ever possibly imagine and you did it all on your own. Without family, without a husband, without anything."

Nina smirked bashfully and shook her head. "I love you, Angela. It is easy to be wonderful for you. And it's true. I never had the love of a man to give me strength." For a moment, she peered up at the cupboard where Angela kept the biscuit tin. Then she went on. "There is no room for that kind of love in a time of war. In war, romantic love dies before it even has a chance to live. And so, I have never been able to give you much help with your troubles with William. But the love of a family... that I know. I lost my parents, but I never forgot that sort of love. That is what kept me alive. Even though I was aware that the family I'd known was gone, I had to survive to give my children, and my children's children, a chance at that kind of love."

She fixed her granddaughter with a piercing penetration and, in a flash of lightning, the full intensity of her wise grey-blue eyes bore into Angela's.

"Now, so many years later, you have that kind of love, Angela. You *do* have it. Do not ever forget that."

Silence fell once more over the two women at the table and, together, they listened to the rain.

They both heard the same sound, but it carried their thoughts to different places. The relentless sameness of the water hitting the roof made one of them think about the monotony of her present and the bleak, grey future she feared might lie ahead. For the other, the sound of English rain took her deep into her past, to the various storms she'd weathered so many years before.

# CHAPTER 9:
## ENGLAND, 1946

As the ship docked in London, the heavy drops of rain that had fallen throughout the crossing slowly gave way to a light, fine mist; Nina felt the tiny pricks of water tickling her face as the transport disgorged its passengers. She followed them onto the slick, wooden planks of the docks, watching them shuffle along with their baggage in their hands. She was carrying nothing more than her red biscuit tin tucked under her arm, and every time she glanced at it, she could hardly believe it had survived the events of the previous months. For that matter, she could hardly believe she had survived them herself.

The light mist felt familiar; in early spring, fine rains just like this would sweep across the thawing streets of Braunschweig, heralding the new growth of the coming season. Nina squinted through the moisture, trying to find something else that reminded her of home. Before she'd spotted anything that looked even vaguely familiar amidst the fog-wreathed stretch of boats and black-clad figures, the crates of cargo, and the indistinct shapes of seabirds swooping overhead, however, she felt two hands settle on her bony shoulders and turn her towards a reddish face, which sat atop a naval uniform.

She knew the man to be one of the sailors from the ship that had carried her across the channel, and he spoke to her in a language she could barely understand, especially when she was distracted or frightened—like she was now. Even so, she was able to deduce that he wanted her to walk over to the line of hackney carriages that were waiting to carry away the disembarking refugees. The line was so long it stretched all along the docks before fading away into the mist.

Nodding, Nina let him direct her towards one of them.

Next to its door stood another man wearing a dark wool suit. He asked her for the piece of paper she'd been given, which bore her name and some other information in English, none of which she'd been able to decipher. He glanced at it, nodded to her, and then opened the door.

She climbed in awkwardly, gently putting a hand on her swollen belly. As she touched this strange new feature of her anatomy—which had been growing ever larger over the past few months—horrible recollections erupted in her mind, nearly stopping her in her tracks.

She fruitlessly endeavoured to chase the memories away

by focusing on the sound of seabirds and the sensation of damp cold in the air, and eventually managed to climb aboard. The man followed her in and shut the door behind them. Nina picked out the word 'hospital' from his brief exchange with their driver, and when they stopped talking she leaned back into the seat and looked out through the window, taking in this strange new city.

As the hackney carriage pulled away from the docks, the salty air that had kept Nina company during the crossing gave way to an unfamiliar, toxic scent. There hadn't been any smog in Braunschweig, at least none as concentrated or as foul as this, as there had hardly been any cars at all. But here the streets were full of them, jockeying for position in the post-war hustle and bustle, closing in around the carriage like moving steel walls erected between Nina and her old life. She jumped at each and every cry of their horns, then jumped again as those cries were echoed by indignant pedestrians darting through the traffic. In her mind, the sudden loud noises morphed into the sound of bombs and the screams of dying men that had accosted her ears during those dark days in Berlin, when every moment had seemed like it would be her last.

She shook her head, trying to clear it of the past and attempting to occupy herself with mentally translating the English words that reached her through the carriage's windowpane. She'd learned some basics during her months under the care of the British Red Cross, and now she needed to start putting them into practice in earnest.

With every block she passed the city seemed to grow larger, its soot-stained bricks haemorrhaging skyward, reminding Nina of just how far she was from home.

*Home doesn't exist anymore,* she reminded herself, juxtaposing the bombed-out buildings of Berlin with the ones she now saw whizzing past her. *Germany is dead. And the person I was, the person who lived in that lost country, died there too.*

She felt a sharp kick from inside her stomach, making her wince.

She hadn't truly been in a large city since they'd taken her away from the ruins of Berlin in the Red Cross ambulance, emaciated, bloodied, and terrified. And, looking out the window now, so much of what she saw brought her back to the days she'd spent there, trying desperately to survive the horrifying chaos all around her.

At the home for displaced female refugees just outside Berlin, where the Red Cross had housed her before she'd been sent on to London, there hadn't been many men. But now, every blond-haired man the carriage passed by reminded her of the boy who'd saved her, who'd given his own life trying to better hers.

As had happened nearly every day in the first weeks after she'd been rescued, she felt tears rise in her eyes, but she willed them back into her tear ducts, reminding herself that she was safe here. She was being looked after. She had survived.

The carriage pulled up to the hospital and she disembarked, being directed through a series of corridors, into a lift, and then left into a small, clean waiting room. Soon after, a young doctor appeared and beckoned her into an examination room. She could tell by his close-cropped haircut that he'd served in the army, by the determined nature of his smile that he'd seen some of the same terrible things as she had, and that he was using all of his strength to wall them off inside himself.

"I'm sorry, but our doctor who speaks German is not here today," he said, shrugging slightly in apology, "so I'm afraid you're stuck with me, dear. Do you speak any English?"

"A—a little." The words felt small and slippery in Nina's mouth, but she did her best to pronounce them properly.

The doctor looked considerably relieved. "You are a very smart girl to have picked up English from the Red Cross workers. I take it they treated you well?"

She nodded, smiling as best she could. "Very well."

"How long did they have you over at the refugee centre, then?"

"Eight... ehhh, eight..."

"Months?" he offered, finishing the sentence for her. "Well, that sounds about right," he continued, looking at her belly. "It would appear you're almost due."

With this last statement she noticed a tense quality that had crept into his voice, the consonants of his words coming out of his mouth like tiny little punches against the air. Nina felt herself blushing, and she welcomed the feeling of embarrassment rising from her hips to the top of her head; it was strong enough to overwhelm some of the other emotions she felt whenever she thought of her unborn child.

He kept looking at her belly, unable to meet her gaze, and the strange tension in his voice mixed with tactful delicacy as he asked, "Is the father one of our boys? Or...?"

At this, Nina couldn't hold on any longer. She saw the faces of all three of them as if they were right in front of her. The smell of them washed over her once again, overwhelming the slight hint of disinfectant in the hospital's air. When Nina finally managed to wrestle her senses back to the present, she began sobbing and shaking uncontrollably.

"Berlin," she gasped in between sobs. "Berlin. *Die russichen— nein.* Russian *Soldat*—sol…soldiers." She took a few steps back until she was leaning against one of the office walls for support.

The doctor was regarding her with a wilfully blank look on his face, but as she stared at him through her tears, she saw his face growing redder. His eyes bulged slightly and he blew out his cheeks.

For a moment Nina thought he was about to strike her, but instead he said, in a voice made brittle by forced politeness, "Would you please excuse me?" Then he sped out the door, living Nina alone.

She heard an eruption of curses shouted by the doctor, inadequately muffled by the thin wall that separated them. She shook at the loud bang of a piece of furniture striking something in the other room, then she continued to stand there, still shaking unsteadily for a few moments and unsure of what she should do until the door opened slowly.

The doctor re-entered, perspiring slightly, his hair dishevelled. "I apologise for the noise," he said after a moment.

Nina nodded, noticing that—like hers—his hands were trembling.

"It's just… you're not alone, you see. You're the fourth girl today and I—what is your name?"

"Aldina Schaeffer. Everyone says to me, Nina."

The doctor nodded. "You don't have to be afraid anymore, I promise. We're going to take very good care of both you and your baby. You're safe now. I'll send a nurse right over. She'll be in to examine you in just a few moments." As he spoke, a whole spectrum of emotions flashed across his face. He knit his brows together in pity, then tried to smile at her encouragingly, but in the next moment his lips tightened in anger and he fled the room, slamming the door behind him.

Again, Nina shook at the sound. That noise, on top of the memories menacing her from her past, was just too much. She tried to remind herself over and over that it was just a door—a door, not an exploding shell or a building collapsing—but her mind was in no fit state to listen to reason.

As she stood there in the doctor's office, she felt herself carried back months into the past, back to Berlin, where day after day, the bombs had fallen.

She was lying on the ground in what had previously been someone's rather luxuriant dining room. The once tasteful wallpaper was ripped, and it dangled off the wall in several places, all of it coated in a thick layer of dust. Chairs—some broken, some simply toppled over—dotted the room like floating debris after a shipwreck. Shattered glass had piled up on the floor below every window—and in front of an elegant cabinet, which was now pocked with bullet holes, having been raided of whatever adornments or keepsakes it had once housed.

Another burst of machine gun fire rang out.

Again, she threw herself behind the dining table that had been turned on its side, hoping that if the bullets found their way into her hideout the table's thick oaken boards would be enough to stop them. Once, a hunk of shrapnel the size of her hand had come screaming through the window and had stuck into the tabletop where it lodged, vibrating for at least a full minute after a bomb had taken out a building just across the street.

Nina crawled across the room on dirty hands and knees. She reached the biscuit tin, which she'd left tucked in a corner of the room, and even though she knew what she'd find, she opened its lid anyway. Empty—just like the last time, and the time before that.

Her stomach growled. She had no idea what she'd do about food. She couldn't even begin to imagine venturing out of the building; even if she did make it outside and actually survived those first few breaths of fresh air, she'd have no idea where to look for anything to eat. She'd tried to take something from the kitchen, but it had been completely stripped, some other looter clearly having had the same idea long before her. She'd been hiding here for three whole days; for two of them, she'd gone hungry.

More gunfire, even closer this time.

It was so loud, so bone-rattling and deafening, that Nina couldn't bring herself to cross the room and take cover; instead, she curled up as tight as she could into a ball in the corner, trying to make herself so small that she'd disappear. Between the salvos of bullets, she began to hear another sound: footsteps—footsteps running inside the house. They were getting closer.

The new fear this sound generated in her was enough to pick her up out of the corner, and she was just about to dive behind the table and try to hide when the door burst open.

A lone soldier, adorned in the grey uniform of the vanquished Third Reich, entered the room.

The first thing Nina noticed about him was that he was unarmed. His wild eyes flew around the room, propelled by pure adrenaline, and when they met Nina's, they widened in shock. The second thing she noticed were his eyes. They were sapphire blue, and with his blond hair he looked like the poster child for the 'pure Aryan line'. As this thought crossed her mind, Nina quickly ascertained that he too was a child; he couldn't have been more than two years older than she was. Sixteen, maybe seventeen years of age.

The two of them stood there, frozen, for several moments as the abrupt and eerie silence that always fell after an exchange of fire settled around them.

The boy took a step towards her, but she flinched and shrunk away from him.

"It's alright," he said. "I promise I will not hurt you."

His voice was high-pitched and sweet, a voice totally out of place coming from someone wearing a soldier's uniform. Still, Nina shrank further away from him, gripped by unshakable animal fear.

The boy reached into one of his pockets, and then, slowly, he withdrew a bar of chocolate. As Nina's stomach rumbled, he removed its wrapper and invited her to take the confection from his hand. "Here. Here, take it. You must be hungry."

Faced with the chocolate bar, a different kind of animal instinct rose up inside Nina; she reached a trembling hand towards the boy and, once it was in reach, snatched the chocolate and wolfed it down in a couple of desperate bites.

"There you go," he said, laughing. "So you were hungry? Look. I've got more food. Some water too." Slowly, so as not to startle her, he walked over to her makeshift fortress behind the overturned table and sat down on the floor. He pulled out a standard army ration and set it down in front of him. Then he removed his canteen from its place on his belt, took a few long sips from it, and placed it next to the ration.

"Come on," he said, patting the filthy floorboard next to him, "you've got to eat something other than chocolate."

The feeling of food in her body had restored at least some of Nina's humanity, but eating that little bit had made her realise just how incredibly hungry she was.

She crossed the room and sat down with the boy, gratefully taking sips of water from his canteen and then digging into the ration.

He watched her as she licked out the inside of the can, getting every last drop of sustenance it provided. When she set the can down, his smile turned into a frown. "Hmm. I wish I had more to offer you. That was my last ration."

"No," Nina said, finally able to speak, "it's alright. I was starving. I think you just saved my life. My name is Aldina. Or Nina for short. Thank you."

"I'm Horst." He gave her an appraising look, his eyes running up from her scuffed shoes to her dirty dress—still stained down the front with her blood—and up to the youthful beauty peeking out from beneath the grime caking her face. "Tell me, Nina. How is it that you ended up here? As you can see, this isn't the ideal place for a girl such as yourself to be spending her time."

In spite of the dire situation, Nina couldn't help but blush and giggle at his words. She told Horst how it was that she'd come to be hiding in the crumbling house in Berlin, about her family in Braunschweig and how they'd arranged for her failed escape, and then about her life before the war, her town, and her hopes and dreams that now seemed like nothing more than the fantasies of a small child. "What about you?" she asked once she'd told him all there was to tell. "You look like a soldier, but what have you done with your gun?"

Horst's face underwent a slow transformation. An odd, faraway look had covered his face as she'd been talking, which made him look even younger than he was. But now his face hardened under the weight of the current reality, his eyes dulling and his voice growing hollow as he spoke.

"I lost it," he explained. "A bomb went off and knocked me over; its force ripped my rifle away and sent it flying out into the open. There was so much gunfire I was too afraid to go get it. The enemy advanced and we tried to retreat properly, but they were everywhere. Our whole unit was getting torn apart, though it wasn't really a unit, just a band of old men with pitchforks and schoolboys with guns. We started to run in all different directions, very afraid. I don't even remember what happened next. I just ran away from the sound of the shooting. The next thing I knew, I was looking at you."

He fell silent all of a sudden, his shoulders drooping.

Nina put a hand on his forearm. "I would have died if your fear hadn't carried you here to this very building," she told him. "I've been so afraid these past few days; I've barely been able to move."

Heartened by Nina's warm hand on his arm, some strength and personality returned to Horst's voice. "Good. I don't want you moving anywhere. At all. It's too dangerous out there. Whatever you do, don't go outside or anywhere near the doorway or windows." Then he stopped and thought for a moment. "Hmmm. But you are going to need to eat, aren't you? Look. It's getting dark. I have to go back out there and try and find the rest of my unit. If I make it, I'll be back tomorrow with more food."

Nina dug her fingernails into his wrist and squeezed it with all her might. "No!" she shouted. "Please, don't go! What if something happens to you?! Please don't leave me all alone again."

Horst smiled at her bitterly. "I have to, otherwise we'll both die—you of hunger, and me from a bullet to my head for desertion—but I'll be back, I promise.

He left, and from the moment the door closed behind him until the first rays of morning sun crept in through one of the shattered windows, Nina thought of Horst's face, of the bravery and kindness he'd so effortlessly shown her.

Growing up in Braunschweig, Nina had always had a fairly positive view of humanity; everyone she knew seemed to treat everyone else with a reasonable amount of respect and kindness, and people were generally happy and willing to help each other. But ever since her supposed saviour had left her bleeding and battered on a distant street, her view of humankind had altered considerably. It had seemed like she'd never be able to trust anyone ever again. Now, with Horst's smile in her mind and the last of his food in her stomach, she felt like she'd been wrong to let that horrific experience affect her so. He'd reminded her of the good in people.

Throughout the morning she had to resist the urge to sit at the window and look out into the street, hoping for a sign of Horst's return. Instead she paced around the room, her mind racing, praying that nothing terrible had happened to him. She didn't feel hungry or thirsty or even particularly afraid, just anxious about what had become of the boy who'd saved her.

The day felt like it would never end, and when she'd finally grown tired of pacing around, and of sitting on the hard floor, she lay down to wait.

Lazily, her eyelids blinked open; without even realising it, she'd drifted off to sleep. As her vision came back into focus, she saw the very sight she'd just been dreaming of: Horst's face, smiling at her, his arms full of army rations.

He took a step towards her. Then another. Then, something strange happened to his chest and his smile disappeared, immediately being replaced by a terrifying look of surprise.

The greeting Nina had just been about to give him caught in her throat, where it turned into a mangled scream of pure horror.

The small black triangle poking out from the front of Horst's uniform trembled slightly and then jutted forward, transforming itself—in a terrible eruption of blood—into the full head of a bayonet.

Horst's eyes were fixed on Nina's, an expression of desperate fear etched into them. He opened his mouth but nothing emerged but a sickening gurgle. Then his body jerked to the side as if operated by an aggressive puppeteer. The blade disappeared and he crumpled to the floor in a heap.

A man's voice said something in a language that Nina, in her disbelief and anguish, couldn't place, and then another man's laugh echoed from the hallway into the room. One by one, three soldiers wearing filthy uniforms—with a blood-red star in the centre of each of their caps—strode into the room.

The first one of them through the door shoved Horst's still gurgling and gasping body to the side with his foot, then his eyes swept the room, falling on Nina. He smiled and uttered something to his companions, one of whom laughed again.

Nina was frozen with terror. She was still lying on the floor where she'd been sleeping, and although she tried to make herself stand and run, the three of them had crossed the room before she could even move a muscle. When she attempted to roll away, a combat boot connected with her forehead with full force, making her see stars. Before her vision had even started to return, she felt boots stomp down on either one of her arms, pinning her down with excessive weight. Nina continued to struggle by kicking her legs and screaming hysterically, and although she couldn't understand a word of what the soldiers were saying, she'd now been able to place the language as Russian. Even so, unintelligible though their words were, she could still hear the evil in their voices.

Hands closed around her ankles and, for a moment, she wriggled one of her legs free and felt her shoe connect with one of their faces, eliciting a curse from near her feet, another bout of laughter from near her head, and a mouthful of saliva that landed on her face. In seconds her free leg was back in the soldier's grip.

She would never forget the kick to her ribs, which hurt more than any pain she'd ever felt in her entire life. She would never forget the sound of their laughter, nor her dress tearing like a thin sheet of paper.

She would never forget the repeated violation of her womanhood.

The bright light of the first sunny day Nina had seen since she arrived in London shone into the small blue eyes staring up at her in wonder. She wrapped the blanket tighter around the baby girl in her arms, protecting her against the slight outdoor chill, and watched as a cab pulled up to the curb in front of the hospital. She rocked her tiny daughter back and forth and gently kissed her head. She'd never touched or seen anything more perfect in her life.

The pain that had caused Nina to become pregnant was nothing compared to the pain she'd felt delivering her baby. But, whereas that first pain had been followed by a nearly insufferable cocktail of all the most horrible emotions a human being could ever experience, when this second pain had terminated, Nina felt flooded with joy and a relief so pure she'd never imagined anything like it.

For months she'd been wracked by anxiety about what she would do with the child—she hadn't even been sure if she could love it, let alone raise it—but at that moment in the hospital, the first time she'd felt the warm weight of her baby in her arms, she'd known she would do anything for the little girl. *Her* little girl.

Her daughter's first act in life had been to instantly and effortlessly remind Nina that, in spite of what she'd been through, she was still capable of feeling love and joy, just as Horst had reminded Nina that people were still capable of acts of kindness, even in a world turned so cruel. She'd instantly known what to name the baby: Hjördis—the female version of her fallen hero's name.

The cab driver stepped out of his vehicle and opened the back door for her, and when he did an old woman's hand emerged from the darkness inside, beckoning her to enter. Nina did so and, just like that, they were pulling away from the hospital, and away from the kind staff who'd helped Nina deliver her baby and recover from the ordeal.

"You are aware of where you're going, yes?"

The woman's voice was raspy and harsh. Nina was slightly startled at the abrupt question, asked without any sort of pre-emptive greeting or pleasantry, not even an introduction.

"Yes, I—I think so. It's called Birdwood?"

"That is correct. Birdwood Lodge, home for foreign... whatever-we're-supposed-to-call-you pathetic things. Lost, displaced, man-less, barely speaking English. We do what we can for you. Put you to work. Make you of some use. Try to find a place for you here or send you back to... to where you came from."

"Oh," was all Nina could say in response. She hadn't quite understood all of the woman's harsh words, but the tone of voice that communicated them was clear enough. Suddenly, faced with such a different sort of person compared to the helpful hospital staff or Red Cross workers, she felt cold.

"I'm Aldina," she ventured. "What shall I call you?"

"'Ma'am' will suffice. Here we are."

The cab stopped outside a boxy building that looked like it had once been a factory. Bars covered the windows and its dark brick façade caused a shiver to run down Nina's spine. However, once she'd been brought inside, registered, shown to her dormitory, and little Hjördis had been deposited in the nursery, Nina felt surprisingly comfortable.

There were many other girls in the same situation—displaced single mothers from France, Germany, and Holland—all of them survivors, and most of whom faced their situation with a similar strength to Nina.

As she was assigned simple tasks that kept her pleasantly occupied throughout the days, such as cleaning or working in the nursery, many of the other girls became her friends. One French girl in particular, Muriel, struck Nina as particularly kind, and the two of them spent much of their time together, telling stories about the past and talking lovingly of their small children.

The weeks spent at Birdwood Lodge wore on, and Nina's only complaint about the place was that she wasn't permitted to spend much time with Hjördis. Between her workload and the strictly enforced visiting hours that mothers were granted with their children, she often felt an aching longing to touch her child, to hold her close and spend hours rocking her gently back and forth. It seemed to Nina almost as if they were purposefully trying to create a distance between the mothers and the babies, though for the life of her she couldn't understand why.

Two months had now gone by, and while her fondness for her fellow refugees had grown along with her English skills, so too had her longing to be back in her homeland. Although she knew that whatever Germany she'd find upon returning would be very different from the one she'd left behind, she was desperate to try and search for her parents, and for her daughter to grow up in the same culture and with the same language that she had.

She'd wondered for some time how to broach the subject of an eventual return to the Fatherland with Birdwood Lodge's matron—who'd had nothing but scowls and sneers for her and the other girls—but just as she was sitting on her bunk bed trying to devise a way to bring up the subject, she was informed that she was required in the matron's office.

Entering the cramped room, Nina sat down in a chair across the desk from the old woman.

"I have here your release form," the matron informed her. "You are going back to Germany. Your passage has been booked for next week. Don't bother trying to argue the subject. It has already been decided and arranged."

Nina sat stunned for a moment, unable to believe her luck, though finally she was able to say, "Thank you, ma'am. I wanted to ask you how I might be able to return home. I would like nothing more than for my daughter to grow up in the same place I did."

The old woman smiled bitterly. "I said *you* would be returning to Germany; I said nothing of the little girl. Your passage has been arranged, hers has not. She'll remain here, in England. She'll be adopted by a good English family, one whose own child was killed by your kind in the war. Consider your offspring lucky; soon enough she'll be a respectable English woman."

By the time Nina returned to her dormitory, she was still unable to think clearly or even to form any words. It took many minutes of Muriel peppering her with questions before she could fully explain what the matron had said, as well as the feelings of injustice and hopelessness it had generated within her. When she finally finished telling Muriel what had happened, a look of horror crossed her friend's face. Then the French girl's lips set into a tight, determined line.

"They cannot do this to you. Not to any of us."

"But Muriel, I don't know what I can do," Nina replied, sounding defeated. "She said it was already sorted. That everything had been decided."

"I will tell you precisely what you will do!" Muriel snapped. "You will leave this place tonight. You will take Hjördis and leave this place together. I will help you."

Hesitantly, and with butterflies in her belly, Nina nodded.

Fifteen minutes after the bells of the nearby church had pealed their midnight clang, Muriel turned the key (which she'd purloined from one of the matron's underlings) in the door that led to Birdwood Lodge's sparse garden.

"Come now. Quickly," she whispered.

With Hjördis in her arms, Nina slipped quietly through the door. Muriel followed close behind, running to get slightly ahead of Nina and Hjördis and then fumbling with the key ring until she found the key for the gate that would lead Nina into the streets of London. The gate came unlocked with a loud clank that made both girls jump, but no one seemed to hear.

"Muriel, I don't know how I will ever repay you for this," Nina said breathlessly, one of her feet still within Birdwood's walls and the other planted on the unfamiliar streets of the city.

Muriel shrugged in a way so distinctly French that the gesture almost carried the accent with it. "It is nothing," she said. "You can repay me by taking good care of that beautiful angel in your arms." She kissed Nina once on each cheek and then shut and locked the gate behind her. "*Au revoir, mon ami!*" she whispered, and then her footsteps faded into the darkness.

Nina's pulse was pounding in her ears. They had done it. She had successfully escaped with Hjördis.

But the wave of relief washing over her quickly became salted with uncertainty. What would she do now? She and Muriel had planned their flight, but she hadn't thought of what to do afterwards. Where would she go? How would she take care of her baby?

It was late Autumn, the night bitter cold, and Nina wandered the streets of London for hours, shivering and unsure of which direction she ought to venture. Her uncertainty soon gave way to dismay and then to outright panic.

She'd been going round and round in frozen circles for quite some time in search of some kind of boarding house or shelter, but had found neither, instead ending up hopelessly lost. Desperate, she followed the first light and warmth she found, entering a large set of doors emblazoned with the words 'King's Cross Station'.

Though still chilly, it was slightly warmer inside the train station, and Nina made her way to an empty bench and sat down, exhausted. She leaned against the wall, clutching Hjördis to her chest. She was far too tired to keep wracking her brain about what to do next, so she closed her eyes and tried to push all of her anxiety out of her mind.

The next thing she knew, a hand was shaking her shoulder.

"Hello? Excuse me, but are you alright?"

It took Nina a few moments to accept that the female voice was speaking to her in German and not English. At first she thought she was dreaming, but as she blinked her eyes and groggily looked up, she saw a finely dressed woman of middle age, staring down at her with a look of genuine concern on her face.

"Or do you speak English?" the woman said now, switching languages effortlessly. "I thought you might have been a German girl, here as a refugee."

"I am," Nina replied. "I am."

The woman smiled down at her warmly. "See? I always trust my intuition and rarely has it ever led me astray. My name is Dorothy Ashley-Cooper. What's yours, dear?"

"Nina Schaeffer."

"And this little darling?" she asked, gesturing to the bundle in Nina's arms.

"Hjördis. My daughter, Hjördis."

"It's nice to meet you both," she said softly, squatting down to be at Nina's eye level. "Please, call me Dorothy. So, tell me, Nina, where are you off to this morning? Waiting for a train?"

Nina's bottom lip began to tremble. She didn't know what to say. She had no idea how to answer that question even to herself, let alone to this upper-class woman who'd found her asleep in a train station like a common vagrant. She shook her head.

"Well, then. I'm just on my way back home from buying some things to prepare a simple family dinner we are having this evening. How would you like to join us as our guest?"

Nina's eyes lit up. "Really?" she said. "Do you mean it?"

Dorothy Ashley-Cooper smiled again. "Come for dinner and see how Hathaway Hall suits you. I have some small children of my own and I've been searching for a governess. Perhaps, after tonight's dinner, you and Hjördis could stay with us for a little longer. If you feel at home, of course."

In response, Nina burst into grateful tears.

# Chapter 10:
## Syria, 2016

Angela opened her eyes and then blinked several times, trying to clear her vision and take in her surroundings. Her throat was parched. She felt dizzy and nauseous. Dimly, as if from somewhere on the far side of the dense narcotic cloud that was currently wreathing around her body, a sharp pain in her left leg pulsed incessantly.

"There she is. Back in the land of the living once again."

The man's accented voice seemed as if it was coming from impossibly far away. But, as Angela's eyesight returned, the shape of a figure sitting next to her bed slowly began to materialise.

"Where... where am I?" she croaked.

"You are in an old primary school, deep in rebel-controlled

Aleppo. But, as I'm sure you've noticed, you are not here to learn your... how do you say it? Your ABCs?"

There was something about the voice's musicality—and the way each word seemed imbued ever so slightly with a warm sense of humour—that put her at ease.

"At the beginning of the war, this school was turned into a field hospital," the man continued. "This is why I brought you here after I found you, lying injured among the ruins of an apartment building. But as to why you are in Aleppo in the first place, this is a question I am very curious to know the answer to."

Angela groaned. The more she was able to see, the more nauseous she felt. As she looked around the room, she was able to discern yellow walls and desks stacked up against them, right up to the low ceiling. Turning her head, she saw the edges of her hospital bed and, beyond, many more identical beds stretching away towards the far wall. Her eyes fell on the one closest to her and took in a human shape lying motionless atop it, completely wrapped in bandages.

"What happened to me?" she asked, turning once again to face her companion. His features swam in and out of focus, but from what she could see, he was a young Syrian, probably in his late twenties. He had a thin face that sported a large, bushy moustache, which looked like it belonged to a much older man. His eyes were large, round, and deep brown. They seemed to radiate gentleness and caring.

"I was nearby when the fighting broke out," he said. "I saw you walk into the square and I could not believe my two eyes. What is this woman doing here? I thought. Then the shots started.

I saw you get knocked down by the shockwave of a bomb and then run into an apartment building for cover. The fighting continued for some time and then the building you'd entered was hit by a mortar shell. I ran through the gunfire to this building, looking for you and any other wounded."

Angela's eyes widened at the casual way he described such a selfless act.

"This is my job," he added, shrugging humbly. "I am a medic, a driver, and a translator. Anyway, there, I found you. A piece of shrapnel had lodged in your leg and you had lost consciousness. I carried you to my van and brought you here. The doctors removed the object and sewed you up, good as new."

"Good as new?" she repeated. She couldn't exactly believe that, considering how the pain in her leg was growing by the second.

"It will be several days before you can walk, but walk again you shall. You will be all better soon enough." He smiled at her affectionately.

On hearing she would be incarcerated in the hospital for several days—immobile, trapped, unable to continue her search for Miles while he was facing dangers she had barely survived—a sob rattled her body.

"No!" she moaned. "Days? No, I can't. I can't stay here. I must… I have to get out of here. I have to find him! I have to find Miles! I have to go!"

With a sudden rush of desperate energy she attempted to sit up, but an explosion of agony in her leg and the man's gentle hand on her shoulder softly pushed her back onto the bed. She struggled feebly against both for a few seconds and then reluctantly submitted, settling back into the pillow and weeping softly.

After a few moments, the man asked, "Miles? Are you looking for this man, Miles? Is this why you're in Syria?"

Angela nodded through her tears.

"Do you have a photograph of him, by any chance?"

"My phone, but it's probably run out of power," she whimpered, suddenly aware that under the makeshift hospital gown she had neither her jeans, nor her mobile phone that she always kept in her pocket. Everything she'd brought with her to this terrible place was probably gone. The last of her money, her phone, her Bergen... even the biscuit tin. That didn't even bear thinking about.

The man turned and reached for something on a table by her bedside, and when she followed his arm with her eyes she saw her clothes neatly folded atop the old biscuit tin. Her backpack sat next to the pile of her belongings. As relief flooded through her, she gestured at the jeans and the man reached into her pocket to release the phone.

"Show me, please," he said, placing it in her hands.

With trembling difficulty she unearthed the image of Miles, though she could barely bring herself to look at the face she loved so intensely. Quickly, she handed the device back to the man.

He looked at it for a few seconds and then, in a voice so loud and excited that it echoed throughout the small room, he shouted, "I know this man!"

He looked around at the other patients, a little embarrassed at his outburst, and then lowered his voice. "I know this man. I've seen him many times. I even drove him through the city once. What a strange coincidence; I was just with his fixer moments before I saw you get hit."

Angela could hardly believe her ears. "You... you know him? You've seen Miles? Spoken to him?"

The man was beaming at her, the full wattage of his smile chasing away any little shadows of doubt that had been forming in Angela's mind.

"You are Angela, are you not? Of course you are. Miles told me all about you. Oh, yes he did. His great love, Angela."

Tears flowed hot and free down her cheeks. She cupped a hand over her mouth as if trying to hold within her relief and elation, wanting to retain the incredibly welcome feelings of near-accomplishment that were now coursing through her body. "Yes," she cried. "Yes, I am! Please. Do you know where he is? Oh please, tell me he's alright. That he's safe."

The man's smile faded and a dark expression clouded his face. "This I cannot say," he told her apologetically. "The last time I saw him was over two weeks ago. As I said, I was with his fixer the other day. Even he has not seen Miles. No one I know has heard from him for some time."

*No,* Angela thought. *No, no, no! I was so close. He must be gone.*

Seeing the disappointment eclipse her features, the man patted her arm in an attempt to comfort her. "You must not lose hope. You must not lose hope, ever," he said. "I have seen strange things in this war. Terrible, strange things. But also, miraculous things. People vanishing, then reappearing. It has happened many times. We must believe it can happen again."

Angela looked into his eyes, urging herself to believe him. The longer she held his gaze, the more she felt hope growing inside her. She focused on this hope, willing it to anaesthetise her physical and psychological torture.

"Hold on tightly to that thought," he said to her as he rose from his seat next to the bed. "I am sorry, I must go now. But I promise you that I will ask everyone who may have any news about Miles if they know what has become of him. I will return as soon as I can and tell you all I have learned. Rest, Angela. Rest and heal. All will be well."

He gave her shoulder one last encouraging squeeze and then turned from her bedside, beginning to make his way across the makeshift ward.

"Wait!" Angela weakly called after him, "I haven't thanked you for saving my life!"

He turned towards her and shook his head, grinning. "There is no need."

"At least tell me your name?"

"Idi!" he shouted over his shoulder. "My name is Idi. We shall see each other soon, Angela. Now, you rest."

The branches of the beech tree stretched out over their heads, casting a pattern of interesting shadows over the picnic basket, the blanket, and the two lovers sitting atop it. Everything sparkled with an otherworldly sheen of magic. Wherever the sunlight penetrated the canopy of leaf and wood, it seemed to leave behind a prismatic trail of refracted colour, little rainbows that danced all around Angela and Miles.

Angela gazed out at the small pond in front of them, trying to take it all in. She wanted this moment to last forever. It was perfect—spiritual, almost —and it appeared that it would, indeed, endure eternally.

Although she detected a slight breeze running over her skin, the leaves above her remained motionless. Beside her, Miles was frozen, his mouth curving in that dashing half-smile of his that always crept onto his face right after he told a joke. His hand in hers felt warm, solid, reassuring… and yet his fingers didn't move.

She sighed, trying to put the growing sensation of pressure she could feel in her leg out of her mind, trying to continue enjoying the serenity of perfect bliss.

She reached up and brushed a strand of hair out of Miles' strangely inert brow and, as she did so, she looked down next to him and saw her *Oma*'s old biscuit tin resting on the blanket. *How strange,* she thought. *I've never seen it look like that before.*

Although Angela knew of its century-old history, and could identify with its every scratch and blemish, the biscuit tin now appeared shiny and brand new, bright red and gleaming in the afternoon light. However, as Angela stared at it, it began to age before her eyes. Rust crept up its sides. Dents began to form all across its surface. Little bits of the German mill embossed on the lid faded and lost their sheen. As she watched, transfixed by the impossible ageing of the tin, the sensation of pressure in her leg grew even more.

Before long it had gone from pressure to pain, then to an all-encompassing fire in her extremity that was beginning to blot out all other sensory input. Blackness started to cloud the edges of her vision. The beech tree began to dissolve, and with it the tin, the blanket, the basket, and Miles.

*No*, she thought. *No, please. Just a few more minutes longer. Just let me stay with him for a few minutes more.*

The encroaching blackness gave rise to several strange noises. Voices speaking a strange language. A child crying out in pain. The sound of a cart's wheels squeaking as it rolled across the floor.

With a start, Angela awoke in the temporary clinic just as she had the day before, and the day before that, and the first image she saw upon opening her eyes was Idi's smile.

"And today?" he asked.

Angela grunted, trying to take stock of the throbbing in her leg so she could compare it with yesterday's level of pain. "A little better. I think."

It wasn't the first time she'd dreamed of her picnic with Miles beneath The Lentil Tree, but leaving it behind in the realm of sleep was seldom easy. Blinking a few times, she forced herself to focus on Idi and thus return herself to reality.

"Would you like an injection for the pain?" he asked her. "You look..."

"No," Angela said quickly, wiping away the tears from her eyes, "I'm fine. That's not why I'm crying, Idi. I just miss him so much."

In response he smiled sadly and bowed his head.

"Have you heard anything?" she asked after a moment.

"I'm afraid that, still, the answer is no," Idi replied, his voice solemn. "The people I asked a few days ago reported back to me, and I am sorry, but they had no news for you either."

For the past several days, it had been exactly the same. Angela would wake from dreams of Miles and, finding Idi watching over her at her bedside, would become fuelled with hope, only to have those hopes snatched away once again by his negative response.

During his previous visits, with nothing to report about Miles, Idi had taken to telling her about his life before the war.

After finishing secondary school, he'd attended a trade school where he'd studied welding. He'd told her that he'd loved the accomplishment of bringing materials together, watching them harden and solidify, and that he'd particularly loved fire's warming but destructive powers, especially its ability to leave things stronger than they were before.

When the war initially commenced, a missile struck his home while he'd been at trade school, killing all the other members of his immediate family. His uncle took Idi in and, once he'd recovered emotionally, he began working for the Red Cross.

Seeing Angela's disappointment at there still being no word of Miles, Idi resumed his tale.

He told her about how he learned basic emergency medicine from international volunteers, and how the more time he spent with them, the better his English had become, first in his role of fixer and eventually as a translator for international media sources. He marvelled at the bravery of journalists and the lengths they go to in order to deliver the facts on the Syrian conflict, transmitting to the world the extent of the horrors of their Civil war. He said that with every wounded person he treated, with every child he brought to the clinics—which were scattered around the ruined city—he felt as if he were rebuilding the parts of himself that had been destroyed on that fateful day when he'd lost his family.

"And this is the reason I will do everything I can to help you find your Miles," he told her, finally. "If I had even the slightest chance to find the loved ones this war has taken from me, I'd do everything I could to get them back. I would cross the world to find them, just as you have done. And I'd want all the help I could get. I know that they are gone, my family, but I do not know that this is true of your Miles. Have faith, Angela."

She felt heartened by Idi's determination, his strength and his resilience. She considered how war brings out the most terrible components in people, while also creating heroes—selfless, brave individuals who display the best qualities a human being can possess.

"You know, Idi, you remind me of someone," she said, putting her hand on his.

"Oh yes? And who is that?"

"I never knew him. He was a boy who saved my grandmother's life towards the end of the Second World War. Just like you, he put others' lives before his own."

"I am honoured that you would say such a thing," Idi replied, solemnly.

"Well, it's the truth. But I hope so desperately that you don't have to make the same sacrifice he did. He died in the war, you see, trying to bring my grandmother food when she was starving. Without his kindness, I don't think I would ever have been born.

My grandmother named my own mother after him. He was called Horst, and she was named Hjördis."

Idi was quiet for a few moments. Then, he said, "Tell me about your mother. Has she passed away? What was she like? Was she as adventurous and bold a woman as you?"

Angela blushed and shrugged. "I don't know. I never knew her. Adventurous, maybe, but I don't think we would have gotten along very well. From what my *Oma*—my grandmother, sorry— has told me, she and I were very different. She died of a drug overdose less than a year after I was born."

"I'm so sorry," said Idi. "That must have been very difficult, growing up without her there."

"It was and it wasn't," Angela replied slowly, lost in her thoughts and memories. "My *Oma* was, and still is, like a perfect mother to me, but I've always wished I could have met my real mother. When I was old enough to remember her, of course. She was troubled, yes, but my grandmother says that her troubles weren't her fault; they were an after-effect of the war."

Idi sighed deeply, which was always the signal that his time with Angela at the clinic was up, and that he needed to return to the field. "War touches everyone in mysterious ways," he said. "It is passed on through generations, like a gene. We must learn from its effect on others; we must use those lessons to learn how to live with the burden of such an inheritance." He patted her on the shoulder. "Your doctor told me you are almost ready to begin walking. Keep fighting, Angela. You are nearly there."

As Angela watched him walk through the swinging double doors of the clinic, thoughts of Hjördis remained in her head. She tried with all her might to reach back into the first months of her life and pull out a memory of her mother's face, but try as she might, all she came up with were blurred shadows that blended into the faces of Nina, Christina, and the ageing features of her own. These shadow images of the Schaeffer women each seemed slightly transparent to Angela, and try as she might, lying there alone in her hospital bed, she couldn't make them into anything more solid or concrete.

She drifted off to sleep and dreamed of Germany.

# CHAPTER 11:
## ENGLAND, 1967

Hands, elbows, shoulders, and arms pressed into Hjördis' back, shoving her up against the front of the stage. Whenever the crowd surged forward, she felt her chest squeezed so tightly by the press of bodies that it became hard to breathe for several seconds until the wave of excitement rippling forwards from the back of the underground club subsided. She was drenched in perspiration—both her own and that of the countless individuals compacted all around her—and in this moment, Hjördis had never been happier.

It was perfect. Everything had become perfectly perfect, the loose fragments of her life aligning seamlessly, in exactly the way she'd longed them to be. Here she was, looking up into Mick Jagger's face as The Rolling Stones ripped into another song. Here she was, with Jack's arm draped over her shoulder—Jack, the rail-thin, lead singer of one of the most popular bands in London, who she'd never thought she'd be lucky enough to even kiss, let alone call her boyfriend. Here she was, with LSD pleasantly tickling her brainstem and making the guitar chords sail through the air around her like so many rainbow-coloured zeppelins. For the first time in her life, Hjördis was where she truly belonged.

The path that had led her to this transcendent moment, however, had been long and arduous. All those years of feeling like an outsider at Hathaway Hall, watching the Ashley-Coopers' children grow up with the proverbial silver spoons lodged in their mouths while she, the governess' daughter, wore their hand-me-downs and heard the posh accent she picked up from them emerge from her own mouth, though tainted by hints of the German she spoke with her mother; those years at school where the other children made fun of her for not having a real father, calling her a Nazi bastard; those first semesters at university, during which she'd been completely overwhelmed by the madness of London and had spent more time studying the complex social hierarchies of art school than she had spent studying sculpture, always looking for a way in.

She'd sworn that here, in the big city, she would be the outsider no longer. She'd decided to do whatever it took to ensure she was a part of the vibrant scene of artists, hippies, musicians, and free thinkers who smoked and drank until the sun rose above the campus' brick buildings, which offered far more stimulating things to do than study. And, in this moment, as Jack leaned over and kissed her, as bass notes bludgeoned her bones, she had accomplished exactly what she'd set out to do.

She'd learned the secrets of every dark corner of every hip club in the city. She'd consumed the esoteric pleasures of an entire pharmacy's worth of chemicals. She'd arrived at raucous parties and deafening concerts with a boy she'd spent an entire week admiring, then had left with another she'd decided she liked even more. She'd woken up in bedrooms that marked the bleeding edge of society, the extreme fringe of coolness. And when she'd looked at herself in the mirror, setting her cigarette down in a soap dish to touch up the dark make-up she wore under her striking blue eyes, and running her hands through her short blonde hair she wore in a Twiggy cut, she'd seen a reflection that finally felt like the real her—a her that was a part of something *she* had chosen.

Finally, she had an identity, one that consisted of more than just being That German Girl Who Lives with a Rich Family.

The Stones finished the song and the crowd screamed its appreciation in enthusiastic union. Jack was clapping his big, bony hands over his head and shouting something at the band, his words lost in the din. Hjördis tried to scream too, but the moment she opened her mouth she was smacked with a wave of overwhelming nausea. With a start, she sensed it had nothing to do with the drugs she'd taken. Caught up in the magic of the concert, she'd completely forgotten about the one thing that had been troubling her in spite of the fun she'd been enjoying for the past couple of weeks.

She'd take care of it. She'd be fine. But until then, she felt as if her body had been hijacked.

When another spasm issued from her stomach she realised she had no choice but to signal to Jack that she had to go to the bathroom. He looked at her like she was crazy for leaving in the middle of such an incredible set, but she just shrugged at him and then fought her way out of the crowd, even as the band was beginning their next number.

She barely made it into the graffiti-covered stall in time; immediately, she was sick. The waves of nausea, the heaving contractions in her throat, and the vibrations of near-overwhelming pleasantness emanating from her stoned brain had all converged together in an odd combination of symptoms.

She leaned against the wall of the stall, laughing, overwhelmed by the ridiculousness of the situation. Then her stomach convulsed and she vomited once more into the toilet.

When she finally thought she was finished, she squatted down on the filthy floor and let her laughter give way to tears. It wasn't fair. It truly wasn't fair. Just when everything was falling into place, the worst had had to happen.

*Just my luck*, she thought. *Just when Jack and I had finally got together.*

She massaged her belly and wondered if she would be sick again. *Why couldn't it have been his baby?* she wondered, wiping tears from her eyes. *Why couldn't it have just been Jack's? Then, who knows? Maybe I could have told him. Maybe we would have kept it. I'd have a child with him if he wanted me to. It wouldn't matter as long as we were together.*

She shook her head in frustration. What was she thinking? A child was the last thing she needed right now. What would she do with it during the nights she spent out with her friends? She couldn't very well take it with her to concerts like this one.

It probably wouldn't have mattered either way if it were Jack's baby; she would just have to do the same thing she was currently planning on doing. *But at least I'd be able to tell him. At least he'd come with me to the doctor – wouldn't he?*

She sniffled and blew her nose into a portion of toilet paper.

She wanted to get it over with. Her roommate, Judy, would come with her, and after all, she had nothing to be afraid of. Loads of girls she knew had had it done. Judy had found her the number of someone who'd help her. Tomorrow. She'd make the appointment tomorrow.

"Hjördis? Hjördis, are you in there, babe?"

"Shit," she whispered under her breath. "Yeah, Jackie. Just give me a sec, OK?"

She grabbed another handful of toilet paper and used it to wipe at the remnants of her tears, and at the make-up that had run down her face. *I must look like a right mess*, she thought, furiously trying to erase all signs of distress before she returned to the wonderful world of hedonistic oblivion. Tears didn't belong in that world.

Suddenly, the door to the stall flew inward, smacking into Hjördis' arm.

"Ouch!" she yelled. "Jack, what the hell are you doing? This is the ladies'."

But he was already inside the cubicle, latching the door behind him with one hand and pulling her face towards the wicked grin she loved so dearly with the other.

"Baby, they are tearing it up out there right now. But I couldn't last another instant without you." He kissed her forcefully, depositing all of her troubles into a distant place called irresponsibility. "What are you doing in here anyway?"

She looked down at the floor, embarrassed and unsure of how to respond. "I don't know," she mumbled after a few moments.

Jack lifted her chin with his forefinger, and she looked into his eyes. His pupils looked like twin gaping holes in his face and the dark stubble on his cheeks was beaded with sweat. He swept some of his long, black hair out of his eyes and patted her softly on the cheek.

"Aw, come on now, love," he said. "Don't look so blue! It's just the acid, you know? Sometimes you get a little lost. And you just got yourself a little lost in the loo, that's all! Nothing to feel bad about." He kissed her again. "Now, give us a smile."

It was an effortless gesture, as if smiling at Jack was the only thing she was truly meant to do in life. She felt overwhelmed with love for him. He could take her sadness away in an instant.

"There's my girl! Now, I don't know about you, but I'm beginning to think that fate brought us here to this very toilet for a good reason."

"Oh? And what might that be?" she said slyly.

As the opening chords of 'Paint It Black' vibrated the bathroom walls and Jack's hands ran over Hjördis' body, she experienced that feeling of perfect rightness unfurl inside of her once more.

It wasn't long before she had forgotten why she'd come to the bathroom in the first place.

It was approaching noon the next day when Hjördis turned the key in the lock of her rooming house and crept up the creaky old staircase as quietly as she could manage. Spread thinly atop her exhaustion, she could still feel a layer of giddiness from the drugs. She reached for the knob of the door to the cramped room she and Judy shared and turned it. When she saw inside, her jaw fell open in shock.

The room was uncharacteristically tidy, nearly unrecognisable from the state in which she'd left it. But, even more shocking, her mother was sitting on her freshly made bed.

"I cleaned up a little while I waited for you," said Nina. "I hope you don't mind."

Hjördis gaped at her, unable to reconcile herself to the sight of her mother in this space. *Her* space.

Nina stood up. "Well, come on now," she said, "let's go get some lunch."

Upon leaving the house, they entered a café that was located a few yards from the rooming house, one that Hjördis and Judy often frequented on hung-over mornings such as this. Through the window, the sky was its typical slate grey.

Once the waitress had set down their food—poached eggs and bacon for Nina and buttered toast for Hjördis—Nina cleared her throat and began to speak.

"I received your letter," she said. "About Christmas."

"Is that really why you came all this way?" asked Hjördis. "I'm sorry, Mother. I just have too much study; I won't be able to make it home. You know I miss you terribly, but I'm sure you'll manage without me this one year."

"You wrote it in German, the letter," Nina said, chewing her bacon methodically. "You only write to me in German when something is deeply troubling you. I know this."

Hjördis took a bite of toast and accepted Nina's observation in silence. Her mother was so perceptive. She always knew when Hjördis was trying to secrete something.

"Hjördis, I don't like the thought of spending the holidays without you," she continued, "but if this is what must pass, so be it. I will manage, just as you say. But I have come here because I cannot stand the thought that you are in pain or entangled in some sort of struggle and feel that you can't share your burden with me. And so I have come to offer my help to you and, more importantly, to tell you that there is nothing you can do that would stop me from loving you just as I always have. *Nothing.* You are my child, and I want you to know that whatever it is, whatever has happened or is happening, you don't have to face it alone. Do you understand?"

Hjördis set down her piece of toast. Instinctively, her hand went to her stomach. She lifted her eyes to meet her mother's gaze and saw the earnest look of concern there. And then she lost control of herself; there, in the café, Hjördis broke down crying.

She told Nina everything. About the parties, the drugs, the sculpture classes she was failing because she never showed up to them. She told her about her string of many sexual partners, about finally finding Jack and feeling as if she were no longer experiencing just 'free love,' but rather, true love. She told her about the morning sickness. About the trip to a doctor who'd confirmed her worst fears. Then she did the math for her mother, the same counting back of weeks she and Judy had done, which had determined that she must have become pregnant before she and Jack had ever slept together. And, finally, she told her mother what she planned to do about it.

"I don't know what else to do, Mother!" she sobbed. "This isn't the right time. It isn't the right father. It isn't the right anything! It's all wrong. I need a second chance. I can't keep it, I just can't!"

Through all of this, Nina had not said a word. She'd listened patiently, nodding once in a while and maintaining soft eye contact with her daughter. Once it was clear that Hjördis had confessed all she had to confess, Nina reached across the table and took both of her daughter's hands in hers.

"Listen to me," she said, not unkindly, "the first thing I will tell you now is the most important, and you must believe it completely. I forgive you, I do. You may have made some mistakes since you moved to the city, but you are, and will always be, my daughter. You are not judged. You are not lost. You are only loved. Do you understand?"

Hjördis sniffled and nodded at her mother.

"Now," Nina continued, "about your unborn child. You may—and should—do as you wish. If you decide you do not want to keep the little boy or girl growing inside of you, that is your choice and I will support you completely. But—"

Hjördis opened her mouth to speak, but Nina stopped her by raising a hand for silence.

"But, you must know that every single thing you just said— every one of those fears about this not being the right time, the right place, or the right man—all of that was racing through my own mind in the months after I discovered I was pregnant with you. I was alone and much younger than you. I had lost my entire family.

I was going to a new country with no money, no real grasp of the language, nothing. A child seemed like a final curse, a new problem so huge I couldn't even begin to imagine how I would survive it."

For the first time that morning, Nina smiled, an inner light shining out through her features as she continued, "I couldn't have been more wrong. You are the most wonderful thing that has ever happened to me. You have given my life a meaning that it never possessed before. You have made all of my other troubles seem like petty travails and nothing else. Losing my family was torturous, but I was given a new one in the form of you. I cannot tell you how grateful I am, every day of my life, that no one gave me the option to abort you. My life would have lost its brightest light, its greatest treasure."

Hjördis looked at her mother with flooded eyes. She was swamped with a sudden and overwhelming feeling of love for her, stronger than anything she'd ever felt for Jack or for anyone else she'd met since her arrival in London.

"Mother. Mother, I—I don't know what to do."

Nina picked up her knife and fork once more and returned to her meal, delicately cutting her food into small pieces as she spoke. "Then come home. Come home and think carefully and leave all the things that have confused you here behind for a while. If you should decide to return, they will still be here. But now, I believe you need the peace of Hathaway Hall. Of home."

# CHAPTER 12:
## SYRIA, 2016

Each step Angela attempted across the brown linoleum of the clinic's floor caused a hot, searing pain to slice into her leg. Her hands were digging into the arm of the nurse who was assisting her. Sweat was pouring down her brow. But she was doing it.

Step by laborious step, she was walking again.

As the nurse led her back to bed, the door to the clinic opened and Idi entered. When he laid his eyes on Angela—upright and moving—a cheery smile shone from his face, and he continued to beam as he spoke briefly to one of the doctors before approaching Angela's makeshift bed space.

"Look at this! Look at this!" he shouted happily as he reached her.

"Yes, finally. I'm back on my feet."

Idi grinned as he pulled up a chair. "This, I see," he said, "and I cannot tell you how happy it makes me. It couldn't come at a better time."

"What do you mean?" she enquired, butterflies suddenly engulfing her stomach.

"Well," said Idi, "you being able to walk once more is the second piece of good news I have received today."

"Oh?" Angela tried to keep her emotions under control, but was struggling to do so. "Idi, do you mean that…?"

"Yes!" he shouted, leaping out of the chair. "Yes! I finally found someone who could bring me news of your Miles!"

Angela's stomach lurched.

"A friend of mine was interviewed by him just two weeks ago, very near to here. He said that right after the interview Miles and his fixer split up and Miles embedded himself with some of the rebels, going with them further east. That was the last time he was seen. I told you I'd find something out! Now, you just need to rest a little more and then we'll be able to follow the trail, but it's a very dangerous trail, Angela," he cautiously concluded.

The elation that had blossomed within Angela as he'd initially commenced speaking had now abruptly withered and died.

Seeing the look on her face, Idi looked at her searchingly, slightly disappointed that she wasn't more heartened by the revelation.

"Thank you so much for bringing this wonderful news, Idi," she said after a moment, "but if that was two weeks ago, how am I ever going to find him now? How will I ever know where he went, searching for him on my own?"

Idi smiled again and patted her arm. "I said 'we,' did I not? You will not be alone, Angela. Once you are fully agile, I will be your driver and translator. We will follow the trail and see where it leads. This I promise you. Now, I must be on my way. Continue to rest and continue to walk. Before long, we'll be out there tracking down Miles. You'll see."

Angela lay on her back, looking up at the clear blue sky through the branches of the beech tree above her. *No, The Lentil Tree,* she thought to herself. *That's what we always called it. The Lentil Tree.*

"Right, Miles?" she asked aloud.

There was no response.

She sat up and was startled to find herself alone on the blanket. The picnic basket was open next to her and the remnants of their meal were spread all around her. *How strange. I know he was here just a moment ago.*

"Miles!" she called. "Miles! Where have you gone?"

She strained her ears for a response, for any hint of his reassuring, deep voice. Instead, she heard indistinct sounds in the distance. Whatever they were they seemed to be approaching, getting louder as they did so.

"Miles? Miles!"

Now she could hear the sounds clearly. Gunfire. Explosions. Screams. The deafening clatter of conflict began closing in on her, drowning out her desperate voice.

*My God*, she thought. *I'm in Aleppo. I must be in Aleppo.* But looking around, she saw only the verdant park in Wimbledon, and the branches of the old beech, which Miles had dubbed The Lentil Tree on that first, cherished picnic together.

A deafening explosion rang out and suddenly the sky, the light, everything around her began to change colour, turning to a fiery orange and red texture. Angela lay confused, trying to wrap her mind around the sudden, surreal world into which the tranquil park had been plunged.

It wasn't until she stared directly skywards that she saw the source of the bizarre, orange light.

"No!" Angela screamed. "No!"

The branches of The Lentil Tree were aflame, its entire trunk also being consumed by the vicious fire.

A second later the ground beneath her split apart, the hot flames streaming fiercely upwards from the tree's roots.

"Miles!" she shrieked in horror. "Miles!"

Angela screamed out loudly as she stirred from her nightmare, causing several patients to turn to her in alarm. She had been dreaming, nothing more. She was knotted up in the bed sheets and drenched in perspiration, panting slightly as the dream's terror faded slowly from her mind.

Gradually, Angela accepted that she was safe and secure in the clinic, and physically more improved since she'd first been admitted to the ramshackle medical aid post.

She gingerly propped herself up and then tentatively twisted her body in a bid to dangle her legs over the side of the bed. Delicately, she placed one foot on the floor and then the other.

Seeing what she was doing, a female attendant rushed over to assist her with physical support, offering her arm as a crutch. Angela smiled nervously at the woman as she put her full weight on the injured limb, and although it supported her it wasn't without a small degree of discomfort.

Taking one step, followed by another, and then several more paces without assistance, Angela ultimately circumnavigated the perimeter of the semi-destroyed clinic.

Just as she returned to the bed and wearily placed her hand on its railing, the doors to the clinic burst open with an urgent bang.

She turned towards the sound and saw Idi and another man rush through the doorway, wheeling a stretcher between them. On the stretcher lay a figure covered in bandages. Her eyes met Idi's and that single glance was all it took. In that instant, Angela knew.

As fast as her injured leg would carry her, she moved across the room to a large wooden table, onto which Idi and a male medic were transferring their human burden. She looked down at the wounded man and her worst fears were confirmed. Most of his face was wrapped in bandages, but she had stared into his green eyes far too often to not be aware of the fact that she had found him. Finally, she had found him. And like this.

"Miles! Miles! Oh my God, Miles!" Angela sobbed. "What have they done to you?"

Her identity dawned on the exposed parts of Miles' face, tears starting to form in his eyes. "Angela, what... what are you doing here?" he croaked.

"I came to bring you home! I need you, Miles, you're the only person that matters," she wept, reaching out for his hand and trying to intertwine her fingers with his.

Before she could get a good grip, however, she felt Idi's hands grasp her shoulders from behind and pull her away from Miles.

A doctor rushed into the space vacated by Angela and quickly administered an injection into Miles' upper left arm with a syringe containing a mildly yellow opioid substance. This immediately caused his body to relax and his green eyes to retreat back into his bloodied head. The doctor placed the used syringe on an adjacent table and then set about slowly removing the raggedy, bloodied bandages. It was then that Angela grasped the full scale of his injuries.

A gasp of horror involuntarily discharged from her mouth as her eyes fell on the harrowing void where his right leg should have been.

As shock took hold of Angela, she dimly became aware of the sound of Idi and the doctor arguing heatedly in Arabic next to her.

Finally, Idi grabbed her shoulders and shook her until her eyes came back into focus. "Angela! Angela, listen to me. Look at me and listen and I'll tell you what has happened."

"Al—alright," she stammered.

"Miles was hit by a large chunk of shrapnel," Idi began. "About two days ago, I was told. He was taken to a temporary field hospital but he remains in grave danger. He was moved to this clinic because here there was supposed to be a skilled surgeon who could operate on him."

Idi hesitated.

"And?" Angela asked, her voice laden with desperation.

"Well, there isn't. Neither the surgeon nor the critical medical supplies have arrived and no one seems to know where they are. It is… agony."

"So what do we do? What are they going to do with him?"

Idi sighed and shook his head. "I am told they'll keep him here until the supplies and the surgeon arrive—what else can they do?—but I don't know when that will be." He looked at her, his jaw set. "Or if they will be on time, to be quite honest," he finished.

Seeing Miles' face had turned Angela's will to iron. She stared at Idi, and in a voice that trembled slightly, said, "Miles can't wait. He can't wait for them. They need to get him to a real hospital. Now. Somewhere where he can receive the treatment he requires."

Idi gave her a helpless look. "But what can they do for him? The safest and nearest hospital that could provide care is way back in Amman—we couldn't go to Damascus, that's an impossibility— and it is an eight-hour journey to Amman, providing they don't run into any problems whilst heading for the Jordanian border."

"Good," Angela said, making Idi's eyebrows jump up in confusion, "I've been there before," she continued. "I'll take him there myself, then."

In spite of the gravity of the situation, Angela's sudden demonstration of insane bravery made a mocking smile erupt on Idi's face. "How?" he laughed. "You'll carry him? You won't get far on that leg of yours."

"Whatever it takes," said Angela, her voice deadly serious. "I'm getting him to that hospital, no matter what."

Idi considered the woman in front of him, and when he looked deep into her eyes he saw something there that convinced him she was telling the truth. He shook his head at the conviction in her voice, at the crazy bravery of this westerner who couldn't even speak Arabic, declaring that she'd be willing to carry her lover through a dangerous, afflicted country of which she knew nothing. "*We* will take him there," he said, after a moment of quiet deliberation, "together. We will take him in my van. I think that might be faster than carrying him the whole way, don't you think?"

Angela started shaking and soon collapsed into Idi's arms, whispering, "Thank you. From the bottom of my heart, I thank you."

Idi patted her on the back before turning to the doctor, and the two of them spoke rapidly in Arabic.

At first, it sounded to Angela as if the doctor was challenging Idi's proposition to move Miles, and so Angela prepared herself for a showdown, ready to do whatever it took to transport Miles out of the clinic. After a few minutes, however, the doctor despairingly shrugged, threw up his hands in disbelief, and hastily walked away.

"What did he say?" Angela asked.

"That he can use the extra space. Can you walk?"

She limped over to Miles' side and stroked his arm where he lay, now unconscious from the medication. "Well enough," she replied, unable to take her eyes off Miles' mangled form.

Taking the lead, Idi wheeled Miles out of the clinic, past the stacked desks, and past the injured men, women, and children lying in the tightly packed beds, Angela hobbling along behind them. Now that she finally had Miles in her sights, now that she could see him with her own two eyes and not just as a memory in her mind, she never wanted to let him go.

*What was I thinking! Why did I push him away and drive him here?*

She reflected on the words she had sent to him, the words that had ended their relationship. *Those words*, she thought, *those few little words have cost the man I love his life.*

She shook her head in a forlorn attempt to clear her sense of guilt; that was an emotion she knew wouldn't serve her on the road ahead. Instead she forced herself to remember her *Oma's* strength, and in doing so she remembered her own. It was a strength that had been growing inside her the entire time she'd been in Syria, though she'd hardly been aware of it. Now, as they placed Miles' supine frame into Idi's Red Cross van, she focused on that strength with all her might.

She was going to need every last ounce of it.

# CHAPTER 13:
## ENGLAND, 2015

Angela turned the key in the front door as stealthily as she could. The lock turned over softly and she slowly pushed the door open, entering the dimness of her Wimbledon home. She felt like a rebellious schoolgirl—or, rather, what she imagined an errant pubescent might feel at such an early hour of the day. In her youth, she'd seldom harboured a desire to be associated with the 'hip crowd', those who frequently skipped classes, smoked cigarettes behind the gymnasium, and lived in a fanciful, adolescent world, filled with teenage melodrama that brimmed with inane logic. Now, in her fifties, she was experiencing her first taste of the bittersweet flavour of culpable subterfuge. And, she had to admit, part of her liked it.

On delicately pressing the door closed behind her, she stood in the hallway and briefly pondered on her parallel existence. Her heart began pounding and her hands trembled at the thought of it all, at the sheer, unabashed magnificence of it all—a beautiful, hidden time of life that imbued even the most mundane tasks with amusement and exhilaration. A fresh level of vitality had re-charged her body, lusciously rising up and surprising her during the oddest moments—when taking a morning shower and breaking into song, splurging out on a new costume when shopping in town, or texting Geoff with a humorous tale that she now felt sufficiently witty and self-confident enough to compose.

She passed through the threshold to the kitchen, hung her keys on the hook by the refrigerator, then paused in the shadowy entrance, closing her eyes to briefly reclaim the prodigious exhilaration of the night before, knowing that soon enough the veil of remorse would once again enshroud and mercilessly smother her in self-reproach.

To stave off that undesired yet inevitable emotion, she began to retrace the events of the previous hours.

She recalled the way Miles had made the cab driver laugh with one of his trademark malapropisms, and then the smell of garlic-infused cuisine, which had sent a rich bouquet wafting from the restaurant and across the hotel lobby. She heard Miles casually saying to the receptionist, "Mr. and Mrs. Dunbar," as if the little white lie tumbled easily from his lips each day of his life. She recollected the enforced silence that had fallen across the elevator—comfortable, yet laden with erotic anticipation. In her mind's eye, she recaptured the simple, streamlined décor of the hotel suite as the door to the chamber swung open, then the expectant look on Miles' face as he knelt next to the minibar.

The memories were so electrifying that she couldn't keep still, pacing up and down as she thought of the torrent of bubbles rushing out of the tiny champagne bottle and into the tall glass, and of the all-encompassing thought that had entered her mind as she sat on the edge of the hotel bed: *After all this time, this is finally happening to me.* The softness of the sheets on her bare skin, their intense lovemaking, how they talked well into the night, the light rhythm of Miles' breathing, the—

Angela's hand flew to her mouth to keep herself from screaming.

Nina was sitting at the kitchen table, sipping a cup of tea and looking up at her granddaughter with a bemused half-smile on her face.

"*Oma!*" Angela hissed. "My goodness, you frightened me! Wh—what are you doing up so early?"

Slowly, Nina set her mug down on the table. "Sit down, *mein kind*," she said.

Angela sat, blushing more intensely than she had ever blushed before. Just moments earlier she had been experiencing the symptoms of child-like thrill, but now that she'd been intercepted, blatantly caught in the act of duplicity by an infuriated parent, her mind raced to conjure up a plausible yet fictitious reason for her overnight absence. Her mouth, however, was instantaneously parched, momentarily rendering her incapable of uttering a single word.

"So, darling," Nina began, "tell me. What does it feel like to have finally found true love?" Her smile broke into a full, toothy grin as Angela's jaw fell open in incredulous alarm.

She had not informed anyone but Geoff, but she should have known better; all the precautions in the world could never deceive the aged lady who sat across from her.

"Perhaps you are wondering how your *Oma* knows, hmm? Or perhaps you are wondering why I do not seem vexed or disappointed with you. I will answer both questions, *Angela*. Would you like some tea?" Without waiting for a response, Nina quickly rose to her feet and retrieved a sachet of *pfefferminztee* from an overhead cupboard before boiling some water in the kettle.

As she did so, she spoke to her granddaughter with a warm whisper. "Ever since my birthday party, you have been a different woman. I hear you humming to yourself. You move about with increased energy. You laugh from your heart and, no longer, forcibly from your mind. I watch you looking into the back garden, absorbing the bushy splendour of your potted plants, the bountiful bloom of the apple tree, and the flowered embroidery of the lawn, all while unwittingly grinning at the beauty of nature. My darling child, I see you bathed in true happiness, that of which I have never before witnessed."

Angela shuffled uncomfortably in her seat. She knew it was all true, of course. And, what's more, she knew that her *Oma* was piercingly accurate in her appraisal of her.

"You are a new woman!" Nina continued. "The skin on your face is now completely unblemished, as if you have gone back through time to retrieve the complexion of youth. Your eyes shine brightly. You wear make-up once more. The way you dress. It's as if you have found a new purpose. And, even though I have never myself experienced what you have found, I know that it must be—can only be—that you have found real, true love."

She set a steaming mug of tea down in front of Angela, who cupped her hands around the hot ceramic chalice in a bid to permit its warmth to steady her as this deepest secret of hers was being exposed.

A brief silence enveloped the room and further communication between them was suppressed for several minutes.

Finally, Angela confessed in a near apologetic and mumbling gesture, "Yes. Yes, it is." And then, as she determined that the entire world was not about to end because she had admitted her great secret, she continued more confidently, with a dash of obstinacy lacing her introverted response, "Yes, *Oma*, I am. I'm in love. I'm in love with a man I met at your birthday party. Miles, Miles Dunbar. He's—oh, *Oma*, he's the one I thought would never arrive!" Once she had said those words, Angela could not prevent the uncontrolled expression from streaming from the inner recesses of her soul, divulging all that had to be said, from their very first conversation at the German restaurant, to the increasing pleasure she derived from their meetings at the coffee shop, to their first night together at the hotel.

Through it all, Nina smiled faintly, clasping her granddaughter's hand as she spoke.

While Angela relayed the details of her relationship with Miles, the spectre of guilt grew ever larger, becoming more and more substantial as she cast anxious glances up the stairs where her husband slept fitfully, mortally ill and oblivious.

As she concluded her declaration of culpability, tears formed in her eyes, soon expanding to drench her entire face. "Last night was… was magical," she admitted, "but *Oma*, oh *Oma*, what am I to do? What have I done? I feel horribly disloyal and cheap. I've been so selfish. I'm having—my God, I can't believe I'm saying these words—I'm having an affair. I never thought… I never wanted this to happen! I'm involved in the most barbarous act imaginable to William, to the children… none of them deserve it." She paused, staring at her grandmother for a moment. "How can you smile at me when I'm telling you all of this? I deserve to be punished or screamed at or… or, I don't know, told that I'm as bad a person as I consider myself to be."

Nina snapped her fingers and reached across the table to wipe the tears from Angela's cheeks. Then she leaned back in her chair, sighed, and smiled again. "I will tell you no such thing, Angela. You are torturing yourself with guilt, and I understand why. But I have seen further proof this morning that you hold immense love for William and your family."

"But how could I love William and be so dishonest? Doesn't that make me a terrible, terrible person?" Angela asked, almost pleading.

Nina waved her hand dismissively. "I am no expert on the heart. I have never had a husband or even a lover. But I examine people most carefully. I have my theories on what the heart is capable of. Do you honestly believe that we can love only one person at a time? This is *alberner unsinn*—silly nonsense, Angela. Love is not a singular possession that is put in place for one person and one person only. Never delude yourself into thinking that the heart is so diminutive it only has the scope to cater for one. Now, I ask you: do you love your husband, William?"

"Yes!" Angela said quickly. "Yes, but—"

"And I ask you as well, do you love Miles Dunbar?"

"Yes. God help me, I do."

Nina quaffed a triumphant sip of her tea. "I know you, Angela Mortimer. I know you more than you know yourself, and I know that you are not a woman who could exist in a dream world. And so, you love them both. This we have proved is possible."

"It doesn't make me feel any better about hurting Will. About betraying him," Angela said quietly, sinking back into her chair.

"I understand. That is the tragedy. But you have lived a life of more than fifty years without the scale of love you have now discovered with Miles. And I have lived much longer than half a century without it. That kind of love is a very rare thing. I never knew what it was to be held by a loving man and to live and grow together as one." She clutched Angela's hands in hers. "But, I will experience it through you and Miles. Let me continue to witness a love that no woman in this family of ours has received or revelled in since the days of my mother. My father imparted on my mama the most celebrated gift that any woman being could hope to possess: the lifelong endearment and ceaseless devotion of another. The heart does not adhere to restrictions; when overcome with passion for a human being, the heart, body, and soul shall fight for it, shall tirelessly strive for it, and even die for it. It's worth fighting for—and worth taking risks for."

Angela gasped. "It truly is the most wonderful awakening. It is a renaissance, an impossible but phenomenal renaissance."

Nodding, Nina rose from her chair and carried the empty mugs to the sink. Sunlight was flooding into the kitchen area through the main window, and it wouldn't be long before the family would start to wake.

Once the crockery had been washed and dried, Nina turned to Angela and gazed at her with intensity. "Angela, you are the most important thing in my life, and I will support any decision you make in this matter. The last thing I will say is this. I have seen life snatched away from good people with my own eyes. I know how short it can be. Happiness can last moments while misery can endure for decades. I want you to remain contented and fulfilled as a woman—you deserve it. You must try to find a means to care for William and not hurt him further, and I believe that somehow you shall. But please, you must avoid the hazards of becoming a casualty yourself. You are drinking from a golden chalice, one brimming with a powerful and intoxicating ambrosia. It delivers the unfamiliar taste of unfathomable love; don't lose it by carelessly spilling the nectar you are imbibing. To do so would lead to the destruction of your own existence."

Nina then embraced her granddaughter, kissed her on the cheek, and left her alone to her thoughts.

In the wake of Angela's conversation with her grandmother, her resolve to honour a self-imposed taboo against entering Miles' apartment had progressively weakened. It no longer made sense to share love only in the confines of a hotel room, and the thought of hotels in regard to what they shared felt base, cheap, impersonal, and transient.

The first evening she entered his apartment it emitted a fragrance of rich, tanned leather, presenting to her a utilitarian, bachelor décor. As she walked through, the intimacy she'd felt for Miles deepened ever further, spreading roots and entrenching themselves deep in the bedrock of her soul. It wasn't a particularly beautiful or romantic or luxuriant dwelling, but it was his, and to Angela, it stood higher than the grandest of resplendent palaces she had ever laid eyes on.

She couldn't visit there often, and never for more than a few hours at a time, for reasons both practical and emotional. There were only so many excuses she could manufacture, only so much time she could vanish for; her responsibilities to run a household and nurse a physical stricken spouse made it impossible to remain with Miles for a longer period of time. Over the days when she couldn't be with him, Angela became wrung out and exhausted with swells of guilt, relentlessly paying a high-priced tariff of shame and betrayal, a costly levy that permanently gnawed on her frazzled psyche.

To quell the symptoms of this psychotic torture, she yearned for the only panacea that would ease the suffering of infidelity: to be with Miles again, to hear his Caledonian twang resonate through the high-ceilinged rooms of his nearby domicile, to sip a glass of French wine on his brown leather couch, talking in a manner she never had before, even with *Oma*. When they were together they unashamedly dissected their respective pasts, their jobs, their individual fears, their mysterious challenges in coming to grips with life and all it entailed, their loves and hates, and their love for one another.

At the conclusion of every covert rendezvous, Miles never permitted Angela to depart his presence without uttering the same lines of his dejected adieu: *"No one shall ever follow you, Angela. My life either begins with you, or perish I shall without you."*

Several months had passed since their first night together, an occasion when their inhibitions had been cast aside in the same manner as their clothing. They had kissed and erotically fondled one another before even reaching the bed, unconsciously standing at the entrance of the bathroom, united in groans of mutual pleasure and social abandonment.

Quickly removing his jacket, Miles tore at his shirt with an intensity that led to the buttons being ripped free from the striped, collared garment, and then he released his belt buckle, allowing his trousers to land unceremoniously at his ankles. Angela had adorned herself with a pair of body-hugging, three-quarter-length white trousers, which had proved difficult to remove when in a gripped entanglement with her lover. Miles had detached his bulky arms from around her shaking torso and reached to her waist, wrenching down her pallid leggings.

She could feel the concrete stiffness of his thirsting manhood, exploring and manoeuvring a passage into her sodden womanhood. And, as he penetrated his route up and into the willing conduit of her gaping vagina, Angela became aware that she was still attired in her turquoise-textured underwear.

During the entire duration of the consummation of their union, a violent storm raged outside. It lashed heavy rain against the windows of the room, accompanied by frequent peals of thunder and lightning. The meteorological outbreak lasted for over four hours, the same portion of time as that of their frenzied lovemaking.

Now, lying comfortably in Miles' bed and basking in the tender afterglow of a bout of lovemaking that had felt more familiar—if no less passionate—than that first explosive encounter months before, Angela felt another swell of sensual energy surge through her body as Miles kissed her. She kissed him back, extending her fingers to run freely through his bushy hair.

Then, her phone registered a caller.

It buzzed on the nightstand by the bedside and she let it ring itself out, pushing away the anxiety its alarming tone had contaminated her with.

Moments later, the phone rang again. She pulled away from Miles.

"Oh, let it ring, darling. Stay here, well off the grid with me, for just a few minutes more."

She shook her head and smiled as she recovered the cellular device from the adjacent tabletop, her eyes widening slightly as she read her daughter's name on the screen. "Not all of us can slip off the grid so easily, Miles. Now, hush. Hello? Christina?"

Angela listened in shocked silence as Christina spoke, her blood draining from her anxious face. "Where?" she asked, promptly raising herself up and swinging her legs out from under the fluffy duvet. "Yes, I heard you, but which one? Right. Right. OK. I'll be there as soon as I can." She stood up and began moving around the room, gathering her clothes. "As soon as I can,

Christina! Fifteen minutes? Twenty? I don't know!" Her voice had risen to a hysterical pitch. She stopped dressing for a moment, giving her a chance to loudly inhale and compose herself. "I'll be there, just—just, I'll be there, alright? Right. Thank you for taking him, darling. Oh my God. Yes. Yes, I'll see you there." Angela finished dressing without looking at Miles. Then, with her back still to him, she made straight for the bathroom.

Miles called through the door, his face contorted in concern, "What's happened? Is everything OK? Tell me, Angela!"

She opened the door and looked into Miles' green eyes, immediately softening in reaction to the news she'd just received. His face was pleading to be informed of what had occurred, and to alleviate the pain of bad tidings. *If only he could*, she thought.

She'd managed to make herself as presentable as possible while glancing at the bathroom mirror, although her face was flushed and her hair was uncombed and dishevelled. With a quick sweep of a hairbrush that belonged to Miles, along with an uncaring sweep of her rouge lipstick, she turned to Miles and fretfully declared, "It's William—he's been taken to hospital. I've called for a taxi. Good God, I should have been there. I'll text you the moment I know how badly he's injured himself."

She then hastily kissed Miles on his open mouth and fled in the direction of the exit, and to the cab that awaited her.

The traffic had been unusually light en route to the infirmary—*a small blessing*, she silently said to herself—and after paying the cabbie she ran up to the hospital's automatic doors, which immediately slid open. Then, following several frustrating conversations at the reception desk, she finally found them.

John leaned against the doorjamb, his arms crossed in front of his chest. Christina sat next to the hospital bed, furiously biting her nails. Nina was asleep in the chair opposite, her arm resting on the bed's railing, her head tilted gently against the wall. And between the two women lay William, ghostly wan and still. His normally animated and ruddy face was lifeless, grey, and slack from whatever sedative had been administered to him. His entire right leg was encased in a fresh cast, which stood out from the drab gown he was attired in, emitting a blinding, clinical white effect.

"At least she got here fast," John said mockingly to Christina, without acknowledging the presence of his distraught mother as she arrived on the ward.

Christina looked up and leapt out of her chair. She opened her mouth to speak, but Angela beat her to it.

"What happened? Is he alright?"

"He'll be fine," said Christina. "They just brought him out of surgery. He has a complicated fracture to his femur on his right leg. The broken bone has penetrated through the skin. Pretty nasty, but he'll survive."

Angela pushed past her children and leaned over her husband, stroking the unconscious man's short, wavy hair. "How the hell did it happen?" she yelled.

"Simply enough, he fell," John responded, his tone patronising. "He fell and had no one to help him. You weren't there for him, Mother."

"He was trying to get out of bed," Christina continued. "*Oma* was taking her afternoon nap and didn't know of his fall. It's a damn good thing I decided to come over to bring him the new seeds I'd bought at the plant nursery. I heard him calling out from downstairs the moment I arrived home. Otherwise, he might have been lying there for hours, bleeding to death in agony."

"Oh my God," said Angela, rushing over to her daughter and embracing her. "Thank you, Christina. Thank you."

Christina pulled away, looking at her mother with a mixture of concern and suspicion. "Where were you?" she asked. "I thought you'd be home. He was up there calling for help for a long time."

Angela's face crumbled as she began to stammer out the lie she'd prepared during the cab ride. The young journalist she'd been mentoring in her spare time. A coffee together and then some sort of fieldwork.

But before she could continue further with the masquerade, a feeble whimper caused both women to whirl around and face an injured husband and father.

Through his obvious torment, William attempted to smile— rather ineffectually—at his family, and all questions for Angela were placed to one side, for the meantime at least.

*They choose to ignore their neglectful mother, just as she's ignored them*, thought Angela. *It's no more than I deserve.*

She glanced over at Nina as she dozed, and for the first time in her life, Angela came to terms with how aged and frail her *Oma* had become in recent times. She peered back at her children, now speaking affectionately and attentively with their infirm patriarch. This was her family. This was her life. She'd been living in a fantasy, play-acting the role of someone free from responsibility and open to life's sudden adventures, when really, she was not. They needed her and she needed to be there for them.

Angela's hand flew to her mouth in disbelief. *What have I been doing? What have I done?* she ruefully thought.

At that moment, the phone vibrated in her pocket. She stepped into the corridor and viewed the screen.

*I'm here for you. Any time of day or night,*
*I'm here at the press of a button. I love*
*you more than life itself. I'll wait for you,*
*no matter how long it takes. I'll wait*
*forever if I must, my darling, Angela."*
*Miles. xxx*

She absorbed the content of the text after reading it through several times, wracking her brain for a reply. Finally, she placed the device back into her pocket without even responding.

*It has to stop,* she thought. *I have experienced deep and incredible love with a very great man for the first time in my life, and now I must release him. It can't go on. I can't do this to them ever again.*

After dabbing the tears from her eyes, she strolled back into the Intensive Care Unit and occupied a chair next to William's bed.

# CHAPTER 14:
## SYRIA, 2016

The weather-beaten Red Cross vehicle ploughed precariously along a road that was no longer visible. The sandstorm had whipped up a vortex of desert sand and airborne scree—loose, broken stones, which had been violently vacuumed from the surrounding higher plains. The aggressive meteorological tempest had churned up a cataclysmic maelstrom of life-threatening horror, blackening the sky and completely hindering visual access to the expansive, desolate wilderness through which they cautiously moved.

Angela had positioned herself in the passenger seat next to Idi. He was staring impassively through the windshield, as if to transmit a signal of reassurance to her as they confronted the howling forces of nature heralding their clamour of devastation—a harrowing phenomenon Angela had never before witnessed during the course of her entire existence. The screeching wind brought to her ear a mocking, bragging statement of hurricane superiority, which stutteringly broadcast the onset of imminent obliteration, not survival. The immensity of the energy it delivered—and that of its voracious constituents—led Angela to ponder if God's hand was at work here, doling out punishment for her loving a man other than her husband.

She quickly dismissed the thought from her mind and turned to cast an apprehensive glance at Miles. He was laid out on the stretcher behind her, completely oblivious to the effects of damnation that were currently encircling their ailing mode of transport. She flicked on Idi's heavy-duty torch and, through the beacon of its penetrating yellow ray, managed to tighten the straps that held Miles in position on the stretcher. She then examined the transparent cannula that was intravenously dripping vital fluids to fuel his wracked body—a critical cocktail of vitamins, minerals, and electrolytes that would deter the prospect of dehydration, and his ultimate death.

He remained still in his unconsciousness, an expression on his face that reflected silent, internal sufferance. The hospital dressing on what remained of his upper leg appeared to be holding out, with no evidence of blood emerging to the surface of the bandaging.

She extended her arm to wipe his furrowed brow, then lifted his hand to her blotched and distraught complexion to dry the tears from her water-laden eyes. As the winds buffeted and wobbled the brittle vehicle, she leant forward and kissed his cracked, arid lips, whispering, *"Dream of us beneath our tree, my darling man, the tree of life, sprouting a life for us both."* Angela then wiped away a trickle of perspiration from her moist forehead before reaching down for the water bottle at her feet. Appreciatively, she quaffed a large gulp of the tepid fluid it contained and then set the plastic flagon back down on the floor of the cabin.

Peering helplessly through the cab window, Angela quizzed Idi on the estimated duration of the cyclonic frenzy that engulfed them. "How long do these things usually last?" she enquired in near desperation.

"I remember once," said, Idi, "a storm that lasted for five days."

"Five... days?!" Angela exclaimed.

"I was very small, and I thought it a blessing from God as I did not have to attend school." He smiled ruefully to himself. "At that age, I did not comprehend the destruction that sandstorms could bring. People dead. So much food and property ruined. It was terrible. But this one will not be the same as that."

"How do you know?" Angela asked, anticipating some promising news to emerge from his mouth. A faint groan from the back of the van prompted her to cast another troubled look at Miles' motionless form.

"Because," replied Idi, "it cannot be the same. If this sandstorm lasts five days, we will all die here. And this, I promise you, is not our fate. The storm will clear. All we must do is wait. Conserve our energy and our supplies, and wait."

Angela looked down at the water bottle she had just imbibed

from and Idi caught sight of her guilt-ridden expression.

"If you are thirsty, Angela, please drink. Dehydration is our worst enemy here." He then began to rummage through his supplies behind the driver's seat and soon freed a two-litre-sized bottle filled with drinking water, holding it up to her. "But this is all we have left. Once Miles' last IV runs out, he will need liquids more than either of us. And we still have a long way to go."

They had driven for four hours before the sandstorm descended, the halfway point to the Jordanian border. Whenever Angela carefully scanned Miles' stricken body she knew his life was unsteadily hanging in the balance, but once they had reached beyond the outskirts of Aleppo and ferried into the desert, she had discharged an audible sigh of relief.

She'd done it. She had bloody well done it. She'd actually found Miles in that tragic excuse for a city, and had triumphantly evacuated him from an arena of militia madness. She had rescued her lover. They were together again—in a life-threatening situation, yes, but they were as one and that was all that really mattered.

Angela recalled the moment she woke up in Tommy's car, first laying eyes on Aleppo. How surreal it had appeared! How utterly out of her depth she had been. But, just as her *Oma* before her, she had survived.

A small ember of pride glowed inside her chest and her heart picked up a faster, pulsating rhythm as they motored further into the desert, each life-affirming throb bringing her closer to the border of Jordan and Miles ever nearer to safety, medical treatment, and freedom.

Then Idi had pointed through the windshield at the

approaching wall of sand and, following several minutes of mounting disbelief, their whole world had been plunged into a sphere of unnatural darkness and desolation.

Idi eventually pulled over and cut the engine. He ensured the windows to the vehicle were securely shut and then turned the dials of the vents to a closed position, before hastily venturing into the rear of the van and packing the rims and seals of the back doors with a number of Red Cross blankets.

The storm raged for over four hours. They sat huddled together as if sailors being thrown about in a lightweight craft, jostled and tossed as the wrath of oceanic disorder toyed with their human insignificance. Angela sat with Miles during the worst of the conditions, fondling the last vial of morphine. Idi had administered the primary injection into Miles' left thigh sometime earlier, and now Angela determined that the effects of that injection would soon wear off. Miles could not be denied the last of the opiate drug, and she quietly mused that the prolonged weather might ultimately kill him.

"Ah! Hah!" yelled Idi from behind the steering wheel. "Look, Angela! Look!" Idi was pointing upward through the windshield.

His ecstatic words shook Angela out of her solemn frame of mind and she craned her neck to look upwards in the direction of the sky. "I don't see anything. What is it, Idi?"

"Do you not? Look harder. Look! There! And there!"

"Oh, Christ!" Angela gasped. "Oh, yes! I see it now!"

As she squinted, tiny strips of blue became visible and, as the pair watched excitedly, the cerulean texture grew wider and wider until the sky spread above them in a giant canvas of resplendent azure once more. Within the space of fifteen minutes, it was as if the sandstorm had never occurred. Once again the limitless desert floor appeared clear, vast, and impassive, stretching out before them.

Idi and Angela hugged each other over the centre console and then Idi turned the key. The engine roared into life and they cheered in excited unison.

"Do you see, Miles?" Angela called over her shoulder. "We're getting out of here! We're back in business, darling." There was no response. Angela and Idi's eyes met.

"Let him rest," he told her. "That is the best thing for him at the moment."

As they drove on, Angela rolled down her window and felt the cooler, rushing air immediately dry her clammy facial skin. Idi hummed tunelessly as he held them on a steady course, and as they continued on their journey Angela sensed an ember of hope rekindling itself inside her.

They motored on for another fifteen kilometres before sighting a dot on the horizon, and as they drove closer, it took the shape and form of a drab, squat building located at the side of the road, with a metal barrier blocking the highway and their path forward.

"Idi? Idi, what is that?" asked Angela, suddenly anxious.

He sighed. "It is a military checkpoint. Do not worry. I will speak to them. We will be on our way again soon."

He stopped the van next to the small building and two men, each carrying an assault rifle, approached the window. Idi spoke with them politely but urgently in Arabic. The soldier he'd been speaking with nodded curtly and then ambled from the window towards the rear of the van. Idi unbuckled his seatbelt and started to alight from the vehicle.

"Is everything alright?" Angela asked. "What's going on?"

"Quite alright," Idi responded as he looked back, forcing a tense smile. "I just need to open the rear doors. I told them that we are evacuating an important foreign journalist and that we must be allowed to pass through. If not, there will be an international outcry." He winked at her and exited the van.

She heard footsteps behind and a series of clicks, then the makeshift medical chamber was instantaneously flooded with light as the doors were pulled open. Another weak groan emerged from beneath the bandages that swathed Miles' face.

*Hold on, my love*, she thought. *Just hold on.*

After several minutes had passed and more words were exchanged in Arabic, the doors slammed shut. Angela winced at the sudden sound they made, hoping the din would not awaken Miles.

Idi opened the driver's door, raised himself into the van, and then looked behind him, frowning. "It looks like he is awake and in considerable pain. Let's hurry." He started the van and moved off in a southerly direction.

Angela could hardly speak; the sound of Miles' suffering was too much for her to bear.

Finally, when she could take it no longer, she burst out, "Can't you drive any faster, Idi? Please! All these delays are going to kill him. Oh my God, he's in agony!"

Before Idi could reply, a croaked word issued from behind them.

"Water… water."

In an instant Angela had leapt from her seat and vaulted to Miles' side. She rummaged around until she found the water bottle and then dribbled small amounts of the lukewarm fluid between Miles' cracked lips.

"There. There you are," she said, forcing herself to hold back her tears.

She clambered deep inside herself to manufacture as much of her *Oma*'s resolute strength as she could, and then, in a level, unruffled voice, she whispered, "You're going to be alright, Miles. You're going to be alright."

Miles' mouth moved without producing any intelligible words. Angela leaned her head close to his mouth.

"More," he rasped, "please."

Angela delivered more drops of water and glanced at the empty IV bag—hanging flaccidly above her, swinging from side to side with the van's movement—shuddering at its lack of content. She then crouched next to Miles as he slipped in and out of consciousness.

Her injured leg throbbed, reacting in searing protest with each transfer of her body weight, just as the shrouding dusk heralded the end of another day in Hell. She dabbed at the sweat on Miles' brow and considered that the evening fall in temperature would provide him with a cool respite from the suffocating heat of the day. Then, she felt the van slow.

Angela leaned over Miles' supine body to peer through the windshield. A little town sat before them, its buildings growing larger in the slanted light of sunset.

"Idi?" she said.

He didn't respond immediately, remaining focused on manoeuvring through the narrow streets of the near-silent metropolis.

"Idi?"

"We must stop for a moment," he said softly.

Anger and desperation rose in Angela's throat. "What? No! We can't afford to stop again. Not another delay. I'm afraid he won't last much longer, Idi."

He pulled over, bringing the vehicle to an abrupt halt, then turned to face her. "He'll die if he doesn't have sufficient fluid, Angela," he explained. "He can hold on a few minutes longer while I try to find some. He is strong."

She opened her mouth to reply, then, thinking better of it, said nothing. She knew he was right. She had come to trust Idi as much as she trusted anyone in the world. Looking down at the empty water bottle, there was no alternative but to keep faith with him.

"I'll be right back," he said, placing a comforting hand on her shoulder. "Sit where you are, now."

When he left, the loud report of the door closing behind him echoed throughout the van as if a mighty detonation had just occurred in the cabin. Angela peered through the windscreen and sighted the first stars assembling in the darkening cobalt sky, at which point she took a sharp intake of breath—in a forlorn quest to calm her straining nerves—and waited.

No more than a minute had passed before Miles' faint coughing grabbed her full attention. One of his hands rose off the stretcher, flailing around weakly in the air. She took it in hers and squeezed it tightly. "Angela?" he gasped. "Angela, is that you?"

"Yes, Miles. Yes, I'm right here."

He let out a heartbreaking, pitiful whimper and, between short, shallow breaths and grunts of pain, he searched blindly for words. "Angela. My God, what have I done?"

"It's alright. Just rest. Idi will be back in a moment and we'll get you to the hospital; we'll get you all fixed up." Suddenly, his breathing appeared to stabilise, and a sharper focus formed in his eyes as he attempted to raise himself. "Easy now," she said, gently pressing him back down with her arms. "Easy."

"Angela." His voice had a sudden clarity to it, and her heart soared upon hearing the real Miles, the assured, strong tone of voice she'd thought she may never hear again. "Angela, listen. I—I don't know what's going to happen, but—"

"I just told you what's going to happen. We're going to the hospital."

"No—stop that. We don't know that, so just… just listen, alright?" His eyes bore into hers with a fierceness and determination that froze her to the spot. "I don't know what's going to happen and I—I need to tell you something."

"Okay," she quietly acknowledged.

"Angela, I know things between us ended badly. And I—I soon understood that I was wrong to try and hang on. To not give you the space you needed. To put my feelings before yours when you were trying to do right by your family, but…" He closed his eyes for a moment as a wave of pain hit him. "But, I need you to know that I kept trying to speak with you, kept sending you all of those pathetic messages, because I love you so dearly. You are the most important, most incredible, most wonderful thing that has ever happened to me. In all of my travels, in everything I have ever done, I have not encountered one single moment, one single experience, that made me feel as fulfilled as I felt when looking into your eyes. You are what everything in my life was leading up to. You're the answer to all the questions I'd asked myself for years, and—"

With his remaining strength, he extended his arm and wiped the tears from Angela's cheek, cupping the side of her face in his bandaged hand.

"And no matter what happens," he continued, "I need you to know this. And, I need you to please, please, forgive me, Angela. It's my bloody fault that you're here, stranded in the desert. It's my bloody stupid fault that *I'm* here, wounded and tearing you apart inside. I just... I just... I didn't know what to do without you in England. I didn't know what to do at all, and I just felt so worthless, and—"

"Shhhh," Angela said, putting their clasped hands to his lips. "That's quite enough, my love. Things are what they are. What has happened has happened. And right now, there is nowhere I'd rather be in this entire world than here by your side, Miles. You are loved more than I thought I could love anyone or anything. And I take some of the burden, too. I may have had my reasons, but to push a love like ours away... well, at the time I felt it was the only option available to me. I'm so, so sorry, my darling."

He started to speak as the colour drained from his face, then he collapsed back onto the stretcher, now exhausted by the exertion of speech. Angela placed her head onto his chest, listening to his faint heartbeat, and wept.

"Oh, where are you, Idi?" she cried out in wearied anguish.

Then, as the earlier shades of night transformed into pitch-black darkness, her thoughts turned to Saad. She'd already been abandoned once. What would happen to them if Idi simply vanished? If he never came back?

The moment that notion crossed her mind a gunshot rang out, followed by a full burst of automatic fire from no more than a couple of hundred yards away. She squatted in horror and terrified incredulity.

As the shots grew closer, it became apparent that the van and its occupants were not just spectators to a running street battle; they were a part of it.

The gunfire appeared to be coming from all directions at once, and deafening reports of pistols and rifles were beginning to close in. Two bullets ripped through the side of the vehicle and Angela threw her body across Miles' limp frame to protect him. A third bullet penetrated the thin metallic skin of the van and creased Angela's right forearm. It felt as if scalding water had been poured onto her exposed flesh, and when she looked down to examine the wound, the scant light denied her the chance to evaluate the extent of her injury. Instead she ran her hand across the wound in the fearsome darkness, confirming that the projectile had just grazed her flesh. She could smell blood, her blood.

"Idi!" she screamed, compressing all her strength and fear into the single syllable. "Idi!"

A moment later the door flew open and Idi tumbled into the

front seat, his eyes wide but retaining their focused efficiency. He lobbed a couple of gallon-sized plastic containers of water onto the passenger seat and then, with gunfire still raging outside, he started the van and hit the accelerator with a powerful right-footed thrust.

As they sped forward and got clear of the killing zone, Idi's door flapped open at the very moment the windscreen shattered. Grabbing the black torch, he knocked out the remaining fragments of glass from its frame and drove on through the ordeal.

Angela screamed out loudly at the sight of Idi's bloodied face; he'd sustained several lacerations to his cheeks and upper torso from the flying chunks of glassed debris that had filled the cabin at the point of impact. Angela attempted to wipe at the injuries with a trembling hand.

"No need!" he cried out to her. "I'm OK. My eyes can still see!"

They journeyed for an hour before speaking again, the only sounds to be heard being the straining din of the engine and the vehicle's tyres crunching on the ground beneath.

Idi eventually broke the silence and turned to Angela, smiling in relief. "I'm sorry I took so long. Very long queue."

They laughed a laugh of unapologetic relief. After all, only one hour earlier, each doubted that they'd live to ever laugh again.

Angela threw her arms around his neck and hugged him from behind the front seat as he continued to drive on.

Idi then suggested that they pull over in order to re-fuel the vehicle with the eight jerry cans that had been strapped to either side of the van before their departure from Aleppo. "Thank Allah none of them were hit by bullets," he gratefully and loudly yelled, extending his outstretched arms in the direction of the sky.

As he alighted the vehicle, Angela shuddered at his words; she had figured that bullets alone could have killed them, but the thought of perishing as a result of burning to death in an enclosed inferno made her knees tremble.

As Idi filled the tank, she removed the last vial of morphine from her trouser pocket, unwrapping its packaging and then attaching a syringe to the tube of opiate. Kneeling next to the stretcher, she felt for the fleshiest area of Miles' left thigh, then thrust the short syringe into his limb through his leggings. Despite the surrounding darkness, she could see a trace of painlessness sweep across the haggard complexion of the man she loved as it took effect.

"Sleep well, my darling, this will all soon be over." Angela then attended to her injured arm as she inwardly craved for sleep—the best kind of sleep, the kind she experienced when in the arms of Miles.

Idi returned to the driver's seat after his refuelling travail and turned over the ignition, but they had moved forward no more than a few yards when they heard a knocking sound tapping out from the engine. Idi gave the accelerator a double-tap with his foot and the vehicle's speed began to increase, but the ominous noise remained.

Angela and Idi looked at one other, exchanging a concerned expression. They each knew there was nothing else to do but to keep moving south.

# Chapter 15:
## England, 2015

Pushing lightly on the bedroom door with the aid of her backside, Angela entered the sleeping chamber, balancing a tray containing hot vegetable soup and a thin slice of dark German rye bread in one hand, accompanied by a steaming mug of herbal tea in the other.

"Lunchtime, darling!" she cheerily announced with a forced but comforting clarity. Then, rather cautiously, she strode across the carpeted floor of what had once been the master bedroom.

In a functional sense, it still remained so, but over the last few months the lightly decorated boudoir had taken on the appearance of an Oncology ward within an infirmary or specialist hospice. Bottles, which contained medications and herbal supplements, littered the bedside tables, and the railings and cables of William's adjustable hospital bed promoted a distinctly medical atmosphere.

As she adjusted his pillows, he depressed a small button on the remote control device and leveraged his upper body into a sitting position. He had become significantly weaker in recent days, and the simple act of raising himself now caused distress and several moments of exacting wheezing. His yellowish skin was drawn and paper-thin, but he managed to exhibit a grateful smile as she placed the simple meal onto his lap.

"Do you need anything else?" Angela asked, leaning over to kiss his moist forehead.

"No, love, I'm fine," he declared in a voice that sounded as if it had been dragged across heavy-duty sandpaper. He gave her wrist a limp squeeze of affection and then spooned a small mouthful of the broth into his mouth.

She lingered by the bed as he slowly devoured the flavoursome consommé, inwardly cheered that his appetite had finally returned; during the previous fortnight, he had refused most of the food prepared for him, other than several inadequate nibbles from a platter of poached cod or scrambled egg. Since his leg cast had been removed, his dour demeanour—along with his disenchanted taste buds—had enlivened measurably.

As Angela turned to leave William to quietly consume his meal, she felt her phone vibrate in the pocket of her apron and, striding perfunctorily from the bedroom, she pulled out the device and scanned the screen.

She had received a text message from 'Geoff'.

Angela stifled a gasp of helpless frustration, closed the

bedroom door behind her, and ventured into the bathroom along the hallway, where she leaned against the shower cubicle for support. The phone number attached to the name 'Geoff' did not belong to her flamboyant, globetrotting, lifelong best friend, as Geoff's number was listed as 'Bug'. The bogus appellation camouflaged the originator's true identity: Miles.

As she examined the despairing content of the text, Angela's legs buckled slightly as she absorbed the brief communiqué.

*Can you please call? Even if I*
*can't see you, I need to hear*
*your voice.*
*Miles xx*

As temperate tears launched in her eyes, she smiled faintly at the idiosyncratic manner in which he signed off, as one may do when penning a letter, in an old-fashioned but enchanting kind of way.

Without responding, she placed the phone into her pocket and turned on the cold tap of the shower to cloak the sounds of her sobbing. Recently, these maudlin interludes had become a staple of Angela's routine. Since severing her clandestine relationship with Miles, she could not respond to him or converse with him, and even one brief utterance from Miles always seemed far too much for her to bear.

She removed the phone from her apron once again and placed it close to her mouth, whispering, *"I shall love you for all time, my precious, much-loved man, but I have no way out."* She then kissed the screen before crumpling onto a fluffy mat next to the bath.

William's recent injury and enforced hospitalisation had registered within Angela that it would be impossible to keep seeing Miles, but now that they were apart, trying to exorcise him from her melancholic existence was proving equally impossible. Caring for William took up the majority of Angela's days and flagging energy, and for this she was grateful. Yet in each second that wasn't consumed with tending to William's needs, she was overcome with an overwhelming impulse to weep alone in whatever private, dark corner was made available to her. She knew she was causing Miles intolerable pain from the rejection he endured, and she too could never get through a whole day without squirming in psychotic and emotional disquiet, yearning to tell him, yet she was reluctantly managing to resist this impulse.

Before returning to the bedroom to recover William's dishes, she rinsed her eyes and applied a small quantity of face cream to erase any evidence of weeping.

William lay asleep. Angela adjusted the bed to a horizontal position with the aid of the remote control and arranged the pillows and duvet before returning to the downstairs kitchen area.

As she set the tray down on the worktop, she detected the sound of Nina clearing her throat from behind her. Angela's shoulders sank. Her *Oma* had heard her weeping.

"Angela?"

She twisted slowly to face Nina, and the pitying look she could see in her grandmother's eyes told her she'd been correct in her assumption. Angela's lip trembled as she attempted to talk.

"You don't have to say anything, dear. Not if you don't want to," said Nina.

Angela sat down at the kitchen table. "Oh, *God!*" she wearily cried out. "I had to do it. I had to do the responsible thing. But it's tearing me apart. I miss him so much. And now... now I fear that you must be disappointed in me. I didn't take your advice. I didn't follow my heart."

"You did what you had to do," said Nina. "You did what you thought was right. As I told you, I support whatever you decide to do with your life. I could never feel anything but love and pride when I look at you, *Angela*. Please, remember that."

"But what do I do now, *Oma*? I've thrown away the most important thing in my life."

"Not thrown away," said Nina, placing her hand on Angela's shoulder. "Just put on hold. He understands that you are taking care of your family. Perhaps this is just another chapter in your relationship. Keep following your instincts. They will lead you on the right path."

The two women remained in the kitchen for some time, sharing a silence that instilled a sense of mutual comfort: a state of grace that more than a million words could not possibly create.

The leaves were shrivelled and crisp as the arrival of winter made its annual presence known, heralding a seasonal reminder that yet another year was quickly drawing to a close. The withered foliage that floated from the branches above plummeted softly down to create an abundant carpet of brown and green freckles across the garden lawn. The balmy, dry summer had finally surrendered to prolonged chilly spells, interjected with lengthy outbreaks of depressing drizzle and occasional heavy overnight rain. The days had drawn in and natural illumination was in short supply; the shades of night extinguished meaningful iridescence by mid-afternoon of each receding day. Yet the changing meteorological conditions swept in a refreshingly congenial and unexpected breeze of reawakening to the Mortimer household.

Angela and Christina were engaged in the preparations for Christmas dinner.

"Where did you learn the recipe for these yams?" Angela queried as she opened the oven door to monitor the progress of the baked tubers, releasing a waft of fragrant vapour. "They smell incredible."

"One of the American girls at university taught me. Her family in Kansas eats them, especially at Thanksgiving," Christina answered. "I hope you all like them. Something new and tasty to bring to the festive table! I just hope they're as scrumptious as your roast potatoes, Mum."

The unexpected compliment caused Angela to smile. A new recipe was the very least that Christina had re-introduced into her life; since returning home to assist in nursing her ailing father, she and Angela had collaborated and bonded as a highly-functional, familial duo, a care-providing unit, operating in perfect symbiosis on three demanding fronts—a trinity of domestic demands that revolved around William, an ailing grandmother, and that of home maintenance.

Angela frequently claimed recurrent interludes to ask Christina about her life, enquiring enthusiastically about her daughter's new career in teaching, and also encouraging her to converse about her university years and the opinions she'd forged on worldwide issues.

This had more benefits than Angela had anticipated; the more Christina's presence grew in her life, the more bearable Miles' absence became. Bridges were being restored and rebuilt, enabling one other to cross and reach the previously unreachable. They had traversed the Rubicon of bloodline anonymity and entered the Promised Land of hope and optimism through laughter, touch, and conversation. Christina was substituting for Miles, but on another level.

Angela extended her arm to wipe a residue of grated cheese from her daughter's flushed cheek, light-heartedly commenting, "Just in case you're wondering, Christina, no matter how the yams turn out, I shall always love you." Angela did not wait for a reply to her pledge of affection; she returned to the oven and examined once more the browning contents of the stove.

Christina walked over to Angela and, from behind, wrapped her arms around Angela's waist as she quietly announced, "And I shall always love you, Mum."

Angela smiled as she squeezed her daughter's arm.

The dinner table was laden with a plentiful array of traditional German cuisine taken from recipes passed down through the Schaeffer dynasty, including apple and sausage stuffing, red cabbage, and cricket ball-sized dumplings. Angela was thankful for preserving some of the last remaining apples from the tree, several of which were used to produce a flagon of *Rumtopf*, a fruity but potent combination of sliced apple and spiced rum. A large, well-basted turkey occupied centre stage on the table.

During healthier times, William had taken immense delight in carving whatever choice of meat they had opted to devour on Christmas Day, but on this occasion the task fell to Christina.

Ready to follow the seasonal banquet, a sweet-smelling Stollen sat nestling in the warm oven. Nina had originally taught her granddaughter how to create the cake-like fruit bread treat; over time, however, she'd marvelled at Angela's special interpretation of the recipe. Lusciously crammed with candied orange peel, lemon, raisins, and almonds, it was unique in comparison to her own version of the rich delicacy. Nina determined that Angela's meticulous measure of cardamom and cinnamon held the secret to her culinary success.

Surrounded by William, Nina, and Christina, Angela felt a surge of contentment flow inside her for the first time since she'd ended the affair with Miles. Yet her mind continued to drift in his direction. *I just can't let go, not even on days like this*, she thought to herself.

Her mind quickly flitted to John, her absent son. He had elected to spend Christmas with his fiancée and her family, with a promise to call home later in the day. Angela and the family had known of his intentions for some weeks, yet his non-attendance still cast a silent shadow; the wholesome good cheer that permeated the dining room was made lesser by virtue of John's decision to celebrate the day elsewhere.

As the main course of the feast was consumed, Nina rose to her feet. The aged, frail lady lifted her glass of wine and beamed at the family members gathered around her. "I would like to make a toast to all of you," she began.

Angela, who had already quaffed her second glass of wine, reached for the bottle to pour herself a third.

"Here we sit," Nina continued, "three generations of Schaeffer women, and a wonderful, strong man in our lives." She smiled at them all. "I have fought very hard during my time on earth to enjoy moments such as these. I love you all dearly and I thank you, Angela, and you, Christina, for all you have done for William and me these past months. I'm so proud of you. You make getting old a wonderful adventure. *Gott segne sie alle.*"

"Here, here!" said William, with as much gusto as he could muster.

Nina gesticulated in a conservative but appreciative manner, nodding her head graciously at each member of the family, and then lifted her glass and drank from it. Everyone followed suit.

Christina then stood and initiated the process of removing the crockery and serving dishes from the dining table. Angela rose to assist her daughter in the task, but Christina flashed her a smile and waved her off. "I've got it, Mum," she said. "I'll take these into the kitchen and be back with the Stollen!"

Angela smiled as she consumed another sip of wine. Given the turmoil of the passing year, she could not have asked for a better Christmas.

William and Nina had now moved to the comfort of the large sofa and were leaning back into it, as if delivering confirmation of their yen for a short nap. Angela opted to retrieve her phone from the bookcase. John and Bug would have transmitted goodwill messages to both her and the family, she determined, and it would be best to reciprocate their greetings before Christina served the Stollen.

As she scrolled through the list of messages, she caught sight of the name 'Geoff', the only contact he had made with her in several weeks. Shakily, she opened the message and devoured the words it contained.

> *Who needs a Christmas tree with*
> *nicely wrapped presents beneath?*
> *Not I, the most beautiful sight is*
> *our Lentil Tree, with you and me*
> *lying under it. I love you now as I*
> *shall always love you. Across all*
> *seasons, for all time.*
> *Miles xx*

Suddenly, the high, impregnable walls of defiance and sacrifice that Angela had constructed within her psyche immediately crumbled, lying demolished at the pit of her stomach. The wine she'd consumed over dinner fuelled her need to respond, to raise her from the encirclement of denial by replying to him, so she retreated to the upstairs bathroom and keyed a hasty, maudlin riposte.

> *Never a day goes by when I don't*
> *capture an image of us lying under*
> *the Tree. I love you, my darling, I*
> *just can't reach you.*
> *Angela*

Angela watched Christina from the lounge as her daughter clipped and manicured the vast assortment of fuchsia, hydrangea, and chrysanthemums in readiness for spring. Christina was tending to her father's plants in the greenhouse at the foot of the garden, ensuring they received the care and attention they required during the winter months. William no longer had the strength or will to venture beyond the threshold of his bedroom, but occasionally he shuffled to the window to admire the botanical landscape he had shaped and maintained over many years.

From where she sat indoors, Angela sighed in frustration at her inability to make *Bug* understand the realities of life—her life, and that of her family's needs. If that meant that she had to feel trapped, frustrated, and constantly beset by a never-ceasing longing for the man she loved, then so be it. This, she thought, was her fate. Regardless of what she said to Bug in their frequent texting conversations, however, she just couldn't make him see the importance of her sacrifice.

She turned away from the window and climbed the stairs to the bedroom to check on William. The Macmillan Nurse had visited him earlier that morning; recently, he had begun to look forward to receiving visits from her, listening to her chatty upbeat conversation and all that had been going on in her own life since her previous appointment with him. Even so, each day his appearance gave way to further deterioration. Each day brought with it yet another shock, and his decline was advancing faster than they'd been led to believe at the onset of his illness.

Angela steeled herself for more distress as she entered the room and the whiff of infirmity filled her nostrils. She had become accustomed to the unpleasant pungency, accepting that odour and disease formed a relationship that was impossible to eradicate. She forced a broad smile of cheeriness to form over her face as she strode to her husband's bedside.

"How are we doing today, soldier?" she asked him, occupying a chair next to where he lay and taking his frail hand in hers.

"Ah, there's my angel," he said in a hoarse voice, smirking up at her. "Doing just fine, thank you. Another day in paradise." Angela laughed. He rubbed her hand with his thumb and gazed into her eyes for a few moments before he spoke again. "Do you remember our lunch date in Regent's Park?"

"Our 'lunch-on-the-run?' Of course I do. The best fish and chips I ever tasted." Angela looked off into the distance, allowing the pleasant memory to flood back. "I'd thought you were going to take us to some stuffy old restaurant, and it saddened me to possibly be cooped up inside on such a beautiful day. But you picked me up in that old Morris Minor car of yours with a greasy brown bag of food resting on your lap and drove us to the park. It was as if you had read my mind, Will."

He smiled agreeably. "You talked so passionately about journalism," he recalled, "about all the pros and cons of it. All I had to offer you was a lesson on the intricacies of cricket," he chuckled to himself. "Even then, I knew we were very different. You, so passionate. And I, well… just a hopelessly average man. But I hoped—I prayed—that you could love me anyway. That you could love me as completely as I'd always loved you."

Angela blotted at the tears in her eyes. "Oh Will, don't say that. I never thought of you as average. You were—you *are*—always just you, yourself: the good, decent, kind man I married. The father of my children. The man I love."

He patted her hand and beamed at her. And then, still in a conversational and pleasant tone, he said, "Or one of them, I suppose."

Angela felt her heart drop. "What?"

"Angela. Come now," he said, a wistful hint of sadness shrouding his face. "I am at the very end of my life. We don't need to keep up any sort of pretence. I have always felt your love for me, and it has been all that I've ever needed to be happy in my life; it's been a life-giving force and I never once felt it waver. But I am no fool. I have loved you with all I have, and although we shared some wonderful happiness, my love alone never made you as elated, as fully charged, as fulfilled as you were a few months ago."

Her mouth fell open. She attempted to speak, but he quickly continued.

"All of these recent plans with friends, mentoring a young journalist... I'm no fool, darling. I've seen enough of life to acquaint myself with the complexion of love," he sighed. "I only wish that, back then, I had dared to bring it up with you and to tell you to follow your heart."

Angela stared at him, confused. "What do you mean?"

"Angie, my darling. You are a beautiful woman who deserves to be loved," he continued, his voice barely more than a whisper. "Loved in the way you need to be loved at your very core. I wish I could have been the one to give you that love. All of it. I need you to know that your love and companionship have been the only things I've ever required. Perhaps I was being selfish, holding on to you for so long, but you gave me everything I could have ever asked for and more. And, at the time, I couldn't imagine losing you. Now, I think what would have made me the happiest—what would still make me the happiest—is seeing you smile the way you smiled when you started seeing whoever it was you were seeing. I don't need to know the details," he added quickly, smiling himself, "it doesn't matter. But you—responsible, caring wife that you are—stuck by me when I needed you the most. You put your family first. You were here for me even when you didn't want to be, and I cannot thank you enough for that."

"Oh, Will," Angela gasped, "I don't deserve a man as good as you! I don't want you to go! How can you be like this? How can you just accept it? Accept *me* after what I did?"

He shook his head. "I see now that all you did was live. All you did was seek happiness. And that is all I've ever wanted for you. You must promise me that you will rid yourself of whatever guilt you feel. Please, Angie, promise me that once I'm—once I'm not around anymore—you'll be as happy as you were during those months again. If I know that, then I will rest in peace."

Angela buried her head in William's chest and sobbed. He stroked her hair as she wept, murmuring to her that it was all going to be alright.

In one of his last acts on this earth he'd lifted a weight off her shoulders that had sat so heavy and for so long that she'd thought she'd never have the strength to haul it off. Not even her *Oma* could have done so; only William could provide her with that relief. And he had.

When her ability to form words returned, Angela whispered through her tears, "I love you, William."

Angela and Christina began withdrawing the cleaned plates and platters from the dishwasher, gingerly returning them to the overhead kitchen cabinets. Following the funeral, they had entertained a small gathering of people at home, comprising a few of William's former colleagues, some members of the golf club, and the wider family.

Angela had been opposed to the idea of people morbidly standing around in the lounge, nibbling on stuffed vol-au-vents and small triangular sandwiches and sipping on lacklustre sherry. William would have abhorred the thought of individuals grouped in a morose huddle, murmuring and mumbling their regrets at his passing.

So, instead, she had decided to cook for 18 people and had prepared her late husband's most mouth-watering meal: duck leg with black lentils and mashed potato in a rich, dark sauce. In order to quell the possibility of dourness enshrouding her bereaved home, Angela had also provided background music—a recorded assembly of William's most loved artists, ranging from Sinatra to Celine Dion. More tears would fall later, but for the moment, this was a celebration of the life of the late William Mortimer.

*There was much to celebrate*, Angela ascertained.

Nina was exhausted. From the moment of waking earlier that morning, she had mutedly wept throughout the entirety of the day. William's long and painful passage to the grave had ultimately led to the loss of not merely an impassioned son-in-law, but that of a treasured companion. She headed straight to bed, leaving a widowed wife and a brace of orphaned offspring to stand in the quietness of the kitchen area.

Once the last platter had been placed in a recess within the cupboard, they each stood in silence, unsure of what more they could say. Finally, Christina broke the heavy silence.

"How's Geoff?" she asked.

"What?" Angela replied. Her thoughts had only been on William, reliving their lives together over and over in her head.

"Geoff. Is he well? I figured he must have texted you at some point today to send his condolences from wherever in the world he's set up shop."

"Oh, right," said Angela, still feeling dazed, "I don't know if he's been in touch or not. I was so out of sorts this morning before the service I forgot to take my phone. It's still in my bedroom. I'll go upstairs and grab it now. Will you be alright?"

Christina acknowledged her mother with a mild gesture of the head, then walked over and tightly embraced her. John did likewise, creating a sphere of collective grief. They remained locked in that embrace until the final teardrop of the day fell.

As Angela entered the sleeping chamber, William's absence struck her with the force of a tidal wave; to enter and not see his gaunt face looking up at her—either smiling or grimacing in pain from the bed—shrouded her mind with an unsettling swathe of raw and unfamiliar loneliness, punctuated with fear and faint foreboding.

The mobile phone lay on the bedside table, and she opened it to find a message from 'Geoff'.

Angela quivered as she raised a hand to her brow. *No, no,* she reminded herself, *it's not Geoff. Not Bug. It's from Miles.*

In the days that had followed William's passing, Angela had been incapable of responding to the majority Miles' messages, leaving most of them unopened, but now she read the lines from his latest transmission in tortured disbelief.

*No. This can't be happening. This can't happen,* she thought to herself. She read the message repeatedly as she attempted to mentally process the impact of his words:

> *There is no place for me at this time. You must remain with your family and pick up the pieces of your life once more, and I must stand aside. I've taken a reporting assignment in Syria. Aleppo, to be specific. There is no better way to clear my mind from never-ending thoughts of you. I'm now at Heathrow waiting to board my flight to Jordan. Maybe when I return, things will be different for us. I love you. Miles. Xx*

Nina and Angela were sitting in the lounge, a fresh pot of tea resting on the rectangular red maple table in front of them. The warmth generated from the central heating system filled the room with a more acceptable temperature than that of outside, where a dense layer of frost carpeted the ground and decorated the tree branches with a deposit of wintery whiteness as if icing on a cake.

Despite the comforting snugness of being indoors, Angela felt as if she were sitting outside and unhealthily exposed to the frigid air, wearing little more than a thin summer blouse and Bermuda shorts. In addition to the seasonal chill, she was trembling with anxiety. Only Nina's presence was able to prevent her from reaching a state of full-blown hysteria.

Since the moment she'd read Miles' final message, her agitation and visible desperation had only grown. Christina determined that her mother was still coming to terms with the recent passing of her father, hence the struggles to lift her from her intense mourning, but *Oma* knew better. She had cast anxious looks whenever her granddaughter's hands began to tremble, had noted Angela's strained tones of voice and poorly concealed tears.

So, when the time came for Christina to resume her teaching duties, Nina suggested to Angela that they spend some time together to discuss the source of her melancholic behaviour.

"Oh, *Oma*, I've spent this last week trying to get in contact with Miles. I've reached out to the news agencies he's worked for in the past, his co-workers and friends too. I've even called the Foreign Office. Yet not one of them can tell me where he is—only that he's disappeared somewhere in the most dangerous active warzone on the whole bloody planet!" She shook her head in disbelief. "I feel so scared; anything could happen to him out there! Or could have already happened to him! I just feel so helpless. He's not a young man anymore. How did he contemplate, for one single moment, that he'd be able to endure—for an unspecified period—in some battered, hostile excuse of a city?"

Nina had expected the theme of their conversation, and was well prepared with counsel for her fretting, highly distressed granddaughter. "Helpless, you said?" The old woman chewed pensively on a biscuit and engaged Angela with an incredulous gaze.

"Well, yes," Angela stuttered back. "Of course I feel helpless. After what William told me, and then losing him and my only purpose in life, just when I thought I might be able to get back what I'd shunted aside with Miles, he's just… gone! Halfway around the world, and to war no less! Who wouldn't feel helpless?"

"Afraid, yes. This I could understand. Upset, yes. Overwhelmed. That I understand. But helpless? No, *child*. This is simply not true. You are selling yourself short, ignoring your agency as a powerful and resourceful woman."

Angela's brow furrowed. "What do you mean?"

"I mean," said Nina, setting down her cup of tea on the table and straightening her back, "that there is still something you can do." The look in her eyes grew more intense, something Angela had not thought possible.

"*Oma*, I told you, I called his—"

"*Geh nach Aleppo und bring ihn nach hause!*"

Angela's teaspoon clattered to the floor as the old woman leapt up from her position on the couch. Despite Nina's small stature, she seemed to tower over Angela, her eyes burning like twin flames and her face flushed with passion. Angela gaped at her in incredulous amazement.

"*Geh nach Aleppo und bring ihn nach house!*" she repeated. "What is it, my Angela? Have you lost your German tongue?

Is this why you stare at me as if you do not understand the words I am saying to you? Must I translate? Go to Aleppo and bring him home, I said. Go to Aleppo and bring him home!" The old woman began to pace around, clearly in an agitated state. "You are not a weak, pathetic thing! You are a woman! You are my granddaughter! You are a Schaeffer! This man is your happiness, your love, your world. You cannot sit idly by and allow him to be snatched from you! Go and bring him back!"

It was several long moments before Angela could find the words to reply, and Nina permitted the silence to settle on her granddaughter, giving her time to think and to let the gravity of what she was saying sink in.

"*Oma*," she said eventually, "are you aware of what you are suggesting? It's a war. It's the Syrian Civil War! How will I even get there? And, when I'm there, how will I even begin to find him?"

Nina sighed and then smiled. "Look inside your heart. Look. And then ask yourself if any of that matters? Ask yourself if it isn't worth it to find a way? You spent your life as a journalist. You know people who can help you leap the initial barriers. Do not allow fear to control you. Be brave. Be driven by the love you hold for one another. Everything in your life has led you to this precise moment. You are more prepared than you believe yourself to be. What will you choose? Fear? Or bravery?"

Angela waggled her head. "I—I can't believe you. I can't believe you would tell me to do this, *Oma*. I might—I might die there. Or become injured. Or kidnapped. Or God knows what! What would you do if that happened to me?"

Nina sat back down on the couch and placed a hand on

Angela's head. "I would die inside—it would destroy me more than you can imagine—but I am willing to risk impossible pain if it means you have a chance for incredible happiness. And, also, a chance to save you from the excruciating, inner burning that comes with age when reflecting on a loveless, meaningless existence in antiquity. Do you understand me now?"

Angela stared at her blankly.

Eventually, Nina sighed and then continued. "Maybe you cannot. That is alright; I'm grateful you do not understand. You have not lost loved ones in the way that I have. William, yes. William has just passed. But this was a natural death, although way before his time." She shuddered under the swell of memories striking her all at once. "I have lost my parents. My brother, Werner. My saviour, Horst. My daughter, Hjördis. All too soon. All before their time. All taken from me. Ripped from me by war and drugs. Do you know the things I would do if you were to give me even the smallest, faintest chance to save them? Do you know the things I would risk?"

She picked up her cup of tea and took a slow, thoughtful sip of the now lukewarm beverage. "Angela, I am grateful for the life I've lived and for the creation of you and our family. My heart was fragmented with each of the losses I endured when I was nothing but a child myself; the inner hurt and confusion of their demises still pervades my soul to this day, lingering as if a very bad smell. For years, many years, I have raised questions within my mind, of how different the complexion of my life would have been if these people had not perished so needlessly, leaving my life, but never departing from my heart. This is the most terrible fate I can imagine for you, Angela, that of true helplessness. If Miles were already dead—lost forever, irrevocably—that is helplessness. But now, *child,* you can try and do something. And I know, from the pit of my soul, that you would not survive in this world by leaving him to his fate. It would crush you. It would destroy you. If you try, if you go and seek him, you at least have a chance at lifelong peace. Whether you find him or not, you will never live with the regret of not having at least tried to take part in the chase for true love. I would risk my pain—my life, even—to give you that chance." She took her granddaughter's hands in hers. "Will you?"

The chaos of thoughts and fears and high-pitched voices that had screamed a chorus of anxiety in Angela's skull for the past week all seemed to fade the longer she held on to her *Oma*'s hands. The clouds inside her seemed to dissipate, and in their place a simple chain of events began to take shape—one in which action followed action, step followed step, and every question that arose could be simply answered by asking herself: *Can I live with myself if I don't try to find him? No! Can I live without him at all? No!*

"I can ask my old contacts how to cross the border."

"Yes."

"I can examine the areas where he was last seen. I can follow his tracks."

"Yes!"

"I can go to Aleppo and bring him home."

"*Ja!*"

"Oh my God, *Oma.* You're right! I have to. I can't exist without him. I wouldn't last more than a few months. I feel too old. I feel scared. But, I don't think I have a choice, do I?"

Nina smiled at her and kissed her on the cheek. "All we can do in the face of war is try to be the best people we can be. To strive for our greatest self and for those who mean the most to us. You know who that self is. You know what she has to do."

"*Geh nach Aleppo und bring ihn nach hause*," Angela replied.

She peered at the frozen garden from the lounge window and clung to the warmth of the radiator. For the first time in days, Angela allowed its warmth to penetrate the marrow of her bones.

# CHAPTER 16:
## SYRIA, 2016

"It can't be more than ten kilometres, now. We're almost there!"

Idi's words sparked warmth and life into Angela. Up until this point, the journey had been exhaustingly protracted and asymmetrically rough, with large stretches of the byways and highways they had driven on being severely damaged and consisting of deep craters and difficult-to-see potholes. The cheerless, caliginous night made driving all the more hazardous; the vehicle's dim headlamps failed to adequately illuminate the road and all the hazardous cavities that lay ahead. More often than not, Idi's belated warnings to prepare for yet another jolt and shudder did little to ease the unsettling discomfort of Angela's throbbing haunches. The bitter cold had played a significant role in adding to this discomfort, as the heating system of the ramshackle craft was no longer functioning; the acute drop in overnight temperature had led to bouts of involuntary shivering for them both. Angela's light summer attire was no defence against the glacial chill that percolated through each aperture and crevice of the faltering automobile, though Miles remained swaddled under a trinity of fleecy, red-coloured thermal blankets.

Angela had frequently monitored his condition during the passage southwards, making sure that he remained warm and securely strapped to the stretcher with no hint of bleeding seeping through his inapposite bandaging. Despite her indefatigable attentions, his face was contorted and markedly ragged; the trauma of the injury and the expanse of the suffering that had accompanied the mutilation of his lower leg had led to disfiguring creases forming on his face and forehead. Angela dwelt on the possibility that he may never be able to recapture his boyish good looks once this terrible ordeal was finally over, but she cared little about this likelihood; she cared only for the man she had come to love and his timely arrival at a Jordanian hospital.

Her leg had throbbed with unrelenting frequency over the previous couple of hours, but Idi's unexpected declaration had instantaneously anaesthetised the pain within her scarred, maltreated body.

They were finally nearing the doorstep to survival. The conclusion to this catastrophic odyssey was less than an hour away.

*Miles is almost safe,* she inwardly declared, a positive vibe of triumphalism embroidering her thoughts.

Idi made another comment, but his words were lost to Angela in the ear-piercing repetitive din from the van's sagging engine, which had transformed into screams of mechanical pandemonium issuing constantly from beneath the bonnet of the stricken vehicle. Since the time of their narrow escape from the firefight in the village, the disconcerting noise had grown louder with the passage of hours and the distance they covered.

"What did you say, Idi?" shouted Angela, whilst pointing to her ears.

"I said, I think it's time to give him the pain medicine!" Idi shouted back.

"I gave Miles the second shot of morphine at the village. I thought we carried only two doses!"

"No," said Idi, "we have a little more than that. Go to the rear and open the large white medical container that is next to Miles' head. Unbolt it and recover the box that has Zomorph Capsules printed on it. This stuff is taken orally. I just hope he will be able to swallow them with some water."

"Oh, thank Christ!" she wailed. "I can't stand to hear him suffering any longer." Angela climbed into the back of the van, where Miles was tossing and turning feebly on the stretcher. During the previous thirty minutes, his ubiquitous mewls had reduced to a series of querulous tones laced in painful dissatisfaction and hopelessness, filling Angela with heightened levels of fear and draining distress. Idi had been determinedly resolute about administering more pain medication, and now they had no other choice but to relieve the torturous scourge of his mammoth wound.

Angela fumbled around until she found the boxed, blister-packed medication and withdrew two tablets. Then, before placing them into his mouth, she crushed them with the aid of the vehicle's black torch. She poured a little water between Miles' lips to moisten his dry palate and dribbled a little more of the cool fluid into a small paper beaker, before adding the mashed medication.

Angela raised Miles' head and tilted the cup to his chapped, dried-out lips. Remaining by his side, she clasped his unshaven face with her cracked hands and asked, "Is there anything you want, darling? We are nearly at the border, so there's not much longer to go now."

Miles gazed up at her, the faintest hint of a smile beginning to form on his bedraggled face. "I need to pee," he hoarsely announced.

Angela responded to his words by reaching for the empty plastic water bottle that had been rolling around on the floor of the cabin ever since Idi had refuelled the vehicle at the roadside a few hours before. Removing a pair of scissors from the same large white medical box that held the morphine tablets, she then punctured the unfilled container and began cutting around the neck of the bottle to create a larger aperture in which Miles could relieve himself. Pushing the blankets and his clothing aside, she placed the newly fashioned urinal between his legs and guided his limp, wilted penis into the chamber of the modified carafe.

It took over a minute before the cascade of yellow urine ceased to flow from him. Once she had adjusted his clothing and placed the blankets back over him, he closed his eyes and drifted into a tormented slumber. She put a hand on his sternum and felt for his chest to rise and fall, breathing a sigh of relief when his respiratory capability was confirmed.

Once back in the front seat, she flicked on the overhead cab-light to try to identify if possible blood traces were present in Miles' urine.

Idi was aware of what she was attempting to ascertain. "You will require a microscope to do that, Angela," he uttered authoritatively, his voice also beginning to emit tones of exhaustion.

She rolled down the passenger window and emptied the bottle as they moved along.

The disconcerting mechanical uncertainty reached a crescendo as a loud snapping noise, combined with a forceful hissing rasp, erupted from beneath the vehicle. The van slowed in spasmodic jerks and sluggishly came to a halt in the middle of the dark, empty road. The whine of a disabled engine rang out as Idi twisted the key in the ignition.

"Idi?" Angela asked, trying to eliminate any trace of panic from her voice. "Idi, please tell me that isn't as bad as it sounds."

Idi did not respond. Instead, he alighted from the cab and lifted the bonnet. On doing so, a cloud of dark, acrid smoke rose into the night sky. He coughed and squinted through it at the engine, waving his hand in front of his face to clear his vision before bending forward and pointing his battery-powered torch at the overheated machinery.

From where Angela sat, he was little more than a dark shadow, moving methodically from left to right and exhibiting a ghostly silhouette locked between rays of light and surface, hovering in front of her as if an apparition making a spiritual appearance.

*This can't be happening*, she thought. *This can't be happening. We're so close!*

Angela held her breath as Idi slammed the hood shut, shaking his head in agitation. "It's useless," he said, re-entering the van. "I can barely see, but something is very wrong. I am a medic, not a mechanic; but one thing is for sure, we are not going any further, Angela. We are stranded until assistance arrives."

She could not immediately respond to Idi's damning analysis; the news had brought with it a disabling, immobilising effect on her vocal chords, as if a large lump had formed in her throat and had drained the last dribble of saliva from her parched oral cavity. She turned and glanced at Miles as he lay in his narcotic haze, her eyes resting on his wounded frame and ravaged appearance.

"I'll call the Red Cross on the satellite phone," screeched Idi, "they will send someone who can either fix the problem or tow us to the border. I can't say how long it will take for them to reach us, though—it could be hours, maybe longer. Who knows?"

Angela studied Miles' face as would a connoisseur of fine arts, visually engaging in the celebrated beauty of a painting created by either Monet or Rembrandt.

"Angela. Angela, did you hear what I said? We are stranded; our lives are in danger right now."

As if lost in the tranquil passages of another time, another place, she captured an image of a beech tree, its branches spreading protectively above her and Miles. They were lying together hand in hand, in torpid silence, admiring the tassel-like catkins hanging from long stalks as they swayed gently in the breeze of a warm, summer puff of air.

She recalled the day when Miles explained the significance of the woody perennial plant, in that both male and female plants sprouted from its long boughs. He had laughed when he classed himself as a male catkin and Angela as the elegant white flower nestling in a small cradling chalice, "Way up high."

As the impression of the serene pool below the tree came into view and stretched before her, she was abruptly prodded back to the present.

"Angela?"

"Yes, Idi. I heard you." She inhaled deeply and exhaled with positive force, her cheeks blown. "Will you help me bring him out, Idi?"

Silent incredulity briefly ensued before Idi replied, "Out?"

"Yes. Out of the van. Onto his stretcher."

"But—"

"Idi, Miles is getting to that hospital in Jordan. If the van can't take him, so be it. I will." Through the gloom of early morning darkness, she saw his eyes widen in disbelief.

"You will?" he said, in shock. "You'll do what? Push or pull him on the stretcher the rest of the way?"

"Yes."

"Through the desert."

"Yes."

"On your bad leg."

"Yes. Please, Idi. We're wasting time here."

He let out a long, low whistle. "Angela, I know you are hell-bent on saving Miles, but do not throw your own life away as well. It is very cold still, and when the cold gives way, it will become very, very hot. *And* you're injured. I cannot advise you to do this."

She took his hand. "I can't thank you enough for all you've done, Idi," she told him. "You've saved my life. You found Miles. You've brought us this far. You have been my guardian angel. But right now, I'm not the one who needs guarding." She gestured to the stretcher. "He does. Now, will you help me, or do I need to move him out of the van on my own?"

Idi smiled in spite of himself. What else could he do? Here, before him, was a woman driven to the point of near madness by pure love. He looked at Miles and knew there was no way he would survive if they waited for reinforcement. He accepted that he could not justifiably prevent her from attempting to reach the border on foot, and to stress the hazards of putting her own life on the line was also futile, as her life and that of Miles comprised one life, one body, entwined in a love that no man could question. "At least wait until first light," he said, finally.

"Look." Angela pointed through the windshield where the sky was beginning to turn from inky black to indigo. "He can't wait any longer."

Slowly, Idi nodded.

They alighted from the van and unbolted the double doors. Then, together, they disconnected Miles' IV and carefully extricated his wheeled stretcher from the vehicle. His head lolled with the judder of the movement, but he remained oblivious to the jostling of their attempts to extract him from the bunk area.

Just hopping out of the van had made pain slam into Angela's leg like a demolition ball, but she pushed it out of her mind as best she could and pulled a blanket over Miles.

Idi handed Angela one of the large water bottles and forced her to drink five generous gulps before putting it in her backpack. Her first two gulps she did not swallow; she swigged on the water and then placed her lips on Miles' mouth, slowly squirting the fluid into him.

As she was about to zip the pack closed, Angela reached inside and touched the biscuit tin, saying a quick prayer to her *Oma* for strength and luck. She then shrugged the backpack onto her shoulders and looked out at the strip of emptiness before her, stretching off into the blackness. She gripped the stretcher's railing tightly and shivered. "How far did you say it was again?"

"About ten clicks, if you stay on this road," Idi replied sombrely. "Are you sure you want to do this?"

"I have never been so sure of anything in my life. There are no alternatives left to us."

"I would come with you," Idi said, "but I must wait with the van. I cannot leave it abandoned. If fate smiles on me and someone comes and fixes it soon, I promise I will drive as fast as I can to take you the rest of the way. But do not count on that. It is far more likely that I will be waiting here for many hours."

Angela released the stretcher from her grasp and firmly embraced him. "Oh, Idi! I'll never be able to repay you for all you've done. Please. Please take the rest of the money I have with me. It's not much but I want you to have it."

Idi vehemently refused her request. "I could not do that in a million years, Angela. Everything I did for you I would do again—it is God's will. Repay me by surviving. Please, Angela. Survive, both of you."

Angela kissed Idi on the cheek and tightened the straps that secured Miles to the stretcher, firmly gripping its railings. *Stay like that, please Miles*, she thought. *Just you rest now. I'll get us there. I swear it.* She glanced over her shoulder and cast one last look at Idi.

"I'll never forget you, Idi!" she shouted.

He raised his hand in salute as Angela strode forward, completing her first step towards a distant borderline.

She had no reliable means by which to accurately calculate her progress. Her phone was dead and obsolete. Her only indication of time was the searing sun, rising ever higher in a deep blue, cloudless sky. The warmth it had radiated during the early morning had been a welcome respite from the nocturnal cold, energising her and improving Miles' wan and lifeless pallor, but that had long since passed; now the intensity of the sun's heat dried the perspiration on the shirt Hans had gifted Angela as quickly as it left her body. The possibility of dehydration, both for herself and Miles, began to dwell on her mind.

The going underfoot was rocky in places and sandy soft in others, but with each step she felt like she was drying up from the inside out. Since stumbling and falling during the trek, her injured leg had begun to throb once more and a trickle of blood had started to flow down towards her ankle. Now, each step forward was accompanied by a groan of painful repugnance.

*How many hours has it been? How many kilometres? How had Idi known how close they were? What if the border is still miles away? What if Miles doesn't last?*

Angela stopped, then slowly lowered the wheeled stretcher to the ground before removing her backpack—without examining the extent of the damage to her bleeding limb. *It doesn't matter*, she told herself. *It doesn't matter. You're just going to walk. Just keep walking. There's nothing else to do but to keep on walking.*

Freeing the water bottle from the battered Bergen, Angela whimpered at the paltry amount of liquid remaining. She then reached down and removed the blanket from Miles' flushed face. It had been meant to serve as protection from the concentrated and trenchant rays of the fiery sun, but they had cooked him nonetheless. She placed a hand on Miles' forehead. His skin was hot and dry.

"Miles," she croaked. "Miles. Time for some water, darling." His eyelids parted slowly. "Open wide, love, it's time to take some water," she instructed, dribbling the last of their liquid supply into his mouth.

"Where—where are we?" he groaned.

"We're almost at the border, my love. We're almost there."

Suddenly, *compos mentis* awareness returned to him. He moved his head left and right and, visually absorbing a panorama of endless sand extending in both directions, he gasped, "Angela! What are you doing? This… this can't be real. I'm—I'm dreaming?"

"Yes, darling. Go back to sleep. Rest. We'll be there soon."

He eased back onto the stretcher as Angela began pulling once more on the wheeled pallet, walking on as she began stumbling on stony debris far more frequently. They had to be close now. They *had* to be, because if not, surely they would die here, alone in the desert.

But that was not to be their fate, just as Idi had implied during the sandstorm. She wouldn't let it be.

By now she had become weary of pulling the stretcher and decided that pushing it forward instead might ease the strain on her arms and the palms of her hands, each of which was bloodied and blistered. It was no longer yards she was covering with each pace she stepped, merely inches.

A small hillock of rock and sand lay directly ahead, some thirty yards in front of them. On another day, she could have scaled a knoll of this dimension with the speed and agility of someone half her age, but not on this day. Today, in her mind, the small mass ahead took on the mountainous enormity of Everest. It would take the very last of her strength to reach its otherwise insignificant peak.

Angela fell to her knees in submission—yearning that their deaths would come quickly and painlessly—and as she dwelt on their demise, her mind started playing tricks on her. In the distance, she spotted a near-infinite mass of buildings—a huge city, but from another time, with cathedrals, bridges and houses, and fighter aircraft swooping down to drop their hellish payloads on those below. *Berlin*, she thought. *How?*—and then she blinked and the vision disappeared.

She rose and pushed onward, starting to mutter to herself over and over, reciting the credo that had carried her so far. "*Geh nach Aleppo und bring ihn nach hause. Geh nach Aleppo und bring ihn nach hause. Geh nach Aleppo und bring ihn nach hause!*"

"Angela?"

She stopped her chanting. She'd never heard his voice sound so weak, so filled with a child's fear.

"Angela, where are we, love?"

"We're under The Lentil Tree, Miles," she cried. "We're lying under The Lentil Tree on a hot summer's day, having a picnic. And it's—it's beautiful, Miles. Just being here with you is the most beautiful thing life could ever offer."

For a moment, a dazed smile of contentment played across his lips, but then reality reclaimed his senses and his terrified expression returned once again.

"My God, Angela! Why are you doing this?" he said as forcefully as he could manage. "We'll both die out here! I don't care what happens to me, but now I've brought you into this hell and now you'll die too! No, Angela! We're both going to die!"

For a moment, there was only the sound of her footsteps and the squeaking of the stretcher's wheels.

When she'd composed herself slightly, she murmured, "Neither of us is going to die, Miles." She looked up from his twisted features, trying to think of something more reassuring to say as she squinted ahead into the glare. Her mouth fell open.

She blinked and shook her head as she peered through the distorting heat haze, unsure if what she'd just spotted was yet another mirage. But it was still there. Solid-shaped and static. "Oh my God! Oh my God, Miles!" she screamed. "Neither of us *is* going to die! Miles! We're going to make it."

It was nothing more than a small, rectangular construction, but it was growing larger with every second, and she knew exactly what it was: the border.

Angela attempted to quicken her pace, but she was no longer capable of walking. She began laughing hysterically, frantically waving her arms to catch the attention of someone—anyone—

who could help her.

It started as a small puff of dust, then as a powder-puff of sand being stirred up by a current of desert air, becoming larger and clearer as the seconds ticked by. It was a motorised, fast-moving vehicle, coming towards them. But no—not a car; it was a pickup truck.

She sat down on the scalding asphalt, whispering, "Thank you. Oh, thank you, thank you."

The approaching vehicle was a silver Toyota Hilux.

"Angela!" came a familiar voice from the window of the truck as it pulled up beside her. "What the hell do you think you're doing, woman?" Tommy's southern twang was more beautiful than any musical score she had ever listened to. She heard a door open and felt hands under her armpits, lifting her. "Jesus H. Christ, what have you done to yourself? I've got water in the truck. You've got to drink. I'll start by giving some to him. Can you stand?"

"Yes," she whispered. "Yes, I think so. But Miles, Tommy. Oh God, Tommy! We have to get Miles to hospital! Now! Now!"

"Damn right. With the shape you two are in, the hospital is the only place we're making for, no doubt about that. Just look at your damn leg. It's a bloody mess. All the stitches have popped!"

"Doesn't—doesn't matter," she gasped. "Him, Tommy. We need to get him to the hospital!" Tommy looked down at Miles and grew still. "Help me get him in," she pleaded.

They loaded Miles into the bed of the truck, and once they had secured his stretcher, Tommy turned to her in amazement. "You did it, huh? You found your man. Well, I'll be. Come on now. Let's go. Ride up front with me." Angela shook her head. "Angie, you've got some very serious sunburn there and you got to get into the shade. Now!"

"No!" she screamed. "No. Help me up. I won't leave him."

Tommy shook his head in disbelief. But, without another word being exchanged, he hoisted her into the truck next to Miles. He then removed his shirt and threw it at her.

"Saturate this with water and put it over your heads, then start giving that lucky guy all the water he can drink. Holy shit! You are one crazy lady, Angie. Here we go."

Tommy wheeled the truck around and headed towards the border post. Angela was increasingly certain that she was close to fainting, her grip on consciousness slipping slowly away. Blurriness was starting to encroach on the periphery of her vision, but it was not a nauseous sensation; it was probably the sweetest feeling she had ever experienced. She looked down at Miles and, with the last of her strength, she took his hand in hers and kissed it.

"Miles! We did it! We're going home."

He attempted to smile, though it was more a grimace of pain. "I love you," he gasped. "I love you."

"*We'll* be safe, Miles!" she cried, her voice breaking as she saw a strange fixation take hold in his eyes. "We're going to make it, Miles!" Angela kissed his hand as she stressed her words, and then seconds later her whole world became dark.

# CHAPTER 17:
## ENGLAND, 2015

Angela removed the black-rimmed spectacles from her face and placed them on the large island in the centre of the kitchen. She would normally position them atop her head when examining things at close range, but today, with her shimmering, newly washed blonde hair encased in a number of multi-coloured rollers, the convenient habit was denied to her.

She chuckled to herself as she pondered what Miles' reaction would be were he to catch a glimpse of her at that very moment, adorned only in her black tracksuit bottoms and pink bra, and wearing only one sock. The plastic curlers holding her hair in place would be the final straw. "He would run for his life!" she giggled to herself, though instinctively she knew this would be the last thing he would do, no matter how she appeared to him.

Angela examined the contents of the old biscuit tin. It was crammed with an assortment of food—black olives, lentil salad, chopped fruit, Emmental cheese, sliced meats, and a small homemade loaf of *Leberkäse* or 'Liver Cheese'. Miles had first discovered this succulent Bavarian dish many years earlier when skiing on the snow-clad slopes of Garmisch-Partenkirchen, and Angela had decided to surprise him with her own creation of the mouth-watering meatloaf, adding a quantity of mixed spices to further enhance the taste of the shredded corned beef, pork, and bacon ingredients.

As she closed the lid of the impromptu metal picnic hamper and set it beside a bottle of wine and a flagon of sparkling water, she became irritated by the thought that she'd overlooked something. Then, it came to her: the *vanillekipferl* biscuits.

As she lifted the tray containing the freshly baked cookies from her cooling oven and reached out for a plastic container to deposit them in, she pondered on the irony of it all. Miles' preference for German food was a source of fascination to her; he linked his culinary preferences to his Scottish upbringing, and to the national similarities to soups, stews, and bread. "German food is Scottish food with a positive attitude," he had jokingly informed Angela on a couple of occasions.

Once the food was sorted, she ascended the stairs two at a time and flung open the double doors of her wardrobe. She knew exactly what she was going to wear: the yellow dress that Miles always commented on. To him it was a concept of sartorial elegance that always triggered his senses. She'd never considered this item of clothing to be anything other than just that—an item of clothing, one she felt comfortable in, and never anything to set the heart racing in a male suitor. But to Miles, ever since that very first night in that special London restaurant, the dress possessed qualities that provoked in him a sensual stimulus like no other.

Impetuously, she removed the curlers and brushed her slightly damp locks into her preferred, uncomplicated style, then inserted the sparkling black diamond earrings into each lobe. The long daylight hours were expected to be warm and dry, and therefore not a day that demanded her legs be swathed in nylon stockings or pantyhose.

She pushed the drawer that held her lingerie back into place and slipped her feet into a pair of soft black shoes. Then, after a quick application of lipstick, she descended the staircase and prepared to load the car.

As she weaved her way through the mid-morning traffic, it seemed to her as if the weather was encouraging her to embrace all the day had in store for her, including the man she was so uncontrollably drawn to. For once she was free to move, to think, and to experience the enthralling company of Miles, the opportunity to do so having been provided by a series of events that had nicely aligned to give her the perfect chance to get away. John's hiatus from university had allowed him to return to her Wimbledon home for a couple of weeks and, earlier that morning, he had taken William out for an early lunch with a plan to attend an afternoon cricket match. Christina and Nina had secured tickets for an annual flower show in the west side of the city and would also be gone for the bulk of the day.

Cricket had never appealed to Angela and the thought of meandering through sweaty throngs of people at some botanical extravaganza was not an option she was prepared to even consider. What would she have been doing if it weren't for her rendezvous with Miles? Sitting around and reading or pottering in the garden quite probably, disagreeably alone in an empty house. Miles was the perfect means of rescue, therefore, from the plodding loneliness of her life, injecting her days with meaning, with radiance, and with promise.

She reached Maison St. Cassien with time to spare and found him waiting for her on the verandah of the establishment.

On catching sight of her, Miles immediately rose from his seat and placed an order for two coffees. As she joined him at the counter, he turned and placed his hands on her shoulders, kissing her on each cheek. Their eyes engaged for slightly longer than that of their previous assignations, each possibly searching for answers as to where they were being led.

The lady behind the counter tapped one of the filled coffee cups with a teaspoon in a bid to grasp their attention and to briefly break into a private world of which she knew nothing, her only need being to provide the hot beverages and lay hands on payment for the service.

Angela and Miles started with small talk—domestic issues, initially—then moved on to current affairs and the turmoil of illegal immigrants risking their lives in makeshift sailing vessels to reach mainland Europe. It was not the conversation they wanted to engage in or hear; it served merely as a means to break the ice.

They were well aware that their intimacy levels had increased considerably over the previous weeks. Their farewell kiss when bidding each other *adieu* several days before had lasted just a little longer than the one before, and the embrace that had accompanied it felt a little firmer.

Angela clasped Miles' hand under the table, a gesture no one else could detect. It was no longer innocent physical contact, but a touch that came with a yet-to-be deciphered message, one that covertly sent their respective hearts racing. It was as if she were on the edge of a precipice, one that she desperately wanted to leap from to fall completely into his arms.

As they drove to the park in separate cars, Angela could not recall a journey when she'd felt so nervous whilst driving—a thrilling but dangerous kind of nervousness replete with a tingling activity running crazily in the pit of her stomach, making her hands tremble.

As they pulled into the car park and exited their respective vehicles, Angela confessed to Miles that her chosen destination within the verdant recreational area would be some distance from their vehicles, involving a ten-minute walk. "But it's worth the effort," she promptly added.

They removed the picnic items and wandered along the lush, tree-lined path towards a large pond. Angela felt a little on edge being with him in public and so walked slightly apart from him, wary of the urge to clutch his hand.

As if sensing her inherent unease, Miles closed the gap between them. "This is precisely how I dreamed of spending a beautiful summer's day, in the company of a beautiful lassie," he enthusiastically commented.

"What? Walking in the park?"

He smiled, shaking his head. "Don't make it sound so plain. I'm striding through heaven with a luscious girl at my side, my wingless angel, one who is as intelligent as she is stunning, and a damn fine *femme cuisinier too*, or so I have been reliably informed."

Before Angela's embarrassed laughter had ceased, Miles slipped her arm under his, and they continued to amble arm in arm until they came to a curve in the leafy corridor. As they followed the route of the twisting conduit, they were soon faced with the sight of a magnificent, in-bloom beech tree, one that stood proudly on the periphery of a tranquil pond, populated with a natural combination of white water lilies and swarms of dragonflies and damselflies, each jostling for the most lucrative feeding area and breeding rights. A family of ducks could also be seen bobbing and diving for whatever aquatic nibble lay below the surface of the shady pool.

A large wooden bench was positioned centrally under the expansive, deciduous plant, and Angela placed the hulking cool bag on this hackneyed seating before spreading the tartan blanket on the grassy bank.

As she laid out the provisions on the chequered mantle, Miles removed the cork from the wine bottle and poured an equal quantity of the dark *vin de table* into a couple of paper cups. He handed one to Angela, they raised the containers into the air, and in vocal union, elatedly cried out, "Prost!"

Within Angela, two warring factions clashed in skirmishes of indecision and delight. Even so, there was nowhere else she'd rather be than right here, eating and drinking al fresco with Miles.

Each time their skin made contact, her thoughts of William and the symptoms of adulterous culpability callously wrenched her from the romantically opulent present. She began looking around nervously, scanning the blossoming panorama for people possibly known to her, casting furtive glances towards the bend in the track they'd just strolled down.

Detecting her sudden consternation, Miles gently quizzed, "Are you OK, Angela?"

"Oh, it's nothing," she murmured apologetically, right before a fresh wave of optimism ran through her. She smiled at Miles and playfully ordered him to change the subject. "Come, let us sit down and devour our picnic," she insisted, holding his arm as if assisting him to occupy a place closest to her.

The peaceful lushness of their concealed haven in the park—and the absence of humankind that it encouragingly afforded—enabled Angela to freely engage with Miles, and he with her. She talked of her early life, her deceased mother, school, university, her profession, marriage, children, and of Nina, while Miles proved an ardent listener. He could not offer much in the way of personal domestic history, but he described his formative years in Scotland with a marked passion, his eyes sparkling when reflecting on childhood memories of Caledonian days gone by. They were entering a new sphere in their fledgling relationship, talking, laughing, booing, cheering… and touching.

Miles expounded on his heroes, and of those he loathed most during his professional career, also making reference to some of the more gruelling aspects of his 40-year relationship with the news industry. He had seen first-hand the horrors of war and the misery that came with it, how loved ones were savagely lost and how those who actually survived never really did. Angela began to notice an increased level of agitation in his voice whenever he reflected on the atrocities committed on Bosnian, Kosovan, and Croatian soil, and on his enforced impartiality when reporting on the monsters that had inflicted the most indescribable horrors known to mankind, further adding that he constantly masked his feelings of sympathy, anger, and abhorrence.

"This alone," he disconsolately surmised, "was perhaps the main reason I never fell in love. Instead I found love in music, in the arts, and in books, in isolation from it all. I didn't need people, or so I believed. I needed peace and release from a stupefying, senseless world at every opportunity I could seize upon."

Miles' mood lightened whenever he talked of art; it was the most beautiful form of expression known to him. It mattered not if he was staring at political graffiti on the former Berlin Wall or Gerhard Richter's 'window' in Cologne Cathedral; they each inspired life with their kaleidoscope of colours and the message they delivered.

When Angela prompted Miles to define this 'message' he replied, "That's simple, my darling woman. Love over war, the only true cause worth dying for." As he spoke a tear fell from the corner of his right eye, and Angela too felt herself welling up at the emotional impact of his compelling utterances.

He leaned forward to gently kiss her wettened cheek, and this time there would be no resistance or spurning what she so insatiably yearned. Their lips met and remained connected; each time they pulled back from one another it was but for a brief moment, re-engaging again for prolonged periods of mouth-to-mouth connection. They were no longer mature people in the autumn of life, but teenage virgins fuelled by a youthful passion that inflamed their suppressed truthfulness about one another, spreading through their bodies as an untamed forest fire, out of control and with no expectation of being quelled at any point in the future, near or distant.

"Miles, Miles!" she gasped. "Not here. It can't be here, my darling man. We must wait—please, let us wait."

He was breathing in short gasps, his brow perspiring. "I'm so sorry," he responded, sorting out his loosened shirt while doing so.

Angela burst into laughter after hearing his respectful but inane apology. "It takes two to tango, Miles. My God, what a dance it proved to be!" She adjusted the tartan rug and encouraged Miles to eat, "as a necessary distraction to our near-carnal feast," she humorously added.

He sat beside her and once again kissed the nape of her neck. "I am temporarily in a state of heated flux and unmanageable turmoil, Angela. Tell me, how do I suppress these stirrings?" he teased.

"*Etwas linsen essen,*" replied Angela. "It means 'eat your lentils' in German. This is the best earthly source to extinguish the heat of orgasmic craving inside you." She did her best to camouflage the beginnings of a smirk forming on her face.

"Wow. I never knew of the power of lentils in this respect. Where did you learn of this magic formula to place passion on hold, for however long?"

"I have no wish for us to be the ones who transform this

respectable park into a lewd den of moral impropriety," she said, glaring into his eyes with mock severity. "Now, *etwas linsen essen!*"

Miles picked up the dish containing the lentil salad and looked at it disapprovingly. "Is there any truth to the theory that lentils can have such an effect on a man?" he uttered in a state of obvious discomfort.

"No," giggled Angela. "Not a damn word of it is true. I just needed to say something convincing so that we could avoid being arrested for indecent behaviour in a public place."

They both burst out laughing and it was several minutes before they could control their mirth. Tears were leaking out of Angela's eyes; it was the kind of laughter she had only ever shared with Geoff before. The joke carried an impact of hilarity far greater than the sum of its parts.

As the sun began to sink and the late afternoon light transformed into the colour of honey, they lay in each other's arms, looking up at the tree's branches while they related to one another through an alternating combination of words and contented sighs.

"I should probably get back," Angela stated ruefully, following a moment of epigrammatic silence.

"Yes, it's that time, isn't it?" Miles replied, noticing the troubled expression creeping into her face. "Same time next week, then?"

She giggled and slapped him playfully on the leg. "We'll see. We'll see."

They stood up and packed their things, Angela placing the biscuit tin back in the bag, grateful to have brought this container of tradition to keep her grounded as she crossed into this dangerous and uncharted territory.

Miles laid his arm around Angela's shoulder as they looked up at the tree, the two of them sharing an unspoken hesitancy to leave a place that had injected such a sensuous spiritual quality in them both.

"I love this old beech," Miles said. "I feel as if we understand one another. Look at it. It's so old—so much older than some of those young whippersnapper saplings over there—but look at how it grows. Look at how full of life it is, in spite of its years!"

Angela silently agreed. She didn't need to say anything. She put her arm around his waist and pulled him closer to her.

"You know," continued Miles, "I think this tree is missing a befitting title. Henceforth," he bellowed, in a jesting official voice, "let it be known that our noble beech is hereby dubbed, 'The Lentil Tree'. Stay firm and lofty, Lentil Tree, and never forget that you're only as old as the rings within you!"

They chortled and joked about the tree's new designation, then slowly made their way back to the car park. Angela held Miles' hand until the last possible moment, all along the winding pathway that led them back to reality and back to being apart—until the next time.

# CHAPTER 18:
## ENGLAND, 2016

After finally pestering an explanation out of Nina, Christina had reluctantly accepted her mother's necessity to be with Geoff following William's death. But the suddenness of her disappearance was another matter. It was so out of the blue and so wholly unexpected, and it meant that Christina didn't even have the chance to wish her *adieu* and *bon voyage*.

For Christina, these last six weeks had been steeped in mystery, further compounded by the lack of communication during her mother's elongated hiatus from home. There had been no phone calls, merely inconclusive and vague texts that made no mention of Geoff or of how she was spending her days on Arabian soil. Nina stressed to both her and John that grief, and the manner in which it affects those who have lost, arrives in many varieties. The wise old woman had also emphasised that Angela was no exception to the rule in that she needed to find herself once more, well removed from the cheerless, isolated surroundings that shackled her to the past.

Despite *Oma's* empathetic interpretation of Angela's inconclusive evaporation from their midst, Christina determined that her mother had some serious questions to answer—and now that she was coming home, answer them she would.

The drive to Heathrow had been even more sluggish than she had anticipated earlier that morning; a combination of heavy traffic, speed restrictions, and roadworks had added another 30 minutes to the journey time.

Flight BA 146 from Amman was due to land at Terminal 5 shortly after midday. Christina had aimed to arrive at the short-stay pick-up point by 12.30, thus allowing her mother sufficient time to disembark the aircraft and then briskly glide through UK Border Control, Baggage Retrieval, and the Nothing-to-Declare points within the airport.

Christina drummed her fingers impatiently on the steering wheel of her car. She'd been waiting for over 30 minutes now and was beginning to wonder if her mother was having difficulty in locating her luggage, or if she'd perhaps been delayed by an overzealous customs officer who was rifling through her baggage in an unrealistic bid to detect items of contraband.

Again, she glanced at her phone: the Heathrow arrivals app confirmed her mother's aircraft had touched down an hour earlier.

Christina shuddered at the thought of a missed-flight

scenario. "What if she's still in the Middle East?" she fretted aloud. Surely not, not her mother—Angela was a stickler for reaching any disembarkation point with unabashed promptness; her professional life and overall success had been forged on the principle of proficient celerity.

Christina scanned the innumerable numbers of people who were emerging from the terminal onto the concourse to connect with waiting taxis or to be reunited with family and friends, but still she couldn't see her mother.

Finally, she caught sight of her, or at least of someone who bore an uncanny resemblance to her. But then Christina hastily dismissed the notion; her agile, spritely matriarch would not be sitting in a wheelchair, being pushed along by a member of airport staff. It was an impossible consideration.

As they neared the car, she detected that the woman's face was deeply tanned and peeling from the after-effects of too much hot sunshine. Her blonde, grey-flecked hair was un-brushed and a mist of condensation had formed on her spectacle lenses. It was apparent that the lady had sustained an injury to a lower limb, making her movements slow and laborious, as if burdened by some imperceptible weight. She moved as a woman of her *Oma's* age might do, shuffling her feet and wincing in pain with each attempted movement. She was carrying a rectangular box in her claw-like hands.

The wheelchair came to a halt just short of Christina's vehicle, at which point the airport attendant assisted the woman in rising from the wheeled convenience. The unfamiliar figure had spotted Christina's vehicle and, with an enfeebled series of paces, started hobbling towards it. The metal container in her hands was Nina's old biscuit tin.

Christina's jaw dropped as the horror of recognition hit her as if she'd just been punched senseless by a heavyweight pugilist. She emitted a cry of disbelief and then leapt from the car, unashamedly crying out, "Mum, Mum, oh God, Mum! What's happened?"

Christina held her mother in her arms for several moments, and then opened the door and guided Angela's broken frame into the passenger seat.

Up close, her mother appeared even worse than she had at first glance. Angela's lips were cracked and the abrasions on her cheeks had formed several small scabs. She groaned as Christina gently guided her wounded leg into the footwell of the car.

The attendant passed her mother's Bergen to Christine, who thanked him and offered him some cash as a fee for his services. He refused the offer, and said he hoped that Angela would recover from her injuries very soon. He then turned from the car, pushing the wheelchair back into the terminal.

Christina was numbed by Angela's haggard, shredded appearance, leading her into a chasm of complicated and calamitous bewilderment. She was chewed up with anxiety and grief for this woman she hardly recognised, who—by the looks of it—had endured the unthinkable over the last 43 days.

*But what was the unthinkable?* Christina fearfully quizzed herself prior to turning the ignition key, trembling at the harrowing permutations of her mother's suffering. *Let it not be rape, dear God, please, let it not be that.*

The journey to SW19 was, for the most part, steeped in silence.

Christina knew there was little point in searching for answers now to the many questions that would follow in the days ahead; this was neither the time nor the place. Instead, Christina made a lame attempt at establishing a modicum of normalcy before reaching the doorstep of the Surrey house. "Are you comfortable, Mum? We shall soon be home."

"Yes love, I'm OK. I just need a hot bath and some sleep. I shall explain everything later," she replied in exhausted despair.

"Why don't you place that old biscuit tin on the floor and just relax until we reach the driveway?" Christina innocently suggested.

Angela's face immediately crumpled, becoming almost disfigured. The mild reference to the biscuit tin caused her to loudly howl a piercing shriek that led to uncontrollable sobbing. Christina jumped in shock.

Angela was exhibiting an outer shell of emotional ugliness that had been shaped by the grotesque inner reminders of Miles in his final, desolate hours.

Upon seeing her mother shrivel and unexpectedly break down, Christina pulled over onto the side of the road. "Mum! Mum! It's OK. It's OK. Slow down there." She positioned her hand gently on Angela's shoulder, but her mother was inconsolable.

She wailed loudly, filling the car with anguished sobs.

"What... what happened to you? Where were you?" Christina sputtered. As desperate for answers as she was, at this point she simply wanted to hear her mother speak, to give her a sign that there was still a functioning human being buried beneath all the terror and violent anguish.

"Just drive!" Angela finally managed to gasp. "Please, Christina."

"But Mum, I need to know what happened to you. You're a mess and you can barely walk."

"My leg," Angela said, waving her hand dismissively. "I hurt my leg, that's all. Please," Angela whimpered, "please, let's just go home."

"Mum. Do you have any idea how worried I've been since you left? *Oma* seemed to know more than she was prepared to admit; she repeatedly told me that it was a subject for you and me to address together when you returned. So where the hell have you been?"

"Syria," Angela gasped, regaining sufficient composure to respond to her daughter's persistent, unfeigned questioning. "I was in Syria."

"Syria?!" Christina shrieked. "Good God, it goes from bad to worse, Mum. That's—there's a bloody war over there, isn't there? Don't tell me you were shot in the leg! You need to go to a hospital!"

"No," Angela replied, in a bone-weary, submissive mien. "No, I've just hurt my leg, that's all. Now, please Christina. I have told you, so now, can we please go? I'll tell you all you need to know in due course, I promise. But right now, I must get home."

Nina had been peering through the front window for longer than she'd intended. The round trip to Heathrow should have taken no more than a couple of hours, yet nearly three hours had passed since Christina had pulled out of the drive en route to the airport terminal. She reminded herself of her brother Werner's comment whenever he'd felt nervous about things he was unsure of: "*Ich habe schmetterlinge im bauchof!*" he would exclaim in a discomposed and uncharacteristic manner when faced with school exams, or when he'd been forced to become a reluctant associate of the Hitler Youth movement. Nina too was now experiencing the effects of butterflies fluttering in her stomach, flapping in unease regarding the whereabouts of mother and daughter.

Her anxiety was finally quelled as Christina's car entered the driveway, but deep within her the butterflies continued to flail, especially when she examined Angela's shrunken and emaciated appearance as she was assisted from her seat by Christina.

Apprehensively, Nina opened the front door to greet the pair of them, and Angela stumbled into the old woman's arms. As she embraced her *Oma*, the full weight of her sobs re-emerged once more.

Nina and Christina made eye contact over Angela's heaving shoulders and Christina gave the old woman a helpless shrug. "She's been like that since I picked her up," Christina said, her voice breaking. "I don't—I don't know what to do."

As tears began to trickle down Christina's cheeks, Nina closed her eyes, deeply pained at the sight of the two most important people in her life suffering so terribly. But she was strong enough to be there for both of them.

She held Angela tightly with one arm and beckoned Christina towards her with the other. She then embraced them both, letting them cry on each of her shoulders. "Don't worry, *mein kind*," she said to Christina. "I will take it from here. I know it must be frustrating to not understand where your mother went, or what has hurt her so. But try not to worry yourself. She will tell you when she is ready to do so. For now, I think perhaps it is best if you leave her to me."

Christina pulled away, wiping her eyes. She observed her weeping mother for a moment before staring into the crestfallen eyes of her *Oma*. She was confused and disheartened that her mother had failed to confide in her, and was consumed with the uncomfortable feeling that she was interrupting a conversation between the other two women that had yet to take place. "Well, I guess I'll leave you both to it then," she said, attempting to conceal the hint of bitterness in her voice.

Nina led Angela to her bedroom, which was located in the downstairs area of the house; Angela was in no condition to climb the stairs to her own sleeping chamber. Through Angela's sobs, which continued once the door was shut behind them, the only word she seemed capable of uttering was "*Oma*," over and over as she wept.

"I'm here, *liebling*," Nina said gently. "Tell me in your own time. Why don't you set down the biscuit tin and I shall make us some tea?"

This comment triggered Angela's sobs to increase in volume as she clutched the tin even tighter to her bosom.

Nina sat next to her on the bed and waited until Angela's teardrops temporarily abated. Then, after taking a few deep breaths, and as she regained a modicum of composure, Angela revealed the full extent of her expedition to locate Miles, from start to finish. She talked of Tommy and her arrival in Aleppo, about Hans and the Red Cross station, then of Saad's disappearance and setting off into the war-torn city alone. She described the moment her leg was pierced with shrapnel and of convalescing in the old school, and meeting Idi for the first time. She told her grandmother about setting eyes on Miles and of the sickening extent of his injuries, Nina inhaling loudly when learning of the loss of his lower leg. "*Ach du lieber Gott!*" she gasped in desperate incredulity.

The pace of Angela's speech then slowed and reduced in pitch as she recounted the mad-dash flight to the border in Idi's malfunctioning mode of transport, and finally of how she'd pushed Miles through the desert for the remaining distance when the van could go no further.

"Angela," Nina said as Angela finished explaining the relief she'd experienced at seeing Tommy's pick-up truck for the second time, "you are a true warrior. Your strength and perseverance are—"

"No, *Oma!*" Angela raised her voice, cutting the old woman off. "I failed! I failed." She began to stroke the biscuit tin. "This! This is all that's left of him! My poor Miles. The last thing I recall was holding him in my arms, and then I passed out. When I awoke in a hospital, he was gone. I didn't even get to say goodbye! They'd already cremated his body."

"And in the tin?" asked Nina delicately, though she already knew the answer before it was unashamedly uttered.

"His ashes!" Angela sobbed. "He's gone, *Oma*! He's gone! I've lost him forever!"

Angela didn't speak another word or make another sound for the duration of the night. Nina stayed with her for several hours, bringing her tea and some food to soothe her, right up until the moment Angela finally surrendered to sleep, still adorned in her travel clothing and clutching the sealed biscuit tin firmly to her breast.

In the weeks and months that followed, little was discussed regarding Angela's disappearance and the precise nature of what she'd endured and why. Nina had encouraged both Christina and John to avoid broaching the subject until such time as their mother was better equipped to re-live the trauma through a conversation with her embittered and flustered offspring. They had reluctantly agreed.

On the morning following her return to Wimbledon, Christina had made arrangements for her mother to be seen by a doctor at the nearby surgery, and was advised to drive her mother to the surgery early that afternoon. Dr Reginald Pimm had catered for the medical requirements of the Mortimer household for over 15 years; he knew the family well, having become even more familiar with them as a result of William's illness and that of his recent, ultimate demise.

As Angela entered the GP's surgery, the balding, middle-aged practitioner failed to camouflage his astonishment at Angela's worn and emaciated appearance. "I dare say there is no point in asking why you have come to see me today, Angela?" he sternly commented. "What have you done to yourself?"

Before carrying out his examination, the doctor opened the surgery door and called for a nurse to be in attendance as he undertook a full appraisal of Angela's bone-weary and well-pounded frame. After stripping down to her underwear and bra and then lying on the examination table, Angela found she could have easily fallen asleep, if that was at all possible. The full scale of her fatigue had now gripped her entire body and was pulling her into a state of unconsciousness.

"It is not for me to ask where you sustained these injuries, Angela," Dr Pimm stated. "However, I must know the cause of them and when you became the victim of this assault on your body," he added further in a professionally inquisitive manner.

The consultation lasted for no more than twenty-five minutes, and by the end of it Angela had indeed fallen asleep as the doctor navigated his way across her mutilated casing and examined her from head to toe, from her facial injuries to her leg wound, her eyes, ears, skin crevices, nasal passages, and blood pressure all forming his concentrated appraisal of his physically dishevelled patient.

Once the doctor had finished, the nursing assistant gently shook Angela from her unexpected slumber. "Angela, we must now get you dressed; you're going to hospital," she warmly instructed her.

"Why am I going to hospital?" Angela inquired of the uniformed caregiver, finding it difficult to digest this information.

"The doctor shall explain everything to you in a few moments," the nursing assistant replied, "he's arranging for an ambulance to get you there."

Angela's thoughts immediately returned to Miles. She had no idea why she was being admitted to hospital, but, curiously, it felt as if she was taking a step closer to him.

"Angela," Doctor Pimm verbally prodded, "you are a very

fortunate lady. You have survived much of what many others in your age bracket might not have. However, your current condition is one that must be treated. It is not a singular medical condition, but one of several disagreeable ailments. Firstly," he explained, "you are malnourished. Your body weight has reduced considerably. I believe you remain in a state of dehydration and, because of this, your flesh wounds are taking longer to heal. You shall be transferred to hospital via ambulance in a few minutes. You have an IV drip now, pumping some of the vitamins into you that your body has been yelling out for. We shall get you back to your old self in no time at all," he affectionately concluded.

As the paramedics prepared to place Angela onto the stretcher and into the ambulance, Christina took her mother's hand and began sobbing. "I'm so sorry, Mum, I was demanding too much from you. Oh God, Mum, don't leave us. Never leave us again!" she pleaded.

As Angela stared weakly at her only daughter, a teardrop fell from her right eye. Both eyes then closed and Angela lapsed into the state of slumber she'd so yearned for, the one that would allow her to see Miles once more, without further disturbance.

She was hospitalised for nine days—a period that brought with it long spells of reflection, dreams, and nightmares. Slowly, her body weight began to increase and her injuries started to heal. She would be left with a sizeable scar on her leg, but thankfully, this would be the only visible reminder of her venture into Syria to evacuate Miles.

Whilst in hospital, Angela was visited by an appointed counsellor, to analyse her psychological state and her general frame of mind. Once it had been established that she was not a victim of rape or torture, and had simply been caught up in military conflict when attempting to report from the Middle East, there were no more visitations from the psychiatric consultant.

On finally securing release from the infirmary—together with a cocktail of medication, including a course of Diazepam to aid sleep—Angela returned home to prepare for Christmas with her family. Miles too was invited; he would be there, as he would be for the remainder of her life.

It felt different to previous Christmases. Happiness, gratitude, and closeness had forced themselves inside the Wimbledon home, taking up residence as if they were overly ostentatious and not entirely welcome guests, dragging along with them tinselled, sickly-sweet sights and aromas. The house was filled with it all.

The aroma of different foods being cooked—and of warm *Glühwein*—wafted from the kitchen, where Christina, Nina, and John's fiancée Imogene were hard at work, stoking the embers of Christmas cheer as best they could while preparing the Yuletide dinner. John, and Christina's new boyfriend Callum, were there too, trying to loosen up the stiff conversation with sips of eggnog. In the living room, decorations sparkled on the tree tucked in the corner and stockings hung from the fireplace, while fairy lights sent their childish rainbow of colours bouncing off the walls. But none of the holiday spirit that had been arranged with such determination throughout the room could penetrate the darkness that now hung over the decorated dwelling. It was a hollow void, a palpable, black absence of cheer.

For the last several months, the couch had become Angela's

undisputed territory, like a dog's favourite armchair. And now, just as she had for the majority of the days since her return from Syria, she lay there on her side, facing towards its backing, away from the world. She hadn't spent all of her time lying there, of course. Several hours of each day were passed in her bedroom, trying to invigorate herself to rise from bed, staring despondently at the ceiling, or watching her vision melt behind a curtain of tears. When she finally did manage to leave the room, tainted with bittersweet memories of the husband she missed and the lover she'd lost, it was in a fractured state of mind that fluctuated between enervation and unbearable anxiety.

Inevitably, the anxiety and loneliness would get the better of her and she'd leap off the couch and run to the closet, reaching up to the highest shelf where the biscuit tin containing Miles' remains sat. She'd pull it down and carry it back to the couch with her, holding it reverently in her arms. Caressing it usually made her feel better—better enough at least to turn on the television and let whatever programme happened to appear on the screen turn her anguished mind blank.

On that Christmas day she responded to the sounds from where she lay, sometimes identifying with Callum's voice and noting his Scottish accent, so similar to Miles'. Hearing those familiar Celtic tones reverberating through the house forced her to cover her ears, preparing to meet and greet Callum without showing signs of further breakdown.

Christina had never invited a boyfriend home before, so Angela knew she should be happy for her daughter—she should be delighted—but all she felt was cold jealousy and a crushing sense of unfairness, pressing down on her chest like a heavy metal plate.

The voices lowered, reaching Angela as an indistinct, conspiratorial susurrus. She knew they must be talking about her. Straining her ears, she heard John's voice rise slightly, saying, "And we still don't know! We still don't even know what it was all about or what's left her like this!"

"Shhhhh!" Christina's hiss for quiet.

But John kept on going, sounding slightly tipsy. "I don't know if I'm more worried or more angry at this point. It's like something has almost killed her and she can't even tell her own family! *Oma*, can't you just tell us what—"

"Stop that, John!" Christina cut in. "She'll tell us when she's ready. And don't ask *Oma* to betray Mum's trust. You know she wouldn't anyway."

The calm murmurs of Nina's speech floated into the living room and over to Angela's ears. The words were too quiet for her to catch, but she heard a chorus of accent issue from the rest of the family, quelling the outburst.

All that John had said was correct; her whole existence *was* pitiful and embarrassing. She wished she could disappear into the couch cushions beneath her, like an old penny, and yet... it was strange, but hearing them talking about her with such concern made her feel the need to make her presence known in some way, to affirm the fact that she was, in spite of everything, still alive, still a person, still a part of the family.

Laboriously, she picked herself up off the couch and, limping slightly from the leg wound she had accepted would probably never quite heal, she made her way to the kitchen.

Everyone turned to face her at once. Looks of guilt or surprise flashed across the faces of her family, and what she thought was a disgusting, pitying smile of false warmth took up residence on Imogene's features.

"Mum! So good that you're up," said Christina, quickly recovering her composure, "dinner's almost ready. Why don't you go have a seat at the table?"

"I see," said Angela, suddenly cold. "So you don't want me in the kitchen with you all. I've only been here all of five seconds. Am I already ruining the holiday spirit?"

"No! No, that's not what I meant at all! It's just that we were all about to go in there ourselves because the food is nearly done."

Dinner and dessert dragged on beneath a tenuous patina of forced conversation. The words exchanged between the family over the table were little more than a series of monosyllabic, clipped tomes, and Angela was mortified that her presence was ruining such a special night.

She thought back to last Christmas—to Nina's heartfelt toast and to her newfound closeness with her daughter—and wished desperately to have those moments restored to her. But there was nothing she could do to stop herself from casting a black cloud over the whole evening. The more she sought to corral her negativity, the more it fought back and rose against her. Everything reminded her of Miles, of her failure to save him, of the permanence of his loss.

Following dessert, Callum announced that he had to leave. Angela inwardly welcomed his imminent absence as his soft intonations and the intimacy shared between him and Christina had been triggering further grief for her throughout the meal.

John and Imogene also did little to placate or mask her disquiet; Imogene was resting her head on his chest and he was stroking her back. *Just be happy for them!* Angela told herself. *Be happy that they have, at last, found love.*

"I'll just start to clear away these dessert plates," John loudly announced, and as he rose from the table he caught his mother's eye and bellowed, "What the hell is wrong with you, Mum?" He threw his napkin on the carpeted floor as he stood next to Imogene.

"I'm sorry," Angela said in a small voice, "I don't know, I—"

By this point, Christina too had reached the point where the difficult questions simply had to be put to her wretched, broken matriarch. "Listen, Mum. We know whatever you went through over there was something horrid and unimaginable—the proof of that is clearly evident—but even so, we are your children and we have a right to know!" She shook her head. "Mum, you are not well, so share it with us and let us heal as one; we're all affected by the change in you."

Angela felt ensnared, like a trapped animal. It wasn't the right time. How could she tell them now? Especially in the presence of Imogene, someone she barely knew? It was private. And what if they failed to understand? What if they didn't *want* to understand?

Angela stood, picked up her plate and wine glass, and fled from the dining room into the kitchen. Seconds later, the splintering sound of shattered glass rang through the lounge, causing everyone to run in after her.

They found Angela sitting on the floor with her mouth wide open, as if in the process of delivering a silent scream, her hands bleeding from the broken glass.

"Mum! Are you alright?" John cried, the previous anger in his voice having now been replaced by worry.

"He's gone! He's gone, he's gone, he's gone!" Angela shrieked.

"Who's gone?" asked Christina, her concern giving way to sheer terror at seeing her mother as devastated as the broken glass that now covered the floor. "Dad? Are you talking about Dad? Is that what this is all about?"

"No! Miles! My Miles! He was right there. I held him in my arms and then they took him away and when I woke up he was gone! Gone!"

"Who the bloody hell is Miles?" Christina asked, utterly confused.

Hearing his name being uttered from her daughter's mouth drew Angela's mind back into a brief and hellish flashback.

She was pushing him through the desert. She was hearing him scream in pain as the van raced towards the border. She was seeing the bloodied stump where his leg had once been. She was lying in his bed, happy and safe in his apartment as they talked and loved, feeling like the most adored woman on the planet. "Miles... my love... gone."

Nina did not have to examine the faces around her to notice how the emotional make-up of the room had pivoted. Concern and fear and empathy were shifting to anger and disbelief; she could feel it in her bones.

She knew it was her time to step in, to rescue her granddaughter from herself, so she got down on her knees—ignoring the glass shards all around her—and pressed a clean cloth to Angela's cuts. She held her granddaughter's head to her chest and stroked her hair, then she looked up at Angela's children with her sad, wise eyes and said, "A little more than a year ago, your mother fell in love with a man named Miles Dunbar, and he with her. He was an international reporter. I encouraged her to pursue the relationship, to pursue the rare breed of happiness she had found. But your mother's sense of guilt and the thought of neglecting your ailing father and her children was too much to contemplate, so inevitably, she ended the relationship. Miles was heartbroken by your mother's decision to end their union, and in order to cope with his anguish, he accepted a reporting job in Syria. Within a number of weeks, he disappeared, missing. Your mother went there to find him. And she did—your strong, brave mother did find him, in Aleppo, and attempted to bring him home, but he was too badly injured and didn't survive."

"So, wait… let me get this straight," John said slowly, in a voice like ice. "You were cheating on Dad?"

Upon hearing these words Angela's sobs deepened, which only seemed to goad John into continuing further. "That explains everything! That explains why you never cared about him! About us!"

"Or why you were never around," Christina chimed in, in a voice more crushed than angry. "Why you weren't there when Dad fell. Always sneaking about. All the lies you must have told us!"

The disappointment she heard in her daughter's words galvanised Angela; she couldn't let them think that way of her. It just wasn't true. "Of course I cared about your father!" she howled in desperation. "He was my *husband*! You don't even know what it means to have a husband! To have that kind of everlasting and slow-burning love! A true partnership! A deep, eternal friendship! But… when I met Miles, it was a different kind of love. Everything about him…" she trailed off for a moment, choking on her tears. "We were made for each other. *Made* for each other! Don't you understand?"

"I feel sick," John said.

"Please, children," Nina said. "Try to open your minds. Try to see things through your mother's eyes."

John scoffed. "I'm leaving. I can't stand to be in this house another minute."

"I'll stay and help *Oma* clean up this mess," Christina said in an unconvincing voice, "but then… then I think I'm going to stay at Callum's for a while."

The door slammed behind John and Imogene, the sound precipitating a deep wailing to rise out of Angela's chest. It was the sound of an already broken heart breaking yet again.

While Christina and Nina picked up the shards of glass around her, Angela cried on the kitchen floor, utterly broken.

# CHAPTER 19:
## ENGLAND, 2017

Rays of multi-coloured light from the television set perforated the inky blackness of the spacious lounge, bathing the domestic enclave in an ever-shifting, sparkling iridescence of illumination. The shifting colours reminded Angela of a late summer holiday with William and the children in Norway many years previously, where they had witnessed the mesmerising, gaseous sight of the '*Aurora Borealis*'.

No sound accompanied the images flashing across the screen—commercials mostly, punctuated by muted scenes from some American sitcom that held no appeal for Angela whatsoever. Witty people making each other laugh. Carefree people solving the most cursory of problems. Young, beautiful people embracing each other in saccharine gestures of rehearsed love played out under fake studio lighting.

Angela sat up on the couch. She'd been staring at the screen since late afternoon and was beginning to feel the effects of her motionless residency on the sofa. Raising her spectacles from her face and placing them atop her blonde crown, she gently kneaded her enervated eyelids with the index fingers of each hand.

Her walks to the park had proved to be more demanding of late. Her injured leg did not react well to the chilly winter conditions and, although the medical staff had advised her that she should exercise her scarred limb with regular frequency, the process was long and irksome. By the time she returned from her ambles through the leafy pastures of the recreational area, Angela's limp would become more prevalent. Still, the thought of a walking stick to aid her stride was not something she wanted to even consider. No, she would persevere without the assistance of any form of crutch and await her next appointment with the physiotherapist—she felt less disabled after completing a session with him.

Regardless of her physical limitations (and of the mixed weather conditions), Angela would wrap up warmly in her favourite overcoat, don her tartan bonnet and scarf, slip on the lined leather gloves that Miles had presented to her several months before, and remove her umbrella from its stand in the hallway. This routine had become part of her daily life.

Before leaving the house each day she would reclaim the biscuit tin from its position in the kitchen and place it into a canvas shopping carrier, the camel-coloured one with 'Harrods' emblazoned on both sides—another gift from Miles. The day he'd handed it to her, she'd found enclosed inside a bottle of her favourite fragrance, though it had remained an unopened present; he was gone before she ever had the chance to apply the heady bouquet of the French perfume, and as it had been for her to wear and for him to enjoy, now it would remain unopened.

Each morning, Angela returned to the site of The Lentil Tree and perched herself on the bench below. She would sit beneath the tree with her lover for some time, occasionally exchanging pleasantries with the occasional passerby—dog walkers, primarily. For the most part she was alone, but not completely alone. Angela understood that all that resided in the biscuit tin was ash, the human residue or remains of Miles. She had not entered a phase of hallucination, assuming that he could converse with her from his place of entombment in an antiquated metal container; she simply sensed a spiritual closeness to him at this tranquil location, more than any other location she visited.

It was their place and they would continue to share its peace and tranquillity for the remainder of her life. She would reflect on all they had been, all they were, and all they had enjoyed, stroking the tin as she recalled their conversations, their kisses, their lovemaking… and their trek back from hell.

"We nearly made it, Miles, but the journey is not over, my darling man," she uttered softly under her breath.

On this particular day, her feeling of serenity was shattered by a bout of shivering. A chill wind blew across the pond as if signalling the need to head home—home to Nina, to the woman who prevented Angela from aimlessly drifting into a cell of solitary confinement.

Since Christmas, Angela had heard little from her children—the only people she had left besides Nina—and sitting in the park with the tin made her feel less alone. She could not explain it, nor rationalise it, and she didn't attempt to. She would return to the house and slide the tin onto the high shelf in the closet, a point at which Angela's remoteness would break on her like a driving storm of intolerable anonymity.

As she collapsed into the couch her phone lit up on the coffee table in front of her. Listlessly, she watched it vibrate several times, scooting around pathetically on the table's dark wood before she could muster the strength to reach for it. She knew who was contacting her; there was only one person still alive in the whole world that would. She opened the conversation marked 'Bug' and read the message.

*Hello, my darling Mouse! How*
*are we doing today?*
*Curled up with a good book, I*
*hope! Have you heard anything back*
*from the kids?*
*All my love! Bug.*

Angela cursed under her breath. How had it come to this? How had she fallen apart so completely that she couldn't even keep her dearest friend up to date with her life? It had been Geoff who'd encouraged her to write the children handwritten letters; of course he'd be wondering what had come of her efforts to reach out to Christina and John. She quickly keyed her response.

*Bug! I'm so sorry; I should have*
*been in touch before this. I*
*received letters from both of them*
*about a week ago. They have*
*both said they forgive me,*
*but who knows? I sent a text to*
*Christina a few days ago but she*
*hasn't replied. I'm apprehensive*
*about contacting John. A. xx*

*The reply came almost immediately.*

*Reach out to them again.*
*I know it will be difficult, but*
*you must do it, Mouse.*

*I don't know if I can, Bug,*
*They have no wish to speak*
*with me. Thank you for the advice.*
*It's my bloody fault, anyway.*

*Nonsense. Like I said, time*
*heals. Keep trying.*
*You need people in your life,*
*Mouse. You can't just shut*
*yourself away. It's not healthy*
*and it won't help you get better,*
*I can promise you that.*

Angela replaced her phone on the table and wandered back into the lounge, switching on the television. The mindless mediocrity it projected sent a flood of nausea coursing through her. *I'm not alone, Bug. I have Miles,* she thought. *This is just another little break from seeing him.*

Slowly, she stood and limped over to the closet, then reached up into the darkness, fumbling around for the familiar shape of the biscuit tin. Her fingers swiped the top of it, inching it closer and closer to the edge where she'd almost be able to grab it. When Angela's hand was finally about to clasp the container, the tin teetered on the periphery of the shelf and then fell to the floor.

"No!" screamed Angela, as it landed heavily and bounced several times across the solid surface of the flooring.

For one heart-stopping moment, Angela feared the container would explosively burst open, but the lid held. The sharp descent from the high shelf had only added another dent to its already pocked and semi-rusted exterior.

The rush of relief that surged through Angela forced her to her knees. With tears in her eyes, she clutched the tin to her chest and pressed her forehead against it, crying and whispering, "Oh, thank God, thank God!"

She was still doing so when she heard a familiar voice behind her.

"This has to stop, *mein kind*. It cannot go on."

Angela spun around and stared up at the shrunken form of her *Oma*, gazing at her with pained concern through bleary eyes.

"Oh no, *Oma*. Did I wake you?" Angela asked, struggling to reign in her sobs.

"Never mind that," Nina said. "I hate to see you like this, dear."

For a few moments, the two women let an uneasy silence hang in the hallway. It was a ransacked silence, a silence that had already been searched so many times for possible answers and apologies that there was hardly anything left inside it.

Finally, finding something in its barrenness, Nina spoke. "How about you get into bed with your old *Oma* and I'll tell you a story?" she suggested. "Just like when you were a little girl, when you used to curl up beside me and rub your little nose in a state of happy anticipation of what was to come."

Angela sniffled, feeling very much like a little girl already, then once again rubbed her nose as *Oma* led her into the bedroom.

The old woman had become so frail that she could barely climb into her bed, but laboriously, she managed, and Angela joined her. Nina wrapped her frail arms around her granddaughter, stroking her hair, and they lay there for several moments. As Nina felt some of the tension easing its way out of Angela's body, she let her mind work its way back into the past, back across the ocean, back across time to Braunschweig. When she could almost smell the old wood panelling of the ancestral Schaeffer home, and feel the memory of the floorboards beneath her feet, she began to speak in a soft, calming voice right into her granddaughter's ear.

"I'd like to tell you a story about one of the darkest moments of my life," she said.

"Alright," Angela mumbled.

"My brother Werner had been gone for years. The war was raging, destroying everything I loved. I had seen it take away my father's arm, his job, and his happiness. I had seen it steal my mother's verve and smile. And, though I didn't realise it at the time, I had let it rob me of my personality; I had let it transform me into an angry, crotchety, depressed girl. Someone who I knew, deep down, I was not.

"One day, we received a letter. My parents were both out of the house and I thought that perhaps I should wait to open it. But I feared I knew what it contained, and after staring at it on the kitchen counter for some time, I decided I had to see if my worst fears were correct. I opened the letter, and I read—I read that my dear brother Werner had been killed fighting for a Germany I hardly recognised anymore.

"In that moment, my world collapsed around me. I felt everything I knew splinter and break. I felt my last hopes die. I was so consumed with pain that I didn't know what to do with myself. And so I did what I thought all adults did when they felt this way; I rushed to my father's liquor cabinet and I drank every drop of alcohol I could get down. I had never tasted liquor before and I tried to imagine that its burn was a fire to erase my pain. But it only made me feel worse. Worse and worse I felt until I became so dizzy I could no longer stand. I was sick, right there on the floor, and I collapsed, unable to move.

"My parents came home and found me like that. They were concerned, shocked, frightened. Just seeing me like that broke their hearts. Then they read the letter for themselves and I watched them suffer the same terrible pain as I had. When I saw them like that—the two people I loved most in the world just falling to pieces—I felt my consciousness leave my body.

"I looked down at myself, at my own body lying on the floor. I saw that the way I was in that moment, the way I'd been behaving for the previous months, was only causing my mother and father more and more anguish. I saw it so clearly. I was a source of pain for them in their own home when everything outside of it was so ugly. It was not my fault, but I was damaging them rather than helping them live. I realised then that I could make the choice to continue hurting them passively, or I could actively choose to be strong.

"Unsteadily, I stood, then I made coffee to sober myself up while they cried and held each other. I dug through the cupboards and put together supper with whatever I could find. I served it to them and watched as my actions took at least some of the bite out of their sadness. I saw my actions draw the slightest smiles of gratitude from their faces, and I decided, from that day forward, I would be strong for them. And, in doing so, little by little, I regained myself. I worked my way back to being the person I was before all those terrible things came to pass."

Angela lay there in silence. Just listening to the tone of her *Oma*'s voice had calmed her considerably, had made her feel safe and cared for and far less alone. But her mind was still so raw from her grief that it was difficult for her to assimilate Nina's story fully, to truly understand it as it applied to her own life. She tried to just let the words wash over her, trusting that their meaning would open up to her later.

"You see, *mein kind*," Nina concluded, her weak voice barely more than a whisper, "we must be strong. We must. Strong, especially in the face of loss. That is how we grow more love. That is how we survive."

For the next several days, Angela reflected on her *Oma*'s story. She spent hours thinking about what her version of *Oma*'s strength could be. What kind of strength did she need to cultivate in order to grow new love? She began leaving the biscuit tin up in the closet. She took walks in the park without it, passing by The Lentil Tree without stopping or even pausing. She sat on the couch and forced herself to read. She watched television and turned the sound on, trying to immerse herself in the news and documentary channels. But it was useless. She did not feel strength building inside of her. She just felt more alone, her longing for Miles only increasing with every day she didn't lay her hands on the biscuit tin.

The only bearable part of her days was when she would climb into Nina's bed for another story. It became a nightly tradition in which she experienced many of the joys and tragedies of her grandmother's life, conjuring them inside her own mind with such incredible detail that they almost became her memories.

She learned about the time that Werner ran away from home, terrifying her great-grandmother Erna, and how Nina had found him camped out in a tent in the park. She learned about the duets the two children would play on the massive piano in the living room while Johannes looked on, smoking his pipe and smiling as he watched his son and daughter indulge in the passion he so enjoyed. She learned about Nina's first days at Hathaway Hall, about how she'd watched Hjördis grow into a young woman alongside the Ashley-Cooper children, and she learned about the wonderful feeling that would course through Nina's entire being whenever she observed little Angela and little Geoff at play. The stories helped Angela sleep, and they also took the bitter sting of isolation out of her nights. But every morning when she woke, she'd find that all her pain had returned with a vengeance.

Pacing around the house one afternoon, thinking once again about the kind of strength she'd need to turn her life around, she realised that it couldn't possibly be this abstinence. It just wasn't working.

So she rushed to the closet, opened the door, and with trembling hands she pulled down the biscuit tin, clutching it to her chest as she breathed a sigh of relief. Holding its familiar rectangular shape close to her body, she felt closer to Miles than she had in days.

With a sudden flurry of energy, she threw on warm clothing, grabbed a thermos of coffee, and took the tin with her to The Lentil Tree. She sat there sipping her coffee, neither saying nor eating anything for over two hours. She stared at the lake as the sun made its early descent, painting the sky a pale orange. Once again, her *Oma's* words crossed her mind. What kind of strength did she need now?

Suddenly, Angela was struck by the memory of how strong she'd felt on the plane to Jordan. She'd been terrified and anxious right up until the moment she'd realised that she had no other option but to track down Miles. All the uncertainties of the journey that lay before her, all of her fears, had faded away in that single determined instant. She'd realised then that nothing could stop her from being with him. She'd realised that she'd happily die trying to find him. She'd realised that life without Miles would be no life at all. It had felt like she'd had a clear glimpse at her destiny on that fateful flight and, in that moment, she'd been filled with a sense of pure purpose.

*Perhaps that's what I need to do again*, she thought, looking down at the biscuit tin. *Perhaps another journey into the unknown to search for Miles is my destiny, the only purpose I have left.*

That night, as Angela tried to sleep after Nina's nightly story, she heard the old woman whimpering next to her. Nina tossed and turned in her sleep, crying out in the darkness. She'd never done this before, not on any of the other nights since they'd started sleeping in the same bed.

Angela tried not to give it much thought and did her best to get some rest, but the next night it happened again, and the following night as well—Nina crying, "Horst!" or "Werner!" or "Hjördis!" or "Angela!" in her sleep, in a voice so fearful it sounded little like her *Oma*. Angela attempted to waken her grandmother, hoping to spare her from those horrible night terrors, but once she'd woken Nina and calmed her down, listening for her breathing to return to the even rhythm of sleep, inevitably, the nightmares would start again.

The following day, Angela could hear the toll that the troubled sleep was taking in Nina's voice. Her stories started to trail off in the middle, to make less and less sense. She was beginning to forget what year it was, oblivious to the fact that Angela was a grown woman and no longer a young girl.

One night, the two Schaeffer women climbed into bed and Angela waited patiently for her *Oma* to begin the nightly story. Minute after minute of silence passed. Worried, Angela rolled over to face her grandmother.

"*Oma? Oma*, are you alright?" she asked in a voice tinged with fear.

"I—I am… fine. I am here." Nina's voice was so faint Angela could hardly make out the words. "I am sorry, *mein kind*, but I just have no stories left to tell. I'm so very, very tired now."

Angela wrapped her arms around the old woman just as Nina had wrapped her arms around Angela every night for the past several weeks, then she wept silent tears as she waited for sleep to envelop her in its nocturnal embrace.

The following morning, Angela woke to find Nina lying in bed next to her, a peaceful expression on her face. Angela didn't need to feel the coldness of her grandmother's skin. She didn't need to check her pulse. From the instant she woke, she knew.

Her *Oma*, Nina Schaeffer, was gone. Forever.

# Chapter 20:
## England, 2017

Angela entered the small, close-packed Lutheran church in the heart of the city. From the outside, the building had struck her as an establishment that must have housed a firm of solicitors—or, quite possibly, chartered accountants. Other than a weather-beaten, religious plaque at the top of the steps (which led into the place of worship), there was little to suggest that a funeral service was soon to be held within its confines.

A number of black-clad mourners sat huddled on a variety of seating; not pews in the strictest sense, but simply an array of chairs—some plastic, some cushioned, some not—neatly lined up in the centre of the large space. To Angela's way of thinking, the soulless chamber was little more than a converted hall, one that could be quickly transformed into a conference room just as easily as a recreational area for pre-school children to play in. Nothing seemed tangible to her. Not the church, not the pews, nor the assembly of morose silhouettes murmuring quietly to one another before the committal proceedings ultimately commenced.

Nina had been born and raised as a member of the German faith group, but had seldom entered any place of religious worship since fleeing from her home in Braunschweig many years previously. And yet, as Angela walked towards the seat nearest to Nina's coffin, she ascertained that the altar on which the casket rested was indicative of her *Oma's* existence. There was an element of brightness from the flowers that surrounded the casket, and from the large crucifix that dominated overhead, shimmering piercingly from the aid of a floodlight that magnified the ecclesiastical effect on the congregation. There was also the suggestion of blackness; the pitch-black veil, which enshrouded the communion table, served as a reminder that death resided in this place, where only tears and the memories that prompted them would signify the merest hint of continued existence for those who loved Nina most.

Whilst in her dreamlike miasma, each sensory detail swooped across Angela; every edge, every line, was blurred by more than just her tears. It all seemed less believable than the scenes in the stories her *Oma* had shared with her.

She floated through the service like an unseen phantom, as if the consoling hands descending on her shoulder to offer a concerned pat would pass right through her, up until the moment they didn't. Sitting on her plastic chair, on a cushion that was ill-designed to afford even a modicum of added comfort, words reached her as if transmitted from many miles away through a haze of disorientating fogginess.

Christina bravely managed her way through the eulogy, breaking off occasionally to wipe her tear-laden eyes.

When the arrangements for the funeral were being made, Angela had reconciled herself to the reality that she would be incapable of delivering a fitting address to the congregation, one that would articulately describe the reflections of her *Oma*; it would take a lifetime to do so. Nina had been her steadying pillar. With her death, what remained of Angela's soul was in the throes of unpreventable collapse, as if it were a sandcastle quickly eroding with the arrival on an incoming tide.

Angela willed herself to focus on her daughter's words. Despite the tremulous nature of the farewell oration, Christina remained upright and dignified as she exclusively depicted the magical manner in which Nina Schaeffer had transformed her own life, one scarred by the most brutal darkness during the days of her virgin girlhood, into a beam of mature luminosity, so dazzling and warm that anyone she came into contact with felt its glow, *her* glow.

"…the kind of woman who enjoyed nothing more than to offer her wisdom to the ones she loved, without judgment, without self-interest, with only their best interests at heart…"

The line took Angela right back to the many conversations regarding Miles she'd shared with Nina at the kitchen table. The listening ear, the advice and the rationale that came with the warm mugs of tea *Oma* placed in her hands… these memories made Angela's body shake with a sudden, uncontrollable sob.

She looked across the aisle and her eyes fell on her son, who was glaring at her with undisguised bitterness. Whether this was in response to her loud outburst of grief or for the litany of maternal wrongdoings she had committed throughout his life, she couldn't determine; not that it mattered anymore. Forgiveness would be a long time coming, if ever. *He has a life*, she thought. *He has love. As long as he never endures as I do, he'll be alright.*

The journey time to the crematorium from the church was relatively short. John and Geoff acted as two of the four pallbearers and handled the coffin as if it contained a quantity of pennaceous feathers or fallen, withered leaves from The Lentil Tree, the weight of Nina's presence in life being far greater than the lightness of her corporeal remains.

As the service drew to a close, a wave of mourners congregated around Angela. She bobbed among them like an untethered buoy, fluctuating between feelings of burning pain and pure numbness. She blinked and caught sight of her daughter standing in front of her, falling into Angela's arms and sobbing against her chest.

Instinctively, Angela held Christina like she had when her daughter was an infant, stroking her hair for a few moments as if both of them were detached from the present and all it displeasingly contained.

Christina looked up at her with a tear-streaked face and asked, "Was it—was it alright?"

"Yes, yes darling, it was perfect. I couldn't have done it better myself. I couldn't have done it at all. I'm so, so proud of you, Christina." Angela had now moved into the role of comforting mother and it had brought her sharply back to the present.

Christina smiled. "Listen, Mum," she said, "I didn't mention this to you before as you were in such a bad state after *Oma*... after we lost her. But I've organised a little reception at the house. I hope that's OK." She watched as the colour drained from Angela's face and hurriedly added, "It's just that Callum's apartment is so small and I didn't know—"

"No, no. Nonsense. That's quite alright, Christina. Of course. Thank you. That was something else I would not have been able to handle myself. You've developed into a wonderful woman, inheriting *Oma*'s special strength." Angela embraced her daughter once more. "That's what you do after a funeral: you have a reception to rejoice and remember. It would be wrong not to."

She smiled, though inwardly, the thought of being around people—of hearing them reminisce about Nina and having to participate in conversations about a past that Angela would never be able to reclaim—filled her with an icy sensation laced in chilly uneasiness. The guests would fleetingly and respectfully chat about the past and then quietly drift off into their respective futures, returning to their way of life with those they loved most. In contrast, Angela now dallied with the prospect of a life of sheer emptiness. She had emerged into an emotional pauper, treacherously inhabiting a void of nothingness, reflective pain and fathomless emptiness her unbidden bedfellows. *Oh God, Miles, I need you more now than ever*, she wretchedly mused, as if delivering a silent orison into the great unknown.

"Hello, Christina. Mum." John and Imogene had appeared next to them. He and Christina shared a heartfelt hug, as did Imogene and Christina. Angela stood aside awkwardly, wringing her hands.

"Listen, I hate to do this and I know you've arranged the get-together, but Imogene and I need to head back to the city. I have to prepare for a meeting and, well, you know. Life goes on, I suppose."

"That's alright," Christina said, hugging him again. "Let's talk soon, OK? I'm going to head back right now and help set up." She kissed Angela's cheek and enquired, "Are you bringing *Oma* home today, Mum?"

The question caused an initial flurry of confusion in Angela's mind, but as she adjusted to the reality of the query, she replied in the affirmative by mouthing a silent "yes" to Christina.

As she departed the crematorium and headed to the car park, Angela was left in the company of her son and his fiancée.

"Well, Mother," John uttered, "I guess I'll see you soon. Take care."

"John," Angela said, closing the distance between them and taking his hands in hers, "I have come to understand the reasons for your vexation. It has been brewing inside you for far too long, for too many years, and no matter how you view me, I've always thought of you as a perfect son—and forever I shall. I've always loved you and I always will." She looked over at Imogene and then back to John. "And I know you'll make a wonderful father someday."

"Thanks, Mum. I appreciate that," he replied, stiffly.

Mother and son shared an awkward hug, then Imogene embraced Angela with a firmer grasp and whispered that they'd "tie-up again in the very near future."

As they departed and walked away, Angela became associated once more with the dissociative sensation of isolation. She stood there for several moments, feeling utterly, utterly lost, and then, from behind her, she heard the one word that could bring her back from the brink.

"Mouse."

She spun around and threw her arms around Geoff, who was standing with a lop-sided, unsymmetrical smile on his face, adorned in his sharp, tailored black suit and pin-striped shirt.

"Oh, Bug. Bug, I'm so glad you're here!" Angela groaned into his shoulder. "I've lost everyone else. I don't know what to do." She pulled away to peer into his eyes and, together, they wiped the tears from her face. "These last months have been... ever since Miles, Syria, and now *Oma*, I just... I can't..."

"Shhh, shhh. It's alright, little Mouse. It's OK. I've got you."

"I feel incapable of coping. Just, incapable of coping with anything, Bug. And Christina, bless her, has taken care of the reception. It's at the house and I should probably go, but the thought of being there makes me so uneasy. I just don't think I can handle being around anyone."

"Anyone?" asked Geoff, flashing her his trademark roguish smile, although his eyes reflected despondency whilst taking in Angela's anguish.

"No, I suppose not," Angela said, letting out a small laugh. "You're the only person I want to be around. I don't even think I can be in that house without *Oma*, not yet, not now, you know?"

"Well, Mouse, it's perfectly straightforward then, isn't it? I know precisely what we'll do."

"What?"

Geoff placed his arm around Angela's shoulder and escorted

her away from the building. "We'll go to the nearest pub and get utterly smashed. The funeral director shall receive Nina's ashes and you can collect them next week when you're a bit steadier."

"Now?" Angela asked, startled. "But the reception, all these people—"

"Somehow they'll manage without us. Come on. We'll take my car."

The pub smelled as many traditional British pubs smell, and something about that timeless scent set some of Angela's nerves at ease from the moment they crossed the threshold. They were positioned at a small, sticky table, tucked in the far corner next to a stained window. It had started to rain outside, but within the pub it was warm, and having worked their way through a couple of drinks, both Geoff and Angela had been lifted from the melancholic air of earlier in the day.

Geoff launched into tales of his recent travels, regaling her with updates of worldwide oil demand and the development of fossil fuels for future generations. Their conversation then shifted to the days of their childhood at Hathaway Hall. Angela laughed about the time she'd dared Geoff to climb the big oak tree in the garden and how, upon reaching the top, he had been too scared to climb back down. She'd had to coax and coach him for nearly an hour before his feet touched the grass again.

"What a ridiculous child I was!" he exclaimed. "I'd still be up that damn tree to this day if you hadn't been there!" He slammed his empty glass on the table and then stood up. "Be right back with another round. And I think the occasion calls for something a little stronger, as well."

When he strode to the bar Angela immediately felt his absence fall on her as the cold, heavy rain outside would, all the mirth being instantly erased from her mind as she was plunged back into the dreary, depressing present. She sat still, trying to keep her breathing steady, but the crushing loneliness of her current life was just too much and her thoughts turned, inevitably, to Miles.

She knew she'd have been able to deal with the pain of losing Nina if he were still alive. If only she could leave this bar and go to his apartment, if only she could hear his voice just one more time…

Her problem now was that there was nowhere for her to go, nothing for her to do, no action she could take to alleviate her pain. She looked out the window at the rain pouring down onto the pavement and thought about her last trip out to The Lentil Tree. She'd had a revelation then, but had been too afraid to fully face it. It had been staring her right in the face, but she hadn't wanted to see it. The strength she'd had on the plane. The purpose of finding Miles, no matter what the cost. The belief in the impossible that she'd had on the plane to Jordan—that they'd be reunited somehow irrespective of the odds, the danger, the death, and the destruction that had lain ahead. There was a purpose in that. There was hope. It was just a matter of believing. It was just a matter of overcoming fear.

She clenched her jaw, watching the fat drops disappear into the filthy puddles lining the ground. *What else do I have?* she thought. *There's no other choice. Another journey. Another adventure. Another leap towards love. It's the only path that remains.*

Just then, Geoff returned with two more pints and a pair of Jägermeister shots clutched precariously in his hands.

"To *Oma*," he said, after passing Angela the small glass. "May she light up the next world the way she lit up this one!"

Angela didn't know how to respond to those words without losing control of herself, so instead she nodded and drank down the syrupy liquor in one desperate gulp.

"And then there was the time with the stray cat, do you remember?" Geoff asked, smacking his lips and coughing on the alcohol.

He was so good at this, at distracting her from the terrible thoughts that lurked at the edges of her consciousness, but now, he was also distracting her from the plan that was forming in her mind; before the taste of the alcohol had even begun to fade from her mouth, he had her laughing and talking about their efforts to secretly keep a pet at Hathaway Hall, something that had been expressly forbidden. They'd housed the cat in a wine cellar, taking it in turns to sneak away with dinner scraps, and had managed to feed it for weeks before their deception had been discovered. Together they'd convinced Lady Dorothy to let them keep the cat, but they'd never been able to agree on a name.

"Every day he got a new one! Socks. Patches. Burt. Burt was my choice, of course," he said, laughing through another sip of beer. "Poor thing must have been confused out of its mind! No wonder he ran away. Speaking of running away, I have to flee to the little boy's room, if you don't mind. But stay right there, Mouse.

I'll be back with you in a tick."

It was the same thing all over again. As soon as Geoff had left their table, Angela slipped back into the yawning emptiness of feeling utterly alone in the world. But, amidst it all, the one shred of impossible hope glimmered like a knife's sharp edge. Geoff could chase all the darkness away well enough, but only for as long as he was right there in front of her, close enough to reach out and touch.

*He can't be around me forever, making me feel this false sense of belonging*, she reasoned. *He has his own life. Somewhere he belongs. I don't belong anywhere anymore. This is nice, but it's just a diversion. A distraction from what I have to do. From what I know I have to do.* She drained the rest of her glass and set it down carefully on the table.

Soon Geoff returned from the bathroom, and before he was fully in his seat he began to launch into another memory from their past, but Angela stopped him.

"Bug, I have to ask you something. Something important. If I needed you to do something for me, even if it was something difficult, would you do it?" She looked imploringly into his eyes and took both of his hands in hers. "Would you?" As she gazed at him she smiled her most serene and loving smile, willing her face to convey nothing more than trust and friendship.

"Of course, Mouse! Whatever you need. Just tell me what it is and I'll make it happen."

"You promise?" She gripped his hands tighter.

"I swear it. Just tell me what it is."

Angela let out a deep sigh of relief. "I will. But first, let's get out of here. I can't handle another drink."

Geoff's rented Mercedes came to a smooth halt in front of the house.

"Just give me a moment, Bug. Be right back," Angela said, trying to keep her voice from shaking. She hopped out of the car before he could respond, walking across the front lawn and over to the door as quickly as she could.

Inside, the house was deserted, the funeral reception long over. Christina must have gone back to Callum's apartment. *Good*, she thought. *I need to be alone.*

Crossing through the living room, she stopped short, her eyes falling on a large, framed photograph of Nina that had been placed there for the reception. It had been taken sometime in the seventies, when Nina's hair still had that rich, golden texture and her limbs were slim, but not frail. She was looking into the camera with a calm and confident disposition, an expression that suggested she was ready to take on whatever came next with self-assurance, poise, and grace. Angela regarded the photograph for a few moments, feeling the last fragments of resistance draining from her body, then she inhaled deeply and exhaled slowly.

"I won't be long, *Oma*," she said. "I'm going to be strong. I'm going to do it. I'm going to be strong enough to find him again, wherever he's gone." She then headed straight for the closet.

Minutes later, she opened the passenger door to Geoff's car and slid herself inside, the biscuit tin gripped firmly in her hands.

"Drop me off at the park, please, Bug. I just needed to pick this up."

"Your wish is my command," he replied and started the car.

They drove down the familiar route, the car weaving smoothly down the gentle curves of the local thoroughfare, depicting a cultivated order in true Wimbledon fashion. Another shower of light rain stopped as suddenly as it had begun. The clouds parted and sunlight began to peek its way through the fast receding grey veil above them, casting an ethereal sheen on the roads and the pavements as they passed through.

After a few silent minutes, they arrived at the car park. Angela's memories of the first time she'd come to this spot with Miles immediately rose up inside her mind, but on this occasion she brushed them aside, completely focused on the present moment in a way she hadn't been since Syria.

She stepped out of the car and walked around to the driver's side. Geoff rolled down his window and leaned out of it slightly, squinting up at his lifelong friend in the sudden sunlight. "Is this the thing you made me promise to do?" he asked. "To take you to the park?"

"Part of it. Now get out of the car, please."

Geoff obeyed. When he stood before her, Angela smiled as she looked him up and down, studying every detail of his familiar features. Then she enveloped him in a long, slow embrace. "I love you, Bug," she said. "You're my family. The best friend anyone could ever ask for. I want you to go back to your life of adventure and travel and to keep living it well."

He laughed, saying, "I will do just that!" Then he pulled away and held her at arm's length. "And I love you too, Mouse. It will all be OK soon. I promise."

"I know it will be. I know it will. Now," she said, taking a step away, her voice breaking ever so slightly, "off you go, Bug."

"Are you sure?" he asked.

"Oh, yes. I need some time alone, now. I need to walk, to think of the best way to negotiate my next journey in life. I'll spend some time with Miles too; he's never very far from me. I think for the remainder of this day I must search for alternatives."

"Alright, Mouse," Geoff said, winking at her, "but don't stay by yourself for too long. I'm just a phone call away. Come by the hotel later after your walk. I don't think I've finished with you yet."

She giggled at the comment. "I could never be finished with you, Bug. Thank you. I'd like that very much. I think I'll have a lie down when I get back home, but then we'll see. Now, go on. And remember that you promised me."

"Oh yes," he said, climbing back into the car and starting it, "I won't forget. Whatever you ask of me, I shall do it. Don't I always?"

"Goodbye, Bug!" she called out, through a lump in her throat, as he pulled away.

He waved to her through the window, turned, and in seconds he was gone.

When she arrived at The Lentil Tree, the biscuit tin tucked securely under her arm, she took a moment to look up at it, marvelling at its natural beauty—the grooves in its bark, the tiny green hints of new leaves, the optimistic extension of its many branches.

"We picked a good one, didn't we, Miles?" she said, sitting down on the rain-sodden bench beneath the tree and placing the tin in her lap. "You should have seen Christina today. Her eulogy was lovely. The way she gave it in spite of her nerves, in spite of her grief… Oh,

Miles, it was just like something Nina would have done. Bold
brave to the last. And John. John looks like such a grown man I
believe it. He's meticulous, careful—he'll be a good architect. He
great things ahead of him. I can feel it in my bones."

She spent close to an hour speaking, looking out at the po
spreading before her and allowing her thoughts to flow freely an
unguarded, just as she always had when she'd been with Miles at
the café, at his apartment, or in this verdant location that meant
so much to them both. Angela pondered on all they had said and
done beneath the towering beech. They had spent many hours
conversing there, dining there, making decisions there, kissing
there, embracing there, and even making love there, and often
they were still there when they could not be together. Since Miles'
death it had evolved into a spiritual base; she had talked alone
with him here as much as she had during the entire duration of
their liaison of the heart, the mind, and the flesh.

Once she'd finished talking she set down the tin next to her
and stood up, reaching into her deep overcoat pocket and grasping
a small hand-held trowel, the one William had frequently used
when planting bulbs in the garden. Angela started to break up
the ground with the steely pointed implement, still soft and
moist from the day's rain. Then, as the soil began to loosen, she
removed it with her bare hands, forming a deep, rectangular
aperture at the base of the tree.

It took nearly an hour to reach a suitable depth, and although
the light was fading, she had sufficient time to deposit the
container into the newly created sepulchre and then cover it with
the disturbed, dark loam she'd removed earlier.

done, Angela wandered down to the bank of the

vered a flattish white stone that was nestling next to

ds at the water's edge. She then carried it back to the

excavation and pressed it firmly atop the small mound

dy excavated topsoil. She cleaned her hands by running

nrough the shallows of the pond and then shook her arms

neans of drying her palms and fingers.

Before departing, she briefly stood over Miles' catacomb. "I'll

e you soon, my darling," she whispered, before turning for home.

Back at the house, Angela ran a hot bath and submerged herself into a frothy pool of sweet-smelling suds, washing her hair as she did so and removing the last remnants of dirt from her fingernails. Once washed and dried, she adorned herself in the yellow dress, adding a little rouge to her lips and brushing her hair as her black diamond earrings moved in agitation with each stroke of her blonde locks.

Angela then moved about the house, erasing all traces of the funeral wake, apart from the large photograph of her *Oma*. Next she embarked on household chores, cleaning everything—from the kitchen to the bathroom, including Nina's room—before carefully dusting the family pictures of William, the children, and Nina.

Once the home was cleaned to her satisfaction, she entered William's study and sat down on his antiquated but much-loved office chair by the writing bureau. Here she scribed two letters by hand, using the fountain pen that had been presented to William at the time of his enforced retirement; she penned a lengthy letter, followed by a much shorter missive, and sealed them in separate white envelopes. She placed the longer communiqué into the top drawer of the writing desk, then unearthed the wedding band that William had worn since their marriage. She placed it atop the letter and gently closed the drawer.

Angela carried the shorter note with her into the dining room and set it on the large dining table. She went back into the kitchen, pulled out her phone, and walked over to the refrigerator, squinting at a phone number scrawled on one of the magnets and dialling the number of a cleaning agency she'd used in the past.

"Yes, hello. This is the Mortimer residence. Could you please send someone by early evening for the usual cleaning duties? No, no need to do the carpets. Just a routine swipe round. Downstairs and upstairs, please. I am unexpectedly away from tomorrow morning so I would very much appreciate your help. No, not now. Could you send someone here around 6 p.m.? Yes. Yes, that would be wonderful, thank you."

She hung up and then found her text conversation with Geoff on her phone. She typed a brief message to him and sent it, then she placed her phone on the kitchen counter. As she moved to the staircase, she stopped and looked once more at the photograph of Nina Schaeffer, feeling a surge of love well up inside her.

"*Dankeshön*," she said, to the image of her *Oma*.

Angela then climbed the stairs. She did not look back.

# EPILOGUE:
## ENGLAND, 2017

After removing the whitish flat rock from the small mound of earth at the base of the tree, Geoff's hand closed around the first handful of soggy, loose soil. Tossing the earth aside, he reached down again and collected another fistful, placing it to one side.

Again and again he repeated the process, until his fingers finally made contact with smooth, cool metal. He brushed away the last film of dirt and saw the weathered image of an old German mill.

Squatting down on his haunches, he pulled the biscuit tin from the ground and regarded it with an intense gaze. He then lifted the lid from the body of the tin and examined the pile of ash inside, shaking his head.

Geoff turned and reached for the simple white urn positioned on the ground next to him. His fingers closed around it, smudging its pale surface with streaks of brown muddy remnants as he briefly closed his eyes to quell the fall of a renegade teardrop. As he lifted the urn, Geoff's thoughts were restored back to the moment when his mind had been crammed with confusion upon first reading the contents of Angela's text message.

*The drawer in the desk. You promised.*

That was all she had said. He'd failed to see the message for over an hour after it had been forwarded to him—he'd either been in the shower or busily packing for his flight to Bangkok the following day—and when he finally read it, he'd frowned at the pixelated characters on the screen. He'd sent a question mark back in response and had then waited anxiously to hear the tone that would signal the arrival of a new message from Angela.

It was unlike her to delay in responding to Geoff. He therefore opted to call her in an attempt to unravel the mystery of her text, and that of her absence, before recalling that she'd intended to take a nap following her afternoon visit to the park. *A nap that had more than likely become a good night's slumber*, he quietly ascertained. He then determined that if he didn't hear from her by early the next morning, he would call again before heading to the airport.

Geoff's phone burst into life at 7.06 a.m., shortly before the alarm on his device had been set to wake him ahead of his busy day. There was no sense to be made from what Christina was attempting to tell him through her hysterical sobs on the telephone, her words almost unintelligible with grief.

He immediately got dressed and rang the lobby to book a

taxi to Wimbledon. En route to the stricken house, he cancelled his flight to the Far East. He knew the worst before being officially told the worst.

As the cab arrived, Geoff spotted a number of vehicles on the driveway. John and Christina's cars were parked at an odd angle and a police car was tucked in closely behind them, plus an ambulance, which was protruding into the street.

Both Angela's children were inconsolable and offered no greeting to Geoff as he strode into the lounge area. The paramedics were treating Christina for the trauma she was enduring. John seemed in a state of paralysis and was holding a glass of dark rum, his shirt soiled with the tears that were still falling from his crumpled face.

After comforting the children as best he could, Geoff began the process of back-tracking 24 hours in a bid to make sense of Angela's suicide with an overdose of the medication she'd been provided with following Syria. She had been prescribed sleeping tablets and had been issued with even more as the months dragged on, yet she rarely touched them and had apparently created a stockpile for use at another time. That time had arrived for Angela several hours earlier, when she had lain down alone on top of her bed, dressed and made up as if she was soon to attend a ball or similar social event, the merest hint of a smile on her face.

Recalling Angela's text message, Geoff made his way to the writing bureau, and on pulling open the top drawer he laid hands on her note. He read it, and as he did so, the events of the last several hours began to make sense. Even his crushing sadness began to subside as he read the last words Angela had written, over and over, again and again.

During the next 12 days, he—along with John and Christina—had been locked in an abyss of distraught and disbelieving fugue. Her final instructions had been all Geoff had to instil shape and control into the days leading to Angela's funeral, the only handhold he had to keep him clinging to reality.

"It's all done, Mouse. Everything just like you asked," he said to the urn, turning it slowly in his hands. "I went down the to-do list. I took care of it all. I've kept my bloody promise up to this point. I made sure everything you left behind will be donated to the children and the Red Cross under the names Miles Dunbar, Angela Schaeffer, and Nina Schaeffer. That was the easy part." He swallowed, wiping at the new tears appearing in his eyes. "And I did the hard bit as well. I've forgiven you." He sighed. "There really was no way for you to go on without him, was there?" Gingerly, he opened the urn. "Well, Mouse," he continued, his voice breaking, "I suppose all that's left for your old Bug to do now is to help you get back to him. Here goes nothing."

Weeping freely now, Geoff poured Angela's remains into the biscuit tin, praying that a strong wind would not destroy his attempts in undertaking the most hellish travail of his entire life.

He complied with her wishes, exactly as she'd specified in her note, reaching inside and mixing the silvery dust contents with that of Miles', until the remains of them both became an indistinguishable but unified substance. He then reached into his pocket and pulled out Hjördis' golden ring, placing in gently atop the ash. Carefully, he closed the lid and lowered the metal box back into its plot beneath the old beech tree.

Finally, carrying out the last of Angela's specified wishes, he dug a small hole next to the tin and secreted William's wedding band into it. He covered the meadow-like place of entombment with the excavated earth, replaced the flat stone, and slowly rose to his feet.

Geoff looked down at the unmarked resting place where his dearest friend and her lover would rest together for all time. Then he listed his gaze to the branches above him, wiping tears from his cheeks as he whispered, "Goodbye, Mouse. I hope that when you find him this time, you do so in a much better place." Then he smiled. "No, Angela. I don't hope—I *know* you will."

He reached out and gave the tree's bark a gentle pat with his hand. Then he sighed, turned, and walked back to his car as if a man of a much more advanced age; stooped and exhausted.

That afternoon, a gentle wind blew in across the pond. Sunlight streamed through the branches as the leaves of The Lentil Tree fluttered in the mild breeze, creating a soothing and peaceful sound as if transmitting in a language all of its own, heralding the arrival of new but familiar residents now lying below its broad trunk, whispering: "*Aller anfang ist schwer.*"

For Angela and Miles the hard part had been successfully negotiated, and now, eternal peace below The Lentil Tree would be permanent and without end.

## THE END

# Author's Biography

Gordon G. Kinghorn was born and raised in Edinburgh, though he left home at the age of 16 to live in Australia, where he spent over thirty years as a professional soldier. He has travelled extensively throughout the world in both a professional and personal capacity, and has written a multitude of articles on his experiences and on the people who shaped and forged his life and opinions. He has two grown children and now resides in Berkshire, UK. This is his first novel.

Printed in Great Britain
by Amazon